DEATH ON THE VERANDAH

Other titles edited by Cynthia Manson
available from Carroll & Graf

Grifters & Swindlers

Kingpins

Women of Mystery

DEATH
ON THE VERANDAH

Mystery Stories of the South from
Ellery Queen's Mystery Magazine *and*
Alfred Hitchcock Mystery Magazine

Edited by Cynthia Manson

Carroll & Graf Publishers, Inc.
New York

First Carroll & Graf edition 1994

Carroll & Graf Publishers, Inc.
260 Fifth Avenue
New York, NY 10001

Library of Congress Cataloging-in-Publication Data

Death on the verandah : mystery stories of the South from Ellery
  Queen's mystery magazine and Alfred Hitchcock's mystery magazine /
  edited by Cynthia Manson. — 1st Carroll & Graf ed.
     p.   cm.
  ISBN 0-7867-0055-6 : $19.95 ($26.95 Can.)
    1. Detective and mystery stories, American—Southern States.
  2. Southern States—Fiction. I. Manson, Cynthia. II. Ellery
  Queen's mystery magazine. III. Alfred Hitchcock's mystery magazine.
  PS648.D4D425   1994
  813'.0872083275—dc20   94-4668
                                                          CIP

Manufactured in the United States of America

CONTENTS

INTRODUCTION

Death on the Verandah is a collection of stories culled from *Ellery Queen's Mystery Magazine* and *Alfred Hitchcock Mystery Magazine* which combines the key elements of a strong mystery and a southern setting. It is not difficult to understand why the authors included in this anthology would choose the South as their locale. This environment provides a background rich in folklore and cultural tradition. Our perceptions of the South's heritage are clouded by myth. The characters and plots of these stories will both dispel and affirm many of your impressions.

The stories span several decades from the 1920s to the present and include a diverse cast of characters. For example, in Flannery O'Connor's "The Comforts of Home," a juvenile delinquent is the catalyst for the severing of a bond between a mother and her son. In Raymond Carver's story "Tell the Women We're Going," we are witness to the inner demons that drive a man to murder. Mr. Craig's "Jambalaya" presents an "old flame" who is at the heart of a dark crime. Other memorable characters include Eudora Welty's Mr. Marblehall, a southern gentleman whose secret double life is revealed in a most disturbing tale, Melville Davisson Post's eccentric defense attorney Colonel Braxton who finds himself on an impossible-to-win case, and Ed Hoch's infamous sleuth Nick Velvet attempting to steal a most unusual object.

On a lighter note, this Dixieland collection would not be complete without some New Orleans jazz in John Lutz's "The Right to Sing the Blues," or a touch of religion in Clark Howard's "The Last Revival," or a Civil War murder mystery in S. S. Rafferty's "The

Georgia Resurrection,'' or, of course, a good old-fashioned ghost story in Donald Honig's "Voices in Dead Man's Well."

Special attention should be given to "Willie's Story" by Jerry F. Skarky which won the Robert L. Fish Award. It is a powerful story of secrets that come to light when a young black girl is found stabbed to death.

I urge you to read *Death on the Verandah* and enjoy this diverse and compelling collection of mysteries set in the South by some of the masters of the art of the short story.

—Cynthia Manson

THE COMFORTS OF HOME
by *FLANNERY O'CONNOR*

Thomas withdrew to the side of the window and with his head between the wall and the curtain he looked down at the driveway where the car had stopped. His mother and the little slut were getting out of it. His mother emerged slowly, stolid and awkward, and then the little slut's long slightly bowed legs slid out, the dress pulled above the knees. With a shriek of laughter she ran to meet the dog, who bounded, overjoyed, shaking with pleasure, to welcome her. Rage gathered throughout Thomas's large frame with a silent ominous intensity, like a mob assembling.

It was now up to him to pack a suitcase, go to the hotel, and stay there until the house should be cleared.

He did not know where a suitcase was, he disliked to pack, he needed his books, his typewriter was not portable, he was used to an electric blanket, he could not bear to eat in restaurants. His mother, with her daredevil charity, was about to wreck the peace of the house.

The back door slammed and the girl's laugh shot up from the kitchen, through the back hall, up the stairwell and into his room, making for him like a bolt of electricity. He jumped to the side and stood glaring about him. His words of the morning had been unequivocal: "If you bring that girl back into this house, I leave. You can choose—her or me."

11

She had made her choice. An intense pain gripped his throat. It was the first time in his thirty-five years. He felt a sudden burning moisture behind his eyes. Then he steadied himself, overcome by rage. On the contrary: she had not made any choice. She was counting on his attachment to his electric blanket. She would have to be shown.

The girl's laughter rang upward a second time and Thomas winced. He saw again her look of the night before. She had invaded his room. He had waked to find his door open and her in it. There was enough light from the hall to make her visible as she turned toward him. The face was like a comedienne's in a musical comedy—a pointed chin, wide apple cheeks, and feline empty eyes. He had sprung out of his bed and snatched a straight chair and then he had backed her out the door, holding the chair in front of him like an animal trainer driving out a dangerous cat. He had driven her silently down the hall, pausing when he reached it to beat on his mother's door. The girl, with a gasp, turned and fled into the guest room.

In a moment his mother had opened her door and peered out apprehensively. Her face, greasy with whatever she put on it at night, was framed in pink rubber curlers. She looked down the hall where the girl had disappeared. Thomas stood before her, the chair still lifted in front of him as if he were about to quell another beast. "She tried to get in my room," he hissed, pushing in. "I woke up and she was trying to get in my room." He closed the door behind him and his voice rose in outrage. "I won't put up with this! I won't put up with it another day!"

His mother, backed by him to her bed, sat down on the edge of it. She had a heavy body on which sat a thin, mysteriously gaunt and incongruous head.

"I'm telling you for the last time," Thomas said, "I won't put up with this another day." There was an observable tendency in all of her actions. This was, with the best intentions in the world, to make a mockery of virtue, to pursue it with such a mindless intensity that everyone involved was made a fool of and virtue itself became ridiculous. "Not another day," he repeated.

His mother shook her head emphatically, her eyes still on the door.

Thomas put the chair on the floor in front of her and sat down on it. He leaned forward as if he were about to explain something to a defective child.

"That's just another way she's unfortunate," his mother said. "So awful, so awful. She told me the name of it but I forget what it is but it's something she can't help. Something she was born with. Thomas," she said and put her hand to her jaw, "suppose it were you?"

Exasperation blocked his windpipe. "Can't I make you see," he croaked, "that if she can't help herself you can't help her?"

His mother's eyes, intimate but untouchable, were the blue of great distances after sunset. "Nimpermaniac," she murmured.

"Nymphomaniac," he said fiercely. "She doesn't need to supply you with any fancy names. She's a moral moron. That's all you need to know. Born without the moral faculty—like somebody else would be born without a kidney or a leg. Do you understand?"

"I keep thinking it might be you," she said, her hand still on her jaw. "If it were you, how do you think I'd feel if nobody took you in? What if you were a nimpermaniac and not a brilliant smart person and you did what you couldn't help and—"

Thomas felt a deep unbearable loathing for himself as if he were turning slowly into the girl.

"What did she have on?" she asked abruptly, her eyes narrowing.

"Nothing!" he roared. "Now will you get her out of here!"

"How can I turn her out in the cold?" she said. "This morning she was threatening to kill herself again."

"Send her back to jail," Thomas said.

"I would not send *you* back to jail, Thomas," she said.

He got up and snatched the chair and fled the room while he was still able to control himself.

Thomas loved his mother. He loved her because it was his nature to do so, but there were times when he could not endure her love for him. There were times when it became nothing but pure idiot mystery and he sensed about him forces, invisible currents entirely out of his control. She proceeded always from the tritest of considerations—it was the *nice thing to do*—into the most foolhardy engagements with the devil, whom, of course, she never recognized.

The devil for Thomas was only a manner of speaking, but it was a manner appropriate to the situations his mother got into. Had she been in any degree intellectual, he could have proved to her from early Christian history that no excess of virtue is justified, that a moderation of good produces likewise a moderation in evil, that if Antony of Egypt had stayed at home and attended to his sister, no devils would have plagued him.

Thomas was not cynical and so far from being opposed to virtue, he saw it as the principle of order and the only thing that makes life bearable. His own life was made bearable by the fruits of his mother's saner virtues—by the well regulated house she kept and the excellent meals she served. But when virtue got out of hand with her, as now, a sense of devils grew upon him, and there were not mental quirks in himself or the old lady, they were denizens with personalities, present though not visible, who might any moment be expected to shriek or rattle a pot.

The girl had landed in the county jail a month ago on a bad-check charge and his mother had seen her picture in the paper. At the breakfast table she had gazed at it for a long time and then had passed it over the coffee pot to him. "Imagine," she said, "only nineteen years old and in that filthy jail. And she doesn't look like a bad girl."

Thomas glanced at the picture. It showed the face of a shrewd ragamuffin. He observed that the average age for criminality was steadily lowering.

"She looks like a wholesome girl," his mother said.

"Wholesome people don't pass bad checks," Thomas said.

"You don't know what you'd do in a pinch. "

"I wouldn't pass a bad check," Thomas said.

"I think," his mother said, "I'll take her a little box of candy."

If then and there he had put his foot down, nothing else would have happened. His father, had he been living, would have put his foot down at that point. Taking a box of candy was her favorite nice thing to do. When anyone within her social station moved to town, she called and took a box of candy; when any of her friends' children had babies or won a scholarship, she called and took a box of candy; when an old person broke his hip, she was at his bedside with a box of candy. He had been amused at the idea of her taking a box of candy to the jail.

He stood now in his room with the girl's laugh rocketing away in his head and cursed his amusement.

When his mother returned from the visit to the jail, she had burst into his study without knocking and had collapsed full-length on his couch, lifting her small swollen feet up on the arm of it. After a moment, she recovered herself enough to sit up and put a newspaper under them. Then she fell back again. "We don't know how the other half lives," she said.

Thomas knew that though her conversation moved from cliché to cliché there were real experiences behind them. He was less sorry for the girl's being in jail than for his mother having to see her there. He would have spared her all unpleasant sights. "Well," he said and put away his journal, "you had better forget it now. The girl has ample reason to be in jail."

"You can't imagine what all she's been through," she said, sitting up again, "listen." The poor girl, Star, had been brought up by a stepmother with three children of her own, one an almost grown boy who had taken advantage of her in such dreadful ways that she had been forced to run away and find her real mother. Once found, her real mother had sent her to various boarding schools to get rid of her. At each of these, she had been forced to run away by the presence of perverts and sadists so monstrous that their acts defied description.

Thomas could tell that his mother had not been spared the details that she was sparing him. Now and again when she spoke vaguely, her voice shook and he could tell that she was remembering some horror that had been put to her graphically. He had hoped that in a few days the memory of all this would wear off, but it did not. The next day she returned to the jail with Kleenex and cold cream and a few days later, she announced that she had consulted a lawyer.

It was at these times that Thomas truly mourned the death of his father, though he had not been able to endure him in life. The old man would have had none of this foolishness. Untouched by useless compassion, he would (behind her back) have pulled the necessary strings with his crony, the sheriff, and the girl would have been packed off to the state penitentiary to serve her time. He had always been engaged in some enraged action until one morning when (with an angry glance at his wife as if she alone were responsible) he had dropped dead at the breakfast table. Thomas had inherited his father's reason without his ruthlessness and his mother's love of good without her tendency to pursue it. His plan for all practical action was to wait and see what developed.

The lawyer found that the story of the repeated atrocities was for the most part untrue, but when he explained to her that the girl was a psychopathic personality, not insane enough for the asylum, not criminal enough for the jail, not stable enough for society, Thomas's mother was more deeply affected than ever. The girl readily admitted that her story was untrue on account of her being a congenital liar; she lied, she said, because she was insecure. She had passed through the hands of several psychiatrists who had put the finishing touches to her education. She knew there was no hope for her. In the presence of such an affliction as this, his mother seemed bowed down by some painful mystery that nothing would make endurable but a redoubling of effort. To his annoyance, she appeared to look on *him* with compassion, as if her hazy charity no longer made distinctions.

A few days later she burst in and said that the lawyer had got the girl paroled—to her.

Thomas rose from his Morris chair, dropping the review he had been reading. His large bland face contracted in anticipated pain. "You are not," he said, "going to bring that girl here!"

"No, no," she said, "calm yourself, Thomas." She had managed with difficulty to get the girl a job in a pet shop in town and a place to board with a crotchety old lady of her acquaintance. People were not kind. They did not put themselves in the place of someone like Star who had everything against her.

Thomas sat down again and retrieved his review. He seemed just to have escaped some danger which he did not care to make clear to himself. "Nobody can tell you anything," he said, "but in a few days that girl will have left town, having got what she could out of you. You'll never hear from her again."

* * *

Two nights later he came home and opened the parlor door and was speared by a shrill depthless laugh. His mother and the girl sat close to the fireplace where the gas logs were lit. The girl gave the immediate impression of being physically crooked. Her hair was cut like a dog's or an elf's and she was dressed in the latest fashion. She was training on him a long familiar sparkling stare that turned after a second into an intimate grin.

"Thomas!" his mother said, her voice firm with the injunction not to bolt. "This is Star you've heard so much about. Star is going to have supper with us."

The girl called herself Star Drake. The lawyer had found that her real name was Sarah Ham.

Thomas neither moved nor spoke but hung in the door in what seemed a savage perplexity. Finally he said, "How do you do, Sarah," in a tone of such loathing that he was shocked at the sound of it. He reddened, feeling it beneath him to show contempt for any creature so pathetic. He advanced into the room, determined at least on a decent politeness and sat down heavily in a straight chair.

"Thomas writes history," his mother said with a threatening look at him. "He's president of the local Historical Society this year."

The girl leaned forward and gave Thomas an even more pointed attention. "Fabulous!" she said in a throaty voice.

"Right now Thomas is writing about the first settlers in this county," his mother said.

"Fabulous!" the girl repeated.

Thomas by an effort of will managed to look as if he were alone in the room.

"Say, you know who he looks like?" Star asked, her head on one side, taking him in at an angle.

"Oh, someone very distinguished!" his mother said archly.

"This cop I saw in the movie I went to last night," Star said.

"Star," his mother said, "I think you ought to be careful about the kind of movies you go to. I think you ought to see only the best ones. I don't think crime stories would be good for you."

"Oh this was a crime-does-not–pay," Star said, "and I swear this cop looked exactly like him. They were always putting something over on the guy. He would look like he couldn't stand it a minute

longer or he would blow up. He was a riot. And not bad-looking,"
she added with an appreciative leer at Thomas.

"Star," his mother said, "I think it would be grand if you developed a taste for music."

Thomas sighed. His mother rattled on and the girl, paying no
attention to her, let her eyes play over him. The quality of her look
was such that it might have been her hands, resting now on his
knees, now on his neck. Her eyes had a mocking glitter and he knew
that she was well aware he could not stand the sight of her. He
needed nothing to tell him he was in the presence of the very stuff of
corruption, but blameless corruption because there was no responsible
faculty behind it. He was looking at the most unendurable form of
innocence. Absently he asked himself what the attitude of God was
to this, meaning if possible to adopt it.

His mother's behavior throughout the meal was so idiotic that he
could barely stand to look at her, and since he could less stand to
look at Sarah Ham he fixed on the sideboard across the room a
continuous gaze of disapproval and disgust. Every remark of the
girl's his mother met as if it deserved serious attention. She advanced
several plans for the wholesome use of Star's spare time.

Sarah Ham paid no more attention to this advice than if it came
from a parrot. Once when Thomas inadvertently looked in her direction, she winked. As soon as he had swallowed the last spoonful of
dessert, he rose and muttered, "I have to go, I have a meeting."

"Thomas," his mother said, "I want you to take Star home on
your way. I don't want her riding in taxis by herself at night."

For a moment Thomas remained furiously silent. Then he turned
and left the room. Presently he came back with a look of obscure
determination on his face. The girl was ready, meekly waiting at the
parlor door. She cast up at him a great look of admiration and confidence. Thomas did not offer his arm but she took it anyway and
moved out of the house and down the steps, attached to what might
have been a miraculously moving monument.

"Be good!" his mother called.

Sarah Ham snickered and poked him in the ribs.

While getting his coat he had decided that this would be his opportunity to tell the girl that unless she ceased to be a parasite on his

mother, he would see to it, personally, that she was returned to jail. He would let her know that he understood what she was up to, that he was not an innocent, and that there were certain things he would not put up with. At his desk, pen in hand, none was more articulate than Thomas. As soon as he found himself shut into the car with Sarah Ham, terror seized his tongue.

She curled her feet up under her and said, "Alone at last," and giggled.

Thomas swerved the car away from the house and drove fast toward the gate. Once on the highway, he shot forward as if he were being pursued.

"Jesus!" Sarah Ham said, swinging her feet off the seat. "Where's the fire?"

Thomas did not answer. In a few seconds he could feel her edging closer. She stretched, eased nearer, and finally hung her hand limply over his shoulder. "Tomsee doesn't like me," she said, "but I think he's fabulously cute."

Thomas covered the three and a half miles into town in a little over four minutes. The light at the first intersection was red but he ignored it. The old woman lived three blocks beyond. When the car screeched to a halt at the place, he jumped out and ran around to the girl's door and opened it.

She did not move from the car and Thomas was obliged to wait. After a moment one leg emerged, then her small white crooked face appeared and stared up at him. There was something about the look of it that suggested blindness but it was the blindness of those who don't know that they cannot see. Thomas was curiously sickened. The empty eyes moved over him. "Nobody likes me," she said in a sullen tone. "What if you were me and I couldn't stand to ride *you* three miles?"

"My mother likes you," he muttered.

"Her!" the girl said. "She's just about seventy-five years behind the times!"

Breathlessly Thomas said, "If I find you bothering her again, I'll have you put back in jail." There was a dull force behind his voice though it came out barely above a whisper.

"You and who else?" she said and drew back in the car as if

now she did not intend to get out at all. Thomas reached into it, blindly grasped the front of her coat, pulled her out of it, and released her. Then he lunged back to the car and sped off. The other door was still hanging open and her laugh, bodiless but real, bounded up the street as if it were about to jump in the open side of the car and ride away with him. He reached over and slammed the door and then drove toward home, too angry to attend his meeting. He intended to make his mother well aware of his displeasure. He intended to leave no doubt in her mind. The voice of his father rasped in his head.

Numbskull, the old man said, put your foot down now. Show her who's boss before she shows you.

But when Thomas reached home, his mother, wisely, had gone to bed.

The next morning he appeared at the breakfast table, his brow lowered and the thrust of his jaw indicating that he was in a dangerous humor. When he intended to be determined, Thomas began like a bull that, before charging, backs with his head lowered and paws the ground. "All right now, listen," he began, yanking out his chair and sitting down, "I have something to say to you about that girl and I don't intend to say it but once." He drew breath. "She's nothing but a little slut. She makes fun of you behind your back. She means to get everything she can out of you and you are nothing to her."

His mother looked as if she, too, had spent a restless night. She did not dress in the morning but wore her bathrobe and a grey turban around her head, which gave her face a disconcerting omniscient look. He might have been breakfasting with a sibyl.

"You'll have to use canned cream this morning," she said, pouring his coffee. "I forgot the other."

"All right, did you hear me?" Thomas growled.

"I'm not deaf," his mother said and put the pot back on the trivet. "I know I'm nothing but an old bag of wind to her."

"Then why do you persist in this foolhardy—"

"Thomas," she said, and put her hand to the side of her face, "it might be—"

"It is not me!" Thomas said, grasping the table leg at his knee.

She continued to hold her face, shaking her head slightly. "Think of all you have," she began. "All the comforts of home. And morals, Thomas. No bad inclinations, nothing bad you were born with."

Thomas began to breathe like someone who feels the onset of asthma. "You are not logical," he said in a limp voice. "*He* would have put his foot down."

The old lady stiffened. "You," she said, "are not like him."

Thomas opened his mouth silently.

"However," his mother said, in a tone of such subtle accusation that she might have been taking back the compliment, "I won't invite her back again since you're so dead set against her."

"I am not set against her," Thomas said. "I am set against your making a fool of yourself."

As soon as he left the table and closed the door of his study on himself, his father took up a squatting position in his mind. The old man had had the countryman's ability to converse squatting, though he was no countryman but had been born and brought up in the city and only moved to a smaller place later to exploit his talents. With steady skill, he had made them think him one of them. In the midst of a conversation on the courthouse lawn, he would squat and his two or three companions would squat with him with no break in the surface of the talk. By gesture he had lived his lie; he had never deigned to tell one.

Let her run over you, he said. You ain't like me. Not enough to be a man.

Thomas began vigorously to read and presently the image faded. The girl had caused a disturbance in the depths of his being, somewhere out of the reach of his power of analysis. He felt as if he had seen a tornado pass a hundred yards away and had an intimation that it would turn again and head directly for him. He did not get his mind firmly on his work until mid-morning.

Two nights later, his mother and he were sitting in the den after their supper, each reading a section of the evening paper, when the telephone began to ring with the brassy intensity of a fire alarm. Thomas reached for it. As soon as the receiver was in his hand, a shrill female voice screamed into the room, "Come get this girl! Come get her! Drunk! Drunk in my parlor and I won't have it! Lost her job and come back here drunk! I won't have it!"

His mother leapt up and snatched the receiver.

The ghost of Thomas's father rose before him. Call the sheriff, the old man prompted. "Call the sheriff," Thomas said in a loud voice. "Call the sheriff to go there and pick her up."

"We'll be right there," his mother was saying. "We'll come and get her right away. Tell her to get her things together."

"She ain't in no condition to get nothing together!" the voice screamed. "You shouldn't have put something like her off on me! My house is respectable!"

"Tell her to call the sheriff," Thomas shouted.

His mother put down the receiver and looked at him. "I wouldn't turn a dog over to that man," she said.

Thomas sat in the chair with his arms folded and looked fixedly at the wall.

"Think of the poor girl, Thomas," his mother said, "with nothing. Nothing. And we have everything."

When they arrived, Sarah Ham was slumped spraddle-legged against the banister on the boarding-house front steps. Her tam was down on her forehead where the old woman had slammed it and her clothes were bulging out of her suitcase where the old woman had thrown them in. She was carrying on a drunken conversation with herself in a low personal tone. A streak of lipstick ran up one side of her face. She allowed herself to be guided by his mother to the car and put in the back seat without seeming to know who the rescuer was. "Nothing to talk to all day but a pack of goddamned parakeets," she said in a furious whisper.

Thomas, who had not got out of the car at all, or looked at her after the first revolted glance, said, "I'm telling you once and for all, the placc to take her is the jail."

His mother, sitting on the back seat, holding the girl's hand, did not answer.

"All right, take her to the hotel," he said.

"I cannot take a drunk girl to a hotel, Thomas," she said. "You know that."

"Then take her to a hospital."

"She doesn't need a jail or a hotel or a hospital," his mother said, "she needs a home."

"She doesn't need mine," Thomas said.

"Only for tonight, Thomas," the old lady sighed. "Only for tonight."

Since then eight days had passed. The little slut was established in the guest room. Every day his mother set out to find her a job and a place to board, and failed, for the old woman had broadcast a warning. Thomas kept to his room or the den. His home was to him home, workshop, church, as personal as the shell of a turtle and as necessary. He could not believe that it could be violated in this way. His flushed face had a constant look of stunned outrage.

As soon as the girl was up in the morning, her voice throbbed out in a blues song that would rise and waver, then plunge low with insinuations of passion about to be satisfied, and Thomas, at his desk, would lunge up and begin frantically stuffing his ears with Kleenex. Each time he started from one room to another, one floor to another, she would be certain to appear. Each time he was halfway up or down the stairs, she would either meet him and pass, cringing coyly, or go up or down behind him, breathing small, tragic, spearmint-flavored sighs. She appeared to adore Thomas's repugnance to her and to draw it out of him every chance she got as if it added delectably to her martyrdom.

The old man—small, wasp-like, in his yellowed panama hat, his seersucker suit, his pink, carefully soiled shirt, his small string tie—appeared to have taken up his station in Thomas's mind and from there, usually squatting, he shot out the same rasping suggestion every time the boy paused from his forced studies. Put your foot down. Go to see the sheriff.

The sheriff was another edition of Thomas's father except that he wore a checkered shirt and a Texas-type hat and was ten years younger. He was as easily dishonest, and he had genuinely admired the old man. Thomas, like his mother, would have gone far out of his way to avoid his glassy pale-blue gaze. He kept hoping for another solution, for a miracle.

With Sarah Ham in the house, meals were unbearable.

"Tomsee doesn't like me," she said the third or fourth night at the supper table and cast her pouting gaze across at the large rigid figure of Thomas, whose face was set with the look of a man trapped by insufferable odors. "He doesn't want me here. Nobody wants me anywhere."

"Thomas's name is Thomas," his mother interrupted. "Not Tomsee."

"I made Tomsee up," she said. "I think it's cute. He hates me."

"Thomas does not hate you," his mother said. "We are not the kind of people who hate," she added, as if this were an imperfection that had been bred out of them generations ago.

"Oh, I know when I'm not wanted," Sarah Ham continued. "They didn't even want me in jail. If I killed myself I wonder would God want me?"

"Try it and see," Thomas muttered.

The girl screamed with laughter. Then she stopped abruptly, her face puckered, and she began to shake. "The best thing to do," she said, her teeth clattering, "is to kill myself. Then I'll be out of everybody's way. I'll go to hell and be out of God's way. And even the devil won't want me. He'll kick me out of hell, not even in hell—" she wailed.

Thomas rose, picked up his plate and knife and fork, and carried them to the den to finish his supper. After that, he had not eaten another meal at the table but had had his mother serve him at his desk. At these meals, the old man was intensely present to him. He appeared to be tipping backwards in his chair, his thumbs beneath his galluses, while he said such things as, She never ran me away from my own table.

A few nights later, Sarah Ham slashed her wrists with a paring knife and had hysterics. From the den where he was closeted after supper, Thomas heard a shriek, then a series of screams, then his mother's scurrying footsteps through the house. He did not move. His first instance of hope that the girl had cut her throat faded as he realized she could not have done it and continue to scream the way she was doing. He returned to his journal and presently the screams subsided. In a moment his mother burst in with his coat and hat. "We have to take her to the hospital," she said. "She tried to do away with herself. I have a tourniquet on her arm. Oh, Lord, Thomas," she said, "imagine being so low you'd do a thing like that!"

Thomas rose woodenly and put on his hat and coat. "We will take her to the hospital," he said, "and we will leave her there."

"And drive her to despair again?" the old lady cried. "Thomas!"

Standing in the center of his room now, realizing that he had reached the point where action was inevitable, that he must pack, that he must leave, that he must go, Thomas remained immovable.

His fury was directed not at the little slut but at his mother. Even though the doctor had found that she had barely damaged herself and had raised the girl's wrath by laughing at the tourniquet and putting only a streak of iodine on the cut, his mother could not get over the incident. Some new weight of sorrow seemed to have been thrown across her shoulders, and not only Thomas, but Sarah Ham was infuriated by this, for it appeared to be a general sorrow that would have found another object no matter what good fortune came to either of them. The experience of Sarah Ham had plunged the old lady into mourning for the world.

The morning after the attempted suicide, she had gone through the house and collected all the knives and scissors and locked them in a drawer. She emptied a bottle of rat poison down the toilet and took up the roach tablets from the kitchen floor. Then she came to Thomas's study and said in a whisper, "Where is that gun of his? I want you to lock it up."

"The gun is in my drawer," Thomas roared, "and I will not lock it up. If she shoots herself, so much the better!"

"Thomas," his mother said, "she'll hear you!"

"Let her hear me!" Thomas yelled. "Don't you know she has no intention of killing herself? Don't you know her kind never kill themselves? Don't you—"

His mother slipped out the door and closed it to silence him and Sarah Ham's laugh, quite close in the hall, came rattling into his room. "Tomsee'll find out. I'll kill myself and then he'll be sorry he wasn't nice to me. I'll use his own lil gun, his own lil ol' pearl-handled revol-lervuh!'' she shouted and let out a loud tormented-sounding laugh in imitation of a movie monster.

Thomas ground his teeth. He pulled out his drawer and felt for the pistol. It was an inheritance from the old man, whose opinion it had been that every house should contain a loaded gun. He had discharged two bullets one night into the side of a prowler, but Thomas had never shot anything. He had no fear that the girl would use the gun on herself and he closed the drawer. Her kind clung tenaciously to life and were able to wrest some histrionic advantage from every moment.

Several ideas for getting rid of her had entered his head but each of these had been suggestions whose moral tone indicated that they had come from a mind akin to his father's, and Thomas had rejected them. He could not get the girl locked up again until she did something illegal. The old man would have been able with no qualms at all to get her drunk and send her out on the highway in his car, meanwhile notifying the highway patrol of her presence on the road, but Thomas considered this below his moral stature. Suggestions continued to come to him, each more outrageous than the last.

He had not the vaguest hope that the girl would get the gun and shoot herself, but that afternoon when he looked in the drawer the gun was gone. His study locked from the inside, not the out. He cared nothing about the gun, but the thought of Sarah Ham's hands sliding among his papers infuriated him. Now even his study was contaminated. The only place left untouched by her was his bedroom.

That night she entered it.

In the morning at breakfast, he did not eat and did not sit down. He stood beside his chair and delivered his ultimatum while his mother sipped her coffee as if she were both alone in the room and in great pain. "I have stood this," he said, "for as long as I am able. Since I see plainly that you care nothing about me, about my peace or comfort or working conditions, I am about to take the only step open to me. I will give you one more day. If you bring the girl back into this house this afternoon, I leave. You can choose—her or me." He had more to say but at that point his voice cracked and he left the room.

At ten o'clock his mother and Sarah Ham left the house.

At four he heard the car wheels on the gravel and rushed to the window. As the car stopped, the dog stood up, alert, shaking.

Thomas seemed unable to take the first step that would set him walking to the closet in the hall to look for the suitcase. He was like a man handed a knife and told to operate on himself if he wished to live. His huge hands clenched helplessly. His expression was a turmoil of indecision and outrage. His pale-blue eyes seemed to sweat in his broiling face. He closed them for a moment and on the back of his lids, his father's image leered at him. Idiot! the old man hissed, idiot! The criminal slut stole your gun! See the sheriff! See the sheriff!

It was a moment before Thomas opened his eyes. He seemed newly stunned. He stood where he was for at least three minutes, then he turned slowly like a large vessel reversing its direction and faced the door. He stood there a moment longer, then he left, his face set to see the ordeal through.

He did not know where he would find the sheriff. The man made his own rules and kept his own hours. Thomas stopped first at the jail where his office was, but he was not in it. He went to the courthouse and was told by a clerk that the sheriff had gone to the barber shop across the street. "Yonder's the deppity," the clerk said and pointed out the window to the large figure of a man in a checkered shirt, who was leaning against the side of a police car, looking into space.

"It has to be the sheriff," Thomas said and left for the barber shop. As little as he wanted anything to do with the sheriff, he realized that the man was at least intelligent and not simply a mound of sweating flesh.

The barber said the sheriff had just left. Thomas started back to the courthouse and as he stepped onto the sidewalk from the street, he saw a lean, slightly stooped figure gesticulating angrily at the deputy.

Thomas approached with an aggressiveness brought on by nervous agitation. He stopped abruptly three feet away and said in an overloud voice, "Can I have a word with you?" without adding the sheriff's name, which was Farebrother.

Farebrother turned his sharp creased face just enough to take Thomas in, and the deputy did likewise, but neither spoke. The sheriff removed a very small piece of cigarette from his lip and dropped it at his feet. "I told you what to do," he said to the deputy. Then he moved off with a slight nod that indicated Thomas could follow him if he wanted to see him. The deputy slunk around the front of the police car and got inside.

Farebrother, with Thomas following, headed across the courthouse square and stopped beneath a tree that shaded a quarter of the front lawn. He waited, leaning slightly forward, and lit another cigarette.

Thomas began to blurt out his business. As he had not had time to prepare his words, he was barely coherent. By repeating the same thing over several times, he managed at length to get out what he wanted to say. When he finished, the sheriff was still leaning slightly forward, at an angle to him, his eyes on nothing in particular. He remained that way without speaking.

Thomas began again, slower and in a lamer voice, and Farebrother let him continue for some time before he said, "We had her once." He then allowed himself a slow, creased, all-knowing quarter smile.

"I had nothing to do with that," Thomas said. "That was my mother."

Farebrother squatted.

"She was trying to help the girl," Thomas said. "She didn't know she couldn't be helped."

"Bit off more than she could chew, I reckon," the voice below him mused.

"She has nothing to do with this," Thomas said. "She doesn't know I'm here. The girl is dangerous with that gun."

"*He,*" the sheriff said, "never let anything grow under his feet. Particularly nothing a woman planted."

"She might kill somebody with that gun," Thomas said weakly, looking down at the round top of the Texas-type hat.

There was a long time of silence.

"Where's she got it?" Farebrother asked.

"I don't know. She sleeps in the guest room. It must be in there, in her suitcase probably," Thomas said.

Farebrother lapsed into silence again.

"You could come search the guest room," Thomas said in a strained voice. "I can go home and leave the latch off the front door and you can come in quietly and go upstairs and search her room."

Farebrother turned his head so that his eyes looked boldly at Thomas's knees. "You seem to know how it ought to be done," he said. "Want to swap jobs?"

Thomas said nothing because he couldn't think of anything to say, but he waited doggedly. Farebrother removed the cigarette butt from his lips and dropped it on the grass. Beyond him on the courthouse porch a group of loiterers who had been leaning at the left of the door moved over to the right where a patch of sunlight had settled. From one of the upper windows a crumpled piece of paper blew out and drifted down.

"I'll come along about six," Farebrother said. "Leave the latch off the door and keep out of the way—yourself and them two women, too."

Thomas let out a rasping sound of relief meant to be "Thanks," and struck off across the grass like someone released. The phrase, "them two women," stuck like a burr in his brain—the subtlety of the insult to his mother hurting him more than any of Farebrother's references to his own incompetence. As he got into his car, his face suddenly flushed. Had he delivered his mother over to the sheriff—to be a butt for the man's tongue? Was he betraying her to get rid of the little slut? He saw at once that this was not the case. He was doing what he was doing for her own good, to rid her of a parasite that would ruin their peace.

He started his car and drove quickly home, but once he had turned in the driveway he decided it would be better to park some distance from the house and go quietly in by the back door. He parked on the grass and on the grass walked in a circle toward the rear of the house. The sky was lined with mustard-colored streaks. The dog was asleep on the back doormat. At the approach of his master's step, he opened one yellow eye, took him in, and closed it again.

Thomas let himself into the kitchen. It was empty and the house was quiet enough for him to be aware of the loud ticking of the kitchen clock. It was a quarter to six. He tiptoed hurriedly through the hall to the front door and took the latch off it. Then he stood for a moment listening. From behind the closed parlor door, he heard his mother snoring softly and presumed that she had gone to sleep while reading. On the other side of the hall, not three feet from his study, the little slut's black coat and red pocketbook were slung on a chair. He heard water running upstairs and decided she was taking a bath.

He went into his study and sat down at his desk to wait, noting with distaste that every few moments a tremor ran through him. He sat for a minute or two doing nothing. Then he picked up a pen and began to draw squares on the back of an envelope that lay before him. He looked at his watch. It was eleven minutes to six. After a moment he idly drew the center drawer of the desk out over his lap. For a moment he stared at the gun without recognition. Then he gave a yelp and leaped up. She had put it back!

Idiot! his father hissed, idiot! Go plant it in her pocketbook. Don't just stand there. Go plant it in her pocketbook!

Thomas stood staring at the drawer.

Moron! the old man fumed. Quick, while there's time! Go plant it in her pocketbook!

Thomas did not move.

Imbecile! his father cried.

Thomas picked up the gun.

Make haste! the old man ordered.

Thomas started forward, holding the gun away from him. He opened the door and looked at the chair. The black coat and red pocketbook were lying on it almost within reach.

Hurry up, you fool, his father said.

From behind the parlor door, the almost inaudible snores of his mother rose and fell. They seemed to mark an order of time that had nothing to do with the instants left to Thomas. There was no other sound.

Quick, you imbecile, before she wakes up, the old man said.

The snores stopped and Thomas heard the sofa spring groan. He grabbed the red pocketbook. It had a skinlike feel to his touch and as it opened he caught an unmistakable odor of the girl. Wincing, he thrust in the gun and then drew back. His face burned an ugly dull red.

"What is Tomsee putting in my purse?" she called and her pleased laugh bounced down the staircase. Thomas whirled.

She was at the top of the stair, coming down in the manner of a fashion model, one bare leg and then the other thrusting out the front of her kimona in a definite rhythm. "Tomsee is being naughty," she said in a throaty voice. She reached the bottom and cast a possessive leer at Thomas, whose face was now more grey than red. She reached out, pulled the bag open with her finger and peered at the gun.

His mother opened the parlor door and looked out.

"Tomsee put his pistol in my bag!" the girl shrieked.

"Ridiculous," his mother said, yawning. "What would Thomas want to put his pistol in your bag for?"

Thomas stood slightly hunched, his hands hanging helplessly at the wrists as if he had just pulled them out of a pool of blood.

"I don't know what for," the girl said, "but he sure did it," and she proceeded to walk around Thomas, her hands on her hips, her neck thrust forward and her intimate grin fixed on him fiercely. All at once her expression seemed to open as the purse had opened when Thomas touched it. She stood with her head cocked on one side in an attitude of disbelief. "Oh boy," she said slowly, "is he a case."

At that instant, Thomas damned not only the girl but the entire order of the universe that made her possible.

"Thomas wouldn't put a gun in your bag," his mother said. "Thomas is a gentleman."

The girl made a chortling noise. "You can see it in there," she said and pointed to the open purse.

You *found* it in her bag, you dimwit! the old man hissed.

"I found it in her bag!" Thomas shouted. "The dirty criminal slut stole my gun!"

His mother gasped at the sound of the other presence in his voice. The old lady's sybil-like face turned pale.

"Found it, my eye!" Sarah Ham shrieked and started for the pocketbook, but Thomas, as if his arm were guided by his father, caught it first and snatched the gun. The girl in a frenzy lunged at Thomas's throat and would actually have caught him around the neck had not his mother thrown herself forward to protect her.

Fire! the old man yelled.

Thomas fired. The blast was like a sound meant to bring an end to evil in the world. Thomas heard it as a sound that would shatter the laughter of sluts until all shrieks were stilled and nothing was left to disturb the peace of perfect order.

The echo died away in waves. Before the last ones had faded, Farebrother opened the door and put his head inside the hall. His nose wrinkled. His expression for some few seconds was that of a man unwilling to admit surprise. His eyes were clear as glass, reflecting the scene. The old lady lay on the floor between the girl and Thomas.

The sheriff's brain worked instantly like a calculating machine. He saw the facts as if they were already in print: the fellow had intended all along to kill his mother and pin it on the girl. But Farebrother had been too quick for him. They were not yet aware of his head in the door. As he scrutinized the scene, further insights were flashed to him. Over her body, the killer and the slut were about to collapse into each other's arms. The sheriff knew a nasty bit when he saw it. He was accustomed to enter upon scenes that were not as bad as he had hoped to find them, but this one met his expectations.

TELL THE WOMEN
WE'RE GOING

by RAYMOND CARVER

Bill Jamison had always been best friends with Jerry Roberts. The two grew up in the south area, near the old fairgrounds, went through grade school and junior high together, and then on to Eisenhower, where they took as many of the same teachers as they could manage, wore each other's shirts and sweaters and pegged pants, and dated and banged the same girls—whichever came up as a matter of course.

Summers they took jobs together—swamping peaches, picking cherries, stringing hops, anything they could do that paid a little and where there was no boss to get on your ass. And then they bought a car together. The summer before their senior year, they chipped in and bought a red '54 Plymouth for $325.00.

They shared it. It worked out fine.

But Jerry got married before the end of the first semester and dropped out of school to work steady at Robby's Mart.

As for Bill, he'd dated the girl, too. Carol was her name, and she went just fine with Jerry, and Bill went over there every chance he got. It made him feel older, having married friends. He'd go over there for lunch or for supper, and they'd listen to Elvis or to Bill Haley and the Comets.

But sometimes Carol and Jerry would start making out right with Bill still there, and he'd have to get up and excuse himself and take

33

a walk to Dezorn's Service Station to get some Coke because there was only the one bed in the apartment, a hideaway that came down in the living room. Or sometimes Jerry and Carol would head off to the bathroom and Bill would have to move to the kitchen and pretend to be interested in the cupboards and the refrigerator and not trying to listen.

So he stopped going over so much; and then June he graduated, took a job at the Darigold plant, and joined the National Guard. In a year he had a milk route of his own and was going steady with Linda. So Bill and Linda would go over to Jerry and Carol's, drink beer, and listen to records.

Carol and Linda got along fine, and Bill was flattered when Carol said that, confidentially, Linda was "a real person."

Jerry liked Linda, too. "She's great," Jerry said.

When Bill and Linda got married, Jerry was best man. The reception, of course, was at the Donnelly Hotel, Jerry and Bill cutting up together and linking arms and tossing off glasses of spiked punch. But once, in the middle of all this happiness, Bill looked at Jerry and thought how much older Jerry looked, a lot older than twenty-two. By then Jerry was the happy father of two kids and had moved up to assistant manager at Robby's, and Carol had one in the oven again.

They saw each other every Saturday and Sunday, sometimes of-tener if it was a holiday. If the weather was good, they'd be over at Jerry's to barbecue hot dogs and turn the kids loose in the wading pool Jerry had got for next to nothing, like a lot of other things he got from the Mart.

Jerry had a nice house. It was up on a hill overlooking the Naches. There were other houses around, but not too close. Jerry was doing all right. When Bill and Linda and Jerry and Carol got together, it was always at Jerry's place because Jerry had the barbecue and the records and too many kids to drag around.

It was a Sunday at Jerry's place the time it happened.

The women were in the kitchen, straightening up. Jerry's girls were out in the yard throwing a plastic ball into the wading pool, yelling and splashing after it.

Jerry and Bill were sitting in the reclining chairs on the patio, drinking beer and just relaxing.

Bill was doing most of the talking—things about people they knew, about Darigold, about the four-door Pontiac Catalina he was thinking of buying.

Jerry was staring at the clothesline, or at the '68 Chevy hardtop that stood in the garage. Bill was thinking how Jerry was getting to be deep, the way he stared all the time and hardly did any talking at all.

Bill moved in his chair and lighted a cigarette.

He said, "Anything wrong, man? I mean, you know."

Jerry finished his beer and then mashed the can. He shrugged. "You know," he said.

Bill nodded.

Then Jerry said, "How about a little run?"

"Sounds good to me," Bill said. "I'll tell the women we're going."

They took the Naches River highway out to Gleed, Jerry driving. The day was sunny and warm, and air blew through the car.

"Where we headed?" Bill said.

"Let's shoot a few balls."

"Fine with me," Bill said. He felt a whole lot better just seeing Jerry brighten up.

"Guy's got to get out," Jerry said. He looked at Bill. "You know what I mean?"

Bill understood. He liked to get out with the guys from the plant for the Friday-night bowling league. He liked to stop off twice a week after work to have a few beers with Jack Broderick. He knew a guy's got to get out.

"Still standing," Jerry said, as they pulled up onto the gravel in front of the Rec Center.

They went inside, Bill holding the door for Jerry, Jerry punching Bill lightly in the stomach as he went on by.

"Hey there!"

It was Riley.

"Hey, how you boys keeping?"

It was Riley coming around from behind the counter, grinning. He was a heavy man. He had on a short-sleeved Hawaiian shirt that hung outside his jeans. Riley said, "So how you boys been keeping?"

"Ah, dry up and give us a couple of Olys," Jerry said, winking at Bill. "So how you been, Riley?" Jerry said.

Riley said, "So how you boys doing? Where you been keeping yourselves? You boys getting any on the side? Jerry, the last time I seen you, your old lady was six months gone."

Jerry stood a minute and blinked his eyes.

"So how about the Olys?" Bill said.

They took stools near the window. Jerry said, "What kind of place is this, Riley, that it don't have any girls on a Sunday afternoon?"

Riley laughed. He said, "I guess they're all in church praying for it."

They each had five cans of beer and took two hours to play three racks of rotation and two racks of snooker, Riley sitting on a stool and talking and watching them play, Bill always looking at his watch and then looking at Jerry.

Bill said, "So what do you think, Jerry? I mean, what do you think?"

Jerry drained his can, mashed it, then stood for a time turning the can in his hand.

Back on the highway, Jerry opened it up—little jumps of eighty-five and ninety. They'd just passed an old pickup loaded with furniture when they saw the two girls.

"Look at that!" Jerry said, slowing. "I could use some of that."

Jerry drove another mile or so and then pulled off the road. "Let's go back," he said. "Let's try it."

"Jesus," Bill said. "I don't know."

"I could use some," Jerry said.

Bill said, "Yeah, but I don't know."

"For Christ's sake," Jerry said.

Bill glanced at his watch and then looked all around. He said, "You do the talking. I'm rusty."

Jerry hooted as he whipped the car around.

He slowed when he came nearly even with the girls. He pulled the Chevy onto the shoulder across from them. The girls kept on going on their bicycles, but they looked at each other and laughed. The one on the inside was dark-haired, tall, and willowy. The other was light-haired and smaller. They both wore shorts and halters.

"Bitches," Jerry said. He waited for the cars to pass so he could pull a U. "I'll take the brunette," he said. "The little one's yours."

Bill moved his back against the front seat and touched the bridge of his sunglasses.

"They're not going to do anything," Bill said.

"They're going to be on your side," Jerry said. He pulled across the road and drove back. "Get ready."

"Hi," Bill said as the girls bicycled up. "My name's Bill."

"That's nice," the brunette said.

"Where are you going?" Bill said.

The girls didn't answer. The little one laughed. They kept bicycling and Jerry kept driving.

"Oh, come on now. Where are you going?" Bill said.

"Noplace," the little one said.

"Where's noplace?" Bill said.

"Wouldn't you like to know?" the little one said.

"I told you my name," Bill said. "What's yours? My friend's Jerry."

The girls looked at each other and laughed.

A car came up from behind. The driver hit his horn.

"Cram it!" Jerry shouted.

He pulled off a little and let the car go around. Then he pulled back up alongside the girls.

Bill said, "We'll give you a lift. We'll take you where you want. That's a promise. You must be tired riding those bicycles. You look tired. Too much exercise isn't good for a person. Especially for girls."

The girls laughed.

"You see?" Bill said. "Now tell us your names."

"I'm Barbara, she's Sharon," the little one said.

"All right!" Jerry said. "Now find out where they're going."

"Where you girls going?" Bill said. "Barb?"

She laughed. "Noplace," she said. "Just down the road."

"Where down the road?"

"Do you want me to tell them?" she said to the other girl.

"I don't care," the other girl said. "It doesn't make any difference. I'm not going to go anyplace with anybody anyway."

"Where you going?" Bill said. "Are you going to Picture Rock?" The girls laughed.

"That's where they're going," Jerry said. He fed the Chevy gas and pulled up off onto the shoulder so that the girls had to come by on his side.

"Don't be that way," he said. "Come on, we're all introduced." The girls just rode on by.

"I won't bite you!" Jerry shouted.

The brunette glanced back. It seemed to Jerry she was looking at him in the right kind of way. But with a girl you could never be sure.

He gunned it back onto the highway, dirt and pebbles flying from under the tires.

"We'll be seeing you!" Bill called as they went speeding by.

"It's in the bag," Jerry said. "You see the look that one gave me?"

"I don't know," Bill said. "Maybe we should cut for home."

"We got it made!" Jerry said.

He pulled off the road under some trees. The highway forked here at Picture Rock, one road going on to Yakima, the other heading for Naches, Enumclaw, the Chinook Pass, Seattle.

A hundred yards off the road was a high, sloping, black mound of rock, part of a low range of hills, honeycombed with footpaths and small caves, Indian sign-painting here and there on the cave walls. The cliff side of the rock faced the highway and all over it there were things like NACHES 67—GLEED WILDCATS—JESUS SAVES—BEAT YAKIMA—REPENT NOW.

They sat in the car, smoking cigarettes. Mosquitoes came in and tried to get at their hands.

"Wish we had a beer now," Jerry said. "I sure could go for a beer."

Bill said, "Me, too," and looked at his watch . . .

When the girls came into view, Jerry and Bill got out of the car. They leaned against the fender in front.

"Remember," Jerry said, starting away from the car, "the dark one's mine. You got the other one."

The girls dropped their bicycles and started up one of the paths. They disappeared around a bend and then reappeared again, a little higher up. They were standing there and looking down.

"What're you guys following us for?" the brunette called down.

Jerry just started up the path.

The girls turned away and went off again at a trot.

Jerry and Bill kept climbing at a walking pace. Bill was smoking a cigarette, stopping every so often to get a good drag. When the path turned, he looked back and caught a glimpse of the car.

"Move it!" Jerry said.

"I'm coming," Bill said.

They kept climbing. But then Bill had to catch his breath. He couldn't see the car now. He couldn't see the highway, either. To his left and all the way down, he could see a strip of the Naches like a strip of aluminum foil.

Jerry said, "You go right and I'll go straight. We'll cut the cock-teasers off."

Bill nodded. He was too winded to speak.

He went higher for a while, and then the path began to drop, turning toward the valley. He looked and saw the girls. He saw them crouched behind an outcrop. Maybe they were smiling.

Bill took out a cigarette. But he couldn't get it lit. Then Jerry showed up. It didn't matter after that.

Bill had just wanted to make love. Or even to see them naked. On the other hand, it was okay with him if it didn't work out.

He never knew what Jerry wanted. But it started and ended with a rock. Jerry used the same rock on both girls, first on the dark-haired girl called Sharon and then on the one that was supposed to be Bill's.

OLD MR. MARBLEHALL

by *EUDORA WELTY*

Old Mr. Marblehall never did anything, never got married until he was sixty. You can see him out taking a walk. Watch and you'll see how preciously old people come to think they are made—the way they walk, like conspirators, bent over a little, filled with protection. They stand long on the corners but more impatiently than anyone, as if they expect traffic to take notice of them, rear up the horses and throw on the brakes, so they can go where they want to go. That's Mr. Marblehall. He has short white bangs, and a bit of snapdragon in his lapel. He walks with a big polished stick, a present. That's what people think of him. Everybody says to his face, "So well preserved!" Behind his back they say cheerfully, "One foot in the grave." He has on his thick, beautiful, glowing coat—tweed, but he looks as gratified as an animal in its own tingling fur. You see, even in summer he wears it, because he is cold all the time. He looks quaintly secretive and prepared for anything, out walking very luxuriously on Catherine Street.

His wife, back at home in the parlor standing up to think, is a large, elongated old woman with electric-looking hair and curly lips. She has spent her life trying to escape from the parlor-like jaws of self-consciousness. Her late marriage has set in upon her nerves like a retriever nosing and puffing through old dead leaves out in the woods. When she walks around the room she looks remote and nebu-

41

lous, out on the fringe of habitation, and rather as if she must have been cruelly trained—otherwise she couldn't do actual, immediate things, like answering the telephone or putting on a hat. But she has gone further than you'd think: into club work.

Surrounded by other more suitably exclaiming women, she belongs to the Daughters of the American Revolution and the United Daughters of the Confederacy, attending teas. Her long, disquieted figure towering in the candlelight of other women's houses looks like something accidental. Any occasion, and she dresses her hair like a unicorn horn. She even sings, and is requested to sing. She even writes some of the songs she sings ("O Trees in the Evening"). She has a voice that dizzies other ladies like an organ note, and amuses men like a halloo down the well. It's full of a hollow wind and echo, winding out through the wavery hope of her mouth.

Do people know of her perpetual amazement? Back in safety she wonders, her untidy head trembles in the domestic dark. She remembers how everyone in Natchez will suddenly grow quiet around her. Old Mrs. Marblehall, Mr. Marblehall's wife: she even goes out in the rain, which southern women despise above everything, in big neat biscuit-colored galoshes, for which she "ordered off." She is only looking around—servile, undelighted, sleepy, expensive, tortured Mrs. Marblehall, pinning her mind with a pin to her husband's diet. She wants to tempt him, she tells him. What would he like best, that he can have?

There is Mr. Marblehall's ancestral home. It's not so wonderfully large—it has only four columns—but you always look toward it, the way you always glance into tunnels and see nothing. The river is after it now, and the little back garden has assuredly crumbled away, but the box maze is there on the edge like a trap, to confound the Mississippi River. Deep in the red wall waits the front door—it weighs such a lot, it is perfectly solid, all one piece, black mahogany ... And you see—one of *them* is always going in it. There is a knocker shaped like a gasping fish on the door. You have every reason in the world to imagine the inside is dark, with old things about. There's many a big, deathly looking tapestry, wrinkling and thin, many a sofa shaped like an S. Brocades as tall as the wicked queens in Italian tales stand gathered before the windows. Everything is draped and hooded and shaded, of course, unaffectionate but close. Such rosy lamps! The only sound would be a breath against the prisms, a stirring of the chandelier. It's like old eyelids, the house with one of its shutters, in careful working order, slowly opening outward. Then the little son softly comes and stares out like a kitten, with button nose and pointed ears and little fuzz of silky hair running along the top of his head.

The son is the worst of all. Mr. and Mrs. Marblehall had a child! When both of them were terribly old, they had this little, amazing, fascinating son. You can see how people are taken aback, how they jerk and throw up their hands every time they so much as think about it. At least, Mr. Marblehall sees them. He thinks Natchez people do nothing themselves, and really, most of them have done or could do the same thing. This son is six years old now. Close up, he has a monkey look, a very penetrating look. He has very sparse Japanese hair, tiny little pearly teeth, long little wilted fingers. Every day he is slowly and expensively dressed and taken to the Catholic school. He looks quietly and maliciously absurd, out walking with old Mr. Marblenall or old Mrs. Marblehall, placing his small booted foot on a little green worm, while they stop and wait on him. Everybody passing by thinks that he looks quite as if he thinks his parents had him just to show they could. You see, it becomes complicated, full of vindictiveness.

But now, as Mr. Marblehall walks as briskly as possible toward the river where there is sun, you have to merge him back into his proper blur, into the little party-giving town he lives in. Why look twice at him? There has been an old Mr. Marblehall in Natchez ever since the first one arrived back in 1818—with a theatrical presentation of Otway's *Venice,* ending with *A Laughable Combat Between Two Blind Fiddlers*—an actor! Mr. Marblehall isn't so important. His name is on the list, he is forgiven, but nobody gives a hoot about any old Mr. Marblehall. He could die, for all they care; some people even say, "Oh, is he still alive?"

Mr. Marblehall walks and walks, and now and then he is driven in his ancient fringed carriage with the candle burners like empty eyes in front. And yes, he is supposed to travel for his health. But why consider his absence? There isn't any other place besides

Natchez, and even if there were, it would hardly be likely to change Mr. Marblehall if it were brought up against him. Big fingers could pick him up off the Esplanade and take him through the air, his old legs still measuredly walking in a dangle, and set him down where he could continue that same old Natchez stroll of his in the East or the West or Kingdom Come. What difference could anything make now about old Mr. Marblehall—so late? A week or two would go by in Natchez and then there would be Mr. Marblehall, walking down Catherine Street again, still exactly in the same degree alive and old.

People naturally get bored. They say, "Well, he waited till he was sixty years old to marry, and what did he want to marry for?" as though what he did were the excuse for their boredom and their lack of concern. Even the thought of his having a stroke right in front of one of the Pilgrimage houses during Pilgrimage Week makes them only sigh, as if to say it's nobody's fault but his own if he wants to be so insultingly and precariously well preserved. He ought to have a little black boy to follow around after him. Oh, his precious old health, which never had reason to be so inspiring! Mr. Marblehall has a formal, reproachful look as he stands on the corners arranging himself to go out into the traffic to cross the streets. It's as if he's thinking of shaking his stick and saying, "Well, look! I've done it, don't you see?" But really, nobody pays much attention to his look. He is just like other people to them. He could have easily danced with a troupe of angels in Paradise every night, and they wouldn't have guessed. Nobody is likely to find out that he is leading a double life.

The funny thing is he just recently began to lead this double life. He waited until he was sixty years old. Isn't he crazy? Before that, he'd never done anything. He didn't know what to do. Everything was for all the world like his first party. He stood about, and looked in his father's books, and long ago he went to France, but he didn't like it.

Drive out any of these streets in and under the hills and you find yourself lost. You see those scores of little galleried houses nearly alike. See the yellowing China trees at the eaves, the round flower beds in the front yards, like bites in the grass, listen to the screen doors whining, the ice wagons dragging by, the twittering noises of children. Nobody ever looks to see who is living in a house like that. These people come out themselves and sprinkle the hose over the street at this time of day to settle the dust, and after they sit on the porch, they go back into the house, and you hear the radio for the next two hours. It seems to mourn and cry for them. They go to bed early.

Well, old Mr. Marblehall can easily be seen standing beside a row of zinnias growing down the walk in front of that little house, bending over, easy, easy, so as not to strain anything, to stare at the flowers. Of course he planted them! They are covered with brown— each petal is a little heart-shaped pocket of dust. They don't have any smell, you know. It's twilight, all amplified with locusts screaming; nobody could see anything. Just what Mr. Marblehall is bending over the zinnias for is a mystery, any way you look at it. But there he is, quite visible, alive and old, leading his double life.

There's his other wife, standing on the night-stained porch by a potted fern, screaming things to a neighbor. This wife is really worse than the other one. She is more solid, fatter, shorter, and while not so ugly, funnier-looking. She looks like funny furniture—an unornamented stair-post in one of these little houses, with her small monotonous round stupid head—or sometimes like a woodcut of a Bavarian witch, forefinger pointing, with scratches in the air all around her. But she's so static she scarcely moves, from her thick shoulders down past her cylindered brown dress to her short, stubby houseslippers. She stands still and screams to the neighbors.

This wife thinks Mr. Marblehall's name is Mr. Bird. She says, "I declare I told Mr. Bird to go to bed, and look at him! I don't understand him!" All her devotion is combustible and goes up in despair. This wife tells everything she knows. Later, after she tells the neighbors, she will tell Mr. Marblehall. Cymbal-breasted, she fills the house with wifely complaints. She calls, "After I get Mr. Bird to bed, what does he do then? He lies there stretched out with his clothes on and don't have one word to say. Know what he does?"

And she goes on, while her husband bends over the zinnias, to tell what Mr. Marblehall (or Mr. Bird) does in bed. She does tell the truth. He reads *Terror Tales* and *Astonishing Stories*. She can't see anything to them: they scare her to death. These stories are about horrible and fantastic things happening to nude women and scientists. In one of them, when the characters open bureau drawers, they find a woman's leg with a stocking and garter on. Mrs. Bird had to shut the magazine. "The glutinous shadows," these stories say, "the red-eyed, muttering old crone," "the moonlight on her thigh," "an ancient cult of sun worshippers," "an altar suspiciously stained . . ." Mr. Marblehall doesn't feel as terrified as all that, but he reads on and on. He is killing time. It is richness without taste, like some holiday food. The clock gets a fruity bursting tick, to get through midnight—then leisurely, leisurely on. When time is passing it's like a bug in his ear. And then Mr. Bird—he doesn't even want a shade on the light, this wife moans respectably. He reads under a bulb. She can tell you how he goes straight through a stack of magazines. "He might just as well not have a family," she always ends, unjustly, and rolls back into the house as if she had been on a little wheel all this time.

But the worst of them all is the other little boy. Another little boy just like the first one. He wanders around the bungalow full of tiny little schemes and jokes. He has lost his front tooth, and in this way he looks slightly different from Mr. Marblehall's other little boy—more shocking. Otherwise, you couldn't tell them apart if you wanted to. They both have that look of cunning little jugglers, violently small under some spotlight beam, preoccupied and silent, amusing themselves. Both of the children will go into sudden fits and tantrums that frighten their mothers and Mr. Marblehall to death. Then they can get anything they want. But this little boy, the one who's lost the tooth, is the smarter. For a long time he supposed that his mother was totally solid, down to her thick separated ankles. But when she stands there on the porch screaming to the neighbors, she reminds him of those flares that charm him so, that they leave burning in the street at night—the dark solid ball, then, tongue-like, the wicked, yellow, continuous, enslaving blaze on the stem. He knows what his father thinks.

Perhaps one day, while Mr. Marblehall is standing there gently bent over the zinnias, this little boy is going to write on a fence, "Papa leads a double life." He finds out things you wouldn't find out. He is a monkey.

You see, one night he is going to follow Mr. Marblehall (or Mr. Bird) out of the house. Mr. Marblehall has said as usual that he is leaving for one of his health trips. He is one of those correct old gentlemen who are still going to the wells and drinking the waters— exactly like his father, the late old Mr. Marblehall. But why does he leave on foot? This will occur to the little boy.

So he will follow his father. He will follow him all the way across town. He will see the shining river come winding around. He will see the house where Mr. Marblehall turns in at the wrought-iron gate. He will see a big speechless woman come out and lead him in by the heavy door. He will not miss those rosy lamps beyond the many-folded draperies at the windows. He will run around the fountains and around the Japonica trees, past the stone figure of the pigtailed courtier mounted on the goat, down to the back of the house. From there he can look far up at the strange upstairs rooms. In one window the other wife will be standing like a giant, in a long-sleeved gathered nightgown, combing her electric hair and breaking it off each time in the comb. From the next window the other little boy will look out secretly into the night, and see him—or not see him. That would be an interesting thing, a moment of strange telepathies. (Mr. Marblehall can imagine it.) Then in the corner room there will suddenly be turned on the bright, naked light. Aha! Father!

Mr. Marblehall's little boy will easily climb a tree there and peep through the window. There, under a stark shadeless bulb, on a great fourposter with carved griffins, will be Mr. Marblehall, reading *Terror Tales,* stretched out and motionless.

Then everything will come out.

At first, nobody will believe it.

Or maybe the policeman will say, "Stop! How dare you!"

Maybe, better than that, Mr. Marblehall himself will confess his duplicity—how he has led two totally different lives, with completely different families, two sons instead of one. What an astonishing, unbelievable, electrifying confession that would be, and how his two wives would topple over, how his sons would cringe! To say nothing of most men aged sixty-six. So thinks self-consoling Mr. Marblehall.

You will think, what if nothing ever happens? What if there is no climax, even to this amazing life? Suppose old Mr. Marblehall simply remains alive, getting older by the minute, shuttling, still secretly, back and forth?

Nobody cares. Not an inhabitant of Natchez, Mississippi, cares if he is deceived by old Mr. Marblehall. Neither does anyone care that Mr. Marblehall has finally caught on, he thinks, to what people are supposed to do. This is it: they endure something inwardly—for a time secretly; they establish a past, thus they store up life. He has done this; most remarkably, he has even multiplied his life by deception; and plunging deeper and deeper, he speculates upon some glorious finish, a great explosion of revelations . . . the future.

But he still has to kill time, and get through the clocking nights. Otherwise he dreams that he is a great blazing butterfly stitching up a net; which doesn't make sense.

Old Mr. Marblehall! He may have years ahead yet in which to wake up bolt upright in the bed under the naked bulb, his heart thumping, his old eyes watering and wild, imagining that if people knew about his double life, they'd die.

THE FORGOTTEN WITNESS

by *MELVILLE DAVISSON POST*

It was a courtroom in which the leisurely customs of the South persisted. The jurors were at ease, as in a sort of club. They were known to one another. The officers of the court, the attorneys, the judge, the prisoner, and the audience filling the seats behind the railing were likewise known to them.

The courtroom had been scrubbed, and through the long windows, open to the air of the summer morning, came the fresh odor of the distant fields.

The criminal trial about to open was of considerable local interest, as evidenced by the alert bearing of the officials and by the respectful silence of the spectators.

The clerk, a man with the classic face of a Greek poet, and who wore a little yellow rosebud on the lapel of his coat, was the most conspicuous person. But he had neither the spirit nor the vocation of his Hellenic cast. One distinction, however, he maintained—he was the prophetic oracle of this court.

He forecast its decisions.

And when he was sober, as he was on this summer morning, his pronouncements were shrewd and accurate. He knew what the judge would do; what the jury usually would do. He knew legal shifts and subterfuges, the stock defenses, the methods and strategy of every attorney at this bar, and he could forecast the development of that strategy when the case was called.

One factor alone disturbed him: he could never be certain of his estimates of Colonel Braxton. He had known this lawyer always, observed him day after day, but for all that the man remained an enigma to him. And he had come to qualify his forecasts with: "If Colonel Braxton is not of counsel for the defense!"

He was looking at the man now, and wondering what substantial defense he could set up for the notorious crook that he represented; some form of alibi or the obscurities of reasonable doubt. But to what end? The jury knew the prisoner's record, the judge knew it— no legal smokescreen could obscure it.

The clerk waited with a keen interest for the case to open.

And, as always when the curtain rose on the legal drama, he selected Colonel Braxton for the point of interest. The prosecuting attorney had made his statement of the case for the State, after the legal custom obtaining in this court. He had fully explained the charge against the prisoner and the nature of the evidence which he expected to introduce.

It was a clear, accurate statement and shrewdly put.

The facts were certain, and the deductions from circumstances were irresistible.

The sheriff had been robbed, and some ten thousand dollars of the county's money taken. It was the custom in that day for the sheriff to collect the taxes and to travel into the magisterial districts for that purpose. He lived some miles from this little city that was the county seat. He had returned home in the evening with the money he had collected. His wife was absent on a visit and he was alone in the house.

He had not yet retired and was reading a newspaper in his sitting room when he heard a knocking on the door. When he opened it, he had been confronted by a man with a colored handkerchief tied around the lower part of his face, who, at the point of a pistol, compelled him to hand over the money, and then forced him into a closet. The spring lock of the door had snapped, leaving him imprisoned in the darkness.

He had shouted at the top of his lungs, but, as his house was some distance from the highway and there was no other residence near it, he was not heard.

In the morning a farm hand returning to the premises heard the sheriff call, and breaking the lock on the closet found the exhausted man collapsed on the floor.

The prisoner was at once taken into custody. He had been seen near the sheriff's residence on this evening, and was known to have returned to his saloon in the city about midnight.

The prisoner had been positively identified by the sheriff.

The house had been examined by the chief of police, but so many people had entered that nothing could be determined, although the approaches to the house, and even the rug on the floor of the room, had been carefully inspected for footprints.

Colonel Braxton had been among those present at this official inspection.

The whole courtroom waited to hear upon what defense the counsel for the prisoner depended.

The attorney for the defense rose slowly.

He was a big man, with a heavy, putty-colored face, expressionless as a mask, except when he wished to contort it with a stamp of vigor. His black hair was brushed sleek, an immaculate white handkerchief, tucked into his collar, covered the white bosom of his shirt to protect it from the ash of the cigar that was always present, even in the courtroom. The color of the heavy face and its placidity, together with the somnolent air of the man and his drawling voice, gave weight to the common impression that he was a drug addict.

"Your Honor," he said, "and gentlemen of the jury, I shall have no evidence to introduce in behalf of the prisoner. If he is cleared here, he must be cleared on the testimony of the witnesses for the State."

The whole courtroom was astonished.

This was an abandonment of the defense.

A plea of guilty, putting the prisoner on the mercy of the court, would have been better. Someone sitting near the clerk whispered this conclusion. But the clerk did not reply. He sat fingering his classic chin. What did this appalling frankness mean? And he leaned forward to catch any concluding words that the attorney might utter.

But there was no further word.

Colonel Braxton put out his hand like one who, with an effort, thrusts the inevitable aside, then sat down.

Of all persons in the courtroom, the prisoner seemed the most astonished. He remained for a moment looking in amazement at the big, placid body of Colonel Braxton who, with half closed eyes, sat chewing the end of his inevitable cigar. Then he leaned forward and began to whisper. What he said could not be heard, but his manner indicated an elaborate protest. The man was alarmed and urgent. But his insistence had no visible effect.

Colonel Braxton's drawl silenced him.

"Now, now, Charlie," he said, "don't hire a dog to bark for you and then go to barking yourself."

Everybody laughed.

This eccentric lawyer was to the audience like an actor in a play, the central figure of these legal dramas. His mannerisms and his queer digressions packed the courtroom. And his peculiarities were suffered by the judge out of long custom.

But there was a sense of disappointment among the spectators in the crowded room. They had assembled to witness a bitter legal struggle—the determined assault of the prosecution and a dogged, desperate resistance—and here was unconditional surrender.

Only the old clerk was in doubt.

But even to his rich experience this looked like the strategy of despair. How could this attorney hope to clear the prisoner on the State's evidence?

He would be convicted on it.

All the requisites necessary to a conviction would be established: the proof of the robbery, the identification of the prisoner, and his presence near the sheriff's house on the night of the robbery.

Where were the colonel's usual defenses: the alibi, the mysterious stranger? Could he mean to exclude the State's evidence?

That was clearly impossible.

Such a motion lay only when there was no evidence tending to indicate the guilt of the accused.

The conduct of a criminal trial in this jurisdiction followed the form of the early trials in Virginia. This procedure lent itself to the possibility of a long preliminary skirmish before the general engagement opened. It began usually with an attack on the procedure of the grand jury returning the indictment; technical objections to the indictment itself.

Following this rich field of contest, there was the struggle in the courtroom over the selection of a jury. There was the peremptory right to strike a certain number from the panel, and to question every man drawn on what is called a *voir dire* examination. And back of this there were the many and various devices for obtaining a continuance of the case from term to term, until public indignation at the offense had subsided, and the witnesses for the State wandered—or were spirited—away.

In this broad borderland Colonel Braxton was a skilled duelist.

Shrewd, farsighted, and accomplished, it was his custom to attack, like the great generals of antiquity, at the dawn. He did not wait to be assailed. He assailed the State, and continued to attack it to the end.

The prosecuting attorney found himself on the defensive.

Instead of the prisoner, he found himself and his procedure on trial. In desperate cases Colonel Braxton tried everybody but the prisoner. In the notorious Barker case he even tried the judge, assembling all the instances in which the Supreme Court of the State had reversed him for erroneous rulings.

And, in the modern vernacular, he got their goat.

The jury, eminently human, came unconsciously to favor the virile, decisive side. And so, here in this desperate case, it was a greater wonder that Colonel Braxton evaded this whole field of strategy; gave the prosecuting attorney his head; and, to the casual observer, abandoned hope for his client.

Even the judge was surprised.

The old clerk, very carefully dressed as for a social function, balanced doubtfully between two conclusions: was this a mere form of pleading guilty, or had Colonel Braxton discovered at the last moment some element of guilt that had wrecked his defense beyond all hope of patching it together?

The prosecuting attorney had his way.

He put on his witnesses and proved his case. After the usual custom, he called the police first, as though to give his case a foundation in law and order, then incidental witnesses, leaving the county sheriff for the last.

And to all this Colonel Braxton made no objection.

He did not cross-examine.

He dismissed each witness with a courteous wave of the hand or some comment agreeable to his testimony in the case, coupled with a pleasantry.

"Thank you, Scally," he drawled, as the chief of police was turned over to him, "you are right—you are quite right. Charlie was out at the sheriff's house that night, and he did come into town about twelve o'clock. Of course, Charlie says that the sheriff told him confidentially that if he came out to see him that night, he would arrange some way to give him time on his taxes. He hadn't any money to pay them just then."

The prosecuting attorney objected.

"If you want the prisoner's explanation to go before the jury, you will have to have him sworn."

Colonel Braxton waved his hand in affable assent.

"Alfred," he said, addressing the prosecuting attorney, as in a confidential aside, "do you think the jury would believe Charlie any quicker just because he was sworn?"

Again the ripple of laughter ran over the courtroom. And the prisoner sought the ear of his counsel with some whispered protest. Was one's lawyer to impeach one's veracity before the world?

There is a theory in the law that circumstantial evidence, when properly coupled up, is the most conclusive of all forms of evidence. The early English judges commented on it with a stock dictum. Men may lie, but circumstances cannot! Bias, prejudice, fear, the hope of gain, a friend to save, an enemy to convict may influence the testimony of many a witness. But a fact stands for itself.

These silent witnesses, as criminal lawyers have dramatically named them, are beyond the influence of the human will.

And out of such testimony the State built up its case.

The prisoner had been seen loitering near the sheriff's residence on the night of the robbery. He had been seen on the highway to this house, and he had been seen and recognized returning to the city near midnight.

His criminal record and his need of money established the motive.

He would know the local custom of the sheriff, to go out to the magisterial districts to collect the taxes, and thus, familiar with that official custom, he would know that a considerable sum of money would be in the possession of the sheriff at this time. Also, it was common knowledge in the neighborhood that the sheriff's wife was absent on a distant visit, and that, therefore, he would be alone in the house.

All these indisputable evidences clearly showed that the robbery was the work of someone in the community.

The prisoner was the man the shoe fitted.

And seeing that he was unopposed, the prosecuting attorney pushed his advantage beyond his legal right. Each criminal charge should stand on its own bottom. But he got before the jury, by the incidental answers of the police, by hint and by innuendo, all the petty offenses with which the prisoner had been charged; enumerating them as one catalogues the important events in a life.

Against the whole force of this assault Colonel Braxton made only a drawling comment.

"Alfred," he said, "you can't make one black elephant out of two hundred black crow-birds!"

But the prosecuting attorney knew what he was about. When all these loose threads were gathered up, they would make the knot he wished. Colonel Braxton's wit would not save his client.

Sheriff Henderson was a well known figure in the community.

He was a little, slight man with pale-blue eyes set in a shrewd face—a man of scattering enterprises, not all of them successful; too many irons in the fire was the homely comment. But his election to the office of sheriff had seemed to strengthen his credit. It was a lucrative office under the system then obtaining in the state, and a careful official usually retired from it with a modest fortune.

But the present incumbent was not an official of accurate business methods, and if he were required now to make good the loss of this robbery he would be on the way to a bankrupt court. In fact, he was already on the way. The gains that he would receive from his office were to be sequestered by his creditors. He, individually, would come out at the end of his term with nothing. There was a rumor that he would remove to a distant state at the end of his term; that he had purchased a farm there, and that the reason he was alone on the night of the robbery was that his wife had gone to inspect this purchase.

It was hoped by his creditors and bondsmen that this trial might in some manner point the way to a recovery of the money.

The robber had unquestionably concealed it. But where, and in what manner?

The prisoner had been shadowed from the very day. His house, and the saloon that he ran in the environs of the city, had been carefully searched. It was the plan of the prosecution to convict the prisoner with a quick trial and, under the pressure of a long penal sentence, force him to disclose the place in which the money was hidden.

And it was to this end that the State directed its energies.

When the prosecuting attorney turned the sheriff over to Colonel Braxton for cross-examination, the thing was done. The details of the robbery had been accurately and succinctly recited and verified. The sheriff said he had shouted in the closed closet, and it was clearly evident that, as his residence was remote from any other, this shouting could not have been heard. The handkerchief which the robber had worn about the lower part of his face had slipped down while he was forcing the sheriff into the closet and he had seen the man plainly.

It was the prisoner at the bar.

The State closed with that decisive identification.

Unless Colonel Braxton could break down this destructive fact, his client was doomed. Everybody realized it; and the whole courtroom waited, curious to see in what manner he would undertake to negative this disastrous incident.

But he made no allusion to it.

He sat for a few moments, apparently irresolute, as though undetermined whether he would interrogate the witness or permit him to stand aside. Finally he seemed to come to a conclusion. But when he spoke there was no vigor in his voice.

"Mr. Henderson," he said, "in a position of panic, don't you think all men are apt to act unconsciously on simple impulses?"

The witness replied promptly, as with a frank unconcern.

"Yes, Colonel," he said, "I think that's true."

"And we may assume," the attorney continued, "that every normal man will act about like every other normal man?"

"I suppose in a panic we would all act about alike."

"Panic," Colonel Braxton went on, "seems to bring out, unconsciously, primitive acts of self-preservation. We can see it easily demonstrated by the acts of a child in panic ... What does a child do, Mr. Henderson, when we lock him up in a dark closet?"

"He makes a noise," replied the witness, "and tries to get out."

"And how does he make a noise and how does he try to get out?"

"He shouts and he kicks on the door."

"Precisely," said the attorney, "for these are primitive impulses of self-preservation, common to all. Don't you think a man would do the same?"

"I think he would," replied the witness; "it would be the natural thing to do."

Colonel Braxton passed his hand over his placid, inexpressive face.

"Now, Mr. Henderson," he drawled, "isn't this precisely what you did when you were locked in the dark closet?"

"I guess it is, Colonel."

The attorney moved his fingers on the table as though he brushed something away.

"I'm afraid we can't guess here, Mr. Henderson. What is the fact about it?"

"Well, Colonel," replied the witness, "that's the fact about it."

The counsel for the prisoner paused. He seemed disconcerted. He passed his hand again over his face, as in some reflection.

"Of course," he added, "in your case it was no use trying to get out, as the closet was securely locked and the door was made of heavy planks. And it was no use making a noise or shouting, as there was no other residence near you. Persons passing on the distant highway could not possibly have heard the most powerful voice shouting in that locked closet in that closed-up house ... Mr. Henderson," the colonel continued, "do you think an Infinite Intelligence conducts the affairs of the universe?"

The witness, with everyone else, was amazed.

"Why, yes, Colonel," he replied, "I suppose He does."

"It's a pretty big job, don't you think?"

The witness smiled: "I'd call it a tremendously big job."

"Do you think a man could take the place of this Infinite Intelligence, and do it?"

The witness continued to smile: "I don't think any man would be fool enough to try, Colonel."

The big attorney made a sudden explosive sound.

"But they *do* try . . . that's what fills me with wonder . . . they *do* try!"

Then he turned aside, as though diverted to something irrelevant.

"You travel out to the magisterial districts on a horse, don't you?"

"Yes," replied the witness; "the roads are usually bad."

"And you meet with all sorts of weather?"

"Yes—I'm out in nearly every kind of weather."

"And you must dress for that sort of rough travel?"

The witness made an apologetic gesture. He looked down at his heavy clothing and his thick shoes.

"Yes, Colonel," he replied, with a little laugh, "that's the reason I go dressed as I am today. Town clothes and dude shoes wouldn't stand what I go through on the Virginia roads."

Colonel Braxton nodded his head, as one without interest.

"Ah, yes," he said, "I was just wondering how you were dressed on the night of the robbery."

The witness replied at once:

"Why, just like I'm dressed now."

Colonel Braxton made a slight gesture, as of one dismissing a triviality. "Ah! yes," he repeated, "precisely as you are dressed now."

Then he dropped back into his former manner, like one meditating aloud on some profound aspect of human conduct.

"At the little points where events touch the great conduct of human affairs, men undertake to substitute their feeble intelligence for the infinite intelligence of the Ruler of Events. They undertake to set that will aside, and to rearrange the moving of events as they wish them to appear. They are fools enough!—that's a good way to put it, Mr. Henderson—they are fools enough! Now, why do you use that term, Mr. Henderson, that term 'fool enough'?''

"Because no man could do it, Colonel.''

"Ah!'' It was the big booming expletive again. "That's precisely the point. No man can do it!''

He shot a sharp glance at the witness, then dropped into a leisurely drawl.

"The great writers on evidence, Mr. Starkey and Mr. Greenlief, were of the opinion that no human intelligence was able to construct a false consistency of events that could be substituted for the true consistency of events that it undertook to replace. It was an impossible endeavor, for the reason that one would have to know accurately all the varied events that preceded and all the varied events that followed in order to substitute false events that would fit. Now, only an Infinite Intelligence could know all that has happened and all that will happen in the future. No man could know it; therefore, no man can do this. But they are fools enough to try . . . Mr. Henderson, I thank you for the word.''

The whole courtroom smiled.

Colonel Braxton continued, as in a friendly monologue to an auditor that pleased him:

"I have a feeling that every event that happens is in some manner connected with every other event that happens; that they are all intricately enmeshed together. You can't tear the threads out and tie in others. The broken ends will show. The knots will show. And so, Mr. Henderson, as you so admirably put it, no man ought to be fool enough to try. He will do too much or he will do too little. He will forget something, or he will overlook something that will show his facts to be fictitious.''

The prosecuting attorney interrupted:

"What's all this got to do with the case, Colonel?''

The big attorney paused and considered his opponent for a moment, as though he had only now become aware of his presence.

"Well, Alfred,'' he said, "it isn't altogether a didactic lecture. It's preliminary to the calling of a witness.''

The prosecuting attorney smiled, as with an air of victory. "So you are changing horses in the stream, Colonel; I thought you were not going to make a defense."

"Alfred," replied the lawyer, regarding the attorney as with a new and intriguing interest, "where did you get that extraordinary idea?"

"I got it from your opening statement to the jury." The man was pricked by the irony in his opponent's voice and manner. "You said that you would introduce no evidence on behalf of the prisoner . . . If the prisoner was cleared, he would have to be cleared on the testimony of the witnesses for the State—isn't that what you said?"

"That," replied Colonel Braxton gently, "is precisely what I said."

This veiled sarcastic handling got the prosecuting attorney into a bit of temper.

"Then I'd stick to it, and not call a witness for the prisoner."

"I am not going to call a witness for the prisoner," replied Colonel Braxton, "I am going to call one of the State's witnesses."

"What one of the State's witnesses?"

"One you forgot," replied Colonel Braxton.

He beckoned to a big youth sitting on a step below the judge's bench, and sent him out of the courtroom.

The judge, observing the act, addressed him:

"Do you want a subpoena for the witness, Colonel?"

Colonel Braxton looked up at him.

"Your Honor," he said, "this witness will testify without the compelling authority of a writ of subpoena."

The interest in the courtroom quickened. The clerk of the court fingered the rosebud in his coat and reflected on this inexplicable defense. What witness was it that Colonel Braxton was about to call? What witness had the prosecution forgotten? The whole extent of the State's case was known to him.

The sheriff remained in the witness chair. He had not been directed to stand aside. The attorney for the prisoner seemed for a moment in reflection, as though considering whether he had any further query to put. He moved the articles aimlessly on the table before him, pushing them about with his fingers.

Finally, when he addressed the witness, it was with the stock query common in all criminal trials; the stereotyped questions with which the witness in such a case is usually dismissed. Colonel Braxton seemed to have no particular concern about these concluding questions. Did he add them to cover the interval while he waited for the forgotten witness to appear?

"Mr. Henderson," he said, "every part of your testimony is quite as true as every other part, isn't it?"

The witness replied at once, with no equivocation. "It is," he said. "Every statement that I have made is precisely the truth."

Colonel Braxton looked vaguely about the courtroom.

"You shouted in the closet and kicked on the door—it's all the truth?"

The witness assumed an air of indignation at this repeated query.

"Yes, it's the truth," he said, "it's all the truth. Why do you ask the same question over? I—"

But he was interrupted.

While his mouth opened on the unfinished sentence, a strange thing occurred. The swinging doors to the courtroom opened and the big youth and another entered, bearing a long white object between them. They came in slowly and in silence, as though they bore the wraith of a dead man on a cooling-board.

The two men came on with their burden, down the central aisle, and placed it upright against the wall before the jury and the amazed sheriff.

The judge, astonished, put the query that was in every mouth:

"What is this?"

And Colonel Braxton, standing before the sheriff, big, dominant, as though he barred the way against him to some expected exit, answered.

"That, Your Honor," he said, "is the forgotten witness!"

Then, as everybody in the courtroom came to realize what this white, silent thing, standing against the wall, was, he returned to his chair; to his relaxed manner; to his listless interest in events.

"It's the door," he drawled, "to the closet in which the sheriff was locked by the robber ... It's the door the sheriff kicked with his heavy shoes in his efforts to escape ... You will notice that *there isn't the faintest scratch of a mark on the white paint!*"

He paused.

The great, obvious fact stood out incontrovertibly to the eye.

Then his voice continued:

"You see, Your Honor, Mr. Henderson went a bit too far in fabricating his events. If he had been content to stop with the assertion that he shouted in the closet, we could not have refuted him. But when he said that he also kicked the door, he overreached himself, for, behold the door, with its painted surface unmarked, appears in this circuit court to prove the man a liar!

"And now," he added, "if Your Honor will send for the stolen money, I think that the prisoner can be dismissed."

"The stolen money!" echoed the judge. "You know where it is?"

"I have a theory," the listless voice went on. "When the police lifted the rug in the sitting room of the sheriff's house to examine it for footprints, I noticed that a board in the floor was not nailed down ... It might be under that board. Don't you think so, Mr. Henderson?"

On the sheriff's white, guilt-stricken face was written the answer.

COME DOWN FROM THE HILLS

by *JOHN F. SUTER*

Arlan Boley eased his backhoe down the ramp from the flatbed, cut the motor, and climbed off. It was early in the morning in the dry season of late August, but the dew was just starting to rise. Boley knew that the oppressiveness of the air would pass, but he hated it all the same.

"You want me to do the first one along about here?" he asked. He brushed at his crinkly blond hair where a strand of cobweb from an overhanging branch had caught.

Sewell McCutcheon, who was hiring Boley's services for the morning, walked to the edge of the creek and took a look. He picked up a dead sycamore branch and laid it perpendicular to the stream. "One end about here." He walked downstream about fifteen feet and repeated the act with another branch. "Other end here."

Boley glanced across the small creek and, without looking at McCutcheon, asked, "How far out?"

The older man grinned, the ends of his heavy brown mustache lifting. "We do have to be careful about that." He reached into a pocket of his blue-and-white coveralls and took out a twenty-five-foot reel of surveyor's tape. He laid it on the ground, stooped over to remove heavy shoes and socks, and rolled the coveralls to his knees.

He unreeled about a foot of tape and handed the end to Boley.

"Stand right at the edge and hold that," he said, picking up a pointed stake about five feet long.

While Boley held the tape's end, McCutcheon stepped down the low bank and entered the creek. The dark brown hair on his sinewy legs was plastered against the dead-white skin from the knees down. When he reached the other side, he turned around. "She look square to you?"

"A carpenter couldn't do better."

McCutcheon looked down. "Fourteen and a quarter feet. Midway's seven feet, one and a half inches. I don't know about you, Boley, but I hate fractions."

He started back, reeling up tape as he came. "Seven feet, three inches from her side. I'll just give her a little more than half, then she can't complain. Not that she won't."

He plunged the stake in upright at the spot. Then he waded ashore, went to the other boundary, and repeated the performance.

"That's the first one. When you finish," he told Boley, "come down just opposite the house and we'll mark off the second one."

"How deep?" Boley asked.

"Take about two feet off the bottom," McCutcheon said. "Water's low now. When she comes back up, it'll make a good pool there. Trout ought to be happy with it."

"I'll be gettin' to 'er, then," Boley said, going back to his machine. He was already eyeing the spot where he would begin to take the first bite with the scoop. He began to work within minutes. He had moved enough dirt with his backhoe in the past to know what he was doing, even with the added presence of the water that soaked the muck. There was also an abundance of gravel in the piles he was depositing along the bank.

When he judged that he had finished the hole, he lifted the scoop until it was roughly level with the seat. Then he swung the machine around and ran it down the creek toward his next worksite.

The pebble-bottomed stream, one typical of West Virginia, was known as Squirrel Creek. It divided two farms of nearly flat land at an altitude between one and two thousand feet. On the eastern side was McCutcheon's well kept eighty acres. McCutcheon, a recent widower, planned well and worked hard, aided by his son and daughter-in-law. Both sides of the stream were lined with trees whose root systems kept the banks from crumbling and silting the creek bed. This was deliberate on McCutcheon's part, happenstance on his neighbor's.

When Boley came down opposite McCutcheon's white frame two-story, he cut the motor and walked over to where the farmer was sitting on the steps of his porch. The house was on a small rise, with a high foundation that would protect it in the event of an unusually heavy flash flood. Because of this, Boley had to look up a few inches to talk to McCutcheon.

"See anything of her?" he asked.

"Not yet," the farmer answered.

"Maybe this isn't gonna bother her."

McCutcheon rubbed his mustache. "*Everything* about this stream bothers that woman, Arly. One of the biggest trout I ever hooked in there was givin' me one helluva fight one day. I was tryin' to play him over to this side, but I hadn't yet managed it. Then, all of a sudden, outa nowhere came the old woman, screechin' her head off. 'What d'you mean ketchin' *my* fish?' she squawks. And with that she wades right out into the water, grabs the line with both hands, and flops that trout out on the ground at her side of the creek. Whips out a knife I'da never guessed she had and cuts the line. Then off to the house with my catch."

"Well," said Boley, "it was on her half of the creek, wasn't it? Property line down the middle? That why you've been measurin'?"

"Oh, sure," the farmer replied. "I recognize that. But that's not the way she looks at it. Had the fish been over here, she'd still have done it."

"I'd better get at it while it's quiet," Boley said, mentally thankful for his own Geneva's reasonableness.

As he walked to his machine, he heard McCutcheon say, "She must be away somewhere."

Later, Boley finished piling the last of the scooped silt and rocks on the bank of the stream. McCutcheon would later sort out the rocks and use the silt in his garden.

Paid for his work, Boley put the backhoe on the flatbed and fastened it securely. He turned around to head out, when he glanced over the creek toward the brown-painted cottage on the other side. A battered red half-ton pickup was just pulling up to the front of the house, barely visible through the tangle of bushes between stream and house.

A rangy older woman with dyed jet-black hair jumped from the truck and began to force her way toward the creek.

"Arlan Boley!" she screamed. A crow's voice contained more music. "What're you doin' over there?"

Boley put the truck in gear and pushed down the accelerator. He had no wish to talk to Alice Roberts. Leave that to McCutcheon.

Six days later, Boley and his family went into town. While Geneva and the two children were making some minor purchases for the opening of school, Boley went to the courthouse to the sheriff's office.

He had just finished paying his first-half taxes and was pocketing the receipt when he was tapped on the shoulder.

"Guess I'll have to wait till spring now before I can get you for non-payment," a voice said.

Boley recognized the voice of his old friend, the sheriff. "Hi, McKee," he said, turning. "You want that place of mine so bad, make me an offer. I might surprise you."

"No, thanks," McKee replied. "More'n I could handle." He nodded toward the clerk's window. "You payin' with what you got from Sewell McCutcheon?"

"Some. It took a little extra." He looked at McKee with curiosity. "What's the big deal? All I did was scoop him two holes in the creek for trout to loll around in from now on."

"You did more than that, Boley. You might have provided him with a fortune. Or part of one."

Boley nudged McKee's shoulder with his fist, feeling the hardness still existing in McKee's spare frame. "Don't tell me he panned that muck and found gold."

"You're not far off the mark."

Boley's eyes widened. He noticed a tiny lift at the ends of McKee's lips and a small deepening of the lines in the sheriff's tanned face. "Well, get to it and tell me," he said.

"Maybe you heard and maybe you didn't," McKee said, "but a state geologist's been usin' a vacant office here in the courthouse for the last ten days. Been workin' in the lower end of the county tryin' to see if there's a coal seam worth explorin' by that company that owns some of the land. Anyway, today McCutcheon walked in lookin' for him. Said he needed an opinion on an object in his pocket."

"And he got his interview?"

McKee nodded. "It seems he pulled out a fair-sized rock. First glance, could have been quartz or calcite. Kinda dull—but somehow different. This state fellow thought at first it was another pebble, then he took a good look and found it wasn't."

"So what *did* he find it was?"

"A diamond."

Boley had been half anticipating the answer, but he had tried to reject it. His jaw dropped. "No kidding!"

"No kidding."

"McCutcheon's probably turning over every rock out of that stream."

The sheriff dipped his chin. "I'll bet. Geologist said it's what they call an alluvial diamond, and the probability of findin' more is very small. Said it was formed millions of years ago when these mountains were as high as the Himalayas or higher. Somewhere in all that time, water eroded away whatever surrounded this one, and it might have even washed down here from someplace else. Come down from the hills, you might say."

An odd feeling crossed Boley's mind. Several times in the past, fragments of an old ersatz folk song had made themselves recognizable at the fringe of an unpleasant situation. "Just come down from the hills" was in one of the verses.

"What's the matter?" McKee asked.

"Nothing. How big is this rock? What's it worth?"

"A little bigger than the last joint of my thumb, not as big as the whole thumb. Worth? The man told McCutcheon there's no way of knowin' until it's cut. And it might be flawed."

Boley stared into the distance. "I'd better get on home and start seein' what's in the bottom of that run that goes through my property.

Everybody in the county'll be doin' the same thing wherever there's water.'' He paused. ''Or does anybody else know?''

''Only McCutcheon, that geologist, and the two of us,'' McKee said. ''There's sort of an agreement to keep our mouths shut. You never know who would get drawn in here, if the word got out. Don't you even tell Geneva.''

''What's McCutcheon done with the thing?''

''I suggested that he should put it in a safety-deposit box.''

''It's what I'd do. I hope he has,'' Boley said.

The quirk around McKee's mouth had gone. ''You know Alice Roberts?''

''Miner's widow across the creek from McCutcheon?''

''That's the one.''

''No. I've seen her. She evidently knows who I am. I don't think I want to know her.''

''Not good company,'' McKee said. ''I wonder if she's heard about this. Do me a favor, would you? Drop by McCutcheon's place before long. You have a good excuse—checkin' up on the job you did. See what you can find out, but don't let on what you know.''

Boley gave him a thoughtful look. ''Seems to me you know a lot already.''

The following evening, Boley left home on the pretext that he wanted to look at some land where he might be asked to make a ditch for a farmer who wanted to lay plastic pipe from his well pump to a new hog house. Instead, Boley went to McCutcheon's.

He found the farmer sitting alone on his porch. The sun had not quite set. His son and daughter-in-law had gone into town.

''Hello, Sewell,'' Boley said, walking to the foot of the steps. ''Water cleared yet where I dug 'er out?''

''If it ain't by now, it never will,'' McCutcheon said. ''Come up.''

Boley went up and sat in a cane-bottomed rocker like the farmer's. ''Ever since I dug it out, I've been wonderin' why you did that,'' he said. ''After all, you have a pretty good farm pond at the back. Fed by three springs, stocked with bass and blue gills, isn't it?''

McCutcheon smiled. ''That's right. Bass and blue gills. But no trout. Running water's for trout. I like variety.''

"You put all that gunk on your garden yet?"

"Oh, yeah. We just took a bunch of rakes and dragged all the rocks and pebbles out, let the muck dry some, then shoveled 'er into a small wagon, towed 'er to the garden, and that was it."

Boley looked at the gravel drive leading from the house to the main road. "I guess you can bust up the rocks and fill in some potholes when you get more."

McCutcheon seemed uninterested. "I suppose. I have a small rock pile out there. Don't know what I'll do with 'em."

Boley decided that the other man was keeping his secret. He wondered if the son and daughter-in-law knew. And if they could keep quiet. To change the subject, he said, "Anybody ever want to buy your land, Sewell?"

The farmer nodded. "Every now and then some developer comes by. Thing is, this isn't close to the lake and the recreation area, and they don't want to offer much."

"It's a good bit for the three of you to handle."

"Maybe it will be later," McCutcheon agreed. "That's when I'll think again."

Boley jerked his head toward the Roberts property. "I'd think they'd get that over there for the price they want."

"Funny old gal," McCutcheon said. "Her husband was a miner, died of black lung. No children. He never had time to work the property. Thirty-nine acres, came down from his old man. Alice like to wore herself out years ago, tryin' to make somethin' of it, then gave up. Except she thinks the place is worth like the middle of New York City—*and* that the creek belongs to her, clear to where it touches my land. You understand any better?"

"I see the picture," Boley answered, "but I don't understand the last part."

"Neither do I," McCutcheon admitted. "How about a cold beer?"

"Fine," Boley said.

McCutcheon went into the house to get it. He had been gone for several minutes when Boley heard footsteps coming around the house from the rear. He turned and saw Alice Roberts at the foot of the steps. She began to talk in a loud voice. "So. Both of you'll be here together—the two of you who took that diamond out've my crick. And how many more we haven't heard about yet.''

Boley stood up. ''What diamond? I don't know what you're talkin' about, Mrs. Roberts.''

She continued up the steps. Boley guessed her to be in her early sixties, but her vigor was of her forties.

''Don't you lie to me, mister!'' she growled, sitting in the chair he had just vacated. ''You know all about it. I saw you here the day it came out of the water. What cut is he giving you?''

Boley leaned against a porch post. ''I'm not gettin' any cut of any kind, lady. I've been paid for diggin' some dirt and rocks out of the water for McCutcheon. I don't see where any diamond comes into it.''

McCutcheon reappeared at the door, carrying two cans of cold beer. He gave one to Boley. ''Alice,'' he said, ''I didn't know you were here. Could I get you some cola?''

''The only thing you can get me is the diamond you stole from my crick.''

McCutcheon glanced quickly at Boley, who continued to look puzzled. ''There's some mistake, Alice. I never took anything of yours. Did you lose a diamond in the water?''

''No, I did not lose *anything* in the water,'' she snapped. ''You found out a big diamond was in my crick and your crony fished it out. I want it.''

''I made two fishin' holes in my side of the water,'' McCutcheon said. ''I got some rich dirt for my garden and a heap of rocks. You can have every rock in that pile, if you like.''

She got to her feet. ''I'll take you up on that. There might be more diamonds in there that you missed. I'll go get the pickup.'' She went down the steps at a speed that awed Boley.

He turned to McCutcheon. ''What was that all about?''

The farmer began to talk in a low tone. ''Water's down more and she can get across on steppin' stones, so she'll be back in a hurry.'' He proceeded to tell Boley the same story McKee had. Boley did not admit to its familiarity. Instead, he said, ''How did she find out?''

''Beats me,'' McCutcheon answered. ''But if you don't want a bad case of heartburn, you'd better leave right now. I'm used to it. It won't bother me."

"The diamond—"

"Is in the bank."

Boley was unable to tell McKee about this for several days. He had necessary work at home, getting in apples from his small orchard. He was also getting in field corn for a very sick neighbor.

After a little more than a week, he went to the courthouse. On the walk outside he was stopped by a friend. Harry Comstock, a quiet, balding man with thick glasses, drew maps for Border States, Inc. Border States harvested timber and was as efficient as the businesses that got everything from slaughtered pigs except the squeal. At times the company leased land for its operations; at others, it drew on its own land. Some of their holdings abutted the land owned by McCutcheon and Alice Roberts.

"Boley!" Comstock said. "Got a minute?"

"One or two."

"Won't keep you." Comstock squinted in the sun. "Didn't you do some work on Squirrel Creek for Sewell McCutcheon right recently?"

"Yeah. Scooped out a couple of fishin' holes for him," Boley said, hoping no more information was asked for.

"Well, you must have started something. Or maybe it's just coincidence. You know what happened yesterday? He came to the office and made a deal to buy fifty more acres from us to add to his land. All rights."

"Whereabouts?"

"Beginning at the creek and going east five acres, then back upstream."

"I'll bet it costs him," Boley said.

Comstock shook his head. "Not too much. Stuff in there's mostly scrub. Company's been wishing this sort of thing might happen."

Boley began to speak, but Comstock went on. "What makes it *real* interesting is that that wild old Alice Roberts came barging in about an hour later and bought twenty acres on the opposite side of the creek. Only hers is two acres west, the rest upstream. Again, all rights. What's goin' on?''

Boley looked blank. "Beats me. Did Alice Roberts pay for hers now?''

"In cash.''

Boley studied the pavement. "That's the funny part, Harry. I can't give you any answers, most of all about that.''

He went into the courthouse and sought McKee. The sheriff was in.

After McKee had closed his office door, Boley ran through all that had happened, including the recent land purchases.

"I figure what they're doin' is buyin' more land along that stream so they can hunt for more diamonds without Border States gettin' into it,'' he finished.

McKee's head was cocked to one side. "What it really sounds like is that Alice intended to go up there and buy up land on both sides of the water and cut Sewell off. He beat her to enough of it that she didn't want to push, or she would have stirred up Border States.''

"Oh, well,'' said Boley. "It's none of our business.''

"I hope you're right,'' said McKee, his voice dry and astringent. "I wish you'd keep your eyes and ears open, anyway. When there's somethin' in dispute that might be valuable, I always feel I might be on the hot seat. Somebody'll be in this jail out of this, is my guess.''

The following morning, Boley had left home in his four-wheel-drive jeep to help an acquaintance assess the feasibility of gathering bittersweet from a difficult location in the man's woods. With autumn coming, the colorful plant was easily saleable for decorations to tourists passing through town.

He had completed the trip and was starting home after returning the man to his house. Looking down the long corridor of trees before him he couldn't see the highway. The lane swung to the right for a few hundred feet before meeting the paved road. He slowed and made the curve, then stopped abruptly. The lane was blocked by a familiar battered red pickup. Standing beside it was Alice Roberts.

He climbed from the jeep. "Mrs. Roberts. What do you want?''

The woman was expressionless. "Mornin', Boley. I want you to get back in your jeep and follow me."

Boley considered several replies. He answered evenly, "I'm afraid I can't do that. If you have work for me, there are some people ahead of you."

"I never said anything about that," she rasped. "How do you think I found where you were?"

"I suppose you called, and my wife told you."

"I didn't call, but she told me." She moved aside and opened the truck door.

Boley stared. Inside, very pale and very straight, sat Geneva.

There was a movement beside him and Boley's eyes dropped. Alice Roberts was holding a double-barrel shotgun in her hands.

"Woman," he said, "shotgun or no shotgun, if you've hurt Geneva, I'll stomp you to bits."

"Don't get excited, Boley," she replied. "Nobody's hurt—yet. Now, you get behind that wheel and follow me."

Forcing himself to be calm, Boley did as he was told. He watched Alice Roberts climb into the truck and prop the gun between the door and her left side. Then she started, turned, and drove out.

Boley followed, driving mechanically. He paid little attention to direction or time. Rage threatened to take control, but he refused to let it. He might need all of his wits.

He wasn't entirely surprised when he saw that they had reached McCutcheon's farm and were pulling into the drive leading to the front.

The truck stopped directly before the steps to the front porch. With her surprising agility, Alice Roberts came down from the driver's seat carrying the shotgun, darted around the front of the pickup, and opened the other door to urge Geneva out.

Boley pulled up behind the truck and got out. He walked over to his wife and put his arm around her quivering shoulders.

"Arly. What's this all about?" she whispered.

"I'm not sure I know," he murmured.

"Quit talkin'!" snapped the woman. "Just behave yourselves and nobody'll get hurt. Now get up there."

She followed them up to the porch and banged on the screen door. "McCutcheon! You in there? Come out!"

There was no answer. She repeated her demands.

Finally a voice came faintly through the house. "Come on around to the west side."

Boley took Geneva's arms and urged her down from the porch, Alice Roberts' footsteps impatient behind them. They went around the house to the right. Waiting for them, leaning against a beech tree, was Sewell McCutcheon.

The farmer's eyes rounded with surprise. "This is more than I expected," he said. "Why the gun, Alice?"

"To convince you I mean business. If I pointed it at *you*, you might think I was foolin'. I hear these folks got two kids, so you'll think a bit more about it. There's shells in both these chambers."

"What do you want, Alice?"

"I want to see that diamond. I want to look at it. I want to hold it."

"We'd have to go to the bank. It's in a safety-deposit box."

Alice lifted the gun. "You're a liar, Sewell McCutcheon. How do I know? I went to the bank yesterday and asked to rent a box the same size as yours. And what did the girl say? 'We don't have a box rented to Mr. McCutcheon.' Now you get that diamond out here."

McCutcheon looked from one to another of the three. "All right. You go sit on the porch. I have to go in the house. You can't ask me to give my hidin' place away to you."

"I could, but I won't," Alice answered. "And don't you try to call anybody or throw down on me with your own gun."

McCutcheon's only answer was a nod. He went rapidly up to the side door and into the house. Boley led Geneva up to a swing that hung near the front end of the porch and sat down on it with her.

Alice followed. "If you're thinkin' about those other two who live here, fergit it. They went off down to Montgomery earlier." She leaned against a stack of firewood McCutcheon had put up to season.

After what seemed to Boley to be an interminable time, the farmer reappeared. He carried a cylindrical plastic medicine container about two inches long and an inch in diameter.

"We'd best go down into the sun," he said. "You can get a better idea."

He led the way down into the yard toward the stream, out of the shade of the trees surrounding the house. He stopped, opened the container, and shook something into his right palm. He offered it to Alice.

"Here it is."

She plucked it from his hand and peered at it.

"Why, it looks just like a dirty quartz pebble or some of them other rocks," she muttered. "This is a diamond? An uncut one?"

"It is. It's real," McCutcheon answered. "I can prove it, too."

She stared at it, letting the sun shine on it. "Well, some ways you look at it— A real, honest-to-God diamond, pulled outa my crick! McCutcheon, all my life I've wanted one nice thing to call my own."

The farmer pulled at his mustache. "Well, Alice, I'm sorry for you, but it came off my property. It came outa my side."

She raised her eyes to his. "How about you get it cut? Cut in two parts. Let me have half."

McCutcheon reached over and removed the stone from her hand. "Alice, you've been too much trouble to me over the years. Threatenin' these people with a shotgun is just too much."

"Shotgun!" she yelled. "I'll give you shotgun!"

She raised the gun swiftly, reversing it, and grasping the barrels with both hands, she clubbed McCutcheon across the back of the head. He fell to the ground, bleeding.

Stooping, she pried his fingers open and took the stone from them. "I'm not gonna let you take it!" she cried, running to the creek. When she reached the bank, she drew back her arm and threw the diamond as hard as she could into the woods upstream from her house. "Now," she yelled, "it's where it belongs! I might be forever findin' it, but you ain't gonna get it!"

Boley retrieved the gun where she had dropped it. "Go inside and call the sheriff," he told Geneva. "Say we need paramedics for Sewell."

When the sheriff's car and the ambulance came, McCutcheon was unconscious. Alice Roberts sat by the creek, ignoring everything until they took her to the car in handcuffs.

Boley explained the morning's events to McKee, who had come with a deputy. The sheriff heard him out. "Sounds like we've got her for kidnapping and assault, at least."

Alice Roberts, in the police car, heard them. "Kidnapping?" she said. "They's only old empty shells in that gun."

McKee leaned in the window. "But they didn't know that, Alice." To Boley, he said, "And don't you back off on the charge."

"I won't," Boley promised. "I'm just glad it's over."

McKee gave him an odd look. "If you think that, you've got another think comin'. Let's do today's paperwork, then come see me late tomorrow afternoon."

When Boley arrived at his office late the next day, the sheriff closed the door and waved him to a seat. "Things are pretty much as I figured," he said.

"How's McCutcheon?" Boley asked. "And what about Alice?"

"Sewell's not too bad." McKee sat down. "He's gettin' a good goin' over for concussion, but that's about it. Alice is still locked up, which is where I want her." He leaned across the desk. "How's it feel to be a cat's-paw?"

Boley was startled. "There's some kind of set-up in this?"

McKee sat back. "I'll run it past you. Some of this I can't prove and we'll just have to wait and see what happens. Anyway, you know same as I do that one of this county's big hopes is to attract people with money to buy up some of this land. Build themselves a place where they can come weekends or for the summer. The trouble is, we have only one good-sized lake and one nice recreation area. There are lots of other good places, but developers want to pick 'em up for peanuts.

"Alice Roberts, poor soul, has a place that looks like the devil's back yard. But it wouldn't take a lot to make it presentable, and it lays well. Sewell's place looks good. Given the right price, he'd quit and retire."

"I'm beginning to get an idea," Boley said. "McCutcheon decided to start a diamond rush, is that it? Where'd he get the stone?"

"You dug it out for him," McKee replied. "Until then, everything was just what it seemed. You dug two fishin' holes. Then he did find the diamond, and all that hush-hush commenced.

"I'd say he called Alice over and had a talk. Showed her how they could put on an act, building things up to her sluggin' him, so his discovery would really hit the papers."

Boley said, "So they bought that land from Border States hoping to resell and clean up. But where did Alice get the money?"

"Maybe she had some put back. But I'd bet Sewell made her a loan."

"The diamond. Is it real?"

McKee grinned. "It's real. The state man wouldn't lie about that."

"You want me to press the kidnap charge."

"I do. And I've had the hospital keep McCutcheon sedated, partly to keep him from droppin' the assault charge. You hang on until I suggest you drop it."

Boley was still puzzled. "What about the diamond? She threw it into the woods. I saw her."

"You saw her throw something into the woods. Remember I said you might mistake it for dirty quartz or calcite? That's probably what Sewell let her throw away." McKee's amusement grew. "Another reason for keepin' her locked up—I want McCutcheon to have time to go over there and 'find' that stone again." He added a postscript. "Or maybe they'll leave it as an inducement for whoever buys Alice's place."

THE GRAVE GRASS QUIVERS
BY MacKINLAY KANTOR

We were alone, out there in the soft spring sunshine. There was no one to disturb us. We dug silently, carefully.

The clinging, black earth came up at every shovelful—moist and alive with the richness of the prairies. We had been digging for ten minutes, when my shovel struck against something, and something cracked.

After that, it wasn't long before we began to uncover things. "Murdered," Doc said, once, and then he didn't talk any more.

It began in Doc Martindale's office, which, as soon as he retired, was to be my office, on a cool spring afternoon in 1921.

"How's it going?" asked Doc.

"I guess it'll be pretty slow here, to live," I said, childishly.

"Not much excitement," agreed Doc. He went to the door and picked up a copy of the *Cottonwood Herald* which a boy had just tossed over the banisters. . . . "Yes, local news is slow, pretty slow. There's a sample of a Cottonwood thriller."

It told of the plans for Arbor Day. The children of the public schools were going to set out some trees as a memorial to the local boys who had died in the World War.

. . . and selected as their choice, American elms. The trees will be planted on the Louis Wilson farm, above the Coon River. Mr. Wilson has agreed to donate a small plot of ground for this purpose. It is thought that these trees, standing on a high hill above the river and overlooking a majestic view of our city will be a fitting memorial.

Ceremonies are to begin at 2 P.M., and it is urged that all local people attend. Rev. J. Medley Williams of the Baptist Church will deliver a—

Doc pulled his gray beard and laughed. "A few meetings, a church social, once in a while a fire or an auto accident! Once in a blue moon we have a divorce. Life comes—and goes—without much hullabaloo."

Then I had to laugh also, and a bit sheepishly. "I guess I'm rather silly. Of course those are the important things in most people's lives. But I would like to get called in on a nice, exciting murder once in awhile!"

Doc was silent for a moment. He appeared to be thinking heavily, as if he had taken me seriously. "Murders," he said, after a moment. "Once before the war, a Mexican section worker stabbed his wife. Then back in '96, an insane farmer shot his neighbor. But, come to think about it, those are the only murders we've ever had here in all my years of practice." He seemed much impressed. "Think of that, think of that! Only two murders since 1861."

"And who," I inquired idly, "was murdered in 1861?"

He tugged at his beard again, and cleared his throat. "Well," he said, slowly, "it was my father and my brother."

"Oh." And I scarcely knew what to say. "I'm sorry, Doctor, I—"

"No matter." He shrugged. "It's a long time. I was just a boy then."

My curiosity was aroused. "What are the details, Doctor? That is, if you don't—"

"Oh, I don't mind. . . . Sit down and take it easy." He fumbled around for his matches, and his fat, brown cigar had been fogging the room for several minutes before he began.

"My brother Titus—he was a lot older—had run away from home

when he was small, and gone West with some folks. He didn't come back until the spring of '61. And when he came, what a time!''

He laughed his short, dry laugh.

"Titus had struck it rich. He had about seven thousand dollars in gold with him.

"Pa and Titus decided to take the gold to Hamilton. There was a sort of bank opened up there, and the folks were afraid to risk keeping so much money around home.

"They were pretty careful, too, and didn't tell around town much about what they planned. They started out at night, figuring to get clear away from Cottonwood and the settlers who knew them, before daylight. Pa and Titus were big strapping men. They looked very strong, setting up on the board laid across the plank wagon box, and Titus carried a navy revolver on his hip and a Sharps rifle across his knees.''

Doc Martindale shifted his fat, bumpy body in his old swivel chair. "And that,'' he said, "was the last we ever saw them.

"On the evening of the second day after my folks left,'' Dr. Martindale continued, "a farmer from the Salt Creek neighborhood rode up in front of our house, and said that he had seen our team down in a clump of willows by Little Hell Slough, hitched to a wagon, and that the men folks were not with the wagon. The team had been dragging around, and tried to go home, but they got hung up in the willows.''

Old Doc was silent for several minutes.

"That was a terrible night,'' he said, simply. "Before we all got down to Little Hell Slough—most of the neighbors were with us—we found the team in those willows, pretty muddy and hungry, and tangled up in the harness, too.

"None of the stuff in the wagon had been taken except—sure: the gold was gone. The blankets were still there, and Titus's rifle, but his navy revolver wasn't anywhere around. And there was no other sign of Pa and Titus.

"I drove Ma and the girls home, in that wagon. Ma sat there beside me on the board, stiff and solemn. Once she said, 'Georgie, if they're gone and gone for good, you'll get the man who did it. Won't you?' I began to cry, of course. I says, 'Yes, Ma. I'll take care of you always, Ma. . . . But if they're dead, it wasn't a man who killed 'em. It was men. One man wouldn't be a match for Titus alone.' ''

Doc was buried in the thickening shadows of the office. I couldn't see his face anymore.

"Then I went back with the men. We searched the river, up and down the hills around Cottonwood, too, clear down to the East Fork. And never found a thing.

"In that wagon there was just one clue—just one thing which made it certain in our minds that they were dead. That was a little spot of dried blood on the floor of the wagon, right behind the seat. About half as big as your hand. Seemed like, if they'd been shot off the wagon, there'd have been more blood. Then, too, the horses were a fairly young team and they might have cut loose and run away if any shooting had started.

"It was always the general opinion that the murderers had disposed of the bodies in the river. But, personally, I always hung to the idea that Titus and Pa were killed in some mysterious way, and their bodies buried. The fact is that the entire community searched for a week, and then gave it up. No other clue was ever discovered, and no further information of any kind was ever unearthed.

"I didn't quit searching for months. Eli Goble helped me, too; he worked like grim death. But we couldn't find a thing."

I asked, "Who was Eli Goble?"

There was the dull scraping of Doc's shoes on the floor. "Seems to me that you cashed a check this noon, boy. Where did you cash it?"

Somewhat perplexed, I told him, "At the bank across the street."

"Well, that's Eli Goble. And where are you living temporarily—until you can find rooms or an apartment to your liking?"

"At the—Oh, of course, Doctor. The Goble Hotel."

He chuckled. "Everything in this town's Goble, boy. He came here in '59 with a man named Goble, but that wasn't Eli's real name. He had heard that his folks came from Ohio, but didn't know anything about it. You see, his family was killed in the Mint Valley massacre, about 1840, and he had been kidnaped by the Indians. Lived with the Sioux until he was sixteen—could talk the language like a native, too. In fact, lots of folks used to think he was part

Indian. But he wasn't. And during the search, he thought all the trailing experience which he had had when among the Indians, might be of some account. But even that didn't help. We couldn't find a thing.''

I said, slowly, "He's rich, now?"

Doc sighed, and began to hunt around for the light switch. "Suspecting Eli Goble, are you?" He chuckled. "I don't believe anybody ever did, before. He never had a cent to his name for years after that. A few months later he enlisted in the army, served all through the war, and didn't come back here till 1867. In the meantime, through someone he met in the army, he had been trying to get track of his family. And eventually he succeeded. Found the original family, back in Ohio. He got what money was coming to him, brought it out here to Cottonwood, invested it carefully, and made good. He retained the name of Goble, for convenience's sake. Now he's almost ninety, but he's one of the richest men in the state, and one of the tightest. He never lets go of a nickel until the Goddess of Liberty yells for mercy."

The big yellow light hissed into being. It glared down on the white-enameled table, the glistening cabinets and instruments, the old desk and rows of books. Doc Martindale stood there in the middle of the office and nodded his head. "That's the story, boy. Real live mystery, just sixty years old this spring. . . ."

We were just putting on our hats, and Doc was struggling into his old brown slicker, when the telephone rang. Martindale took up the receiver. "Doctor Martindale speaking."

"Oh," he said, after a moment. "Well." And then he winked quickly at me above the telephone. "Did you use any of that stimulant I left last time? . . . Yes. I'm leaving the office, now, to go home, and I'll stop in. Yes."

He replaced the receiver on its hook. "Speak of the devil," he said. "Eli Goble's just had another heart attack. Nothing to get excited about. He has them frequently, but in between times he's up and down and around. We'll stop in to see him for a minute."

The Goble house was only a few minutes' drive from the main business streets. . . . Lights glowed from most of the windows, as we came up the sidewalk. "You can tell that Eli's flat on his back," said Doc. "If he was around, he wouldn't let them burn all that electricity."

The old man watched us from his pillow, with black, red-rimmed eyes, deeply sunk beneath the moldy fuzz of his eyebrows. . . . He was breathing heavily.

"Well, Eli. How do you feel? This is Dr. Patterson, Eli."

The old man seemed to glare broodingly at me.

"Don't feel—so—good," Goble managed with difficulty. "Plagued heart seems—like—played out on me."

Martindale began to open his bag. "Oh, nothing to worry about, Eli. We'll fix it all up right." He made a perfunctory examination. "You'll feel better soon, Eli. Sleep tight."

The old man mumbled and coughed; and we went down the shadowy stairway, through the gloomy, over-ornate hall, and out to the front door.

It was four o'clock the next afternoon when Doc Martindale and I arrived at the office, following a round of calls on widely separated cases. Beyond a few hasty reports to the girl whom Doc Martindale kept in his office during the midday hours, we had enjoyed no contact with the town of Cottonwood since 10 A.M.

When we returned in Doc's old touring car, it was to find the *Cottonwood Herald* spread on the table with plenty of black ink decorating the front page.

ELI GOBLE GIVES PARK TO CITY

Local businessman and Pioneer Settler Decides on Memorial

Plans Changed for Tomorrow's Dedication

At a special meeting of the city council this afternoon, it was unanimously agreed to accept the gift tendered by Eli Goble, revered Civil War veteran and early settler in Cottonwood, who today offered to give the town of Cottonwood some thirty acres of beautiful woodland, to be known as "Goble Memorial Park."

It is understood that Mr. Goble has been ill, and that is the reason for a delay in his plans.

"The grand old man of Crockett County" stipulated in the terms of his gift that the proposed Memorial Grove of trees should be set out somewhere in the new park area. This necessitated a hasty change in plans. Instead of being planted on the north hill, on the Louis Wilson farm above the Coon River, the trees will be set out on the brow of the east hill, which is included in the thirty acres donated by Mr. Goble.

A big parade, forming in the city hall square, and proceeding across the east bridge toward the new park, will officially open the Arbor Day ceremonies at two o'clock tomorrow afternoon. Following an invocation by Rev. J. Medley Williams, the Cottonwood city band will—

We leaned there, side by side with our hands upon the desk, and read that newspaper story.

Doc tapped the paper with his forefinger. "I'll go on record as saying," he declared, "that this is the first thing Eli Goble ever gave away in his life—at least the first thing in which there wasn't some chance of his getting value received out of it. And I don't see what he can get out of this, except glory. . . . Eli doesn't care a rap for glory. Listen to Editor Nollins calling him, 'the grand old man of Crockett County.' That's because Eli holds a mortgage on the *Herald* building."

Two patients drifted in for examination. . . . When I left, an hour later, I looked back to see Doctor Martindale sitting there in his swivel chair, a tired hulk, still reading the *Cottonwood Herald*.

At five-thirty in the morning, Old Doc was beating on my door. I arose, startled, and feeling that nothing short of peritonitis or a breech delivery could have made him summon me so insistently.

He came into the hotel room and waited while I threw on my clothes. "What is it?" I asked, between splashes of cold water.

"We're going out and do a little digging," he said.

I nodded. "Appendectomy? Or what?"

"Nothing so unimportant," Doc replied. And his eyes looked as if he had been awake all night—red-rimmed and circled. . . . "Real digging. No one will know where we are. If Mrs. Gustafson takes a notion to sink and die while we're away, she'll just have to sink and die." He said it with seeming brutality. I was still too sleepy to press him for more details, or to wonder what it was all about.

But when we got out to the curbing in front of the hotel, and I glanced into the rear seat of Doc's car, there lay two spades, a scoop-shovel and a pickax.

I turned with an exclamation of astonishment.

"Get in," said Doc. And I did, without any more words. He drove down Main Street, north on Kowa Avenue, and under the Burlington viaduct. We seemed to be heading north of town. Two minutes later our car was making the Coon River bridge rattle and bang in every loose joint.

"This is the Louis Wilson farm," said Doc. "Hm. I reckon we can turn here past the Cedar school, and drive down the lane past the timber."

At the furthest corner of the cornfield we climbed out, taking the shovels and ax with us. Doc was breathing hoarsely, but the strange pallor had left his face. . . . His eyes were bright and intent; there was something almost furious in their gleam.

He led me through a fringe of oak timberland, skirting two brushy ravines, and coming out on a sloping knoll where one solitary oak tree stood, stunted and twisted by many winds. The grass beneath our feet was coarse, tangled, flat-bladed. Native prairie sod, without a doubt. . . . Far away, a band of crows was circling over the river, cawing with faint and raucous cries.

"This is the north hill," said Doc. "There's the town."

It was a very high hill, this bald mound on which we stood. Beneath us the Coon River swung in a flat band of glistening brown.

The thin, brittle grass of the barren hill was tufted with hundreds of pale, lilac-pastel flowers. The blossoms grew on short, fuzzy stems; the petals shaded from white to purple, with a heart of yellow in each flower.

"They're beautiful," I said, "I never saw anything like them before. What are they?"

"Wind-flowers. Easter flowers. Or I guess the more modern name is pasque-flower. Pretty things, aren't they? One of the earliest we have around here. . . Well, I'm going to get busy.''

Doc dropped the shovel he was carrying, and I was just as willing to relinquish the heavy load in my own arms. I went over and sat down against the gnarled oak tree, which was the only tree on all that bald, brownish hill. A million facts and statements and conjectures seemed boiling in my brain; I could make nothing out of them.

Before my eyes, Doc Martindale was behaving in a very strange manner. He was walking slowly in vague, indefinite circles, his eyes staring at the ground in front of him. Occasionally he would move up beyond the brow of the hill and sweep the surrounding area with his eyes. I had the strange notion that Doctor George Martindale, after unloading the sad story of his youth, had taken two days in going deliberately and completely insane.

He thrust a small piece of stick into the ground, moved away, surveyed the spot carefully, and then came back to set up another stick, several feet from the first. He repeated this process two more times. He now had an uneven rectangle, eight or ten feet long, marked at its corners by the bits of stick. ''We'll try it here,'' he said.

Without another word, he removed his coat, lifted the pickax, and sent its point into the ground.

I cried, ''Wait a minute! Won't people down in the town see us up here?''

''They'll think we're cows or pigs,'' said Doc.

And, as I have said before, we were alone—out there in the thin sunshine of early morning. We dug silently. Neither of us spoke a word. After Doc had penetrated some two feet in depth, at one side of the rectangle, he moved out toward the middle of the space he had marked. I followed, with my shovel.

We had been digging for about ten minutes, when we began to find things.

''Murdered,'' said Doc.

We were finding them, picking out the disordered relics from the rich earth where they had lain so long. Tibiæ, ribs . . . phalanges . . . the rusty remains of an ancient revolver.

Doc straightened up, and spoke to me gently. His face was set and strained; it might have been cast in iron. ''There's a sheet and a grain sack or two in the car,'' he said. ''Will you go over and bring them?''

I was glad of the opportunity to get away for a few minutes. When I came back, Doc had most of the bones covered with his coat. The knees of his trousers were dark and earthy; he had been kneeling in the loose mold of the grave, picking out the smaller fragments.

''I want a witness,'' he said, shortly. ''Take a look at this.'' From beneath the coat he withdrew a human skull and turned it slowly for me to see. There was a complete and noticeable fracture, such as might have been caused by the blow of a sharp ax. ''The other is the same way,'' he added, and replaced the skull tenderly.

Then I spoke for the first time. ''Can you identify them?''

''Easily,'' he said. ''There's a Masonic pocket-piece, the revolver, and knives and things. . . . The pocket-piece is the best bet. It's engraved with Pa's name. Not corroded at all. I rubbed it up and could read the engraving.''

Wisely, he had made no attempt to identify or isolate the separate skeletons. The bones made awkward bundles, in the grain sacks. We worked slowly, carrying them and the shovels back to the car. I was too stunned by the grim reality to ask any questions. We went away and left that uneven black hole in the middle of the blooming wind-flowers.

Back in town, we went to Doc Martindale's garage, behind his little house on Omaha Street, and left the bundles there. Then we hurried to the office; fortunately there had been no phone calls at either house or office. It was after seven o'clock, and yet I had no desire for breakfast.

Doc sat at his desk and thumbed through a stack of old letters and notebooks. ''Clell Howard's living in Long Beach,'' he muttered. ''Got his address somewhere. . . . And Eph Spokesman is with his niece out in Portland. I've got to send telegrams right away.'' Then, strangely enough, he seemed to discover me standing there. ''You go around and look at Mrs. Gustafson and that greenstick fracture and the little Walker boy; tell them I'm busy on an emergency case. Don't say a word to anybody.''

''I won't,'' I promised.

He said, ''And be sure you don't forget the parade. It forms at 2

P.M., at the city hall square. You'll want to see that." And then he turned back to his rummaging.

I had all of the bedfast patients bandaged and dosed and sprayed and examined before 1:30 P.M. At two o'clock I was standing, with a group of pleasant and gossipy citizens, on the steps of the Cottonwood city hall. The triangular "square" was blooming with the gay sweaters and dresses of hundreds of school children who darted wildly underfoot, seething and yelling in a mad half-holiday.

At twenty minutes after two, the crowd was somewhat impatient. There had been a large turnout; the Boy Scouts were there, and the members of the American Legion, chafing and shifting in line. There was even a huge truck, splashed with vivid bunting, on which were the grove of memorial elms all ready to be set out, their dirt-encrusted roots sticking from beneath the scarlet shimmer of flags, like so many witches' claws.

This crowd was waiting for Eli Goble, albeit waiting impatiently. If a man was so kind as to give away thirty acres of land, one could at least expect him to show up for the dedication.

It was almost two-thirty before a big Cadillac touring car slid around the corner by the Phillips's oil station, and the crowds in that vicinity began a desultory hand-clapping. Yes, it was Eli Goble. I could see that bearded, skeleton shape sitting hunched in the rear seat, a Navajo blanket across his knees. His narrow-eyed son, vice-president of the bank, was driving.

Some fortunate fate had directed me to take up my station on those steps, above the mass of children. For I had a clear and unobstructed view of Doc Martindale, accompanied by a fat, pink-faced man who seemed very nervous, emerging from a dark stairway across the street.

I vaulted over the concrete railing beside me, and shouldered through the knotted humanity. Once or twice I had a quick glance at Doc and the pink-faced man, over the heads of the crowd. They were walking rapidly toward the corner where the Goble car was parked; the pink-faced man was drawing a folded paper from his pocket, and he seemed more nervous than ever.

We reached the corner simultaneously. A benign citizen, who wore a white silk badge, "Chairman," fluttering from his coat, was leaning at the side of the car, conversing with Eli Goble and his son.

"Daniel," said Doc Martindale.

The chairman turned.

"Get up on the city hall steps," Doc directed him, "and announce to the crowd that Mr. Goble's physician refuses to allow him to participate in the exercises. Then get them started with their parade."

Daniel began to stammer and sputter.

"Go 'long with you," ordered Doc, firmly. He opened the door of the back seat, and he and the pink-faced man slid in beside Eli Goble. And then Doc saw me standing there. "Get in the front seat, Dr. Patterson," he called, and before I knew it, I was sitting beside Vincent Goble, who was too excited to even bow.

"I don't understand this," he said importantly. "You're carrying things off with a very high hand, Doctor Martindale. It is my father's wish that—"

Doc's lips were thin and firm beneath his scraggly beard. "You keep your mouth shut, Vincent," he said. Vincent Goble gasped. "Drive around the corner on Queen Street, out of this crowd, and pull up at the curb."

The younger man's face was flaming with rage, but he obeyed the command. The Cadillac purred ahead, past the corner, past the alley, past the crowd. A block away it drew up beside the curb.

Vincent Goble and I swung around to face the trio in back. Eli Goble sat in the middle, clutching and contracting his hands against the red triangles of the Navajo blanket.

"Go ahead, Ed," said Doctor Martindale.

The little pink-faced man gasped apologetically, and fluttered the folds of the paper in his hand. He began a whispered jumble of phrases: "As sheriff of Crockett County, it is my duty to place you, Eli Goble, under arrest. You are charged with the murders of Titus Martindale and William Martindale, on or about the twenty-fourth of April, in the year 1861—"

Vincent Goble snarled. The old man still sat there, motionless except for the parchment hands which twisted in his lap. "Ain't true," he managed to whisper. "It—ain't true."

"You cowards!" cried his son. The banker's face was livid.

"You'd devil the very life out of an old man with some crazy superstition like that! You'd—"

Doc Martindale said, "Drive up to the sheriff's office, Vincent.
We want to talk things over."

"Like hell I will! Like—"

Ed Maxon, the sheriff, gulped fearfully. "Yes, Mr. Goble. That's
right. Have to ask you to bring your father up to my office."

And so, we went. Vincent, cursing beneath his breath, Doc Martindale silent as the tomb, Ed Maxon twisting and rubbing a damp hand
around his collar. And Eli Goble sitting there under the blanket, his
eyes like black caverns, and saying: "I—never done it. You'll see.
I never done—that."

"You saw the gold at the house. And made up your mind—"

"No."

"You followed them out there on the east prairie. Or maybe you
were lying there, waiting for them."

"I never—done it."

"Say, Doctor Martindale! If my father should have another heart
attack and die while you're questioning him—"

"Now, Mr. Goble, you—"

"I'm a physician, Vincent. And Eli's my patient. I'll look out for
him if he starts to faint. . . . Eli, you killed them from ambush."

"I never. Never did."

"Then you left the bodies in the wagon, took the team, and drove
out to the north hill. It was a long drive—must have taken hours to
get out there. But you figured that nobody ever went up there, and
it was away from the beaten track, and would be a good place to
hide the bodies."

"I—I—George, I'm an old man. I—"

"Damn you, Martindale! You—"

"Sit down, Vincent, and shut up. I'm not going to fool with anybody today. . . . Let's take your pulse, Eli. . . . Hm. Guess you can
stand it. All right. You buried them out on the north hill. Maybe
you drove the wagon back and forth over the grave—an Indian trick.
Trick you learned from the Sioux. And probably you scattered lots
of grass and brush around."

"No. *No.*"

"Titus had his gun strapped on; you left them in the ground, just as they were. You didn't take anything out of the wagon except those buckskin bags. Then you drove clear around town again, forded the river opposite Salt Creek, and drove over by Little Hell Slough. You left the team there, and skinned out. Took the gold somewhere and hid it, probably."

"Ain't so. Lie. . . ."

"Then you laid low, and waited to join in the search. You were clever, Eli. Clever as an Indian. . . . You helped me search, too. Oh, how we searched! We even went right across that north hill. But we never saw anything that looked like a grave. . . . You kept it covered up, Eli. You were smart."

"Don't. . . . Don't talk so—I can't—"

"By God, you let my father alone!—"

"Now, Mr. Goble. Please. Control yourself. Please—"

"You concluded that seven thousand dollars was a big fortune. Well, it was. Worth waiting for. So you enlisted in the army, took your chances—I'll give you credit for nerve there, Eli—and turned up after the war with that story about finding your relatives and your family property back in Ohio. Yes, you were smart."

"I never—never done it."

"Why did you give this park to the city?"

"Mmmmm. I—"

"The *Herald* carried that Arbor Day announcement, night before last. And right away you had a heart attack. And the next morning you came out with that gift to the city. *Provided*—"

"Vincent. Vincent. Make 'em let me—"

"I'll—"

"Here, hold him!"

"I've got him. Now, Mr. Goble, you'll have to sit down."

"Don't be a fool, Vincent. This is true—all true. It's taken me sixty years to find out, but I've found out. . . . You gave that park to the city of Cottonwood, Eli Goble, *provided* that they set out the memorial grove over there, on the east hill, instead of on the north hill. You didn't want anybody digging on the north hill, did you? It had never occurred to you to buy Louis Wilson's farm, so there wouldn't be a chance of people digging that ground up.''

''No. . . . Don't talk so, George! . . . Old. I'm an old an'—''

''Well, it was the first thing you ever gave away, in your life. And it set me to thinking. I thought, 'Why didn't Eli want that memorial grove planted up there?' And then, I began to understand things. I went up there this morning. Doctor Patterson was with me—I have a witness to what I am now about to relate. He saw me dig; he saw me find things. I found *them*, Eli.''

Vincent Goble was slumped forward, his head buried in his hands. Eli sat there in the sheriff's big chair, staring across the table. He seemed to be looking squarely through the opposite wall.

''They were murdered, Eli. Their skulls had been broken. A heavy, sharp blow at the back of each skull. I found them.''

The old man's lips were gray and rubbery. He whispered. ''No, I never done it. Can't prove it was me.''

''A hatchet, Eli. Someone had thrown a hatchet—or maybe two hatchets, in quick succession. They were sitting on that wagon board, in the bright moonlight. It would have been easy for anyone who could throw a tomahawk.''

Doc fumbled in the breast pocket of his coat, and brought out three folded squares of yellow paper. ''I'll read to you all,'' he said calmly. ''Three telegrams. The first one I sent myself, early this morning, to Clell Howard, in Long Beach, California, and to Ephriam Spokesman in Portland, Oregon. . . Remember those names, Eli? . . . Clell was mayor here, once. And Eph Spokesman—everybody knew him. Here's my telegram: 'Please reply by wire completely and at my expense. During the old days at Cottonwood, what man was skillful at throwing a knife or hatchet. Search your recollection and reply at once.'

''Here's the first reply I got. It came from Ephriam Spokesman's niece. Came about eleven o'clock. You can read it yourselves, gentlemen. It says, 'Uncle Eph very sick but says man named Goble thought to be a half-breed was only one who could throw hatchet. Wants to hear full details why you ask.'

''Along about eleven-forty-five, I got a telegram from Clell Howard. Here it is: 'Hello old neighbor regards to you. Am almost ninety but recall perfectly how I lost five dollars betting Eli Goble couldn't stick hatchet ten times in succession in big tree by Halsey blacksmith shop.' ''

The room was perfectly still, except for the hoarse sputtering in Eli Goble's throat. "No," he whispered tremulously. "No."

Doc Martindale pointed to the further corner of the dusty old room. There was a table, which none of us had noticed before, and on that table was a white sheet, rumpled and bulky.... "Eli," said Doc, quietly. "They're over there. In the corner."

The aged man stiffened in his chair. His back arched up, the shoulders quaking; his claw hands seemed wrenching a chunk of wood from the table in front of him.

"Father!" his son cried.

Eli Goble shook his head, and dropped back in his chair, his deep-set eyes dull with a flat, blue light. "The dead," he whispered. "They found me.... They're here in this room. I done it. I killed them. Titus and Bill. Yes. Yes."

Vincent Goble dropped down, his head buried in his arms, and began to sob—big, gulping sobs. The sheriff twisted nervously in his seat.

"George. You—you gonna send me to—prison? You gonna have them—hang me? I'm old ... I done it. Yes."

Doc Martindale cleared his throat. "Yes, you are old, Eli. Lot older than I am. It's too late, now, to do anything about it. I told my mother I'd get the man, and—But I can't see what good it would do, now, to send you to jail or even try you for murder."

Sheriff Maxon wiped his forehead. "The law," he said shrilly, "the law must take its course! Eli Goble, you must—"

"No," said Old Doc, decisively. "I'm running this show, Ed. Without me, without my testimony and the case I've built up, there isn't any show against Eli. I won't prosecute him, or furnish evidence."

"But he confessed to this murder!" shrilled Maxon. "He—"

Doc nodded. "Orally. Yes, but what if Vincent and Dr. Patterson and myself all swear that he never confessed? What if I destroy—the evidence!"

Maxon shook his head and bit his lips.

"How much is your father worth?" asked Doc of Vincent Goble. The banker lifted his face, on which the weary, baffled tears were still wet. "Couple of million, I guess."

"All yours," whispered Eli. "All yours . . ."

"Maybe," Doc nodded. "Seven thousand dollars. Quite a nest egg, in those days. Like fifty thousand, now. Or even more. . . No, gentlemen. Money won't do me any good. It can't bring back Titus and my father. But it can still do good. Yes."

Eli Goble's eyes had closed, like dark windows on which ragged curtains had been drawn. "I've seen 'em—I've seen 'em. Always. Since I got old—they come back. . . I had to give in. Yes."

"You'll go home," said Doc. "I'll give you something to put you to sleep. Then, after you have a little rest and get your strength back, you'll have a lawyer up at your house. . . . You will give, to this county in which you live, one million dollars for the purpose of founding and endowing a modern hospital, where every inhabitant can secure the best medical and surgical attention, free of charge. How does that sound?"

Head still buried in his arms, Vincent Goble nodded drunkenly. His father had opened his eyes and was shivering, still staring through the blank wall ahead of him. "Yes. Anything. . . . I give— anything. But take me away. I want to go—home. . . . I'm old. I don't want to stay in—this room. I don't want to stay with—*them*."

After Eli Goble was in bed, and asleep, Doc and I came out into the damp warmth of the spring afternoon. Martindale looked ten years older than he did the day before. "After this," he said, "after everything is taken care of, I'll let things go. . . You look after the practice beginning next Monday."

Our feet sounded flat and talkative, echoing on the long sidewalk. "One thing," I said. "I can't understand how you found the place. I can see how you reasoned out the rest—about that grove and about Eli Goble's not wanting the trees planted up there. But how did you know where to dig? We could have been up there for days, turning the soil."

Doc felt in his pocket for a cigar which wasn't there. "Wind-flowers," he said quietly. "They were scattered all over that hill.

Beautiful, like you said. . . . But I knew enough to dig where there were no wind-flowers. The grass on that hill looked pretty much alike, all over, but there weren't any flowers growing in that place I marked off. Those little purple flowers are funny. They only grow on native soil. You can't get them to grow where the sod has ever been turned.''

THE GEORGIA RESURRECTION

by S. S. RAFFERTY

"To be sure, Captain Cork, I agree," Tolliver Smyth said, readjusting himself in the high-back cane chair after refilling our drinks. "Superstition is a weakness in the chain of reality, but even a weak link is better than none, especially here in the Georgia plantations."

Out in the darkness, through the heavy muslin screens that gave entry to a slight breeze and yet protected us from the fierce insects that churned out of the swamps, came the rhythms of drums. They had been beating since supper, and although a bit unnerving, the crude timpani was oddly hypnotic. Suddenly Smyth chuckled to himself.

"Was that meant to be a pun, Captain?" he asked. "Calling it *black* magic? Very clever when you come to think of it. The slaves call it *vodo*."

"Yes," Cork said. "I have run into it in the Indies, especially on Hispaniola. It is outlawed there, I believe."

"And frowned on here, sorry to say. What harm can a few drumbeats and a chant or two do, yet it scares the locals hereabout out of their skins. I say, if it keeps the slaves happy and productive, let them conjure away."

"You are most progressive, sir," Cork remarked, hiding his pejorative intent in mild observation. I, of course, could interpret his true feelings, for I know my employer better than any other man in the American colonies. Cork detests the concept of slavery; in fact, it was this abhorrence that had brought us to the Georgia colony in the summer of 1761.

When he first devised a machine for the harvesting of rice, I thought he had finally decided to put his mind to industry rather than the solution of what he calls "social puzzles." But the fervour with which he approached the task and the speed with which he implemented it soon told me his real mission. If he could successfully prove the economy of his intention, he would render slavery unnecessary in these terribly hot and dank deltas, where no white man could toil more than an hour or two at a time.

Tolliver Smyth's plantation was near the Brunswick settlement several miles up one of the many small rivers that finger this remote and sparsely populated area. The Tolliver lands were called a "spread" by its master, in contrast to the smaller farms scattered about the back country. Smyth himself was an amiable young man of thirty who had recently come out from England to try his hand at a frontier fortune. And he had the strong hands for it, despite all his gentlemanly ways.

During supper, before the drums from the slave quarters had started, our main topic of conversation had centered on the harvesting scheme itself, and there was much chiding at my expense because I was the only one of the trio who was beardless. Before we left Charleston, Cork had begun to allow his usually trim barba to spread into a full beard. I found the suggestion that I too grow a beard ludicrous, since the excessive heat of this semi-tropical place would roast a man to the bone.

Cork hadn't prepared me for the mosquitoes and gnats which had been eating me alive since we arrived. However, the bugs did not seem to bother Tunxis, the tamed Quinnipiac Indian who serves as the captain's shadow. His method is to smear himself with a foul mixture of skunk oil and berry juice. It not only helps keep the insects away, but all humankind as well. As usual, he was out of doors somewheres—he refuses to enter under a roof.

We had arrived at Finderlay, as the plantation was called, earlier that day, and were now relaxing as best we could in the incessant heat. Overhead, from the verandah ceiling, swung a broad woven-reed plank that served as a fan, its locomotion provided by some unseen black hand. We were sipping dark rum, Smyth and I having refused to join Cork in his own ritual of eating raw clams liberally laced with vinegar.

"Well, I can see where a Christian community would be upset by occult arts being practiced in their midst," I put in.

Cork looked up from a clamshell. "The only thing that doesn't upset a Christian is another Christian, Oaks," he said, devouring the clam meat, "and then only if he totally agrees with him. It seems you are the only white man on the place, Smyth."

"I plan to marry one of these days, but I have to get Finderlay in shape for womankind, I'm afraid. What is it, Neela? You look like a startled fidget."

The tall black woman who had just come out onto the verandah was indeed astir. When we arrived earlier, I had noticed that her button-brown eyes were bright and minikin gay; they were now horse-wide with fear. She didn't speak, and merely cocked her head toward the front of the house.

"What the deuce has gotten into you, girl?" Smyth said impatiently. "Are there callers?"

She merely nodded.

"Then show them out here," Smyth told her. "Must be the devil himself," he said as we waited. "She's usually a calm woman."

Seconds later we had evidence of her consternation. I felt my own throat tighten as they loomed into view through the candle haze, presenting us with a bizarre duo of ominous dimensions.

Though the temperature had to be well over ninety degrees, and the humidity thickly oppressive, both men were dressed in winter greatcoats of immense bulk and mourning blackness. Despite their out-of-season bundlement, they showed no signs of discomfort; their alabaster faces glistened like hoarfrost on chipped stone. They could have been citizens of the netherworld, and instinctively I was repelled by them.

The taller of the two was heavyset, with a leonine head and a cavernous mouth that echoed his speech in deep drum tones. The other man was snipe-like in stature, with pathetically thin legs supporting an immense upper torso; when he spoke, he had a habit of turning his oblong head from side to side as if he were unable to see over his sharply pointed nose.

The latter announced himself as Zachary Gooms, and the black scarf trailing from the rim of his tricorner had already told us his profession of gravesman. The taller one announced that he was Simon Cratch, who made his living as a hangman. This was certainly strange postprandial companionship, and Smyth seemed annoyed at the intrusion by men of such low station.

"We bury our own here at Finderlay, Gooms, and slaves are too expensive to hang, Cratch, no matter what the crime."

"Well, sir," Cratch said uneasily, "we thought we could save you some trouble, since we understand you let your Nigras practice heathen religion."

"What my people do on Finderlay is my affair," Smyth said sternly. "What *trouble* are you talking about?"

"Well, sir, Gooms is the local man, so I'll let him tell it," Cratch acceded to his companion.

Smyth raised a hand in tacit approval. "Go on, Gooms, I thought you looked familiar. You have a coffin shop in Brunswick."

"Correct, sir, coffins and burials and fine furniture, if you wish. But even as the official county gravesman, it's a poor living. Now the coffins are gaining favor with the townsfolk, although you people out in the back country still make your own. But the furniture's another matter, with people sending to England for it."

"At least you can make a living," Cratch lamented. "I purposely came to Georgia thinking there would be a great need for my services."

"Why is that?" Cork queried.

Cratch looked at Smyth, who said, "This is Captain Jeremy Cork and his yeoman, Wellman Oaks."

"Well, Captain Cork," Cratch went on, "it seemed to me that since many of the felons were being transported from our jails at home to Georgia, and felons never changing their ways, as you know, there would be a brisk business for me.

"But it turned out not to be the case, and I near starved for lack of commissions. To add to my misfortune and a stroke of bad timing,

I requested transfer back to England and was granted it. Of course now the Escape Commission is a-comin' over and there'll be lots of work for the new man at the derrick.''

"Escape Commission? Sounds royal and self-contradictory," I said.

"Its mission has received quite a broadcast in these parts, gentlemen," Smyth explained. "Not only are the colonists perturbed by the legally transported convicts, but terror is slowly building up over the escaped cutthroats who somehow make it to these shores and seek refuge among old criminal friends."

"Yes," Cork said, "several newspapers in the north have come out quite strongly for an end to transportation."

"Aye, and woe to my timing of transfer," Cratch consoled himself. "The Commission will bring with them a warder from each of the main prisons who know these escaped scoundrels on sight. They'll be full gibbets from here to Canada, they will. Now as luck would have it I missed my ship at Brunswick and happened by Mr. Gooms's shop. I wouldn't want the foul deed on my record."

"Foul deed? What are you talking about, man?" Smyth was irritated and abrupt. Cork seemed interested, however, and tried to calm our host.

"Perhaps these fellows have a tale to tell, Smyth. It will pass the evening. Why don't you two sit down?"

Smyth nodded agreement and they took seats.

"Well, gentlemen, the problem seems to be Arthur Briddleton here." As Gooms said it, he took a white plaster sculpture from under his greatcoat and laid it on the table. The object was a man's face in repose. The nose was aquiline, the skin smooth and unlined. It was the death mask of a man in his late twenties.

"You are quite expert in the art of death masks, Gooms. Is that one of your services to clients?" Cork asked.

"No, sir, it's more trouble than it's worth to me, but the governor has ordered that one be made of every executed criminal."

I shot a quick glance in Cork's direction, but he ignored me. Just six months ago he had suggested this method of verifying the death of criminals to Major Philip Tell, a special King's agent at large. I could see that Tell had wasted no time in turning Cork's advice to his own advantage. However, I could not fault the major, for I could see little profit in the business. Cork was speaking again. "And this, you say, is Arthur Briddleton's face?"

"Well, sir," Simon Cratch's voice boomed over us like cannon fire, "that's the heart of the matter, so to speak. I say that's *not* the face of the man called Briddleton who I hanged on Monday last, and Mr. Gooms insists that it is."

"Nay, Mr. Cratch, that's not correct. I claim that is the death mask of the body I picked up at the gibbet at Landsdown crossing at sundown on Monday last. I never knew Arthur Briddleton and could not swear what he looked like. I say the man hanging there bore the face you see in the mask."

"Gentlemen," Cork said, raising an open palm, "if you will let me ask a few questions to put the problem in its traces, I think we can be of help. Would you care for a drink?"

Gooms said no, but Cratch eyed the bottle near Cork's plate of clams. "Would that be vinegar I smell, sir?"

Cork nodded. "Yes, I believe a red wine gone sour, and quite tart."

"Then I'll happily take a cup. Helps with the heat."

My own mouth felt like cotton as I watched him drink down the acetose liquid and wondered if indeed it did keep one cool. Cork proceeded with a methodical interrogation, from which I have summarized the following.

On the previous Sunday (this being a Thursday evening), a stranger to the locality, who gave his name as Arthur Briddleton, was seized while stealing a horse in an inland village known as Landsdown. He was immediately brought to the local Justice of the Peace, who tried and convicted him. The punishment, as usual, was hanging. There was some argument about executing a man on the Sabbath, and it was decided to hold it on the following day.

"And most fortunate for Briddleton at that," Cratch said. "I was on my way up from Waverly to take a ship at Brunswick for England when I heard there was supposed to be a hanging at Landsdown. Believe me, I'm not one to miss a fee. Lucky lad, Briddleton."

"Lucky?" I echoed unconsciously.

"Certainly, Mr. Oaks," Cratch said with a wink. "A man condemned to death can suffer on the string, for if the noose is applied by some amateur, the hanging can be most unpleasant. But old Simon Cratch was handy, and he went swiftly and sweetly. But that mask isn't Arthur Briddleton.''

"And just what did your Briddleton look like?'' Cork asked.

"Well, the first thing I noticed when I happened to stop by Gooms's shop and saw the mask was that the scar along the left cheek was missing. Then the nose was different. This one is quite pointed, whereas the nose of the man on the gallows was flatlike.''

"Of course this was a public execution,'' Cork said.

"Out in the open, but with no witnesses except the J.P., Bill Tooks. Folks want justice, gentlemen, but they don't like to see it dispatched. I put him on the string about two in the afternoon and went my way, for I had the ship to catch. As luck would have it, I missed her. Now, by the look you're aiming at me, Captain, I know you're asking yourself, was the man dead, and I can assure you he was. I've put fifty men on the derrick in my day, and not a manjack of them ever walked away.'' He sat back with a self-satisfied smug, "I'll take some more of that vinegar, if you please, sir. It's got a fine bite.''

Cork refilled the cup and turned to Zachary Gooms. "Now will you tell your part in all this?''

"Glad to,'' the gravesman said, clearing his throat. "When I heard the nine tolls plus one for a dead man on the Landsdown bell, I knew I was needed for a felon burial. It's part of my contract to care for public graves, and when the bell is rung nine times and one, it's to tell me to come at sundown. The body is left on the gibbet till that time as an example, although most people avoid the Crossing when a body has swung.

"Well, sir, I took my cart out there to that deserted gibbet and brought the corpse back to Brunswick. As I was passing through the delta road by your bottom acreage, Mr. Smyth, I came upon a group of your Nigras dancing and cavorting in a grove just off the road. It was like a witch's sabbath, it was, with drums and rattles and the like. Most hellish.

"I can't tell you how uneasy I was, and I gave the horse a crack to get out of the neighborhood, for I wanted no truck with black devils. Then, damnation, my old Ned rears up and pushes the cart into a gulley. The noises attracted the nigras, and they came running to see. I'll say this for your boys, Mr. Smyth, they were most helpful. They got the cart back on the road and I was off like cannon-shot. I got back to Brunswick, made the mask, and buried the body outside town to the west, in the poor field, in an unmarked grave. The face you see in that mask is the face of the man I buried. I swear to it, sir!''

Tolliver Smyth, who had been sitting with his booted feet spread in front of him during the narration, now stood up menacingly. "Are you implying that my slaves had something to do with this?"

"Now, Mr. Smyth, sir," Gooms said hesitantly, "I just state the facts."

"Despite the heat," Cork put in, "let's keep cool heads. Did you look at the corpse when you took it down at the gibbet, Gooms?"

"It was hard to see in lanternlight, Captain. The first good look I got of him was when I reached my shop."

"Then the bodies could have been switched on the gibbet," Cork suggested.

"Switched!" Gooms said in confusion, "I never thought of that. I thought those black devils put a spell on the body. You know, used magic."

"Gooms," Cork said, "it is best to look to reality for an answer before bringing in the occult. Consider your own precarious position, sir. You bury a body that does not resemble the hanged man. That, my lad, is suspicious."

Gooms was visibly disturbed. "Why would I do anything like that? I made the mask, didn't I?"

"Of course, but you assumed that Cratch would be off to England and the J.P. at Landsdown would never see the mask, since it would be sent to the officials in Savannah."

"I beg you, sir," the gravesman pleaded, "I am an honest man."

"And you shall have a chance to prove it."

"Thank God for that," Gooms said fervently, "but how can I?"

"With the greatest ease—by resurrection." As Cork said the word, a sudden silence fell over the company. Gooms looked horrified, and

Cratch—yes, even that grim hangman seemed uneasy. Tolliver Smyth was shocked. For myself, I was appalled.

"Dig up the body?" I said. "Why, that's sacrilegious!"

"Well, my fellows, you can't have it both ways," the captain admonished us all. "We have a dispute over identity, so we must let the corpse speak for itself."

"Begging the Captain's pardon," Cratch said, "I'm as hard a man as any—but resurrection! I'd as soon forget the whole affair. In fact, the more I look at this mask, the only thing different is the scar and the nose."

"But I can't forget it; nor can you, Smyth," Cork said. "These fellows have made a serious accusation against your slaves, and it's bound to start disquieting rumors. No, the body *must* be resurrected at once. Let's see, buried just four days ago. Hmmm, should be still in fine condition for identification."

"Well, an official will have to pass on it," Gooms said humbly. "I'm all for it, but I'll not take it on my own head."

"To be sure. Let us keep it legal," Cork advised. "And who better to order Briddleton resurrected than the man who sentenced him to the grave? Now get you both to this J.P. and resolve the issue."

Both men got up to leave when Cork stopped them. "Oh, yes, you lads had better leave the death mask here, for safekeeping."

After our eerie visitors had left, Smyth suggested we turn in, for we had a long day ahead of us in the rice fields. I was all for it and, despite the heat, dropped off to sleep in minutes. It was still dark of night when I sat bolt upright in bed, a hand covering my mouth.

"By Jerusalem, Oaks, be quiet," Cork's voice whispered. "Come, get dressed, we have work to do."

Minutes later we were out of the main house, prowling about the outbuildings. We came upon a small shed, and Cork slipped inside, returned in a trice, and tapped my shoulder. "Come in, I've found it," he said.

Once inside he shut the door and relit a candle. It was nothing more than a workshed, quite like any that one would expect to find on a self-sustaining plantation which makes everything from shoes to shingles for itself. I watched the captain as he uncovered a barrel of chalky white powder and scooped some into a bowl. To this he added water from a bucket in a corner, and proceeded to beat the mixture into a paste.

"It is fortunate that the Smyth main house has plaster walls, and that the materials are at hand," Cork said.

He dumped the paste onto a worktable, and then, to my surprise, took the Briddleton mask from inside his shirt. He lay the mask next to the heap of white paste and began to shape the stuff into a facsimile, smoothing the features of a face on it. I watched him work in silence, and after half an hour he stepped back and cupped his bearded chin with his hand, as if admiring a masterpiece.

"If your creation is supposed to match the original, I can assure you that you are no sculptor, Captain."

"It will do. Same general shape, similar nose, eyes. Yes, it will do fine. Now this will have to dry before we can move it." He picked up the original and tucked it back into his shirt. "Now we shall take a little stroll, old son," he said, going out into the moonlit, drum-beating night.

We were only ten yards from the workshed when he stopped and put both hands to his mouth, one cupped over the other, and delivered the most perfect imitation of a lake loon I have ever heard. I have tried it myself several times and failed, to Tunxis' amusement, for this is how the savage and Cork sometimes communicate. At the edge of a clearing I could hear the return call and knew that Tunxis was nearby. Cork walked off to meet him. When he returned to me, I said, "This is all so befuddling."

"That is because your mind is on other things. Come, our stroll is not over."

I followed him across the clearing into the underbrush, and ten minutes later found myself in a deep swamp, gingerly trodding along a hummock that snaked its way across the dark black water, hiding God knows what in its depths. Ahead of us the drums grew louder. I was amazed at the way Cork so assuredly picked his way along, till I realized that Tunxis must have marked the trail for him. We stopped for a moment while he got his bearings, and I asked him where we were headed.

"One of the sad thoughts in my life, Oaks, is that my adventures have kept you from romance. Tonight we shall rectify the oversight. Ah, there are lights ahead, and our destination.''

The hummock suddenly broadened into a small island that rose slowly out of the swamps. Giant mangroves tentacled out of the water to make it a fortress, an evil bastion.

When we came into the clearing, the drums suddenly stopped. A group of black men and women were sitting by a fire, looking at us in wonderment. A huge muscular fellow rose slowly to his feet and came toward us.

''Why, it's the cappin' who's visitin' the mastah,'' he said with a smile of relief. ''You musta lost your way. Load a danger in the swamp at night, sirs. Come, I take you back so's you don't get ate by a 'gator.''

·''You are called Big Blue, I believe. I saw you this afternoon in the fields. You're a good worker.''

The man smiled at the flattery. ''Big Blue worth ten men, the mastah say. Make's Big Blue head man. Come, I take you back, sirs.''

''No. First I must see the *mambo*.''

Big Blue's amiable face froze in terror. ''No *mambo* here at Finderlay, sir. No *vodo*. No priest woman, no sir.''

''A *zohop* then, one who knows the plants and leaves. My friend here is in need of *vervain*.'' As he said it, he placed his hands over his heart and feigned a swoon, which brought hearty laughter from the campfire. Although it broke the tension, I didn't like having it done at my expense. I assumed *vervain* had something to do with the romance he had alluded to.

Amid all the laughter an ancient Negress emerged from the shack and sat herself on a tree stump. She was old and wizened; a bright red bandanna covered her head, while a gingham shawl hid her shrunken body. She let out a cackle and motioned us forward.

When we reached her, Cork bowed slightly and handed her two coins. ''This is Mamabin,'' Big Blue said. ''Very old, very much head for dreams.''

The crone looked up at Cork and told him, ''You are as high as a tree, which means your head always clear. How do you come by the tongue of the swamps?''

"I have put time in the Indies, old mother."

"Pirate?" she shouted.

"No, mother, a traveller. Please, a *vervain* for my friend."

She cocked an eye at me and looked me over from head to toe. "Hard to do, hard to do, but we try." She put her hand into a grass-woven satchel at her feet and took out a handful of leaves. She scrutinized her palm and then selected five leaves of equal size and handed them to me. They were nothing more than oleander leaves.

"Pin one each to the corner of your pillow and one in the center. Then you sleep and dream of lady you will marry." It was all nonsense, but I took them and thanked her.

"Tell me, old mother," Cork said, "what is the way to make a zombi walk?"

She immediately cringed, and he was quick to calm her.

"I know you don't make zombi, but I have great interest, and it may help your master."

"Masta Tolliver good man," she said. "No whips here at Finderlay. Make Blue head man. Good masta. Someone has spell on him?"

"Not yet, but in case it happens."

"They say make zombi drink salt water and he speak."

"You are very wise, old mother. I am told you can make zombi if you hang a dead man from his heels and take three drops from his nose."

She tossed her head back and cackled. "That would be a pizen, child."

"Or is it a pin stuck into a lime while still on the tree from sunup to sunup and then squeezing the juice?"

She cackled again. "More pizen."

"Or is it the black-leaf tea, old mother?"

At this remark she went silent. "Houngan. You houngan."

"I know more of magic than these people should hear, old mother. Come, let us go inside where we can talk."

He was in with her for almost half an hour, while I stood in the campfire-lit grove a bit uneasily. He finally came out, and we left the place hurriedly. Once back at the main plantation, we picked up the now dry, rude copy of the death mask, and crept up to our rooms.

"I take it she is a witch of some kind," I said to him before going into my own bedchamber.

"More an herbal magician, or a *docteur feuilles*, as the French colonists call them. These old tribal rites and beliefs brought over from Africa have been diluted and fragmented by time and locale, but the basics are still there. That's what I was after tonight."

"And did you get it?"

"Sweet dreams, old son," he said, shutting his door.

All this confusion had muddled my mind, and only sleep could clear it. I fell asleep for the second time that night with a bit of difficulty, for the oleander leaves on my pillow kept scratching my ear.

For the next two days we heard nothing from Cratch or Gooms and had little time to think of their problem. We were up with the sun and into the rice fields, where Cork made elaborate calculations and closely observed the method of harvesting. I spent most of my time swatting bugs. Each night Cork spent long hours at his drawings, leaving me to bide my time with Tolliver Smyth, who proved to be a well-read fellow.

Even Saturday night could not drag the captain from his work, and Smyth and I repaired to drink once again on the verandah.

"One of my men, Big Blue, tells me that you paid a visit to the old woman in the swamps," he said, lighting a seegar. "Best be careful back in there. Hundred of quicksand places that could swallow a man forever."

I shuddered inwardly and thanked the Lord for Tunxis' trailblazing ability. I hadn't seen the savage since that night, and wondered where he was off to. But he does that now and again, so I paid it no heed.

"I'm afraid your visit has spoiled me, for I shall miss our talks and fellowship when you are gone," Smyth said.

"Not many neighbors?"

"These plantations are so vast that there is little sociality, and then in the small villages they don't take to strangers, at least not to me."

"They think you are too easy on the slaves?"

"Yes. Always talk of keeping them down for fear of an uprising. If the poor devils do a day's work, let them be. But then maybe it's me personally they don't like. After all, Bill Tooks is as new out here as I am, and the locals took to him like a duck to water. Elected him J.P. and all that."

"Never confuse competence with popularity." We looked up to see Cork coming out onto the verandah from the house. "It is one of the flaws of the human race. We seem to have visitors, gentlemen."

Out in the darkness was the sound of horse hooves, and one of the house slaves ran into the yard with a torch illuminating the arriving party. Three men were ahorse—Gooms, Cratch, and an unknown man. The fourth person on foot was known well to me.

"Take a care, sirs!" Cork shouted. "That's a war chief of the Quinnipiac you have bound by rope and lead on a halter."

"Runaway slave from the West Indies, if I have it right," growled the stranger. He was a fierce man with a black beard and wore rough back-country clothes. Smyth got to his feet and was seemingly about to corroborate Cork, when the captain stopped him.

"Never shout a truth when you can exhibit it," he said to our host. "Very well, sir, you operate at your own peril."

Then, to Tunxis he said something in Indian jabber, and in a second the redskin's hands were not only free, but whipping the tether and the stranger from his horse.

"Help the gentlemen up, Tunxis, and dust him off a bit. I suggest you let him do it, sir, for he could have your scalp in a trice if he cared to."

"It's all right, Bill, the Indian is with Captain Cork!" Smyth shouted.

There was much swearing from Justice of the Peace Tooks as the three men climbed to the verandah. Cork went into the yard and talked with Tunxis, who handed him a piece of paper he had concealed in his moccasin.

Tooks was saying, "How was I to know he was a bloody prince or something?" when Cork returned.

"No harm done, Mr. Tooks. An Indian in unfamiliar country walking alone is, of course, suspicious, since the redman is used as a slave in the Indies. I can see that you were only doing your duty as a J.P."

This seemed to placate the man for a few moments, and then he became irritable again. "And I'm here to do my duty, I can assure you. These are strange doings indeed. Never saw the like of it. Gooms and Cratch arguing over who's hung and who's buried. I've been off in the wilderness for two days or I'd have been on this sooner. I'm not opening a man's grave, felon or not, until I find out which one's lying. I'm told you have the death mask, Cork, and I want it produced now."

"Of course, Justice Tooks, I'll fetch it and along the way I'll make you some of my own Apple Knock. Would you rather have more vinegar, Mr. Cratch?"

The hangman smiled. "I'm not against a bit of liquor, sir."

Cork asked me to assist him, and, as we left the verandah, Tooks was growling at Smyth, "If any of your damned darkies had anything to do with this, they'll all hang."

Once inside, Cork sent me to his room to get the mask. He was mixing the Knock when I returned below stairs. How he expected to pass off this childish copy as a death mask, I had no idea. I was preceding him out the door when he tripped me and sent me sprawling forward. The mask flew from my hands and smashed to pieces.

"Oaks, you jackanapes!" he shouted at me. "Now look what you've done. You'll be flogged for this!"

"Is that the mask?" Tooks cried.

"*Was* the mask, I'm afraid, Mr. Justice," Cork apologized. "You must forgive this menial of mine."

I was stunned at such treatment from the man I considered my friend. Seeing my anger, Cork admonished me, "Hold your tongue, man, that's an order!"

"Now that's done it." Tooks was red with anger. "Now I'll have to open the grave."

"I think not, sir," Cork said, handing the drinks around. "The explanation to this is quite simple. Tell me, Mr. Cratch, when did you arrive at Landsdown?"

"Why, Sunday in the forenoon, right after the trial."

"And how did you spend your time, sir? The hanging wasn't until Monday afternoon, which in itself is strange, since executions are normally at dawn."

"I'll tell you what he did, he got himself drunk as a lord." Tooks pointed a finger at Cratch. "Couldn't get the sot awake till almost one on Monday. I wouldn't have paid him a fee in advance if I knew he was a drunkard."

"So we have a bleary-eyed rumpot who says the man hanged is not the man buried. Your proclivity for vinegar is not uncommon among men who drink too much, Cratch. It is the fool's notion that acid thins the blood and makes one sober. In the Pennsylvania colony sauerkraut juice is the common remedy."

"You mean all this trouble was caused by a drunken hangman?" Tooks was now livid. "By thunderation I'll put *him* on the gibbet, I will!"

"Have a care, Mr. Justice, you may not be so lucky next time."

"Lucky? What do you mean, lucky?"

"Well, Mr. Tooks—" Cork took a piece of paper from his pocket "—two days ago I dispatched my Indian friend to Savannah by coaster with an accurate description of the death mask. Now in my report to the governor, I failed to mention that you tried Arthur Briddleton on a Sunday, which is illegal, and thus so was his sentence. I did not mention that you might have committed judicial murder, for it was not my purpose to bring the Royal Governor down on your head. I have an interest in this death-mask system, sir, because I am its inventor. Well, lo and behold, you are a bit of a hero, for Tunxis brings me word that you have successfully tried, convicted, and hung none other than Black Jack Herleigh."

"The escaped highwayman? My word!" Tooks beamed. "He was one of the blackguards mentioned in the Escape Commission's proclamation. Think of it, gentlemen—me, Bill Tooks, captured and hung a notorious robber that all the King's men couldn't keep or find!"

He took a long draught to his success from his Knock and smiled anew. Suddenly, in the instant of a swallow, his face went white and he fell forward on the floor.

"Quick, you two! To the well for cool water!"

"It's no use, Captain Cork," the gravesman said, looking down at Tooks's face. "I knows a corpse when I sees one."

"I said water and fast!" Cork said with a roar that sent both men scurrying outside.

Smyth bent over the body, rolled back the eyelids, then put his head to Tooks's chest.

"Too much excitement, I would guess," Cork said.

Smyth got to his feet and rushed indoors, mumbling, "Damn fool." He returned seconds later and poured liquid from a small blue philtre into Tooks's mouth. The man's eyes began to flutter and his breath came heavy at first and then steadied.

"You're all right, Mr. Tooks," Cork said, kneeling down. "You've had a bit of a fright, that's all. You should take things easier in the future, for I think you may have some trouble with your heart."

Within the hour the Justice of the Peace was on his feet again and as feisty as ever. "You, Cratch, had better be on the next boat out of Brunswick, if you know what's good for you. And you, Zachary Gooms, help me to home. I'm sorry to have caused you trouble, Tolliver. Drop over soon to meet the folks at Landsdown. There's a young widow I'd like you to meet."

When the hoofbeats were out of earshot, we all sat down again to our drinks and relaxed.

"Well, I must say all's well that ends well," I chuckled. "But this affair must have had little zest for you, Captain, since it proved to be no puzzle at all."

He gave me that smirk-a-mouth. "More of a puzzle than you think, old son." He turned to Smyth. "Why don't you take off the false beard, Black Jack? Your own must be grown in fairly well by now."

"Black Jack? Black Jack Herleigh? Come now, Captain."

Then, before my eyes, the planter removed his thick beard and revealed a good seven-days' growth.

"When did you get on to me?" he asked.

"I was sure when you went for the antidote to the datura and gave it to Tooks. If you hadn't, I would have administered my own concoction."

I was astounded. "I don't understand this at all. Isn't Herleigh supposed to be in his grave?"

"Hold fast, Oaks. Let us start from the beginning. You will recall when Cratch and Gooms first brought us the problem, I offered the simplest of solutions. One body, probably Briddleton's, was replaced by another. But whose, and, more pointedly, why? The who, of course, would have required clairvoyance; the why, however, although a puzzling question, was not beyond *all* conjecture."

"Well, I've thought about that," I said, "and fell upon the idea that someone had been murdered and that his corpse had somehow gotten into Gooms's hands for a legal burial."

"Then you didn't think hard enough, Oaks. A murdered corpse could be hidden eternally in the quicksand of the swamps. No, the purpose of the replacement was one of *identity*. Either to hide Briddleton's or to expose the face on the mask. And the answer leans to the latter in light of the Escape Commission's imminent arrival. Briddleton was a complete stranger hereabouts with no friends to identify him. And even if he were an escaped felon, what could be gained by hiding his identity after death?"

"And that's why you sent the original mask to Savannah?" I asked.

Smyth-Herleigh looked agitated. "I thought you said you sent a description, and that those smashed bits of plaster are the remains of the mask."

"A mere diversion, Jack Herleigh, or should I say Tolliver Smyth, for you are forever safe in your new identity. The Commission has now written you off as dead, and will not look for a man who has been officially buried. Hanged and buried. You can be assured that Tooks is so inflated by his capturing and hanging a notorious highwayman that nothing could convince him to the contrary. Black Jack Herleigh is 'dead.' "

"But that's what I don't understand," I said. "If Herleigh—that is, Smyth—posed as a corpse to have his freshly shaved face cast in a mask, how could he fool a gravesman?"

"Because to all intents and purposes he *was* dead, Oaks. He was a zombi until his slaves could dig him out of the grave and put Briddleton's body in his place."

"A zombi? Why, zombies are mere superstition!"

"To the uninitiated, yes, but a person can be suspended in a catatonic deathlike trance with any of several tropical drugs. In South America it is curare; in Hispaniola, datura is used."

"Or mancenillier," Smyth-Herleigh interjected.

"I see you know herbal medicine as well as Mamabin."

"Not really, but she made the sleep draught for me when I learned of the Escape Commission's coming. I was a wild lad in the old days, and took to the highway more for the adventure than for the profit. I never killed anyone, despite the reports of my savagery. My main sin seems to have been escaping from Newgate and cheating the hangman. Out here I planned a new life."

"And you have it, sir."

"Thanks to you, yes. When I learned that a man near my age and build was going to be hanged in Landsdown, I saw my chance to throw the Escape Commission off my trail, so I took the draught and had the slaves put my 'dead' body in place of Briddleton's during the slaves' diversion on the Delta road. But how could you know it was my face in the mask? I had to shave clean for the death mask. Is this false beard so bad?"

"No," Cork said, "it's quite good, in fact. Until Tunxis returned, I had no inkling of a man named Black Jack Herleigh. But I did suspect that the affair had something to do with a runaway criminal, and both yourself and Tooks were new to the neighborhood. I decided on you, for Tooks, in his official capacity, could have made a mask of his own face and sent it along to Savannah without any hanging at all. You proved your mettle tonight when you gave Tooks the antidote for the death-sleep potion I put in his Knock."

"I thought Neela had done it to protect me."

"Your slaves think well of you, Smyth, and I suspect your attitude comes from having spent some time in chains yourself. If you perfect this new scheme of mine for rice production, you may well have no need for them. What the devil are you doing, Oaks?"

"I'm rubbing my shin where you tripped me."

"Sorry, old son, but I had to trip you. It was necessary to the charade."

I was truly touched until he gave me that smirk-a-mouth again.

"Of course, you can trot off to the swamps and have Mamabin fix you a poultice. And while you're there, have her give you new oleander leaves for your pillow. The old ones have scratched the back of your neck, and you are dreaming of the wrong things.''

I decided to ignore him, but he is uncanny. How could he know that I had dreamed of my account books?

VOICES IN DEAD MAN'S WELL
by *DONALD HONIG*

The way they talked about the farm, you'd of thought they wanted something terrible to happen, were waiting for it to happen. The way they talked, even when I was a small boy, you'd of thought there was nothing a man could do about the place. They said it was damned and haunted. But I never believed that, not when I was a small boy. I went there a lot of times then and looked at it. It looked no different from the other farms in the county, except that it was rundown and the house was empty and the barn had half slid back to the earth.

I even looked down into the well once and I didn't see nor hear anything down there. When I went home, I told my mother I'd been there and had looked down into the well. She glared at me and shook me by the arm and yelled at me never to go up there again. "Don't you know what people say about that place!" she yelled.

Her yelling at me never changed my mind, though. I still went there every so often and walked around the moldering old place. When I was a small boy I never heard voices coming out of the well, and it never seemed as if anything bad could happen there if people, and I mean real live people and not ghosts, didn't make it happen.

The farm lay in against the foothills and there were a lot of trees and some good soil if you worked at it hard enough. It was no better than most and no worse than others, except that, for almost fifty years it had stood deserted in the sunlight and under the stars and in the wind and rain and under the snows, unworked and unwanted, with even the hoboes who came into and out of town on the through freight giving it wide berth, having heard about it.

They called it Dead Man's Well. Everybody in the county knew about it and that was what they called it. It got the name during the War Between the States. A big battle had been fought in the area, part of which had taken place right on the farm. The day after the battle, a Confederate colonel rode up to the farmhouse and told the farmer there were a lot of dead bodies strewn out on the pasture and that the farmer would get a dollar per head for each one that he buried, what with the army being unable to spare any men for the detail. The farmer said all right. But he was a crafty one. He hitched his team and drove out with his wagon and gathered up thirty dead soldiers and collected his thirty dollars—insisted that it be in gold, too, not paper money. Later that day the army moved out, and as soon as they were all gone the farmer, not a man to bend his back to work if he could get by with it, began throwing the bodies down the well. The story goes that his wife went out of her mind with panic at the sight of what he was doing. But he went right on with it, pulling the bodies off the wagon and dropping them down the well.

Folks found out about it soon enough and they didn't take kindly to what the farmer had done. Some of them came up to the farm one night and there was harsh words and something happened— nobody ever told just what—and the farmer was left lying on the ground with smoking bullet holes in him. His wife saw that too and it turned her into a jibbering idiot altogether and it took the men two days to hunt her down in the woods and take her away to the asylum.

That's how the legend was begun. Nobody would go near the place after that. Country people whose lives abound with idle nights are good at promoting a legend and making it stick. Those who passed the farm in the late night hours swore that they heard all manner of sounds coming from the well, sounds like souls crying and moaning and bones rattling; this latter, they claimed, was the dead trying in vain to climb up out of their unnatural grave.

So that's how Burt Potter and I were able to buy the farm from the county so cheap. It was a lot of work getting it back into shape again. We had to build up the barn and restore the house. There was weeds to be pulled, lots of growth to be cut away, and just about a thousand other things before we could begin to work her again. It was half a summer's work, but we got her to clicking.

Even then, though, even with things beginning to grow there, it still had a strange ghostly look to it. When it was quiet out there it was dead quiet. You couldn't hear a thing, not even some dog barking or a bird in the woods. Just not a sound. Sometimes I'd stand still and listen to the quiet and it would get to be like something seeping into my blood. It would give me the creeps and I'd start to work around, trying to make as much noise as I could, but whatever sounds I'd make would die the minute I made them, swallowed right up into the quiet. Then I would stop and listen again, and I found myself stopping and listening more and more and longer and longer to the strange quiet that seemed to stretch way out across the fields and go all the way out to the mountains.

The nights were the strangest. When the wind went through the trees, there was this eerie sound just like voices, and that was probably what people heard when they said it was the voices of the ghosts in the well. Folks had warned us we'd never be able to sleep out there because of the voices, but we were young and cocky then and we laughed that off. Both Burt and I had just come back from fighting with the A.E.F. in France and we weren't scared of anything.

One morning the preacher came by. It was in the fall, the first fall we were there. He drove in in his buckboard. It was a Sunday morning and he said he was going to give us a private sermon. Burt and I, we'd been sitting on the steps smoking pipes, we sat there and watched him. He'd never been out to the farm before; in fact, he'd been the one who'd warned us the most passionate against the ghosts.

The preacher, he was a tall, thin man and he wore a long black frock coat, went over to the well and dropped his hat on the ground and clasped his hands and shut his eyes and raised his head and began to pray in the most God-awful voice I ever heard, saying things like save these souls, give them rest; and then, in winding up he said:

"And look after these two young men who are here alone night on night with the restless dead who are trying to storm free and wreck their vengeance upon a cruel, cold, forgetful world.''

Then the preacher looked at us. He looked at us as if we were sitting on a gallows, his eyes round and white and filled with fear. We just looked back at him, our pipes gone out cold. He never said a word further, but just picked up his hat and put it on and backed on away, watching us as if we were too other-worldly and might spring up at him and pitch him into that well. He got into his rig and drove off.

"He's daft," Burt said.

"Maybe," I said.

"What do you mean, 'maybe'?"

"He's a preacher, ain't he?" I said. "He might know something."

"*Know* something?" Burt said, right out loud, as if I was sitting on the other side of the yard. "What's there to know? It's only a well with water in it. It's no different from any well in the county."

"All right, all right," I said, real sharp. "Don't be shouting at me."

Burt had been giving me trouble right along. To begin with, he was a bad egg to go into partnership with. Even when we began, from the first day when we pooled our money and bought the place, we had our differences. Burt was always an ornery kind, the kind that only a saint can get along with. Not ever having been canonized, and with the possibility of that being highly remote, I often found myself wishing that Burt would go on off somewheres and sit in a bear trap or something.

Burt liked his liquor and liked his women, and so, between the indulgence of these two whims of his, I found myself working the farm alone for days on end. Then at the finish of the month when the time came for whacking up what little money we took out of it, Burt would rear up on his mighty tall hind legs and demand a fifty-fifty division.

Once we had a fight, coming back from the field. Burt was a good deal bigger than me and he whipped me good. I was going to let him have it with the scythe, but I stopped myself, remembering how the state was pretty narrow-minded about murder. We'd been talking about the ghosts again; I'd been telling him that the wind really did sound like voices and he'd been telling me back, in that irritating offhand way of his, that I was going off my mind.

Lots of times I wanted to do him justice, but I wasn't that sort. I knew that a type like Burt always found his own executioner sooner or later, and I was content to leave it at that.

Burt would say, "I don't know what's got into you. When we first come out here we was real good friends. Now look at you."

"We was never real good friends," I'd tell him. "So don't try that honey and molasses business on me. I ain't one of your girlfriends."

If you might think that in disliking Burt I was black of heart or something, let me tell you that once when he fell into that well that I saved his life. He'd gotten good and drunk and had fallen over the low wall (people, northerners mostly, who'd heard about what had happened had come down to see the well and chipped off pieces for souvenirs) and I threw him down a rope and saved him.

The more we worked the farm the better it came to look. After about a year some real estate people in town put all superstition aside and offered to buy it from us for a lot of money. But I told them I didn't want to sell. Burt felt the same. A few times I offered to buy up his share, but he wouldn't go for it. And I couldn't blame him, what with me doing most of the work and him sharing in half the profits. It made me pretty sore.

And all along those voices—for some reason, I couldn't figure—were sounding more and more real to me. I remember one night in particular—it was during our second summer there—I was lying in bed, not able to sleep. I was thinking of the farmer who had been murdered and of his wife who had gone off her head right in that very house. Burt was off somewhere, and not tending to his own business, either, when I heard the wind soughing through the trees. I heard it for a long time. I heard it even after it stopped. It made me turn cold. I got out of bed and went outside and sneaked across the yard to the well and looked down into the dark water. Then just to be doing it, I picked up a stone and dropped it straight down there. It seemed like a long time before the splash came up. When I was going back to the house, the wind started again. But this time it didn't bother me and I went right to sleep.

"They were talking about you last night," I told Burt the next morning.

"What's that?" he said.

"The voices. They said you'd better start behaving yourself or they won't tolerate your presence here much longer." I knew he didn't like to hear that, but I figured it was my duty to tell him; that was how it all suddenly seemed to me.

He laughed at me. "That so?" he said.

"That's so," I told him.

"Tell me something, boy. If there's so many voices down there—how many, thirty?—how can you make out what they're all telling you?"

"Because I hear 'em out, that's why," I said.

"How come I don't hear them?"

"Because I'm the one they're talking to."

"Do they mention me by name?" he asked.

"As a matter of fact they do."

So you see that Burt didn't believe in the voices. And I remembered that I never had up until now. This change in me kind of gave me a chill. But why make a joke out of something that the whole county took to heart? That's what I told myself. And you'd think a man, even one like Burt, receiving an honest warning, would take heed. But not him. So if anything happened to him at least I would have a clear conscience. After all, I'd given him the warning, hadn't I?

Then one Saturday night everything happened. I'd finished work at noon, which was my custom on Saturday, and washed and dressed and walked down the road to town and stood around in the square till it got dark, then gone into the picture show and then later was walking home. It was an overcast September night with a round harvest moon peeping in and out of the clouds, shedding just enough light to see the road by.

As I was walking up near our place, old Crazy Nicholson, who owned the place next to ours, came running down his path. And he was a sight to see running, especially in the moonlight, what with his old baggy trousers held up by wide galluses jouncing up and down and the longest white beard ever seen on a man or goat flying around his face. He was aptly named, too. He'd been a young man in A. P. Hill's division at Antietam and had got hit in the head real bad. That might have been sixty years ago, but to old Crazy it was just like now, all the time. He was red-faced and wild-eyed and mistrustful of everything between heaven and earth.

"Wait right there, young fella!" he called to me.

I waited. I'd been waiting, stopped cold in the road watching him run.

"Where's your partner?" the old man demanded, coming on out through his gate, hitching up his pants with his thumbs.

"Who?" I asked.

"Potter. Burt Potter. You ain't got but one partner."

"I don't follow him around," I said.

"Well, somebody ought to. And with a rifle, too. Y'know whut he did?"

"Tell me," I said.

"He snuck in here tonight stinking drunk and took Sally Ann right out of the house." Sally Ann was Crazy Nicholson's granddaughter. Pretty, too.

"He's done that before, I reckon," I said.

"And got by with it, too," the old man said, his little red eyes steaming. "But not anymore. Not any more. By the good gray cloth, he won't do it anymore. He's taken her up to that damned haunted farm of yours and . . ."

"Easy now," I said. "You don't know that for sure."

"He did. He did, I tell you," the old man said. He was near dancing with excitement. "Because he knows I'm scared to go near the place. That's where he always takes her, up there with the voices of the dead."

"Well, I'm going back there now. If she's there I'll send her on back."

He gave me the wildest look that a crazy eighty-year-old man can possibly give.

"You swear?" he asked.

"Cross my heart."

"On a night like this, you don't know what a moon like this does to them. And the wind's coming up now. My little granddaughter, there alone with—"

"I'll go back right now. You just hold on, Mr. Nicholson."

So I left the old man standing there quivering with rage and terror and continued up the road, cursing Burt for the trouble he always caused.

I cut in from the road and hurried up toward the farm. I could see the lamp burning in the house and I knew they were there, or had been there anyway. As I went toward the house, I suddenly saw Burt reeling out of the shadows singing a tune he had probably heard on the radio in town. The sight of him really made my blood boil up. He stopped short when he saw me. He stood there squinting at me, swaying back and forth as if the wind was hitting him like that.

"Why, you ain't Sally Ann," he said.

He looked all undone, what with his white shirt hanging out over his trousers and his jacket on crooked like somebody had been tugging at the shoulders. He staggered toward me.

"Where is she?" I asked.

"She's run off," he said, pushing the hair from out of his eyes. "So what about it?"

"Has she gone home?" I asked, knowing she hadn't, because I hadn't seen her coming down the road.

"Damn if I know," Burt said shaking his head.

"Old Nicholson is about to take after you with a rifle."

Burt laughed. He had a laugh like a cackle. He laughed loud and long into the strong warm wind that was beginning to whip the dried leaves around the yard.

"Now, you cut it out," I said angrily. "Where's she gone?"

"That way," he said, pointing toward the trees.

"This farm's cursed, all right," I said with heat. "Only the curse ain't from the well. It's from you."

He went staggering about then. I grabbed him by the arm.

"Where you going?" I asked.

"Don't know. To find Sally Ann, I reckon."

"Well, I reckon not. You wander far about and the grandfather'll get you. You get on into the house and sleep it off and I'll find her and bring her home. Now wash up and get to bed.''

I pushed him toward the house and that's all a drunken man needs, just a little shove to change his direction, and off he went stumbling toward the house, singing his little tune again, his jacket hung all crooked on his shoulders.

Then I took off toward the trees, the other side of which lay our pasture. I was yelling Sally Ann's name. The wind was blowing real hard now and there was a smell in the air like a rainstorm was coming up. Then I ran plumb into our mule out in the pasture. He was just standing there looking dazed and worried about being out in the dark. I figured Burt had been stumbling around the barn looking for Sally Ann and had let the mule wander out, so I had to abandon looking for Sally Ann for the moment and drag old Ben back and whip his rump a few times and shut him into the barn again. Then I ran back into the trees yelling the girl's name, feeling like a fool and a hero both, with the wind really roaring overhead in the trees now, with the round old moon shining through the leaves like a white face watching everything, hard and cold and sinister. I remember thinking, *The voices are really going to jabber tonight*, and that it was as if something not quite myself had thought that.

I ran all through the pasture, falling down a couple times on the rocks. When I was all out of breath from yelling and running, I stopped and stood there, gasping. Then I saw Sally Ann. She was sitting on the stone wall, looking at me, curious and amused, as if I had been putting on a show for her.

''What are you doing there?'' I asked. I was pretty sore by then. She'd probably been sitting there the whole time watching me run around.

''Waiting for Burt to find me,'' she said.

''Damn it all, I'm taking you back to your grandpa.''

''Where's Burt?''

''Burt's gone to sleep. He's falling down drunk.''

''I thought he'd come chase after me.''

I went over and took her by the arm and got her down from the stone wall.

''Your grandpa's mighty sore,'' I said.

"It's something to occupy his mind," she said. She was a sassy one, all right.

"Never mind that. I'm out here to prevent murder. Come on now. I pretty near lost my mule on account of you, too."

"We was never near the barn," she said.

That made me think: Suppose Burt hadn't been the one to let old Ben wander? Suppose the old man had come up there looking around? The last I'd seen of Burt he was heading for the house, and the barn door had been closed then.

So I left Sally Ann right there and was running again. After all these years, the old man had finally let his anger get the high hand on his fear of the farm.

"Don't let him shoot Burt," I heard Sally Ann yell.

The wind was roaring hard now, sweeping through the trees, making them bend and twist and snarl around me. The whole forest was filled with sounds, louder than I had ever heard them before. I ran through the poplar grove, past the barn and out into the yard. I was running across the yard when I saw the old man in the moonlight, poking around the shed. Then I heard the voices. They were clearer this time than I'd ever heard them before. Even though I was running, I could almost make out what they were saying.

The old man came charging towards me with that rifle slanted across his chest, running like he was charging with Hill's Division again.

"Whut's that?" he asked, coming up to me, his eyes crazy with fright.

I whirled around. I saw Burt's jacket and shirt lying there next to the wall, where he'd dropped them before washing up. The voices were real clear now. They seemed to be right up there at the top, about to jump out.

"Whut's that yelling there?" the old man asked.

"That's the ghosts," I yelled. I yelled it real loud.

"God save us!" the old man yelled, even louder, as the wind spun his white beard back over his shoulder. He ran over to the well and pointed his rifle down there and fired. The shot made an explosion that must have echoed all the way down to the center of the earth.

Then he stepped back, put the rifle on his shoulder, stood up erect, and saluted.

They took the old man away and committed him to the state asylum. And I've got the farm all to myself now, but now after the murder folks are properly convinced that the place is cursed and haunted. I tried to sell it, for dirt cheap, too, but nobody would have it. I don't even work it any more. The weeds are high again. It's got real lonely again.

But I won't leave it now. I don't even think of leaving it anymore. I've been living here alone for six years now and before I can think of leaving I know I've got to hear the voices just once more, like I heard them when Burt had fallen into the well. I keep telling myself that I didn't know Burt was down there, that it wasn't his voice I heard, that what with the wind blowing like a hurricane and all the trees howling a man couldn't be too sure of what he was hearing. The wind has blown a thousand times since then, but I haven't heard anything. I tell myself that if I can just hear the voices once more, I'd know for certain that I didn't make the old man shoot his rifle down there because I'd wanted him to commit a murder for me.

THE RIGHT TO SING
THE BLUES

by JOHN LUTZ

"There's this that you need to know about jazz," Fat Jack McGee told Nudger with a smile. "You don't need to know a thing about it to enjoy it, and that's all you need to know." He tossed back his huge head, jowls quivering, and drained the final sip of brandy from his crystal snifter. "It's feel." He used a white napkin to dab at his lips with a very fat man's peculiar delicacy. "Jazz is pure feel."

"Does Willy Hollister have the feel?" Nudger asked. He pushed his plate away, feeling full to the point of being bloated. The only portion of the gourmet lunch Fat Jack had bought him that remained untouched was the grits.

"Willy Hollister," Fat Jack said, with something like reverence, "plays ultra-fine piano."

A white-vested waiter appeared like a native from around a potted palm, carrying chicory coffee on a silver tray, and placed cups before Nudger and Fat Jack. "Then what's your problem with Hollister?" Nudger asked, sipping the thick rich brew. He rated it delicious. "Didn't you hire him to play his best piano at your club?"

"Hey, there's no problem with his music," Fat Jack said. "But first, Nudger, I gotta know if you can hang around New Orleans till you can clear up this matter." Fat Jack's tiny pinkish eyes glittered with mean humor. "For a fat fee, of course."

Nudger knew the fee would be adequate. Fat Jack had a bank
account as obese as his body, and he had, in fact, paid Nudger a
sizable sum just to travel to New Orleans and sit in the Magnolia
Blossom restaurant over lunch and listen while Fat Jack talked. The
question Nudger now voiced was: "Why me?"

"Because I know a lady from your fair city." Fat Jack mentioned
a name. "She says you're tops at your job; she don't say that
about many.

". . . And because of your collection," Fat Jack added. An ebony
dribble of coffee dangled in liquid suspension from his triple chin,
glittering as he talked. "I hear you collect old jazz records."

"I used to," Nudger said a bit wistfully. "I had Willie the Lion.
Duke Ellington and Mary Ann Williams from their Kansas City
days."

"How come had?" Fat Jack asked.

"I sold the collection," Nudger said. "To pay the rent one dark
month." He gazed beyond green palm fronds, out the window and
through filigreed black wrought iron, at the tourists half a block away
on Bourbon Street, at the odd combination of French and Spanish
architecture and black America and white suits and broiling half-
tropical sun that was New Orleans, where jazz lived as in no other
place. "Damned rent," he muttered.

"Amen." Fat Jack was kidding not even himself. He hadn't worried about paying the rent in years. The drop of coffee released its
grip on his chin, plummeted, and stained his white shirtfront. "So
will you stay around town a while?"

Nudger nodded. His social and business calendars weren't exactly
booked solid.

"Hey, it's not Hollister himself who worries me," Fat Jack said,
"it's Ineida Collins. She's singing at the club now, and if she keeps
practicing, someday she'll be mediocre. I'm not digging at her,
Nudger; that's an honest assessment."

"Then why did you hire her?"

"Because of David Collins. He owns a lot of the French Quarter.
He owns a piece of the highly successful restaurant where we now
sit. In every parish in New Orleans, he has more clout than a ton of
charge cards. And he's as skinny and ornery as I am fat and nice."

Nudger took another sip of coffee.

"And he asked you to hire Ineida Collins?"

"You're onto it. Ineida is his daughter. She wants to make it as a singer. And she will, if Dad has to buy her a recording studio, at double the fair price. Since David Collins also owns the building my club is in, I thought I'd acquiesce when his daughter auditioned for a job. And Ineida isn't really so bad that she embarrasses anyone but herself. I call it diplomacy."

"I thought you were calling it trouble," Nudger said. "I thought that was why you hired me."

Fat Jack nodded, ample jowls spilling over his white collar. "So it became," he said. "Hollister, you see, is a handsome young dude, and within the first week Ineida was at the club, he put some moves on her. They became fast friends. They've now progressed beyond mere friendship."

"You figure he's attracted to Dad's money?"

"Nothing like that," Fat Jack said. "When I hired Ineida, David Collins insisted I keep her identity a secret. It was part of the deal. So she sings under the stage name Ineida Mann, which most likely is a gem from her dad's advertising department."

"I still don't see your problem," Nudger said.

"Hollister doesn't set right with me, and I don't know exactly why. I do know that if he messes up Ineida in some way, David Collins will see to it that I'm playing jazz on the Butte-Boise-Anchorage circuit."

"Nice cities," Nudger remarked, "but not jazz towns. I see your problem."

"So find out about Willy Hollister for me," Fat Jack implored. "Check him out, declare him pass or fail, but put my mind at ease either way. That's all I want, an easeful mind."

"Even we tough private eye guys want that," Nudger said.

Fat Jack removed his napkin from his lap and raised a languid plump hand. A waiter who had been born just to respond to that signal scampered over with the check. Fat Jack accepted a tiny ball-point pen and signed with a ponderous yet elegant flourish. Nudger watched him help himself to a mint. It was like watching the grace and dexterity of an elephant picking up a peanut. Huge as Fat Jack was, he moved as if he weighed no more than ten or twelve pounds.

"I gotta get back, Nudger. Do some paperwork, count some money." He stood up, surprisingly tall in his tan slacks and white linen sport coat. Nudger thought it was a neat coat; he decided he might buy one and wear it winter and summer. "Drop around the club about eight o'clock tonight," Fat Jack said. "I'll fill you in on whatever else you need to know, and I'll show you Willy Hollister and Ineida. Maybe you'll get to hear her sing."

"While she's singing," Nudger said, "maybe we can discuss my fee."

Fat Jack grinned, his vast jowls defying gravity grandly. "Hey, you and me're gonna get along fine." He winked and moved away among the tables, tacking toward the door, dwarfing the other diners.

The waiter refilled Nudger's coffee cup. He sat sipping chicory brew and watching Fat Jack McGee walk down the sunny sidewalk toward Bourbon Street. He sure had a jaunty, bouncy kind of walk for a fat man.

Nudger wasn't as anxious about the fee as Fat Jack thought, though the subject was of more than passing interest. Actually, he had readily taken the case because years ago, at a club in St. Louis, he'd heard Fat Jack McGee play clarinet in the manner that had made him something of a jazz legend, and he'd never forgotten. Real jazz fans are hooked forever.

He needed to hear that clarinet again.

Fat Jack's club was on Dexter, half a block off Bourbon Street. Nudger paused at the entrance and looked up at its red and green neon sign. There was a red neon Fat Jack himself, a portly, herky-jerky, illuminated figure that jumped about with the same seeming lightness and jauntiness as the real Fat Jack.

Trumpet music from inside the club was wafting out almost palpably into the hot humid night. People were coming and going, among them a few obvious tourists, making the Bourbon Street rounds. But Nudger got the impression that most of Fat Jack's customers were folks who took their jazz seriously and were there for music, not atmosphere.

The trumpet stairstepped up to an admirable high C and wild applause. Nudger went inside and looked around. Dim, smoky, lots of people at lots of tables, men in suits and in jeans and T-shirts, women in long dresses and in casual slacks. The small stage was empty now; the band was between sets. Customers were milling around, stacking up at the bar along one wall. Waitresses in "Fat Jack's" T-shirts were bustling about with trays of drinks. Near the left of the stage was a polished, dark, upright piano that gleamed like a new car even in the dimness. Fat Jack's was everything a jazz club should be, Nudger decided.

Feeling at home, he made his way to the bar and after a five-minute wait ordered a mug of draft beer. The mug was frosted, the beer ice-flecked.

The lights brightened and dimmed three times, apparently a signal the regulars at Fat Jack's understood, for they began a general movement back toward their tables. Then the lights dimmed considerably, and the stage, with its gleaming piano, was suddenly the only illuminated area in the place. A tall, graceful man in his early thirties walked onstage to the kind of scattered but enthusiastic applause that suggests respect and a common bond between performer and audience. The man smiled faintly at the applause and sat down at the piano. He had pained, haughty features, and blond hair that curled above the collar of his black Fat Jack's shirt. The muscles in his bare arms were corded; his hands appeared elegant yet very strong. He was Willy Hollister, the main gig, the one the paying customers had come to hear. The place got quiet, and he began to play.

The song was a variation of "Good Woman Gone Bad," an old number originally written for tenor sax. Hollister played it his way, and two bars into it Nudger knew he was better than good and nothing but bad luck could keep him from being great. He was backed by brass and a snare drum, but he didn't need it; he didn't need a thing in this world but that piano and you could tell it just by looking at the rapt expression on his aristocratic face.

"Didn't I tell you it was all there?" Fat Jack said softly beside Nudger. "Whatever else there is about him, the man can play piano."

Nudger nodded silently. Jazz basically is black music, but the fair, blond Hollister played it with all the soul and pain of its genesis.

He finished up the number to riotous applause that quieted only when he swung into another, a blues piece. He sang that one while his hands worked the piano. His voice was as black as his music; in his tone, his inflection, there seemed to dwell centuries of suffering.

"I'm impressed," Nudger said, when the applause for the blues number had died down.

"You and everyone else." Fat Jack was sipping absinthe from a gold-rimmed glass. "Hollister won't be playing here much longer before moving up the show business ladder—not for what I'm paying him, and I'm paying him plenty."

"How did you happen to hire him?"

"He came recommended by a club owner in Chicago. Seems he started out in Cleveland playing small rooms, then moved up to better things in Kansas City, then Rush Street in Chicago. All I had to do was hear him play for five minutes to know I wanted to hire him. It's like catching a Ray Charles or a Garner on the way up."

"So what specifically is there about Hollister that bothers you?" Nudger asked. "Why shouldn't he be seeing Ineida Collins?"

Fat Jack scrunched up his padded features, seeking the word that might convey the thought. "His music is . . . uneven."

"That's hardly a crime," Nudger said, "especially if he can play so well when he's right."

"He ain't as right as I've heard him," Fat Jack said. "Believe me, Hollister can be even better than he was tonight. But it's not really his music that concerns me. Hollister acts strange at times, secretive. Sam Judman, the drummer, went by his apartment last week, found the door unlocked, and let himself in to wait for Hollister to get home. When Hollister discovered him there, he beat him up—with his fists. Can you imagine a piano player like Hollister using his hands for *that*?" Fat Jack looked as if he'd discovered a hair in his drink.

"So he's obsessively secretive. What else?" What am I doing, Nudger asked himself, trying to talk myself out of a job?

But Fat Jack went on. "Hollister has seemed troubled, jumpy and unpredictable, for the last month. He's got problems, and like I told you, if he's seeing Ineida Collins, I got problems, I figure it'd be wise to learn some more about Mr. Hollister."

"The better to know his intentions, as they used to say."

"And in some quarters still say."

The lights did their dimming routine again, the crowd quieted, and Willy Hollister was back at the piano. But this time the center of attention was the tall, dark-haired girl leaning with one hand on the piano, her other hand delicately holding a microphone. Inside her plain navy blue dress was a trim figure. She had nice ankles, a nice smile. Nice was a word that might have been coined for her. A stage name like Ineida Mann didn't fit her at all. She was prom queen and Girl Scouts and PTA and looked as if she'd blush at an off-color joke. But it crossed Nudger's mind that maybe it was simply a role; maybe she was playing for contrast.

Fat Jack knew what Nudger was thinking. "She's as straight and naive as she looks," he said. "But she'd like to be something else, to learn all about life and love in a few easy lessons."

Someone in the backup band had announced Ineida Mann, and she began to sing, the plaintive lyrics of an old blues standard. She had control but no range. Nudger found himself listening to the backup music, which included a smooth clarinet solo. The band liked Ineida and went all out to envelop her in good sound, but the audience at Fat Jack's was too smart for that. Ineida finished to light applause, bowed prettily, and made her exit. Competent but nothing special, and looking as if she'd just wandered in from suburbia. But this was what she wanted and her rich father was getting it for her. Parental love could be as blind as the other kind.

"So how are you going to get started on this thing?" Fat Jack asked. "You want me to introduce you to Hollister and Ineida?"

"Usually I begin a case by discussing my fee and signing a contract," Nudger said.

Fat Jack waved an immaculately manicured, ring-adorned hand. "Don't worry about the fee," he said. "Hey, let's make it whatever you usually charge plus twenty percent plus expenses. Trust me on that."

That sounded fine to Nudger, all except the trusting part. He reached into his inside coat pocket, withdrew his roll of antacid tablets, thumbed back the aluminum foil, and popped one of the white disks into his mouth, all in one practiced, smooth motion.

"What's that stuff for?" Fat Jack asked.

"Nervous stomach," Nudger explained.

"You oughta try this," Fat Jack said, nodding toward his absinthe. "Eventually it eliminates the stomach altogether."

Nudger winced. "I want to talk with Ineida," he said, "but it would be best if we had our conversation away from the club."

Fat Jack pursed his lips and nodded. "I can give you her address. She doesn't live at home with her father; she's in a little apartment over on Beulah Street. It's all part of the making-it-on-her-own illusion. Anything else?"

"Maybe. Do you still play the clarinet?"

Fat Jack cocked his head and looked curiously at Nudger, one tiny eye squinting through the tobacco smoke that hazed the air around the bar. "Now and again, but only on special occasions."

"Why don't we make the price of this job my usual fee plus only ten percent plus you do a set with the clarinet this Saturday night?"

Fat Jack beamed, then threw back his head and let out a roaring laugh that turned heads and seemed to shake the bottles on the back bar. "Agreed! You're a find, Nudger! First you trust me to pay you without a contract, then you lower your fee and ask for a clarinet solo instead of money. There's no place you can spend a clarinet solo! Hey, I like you, but you're not much of a businessman."

Nudger smiled and sipped his beer. Fat Jack hadn't bothered to find out the amount of Nudger's usual fee, so all this talk about percentages meant nothing. If detectives weren't good businessmen, neither were jazz musicians. He handed Fat Jack a pen and a club matchbook. "How about that address?"

Beulah Street was narrow and crooked, lined with low houses of French-Spanish architecture, an array of arches, pastel stucco, and ornamental wrought iron. The houses had long ago been divided into apartments, each with a separate entrance. Behind each apartment was a small courtyard.

Nudger found Ineida Collins's address. It belonged to a pale yellow structure with a weathered tile roof and a riot of multicolored bougainvillea blooming wild halfway up one cracked and often-patched stucco wall.

He glanced at his wristwatch. Ten o'clock. If Ineida wasn't awake by now, he decided, she should be. He stepped up onto the small red brick front porch and worked the lion's head knocker on a plank door supported by huge black iron hinges.

Ineida came to the door without delay. She didn't appear at all sleepy after her late-night stint at Fat Jack's. Her dark hair was tied back in a French braid. She was wearing slacks and a peach-colored silky blouse. Even the harsh sunlight was kind to her; she looked young, as inexperienced and naive as Fat Jack said she was.

Nudger told her he was a writer doing a piece on Fat Jack's club. "I heard you sing last night," he said. "It really was something to see. I thought it might be a good idea if we talked."

It was impossible for her to turn down what in her mind was a celebrity interview. She lit up bright enough to pale the sunlight and invited Nudger inside.

Her apartment was tastefully but inexpensively furnished. There was an imitation Oriental rug on the hardwood floor, lots of rattan furniture, a Casablanca overhead fan rotating its wide flat blades slowly and casting soothing, flickering shadows. Through sheer beige curtains the apartment's courtyard was visible, well tended and colorful.

"Can I get you a cup of coffee, Mr. Nudger?" Ineida asked.

Nudger told her thanks, watched the switch of her trim hips as she walked into the small kitchen. From where he sat he could see a Mr. Coffee brewer on the sink, its glass pot half full. Ineida poured, returned with two mugs of coffee.

"How old are you, Ineida?" he asked.

"Twenty-three."

"Then you haven't been singing for all that many years."

She sat down, placed her steaming coffee mug on a coaster. "About five, actually. I sang in school productions, then studied for a while in New York. I've been singing at Fat Jack's for about two months. I love it."

"The crowd there seems to like you," Nudger lied. He watched her smile and figured the lie was a worthy one. He pretended to take notes while he asked her a string of writer-like questions, pumping up her ego. It was an ego that would inflate only so far. Nudger decided that he liked Ineida Collins and hoped she would hurry up and realize she wasn't Ineida Mann.

"I'm told that you and Will Hollister are pretty good friends."

Her mood changed abruptly. Suspicion shone in her dark eyes, and the youthful smiling mouth became taut and suddenly ten years older.

"You're not a magazine writer," she said, in a betrayed voice.

Nudger's stomach gave a mule-like kick. "No, I'm not," he admitted.

"Then who are you?"

"Someone concerned about your wellbeing." Antacid time. He popped one of the white tablets into his mouth and chewed.

"Father sent you."

"No," Nudger said.

"Liar," she told him. "Get out."

"I'd like to talk with you about Willy Hollister," Nudger persisted. In his business persistence paid, one way or the other. He could only hope it wouldn't be the other.

"Get out," Ineida repeated. "Or I'll call the police."

Within half a minute Nudger was outside again on Beulah Street, looking at the uncompromising barrier of Ineida's closed door. Apparently she was touchy on the subject of Willy Hollister. Nudger slipped another antacid between his lips, turned his back to the warming sun, and began walking.

He'd gone half a block when he realized that he was casting three shadows. He stopped. The middle shadow stopped also, but the larger shadows on either side kept advancing. The large bodies that cast those shadows were suddenly standing in front of Nudger, and two very big men were staring down at him. One was smiling, one wasn't. Considering the kind of smile it was, that didn't make much difference.

"We noticed you talking to Miss Mann," the one on the left said. He had wide cheekbones, dark, pockmarked skin, and gray eyes that gave no quarter. "Whatever you said seemed to upset her." His accent was a cross between a southern drawl and clipped French. Nudger recognized it as Cajun. The Cajuns were a tough, predominantly French people who had settled southern Louisiana but never themselves.

Nudger let himself hope and started to walk on. The second man, who was shorter but had a massive neck and shoulders, shuffled forward like a heavy-weight boxer, to block his way. Nudger swallowed his antacid tablet.

"You nervous, friend?" the boxer asked in the same rich Cajun accent.

"Habitually."

Pockmarked said, "We have an interest in Miss Mann's welfare. What were you talking to her about?"

"The conversation was private. Do you two fellows mind introducing yourselves?"

"We mind," the boxer said. He was smiling again, nastily. Nudger noticed that the tip of his right eyebrow had turned white where it was crossed by a thin scar.

"Then I'm sorry, but we have nothing to talk about."

Pockmarked shook his head patiently in disagreement. "We have this to talk about, my friend. There are parts of this great state of Looziahna that are vast swampland. Not far from where we stand, the bayou is wild. It's the home of a surprising number of alligators. People go into the bayou, and some of them never come out. Who knows about them? After a while, who cares?" The cold gray eyes had diamond chips in them. "You understand my meaning?"

Nudger nodded. He understood. His stomach understood.

"I think we've made ourselves clear," the boxer said. "We aren't nice men, sir. It's our business not to be nice, and it's our pleasure. So a man like yourself, sir, a reasonable man in good health, should listen to us and stay away from Miss Mann."

"You mean Miss Collins."

"I mean Miss Ineida Mann." He said it with the straight face of a true professional.

"Why don't you tell Willy Hollister to stay away from her?" Nudger asked.

"Mr. Hollister is a nice young man of Miss Mann's own choosing," Pockmarked said with an odd courtliness. "You she obviously doesn't like. You upset her. That upsets us."

"And me and Frick don't like to be upset," the boxer said. He closed a powerful hand on the lapel of Nudger's sport jacket, not pushing or pulling in the slightest, merely squeezing the material. Nudger could feel the vibrant force of the man's strength as if it were electrical current. "Behave yourself," the boxer hissed through his fixed smile.

He abruptly released his grip, and both men turned and walked away.

Nudger looked down at his abused lapel. It was as crimped as if it had been wrinkled in a vise for days. He wondered if the dry cleaners could do anything about it when they pressed the coat.

Then he realized he was shaking. He loathed danger and had no taste for violence. He needed another antacid tablet and then, even though it was early, a drink.

New Orleans was turning out to be an exciting city, but not in the way the travel agencies and the chamber of commerce advertised.

"You're no jazz writer," Willy Hollister said to Nudger, in a small back room of Fat Jack's club. It wasn't exactly a dressing room, though at times it served as such. It was a sort of all-purpose place where quick costume changes were made and breaks were taken between sets. The room's pale green paint was faded and peeling, and a steam pipe jutted from floor to ceiling against one wall. Yellowed show posters featuring jazz greats were taped here and there behind the odd assortment of worn furniture. There were mingled scents of stale booze and tobacco smoke.

"But I *am* a jazz fan," Nudger said. "Enough of one to know how good you are, and that you play piano in a way that wasn't self-taught." He smiled. "I'll bet you even read music."

"You have to read music," Hollister said rather haughtily, "to graduate from Juilliard."

Even Nudger knew that Juilliard graduates weren't slouches. "So you have a classical background," he said.

"That's nothing rare; lots of jazz musicians have classical roots."

Nudger studied Hollister as the pianist spoke. Offstage, Hollister appeared older. His blond hair was thinning on top and his features were losing their boyishness, becoming craggy. His complexion was an unhealthy yellowish hue. He was a hunter, was this boy. Life's sad wisdom was in his eyes, resting on its haunches and ready to spring.

"How well do you know Ineida Mann?" Nudger asked.

"Well enough to know you've been bothering her," Hollister replied, with a bored yet wary expression. "We don't know what your angle is, but I suggest you stop. Don't bother trying to get any information out of me, either."

"I'm interested in jazz," Nudger said.

"Among other things."

"Like most people, I have more than one interest."

"Not like me, though," Hollister said. "My only interest is my music."

"What about Miss Mann?"

"That's none of your business." Hollister stood up, neatly but ineffectively snubbed out the cigarette he'd been smoking, and seemed to relish leaving it to smolder to death in the ashtray. "I've got a number coming up in a few minutes." He tucked in his Fat Jack's T-shirt and looked severe. "I don't particularly want to see you any more, Nudger. Whoever, whatever you are, it doesn't mean burned grits to me as long as you leave Ineida alone."

"Before you leave," Nudger said, "can I have your autograph?"

Incredibly, far from being insulted by this sarcasm, Hollister scrawled his signature on a nearby folded newspaper and tossed it to him. Nudger took that as a measure of the man's artistic ego, and despite himself he was impressed. All the ingredients of greatness resided in Willy Hollister, along with something else.

Nudger went back out into the club proper. He peered through the throng of jazz lovers and saw Fat Jack leaning against the bar. As Nudger was making his way across the dim room toward him, he spotted Ineida at one of the tables. She was wearing a green sequined blouse that set off her dark hair and eyes, and Nudger regretted that she couldn't sing as well as she looked. She glanced at him, recognized him, and quickly turned away to listen to a graying, bearded man who was one of her party.

"Hey, Nudger," Fat Jack said, when Nudger had reached the bar, "you sure you know what you're doing, old sleuth? You ain't exactly pussy-footing. Ineida asked me about you, said you'd bothered her at home. *Hollister* asked me who you were. The precinct captain asked me the same question."

Nudger's stomach tightened. "A New Orlean's police captain?"

Fat Jack nodded. "Captain Marrivale." He smiled broad and bold, took a sip of absinthe. "You make ripples big enough to swamp boats."

"What I'd like to do now," Nudger said, "is take a short trip."

"Lots of folks would like for you to do that."

"I need to go to Cleveland, Kansas City, and Chicago," Nudger said. "A couple of days in each city. I've got to find out more about Willy Hollister. Are you willing to pick up the tab?"

"I don't suppose you could get this information with long-distance phone calls?"

"Not and get it right."

"When do you plan on leaving?"

"As soon as I can. Tonight."

Fat Jack nodded. He produced an alligator-covered checkbook, scribbled in it, tore out a check, and handed it to Nudger. Nudger couldn't make out the amount in the faint light. "If you need more, let me know," Fat Jack said. His smile was luminous in the dimness. "Hey, make it a fast trip, Nudger."

A week later Nudger was back in New Orleans, sitting across from Fat Jack McGee in the club owner's second floor office. "There's a pattern," he said, "sometimes subtle, sometimes strong, but always there, like in a forties Ellington piece."

"So tell me about it," Fat Jack said. "I'm an Ellington fan."

"I did some research," Nudger said, "read some old reviews, went to clubs and musicians' union halls and talked to people in the jazz communities where Willy Hoilister played. He always started strong, but his musical career was checkered with flat spots, lapses. During those times, Hollister was just an ordinary performer."

Fat Jack appeared concerned, tucked his chin back into folds of flesh, and said, "That explains why he's falling off here."

"But the man is still making great music," Nudger said.

"Slipping from great to good," Fat Jack said. "Good jazz artists in New Orleans I can hire by the barrelful."

"There's something else about Willy Hollister," Nudger said.

"Something that nobody picked up on because it spanned several years and three cities."

Fat Jack looked interested. If his ears hadn't been almost enveloped by overblown flesh, they would have perked up.

"Hollister had a steady girlfriend in each of these cities. All three women disappeared. Two were rumored to have left town on their own, but nobody knows where they went. The girlfriend in Cleveland, the first one, simply disappeared. She's still on the missing persons list."

"Whoo boy!" Fat Jack said. He began to sweat. He pulled a white handkerchief the size of a flag from the pocket of his sport jacket and mopped his brow, just like Satchmo but without the grin and trumpet.

"Sorry," Nudger said. "I didn't mean to make you uncomfortable."

"You're doing your job, is all," Fat Jack assured him. "But that's bad information to lay on me. You think Hollister had anything to do with the disappearances?"

Nudger shrugged. "Maybe the women themselves, and not Hollister, had to do with it. They were all the sort that traveled light and often. Maybe they left town of their own accord. Maybe for some reason they felt they had to get away from Hollister."

"I wish Ineida would want to get away from him," Fat Jack muttered. "But Jeez, not like that. Her old man'd boil me down for axle grease. But then she's not cut from the same mold as those other girls; she's not what she's trying to be and she's strictly local."

"The only thing she and those other women have in common is Willy Hollister."

Fat Jack leaned back, and the desk chair creaked in protest. Nudger, who had been hired to solve a problem, had so far only brought to light the seriousness of that problem. The big man didn't have to ask "What now?" It was written in capital letters on his face.

"You could fire Willy Hollister," Nudger said.

Fat Jack shook his head. "Ineida would follow him, maybe get mad at me and sic her dad on the club."

"And Hollister is still packing customers into the club every night."

"That, too," Fat Jack admitted. Even the loosest businessman could see the profit in Willy Hollister's genius. "For now," he said, "we'll let things slide while you continue to watch." He dabbed at his forehead again with the wadded handkerchief.

"Hollister doesn't know who I am," Nudger said, "but he knows who I'm not and he's worried. My presence might keep him above-board for a while."

"Fine, as long as a change of scenery isn't involved. I can't afford to have her wind up like those other women, Nudger."

"Speaking of winding up," Nudger said, "Do you know anything about a couple of muscular robots? One has a scar across his right eyebrow and a face like an ex-pug's. His partner has a dark mustache, sniper's eyes, and is named Frick. Possibly the other is Frack. They both talk with thick Cajun accents."

Fat Jack raised his eyebrows. "Rocko Boudreau and Dwayne Frick," he said, with soft, terror-inspired awe. "They work for David Collins."

"I figured they did. They warned me to stay away from Ineida." Nudger felt his intestines twist into advanced Boy Scout knots. He got out his antacid tablets. "They suggested I might take up postmortem residence in the swamp." As he recalled his conversation with Frick and Frack, Nudger again felt a dark near-panic well up in him. Maybe it was because he was here in this small office with the huge and terrified Fat Jack McGee; maybe fear actually was contagious. He offered Fat Jack an antacid tablet.

Fat Jack accepted.

"I'm sure their job is to look after Ineida without her knowing it," Nudger said. "Incidentally, they seem to approve of her seeing Willy Hollister."

"That won't help me if anything happens to Ineida that's in any way connected to the club," Fat Jack said.

Nudger stood up. He was tired. His back still ached from sitting in an airline seat that wouldn't recline, and his stomach was still busy trying to digest itself. "I'll phone you if I hear any more good news."

Fat Jack mumbled something unintelligible and nodded, lost in his own dark apprehensions, a ponderous man grappling with ponderous problems. One of his inflated hands floated up in a parting gesture as Nudger left the stifling office. What he hadn't told Fat Jack was that immediately after each woman had disappeared, Hollister had regained his tragic, soulful touch on the piano.

When Nudger got back to his hotel, he was surprised to open the door to his room and see a man sitting in a chair by the window. It was the big blue armchair that belonged near the door.

When Nudger entered, the man turned as if resenting the interruption, as if it were his room and Nudger the interloper. He stood up and smoothed his light tan suit coat. He was a smallish man with a triangular face and very springy red hair that grew in a sharp widow's peak. His eyes were dark and intense. He resembled a fox. With a quick and graceful motion he put a paw into a pocket for a wallet-sized leather folder, flipped it open to reveal a badge.

"Police Captain Marrivale, I presume," Nudger said. He shut the door.

The redheaded man nodded and replaced his badge in his pocket. "I'm Fred Marrivale," he confirmed. "I heard you were back in town. I think we should talk." He shoved the armchair around to face the room instead of the window and sat back down, as familiar as old shoes.

Nudger pulled out the small wooden desk chair and also sat, facing Marrivale. "Are you here on official business, Captain Marrivale?"

Marrivale smiled. He had tiny sharp teeth behind thin lips. "You know how it is, Nudger, a cop is always a cop."

"Sure. And that's the way it is when we go private," Nudger told him. "A confidential investigator is always that, no matter where he is or whom he's talking to."

"Which is kinda why I'm here," Marrivale said. "It might be better if you were someplace else."

Nudger was incredulous. His nervous stomach believed what he'd just heard, but he didn't. "You're actually telling me to get out of town?"

Marrivale gave a kind of laugh, but there was no glint of amusement in his sharp eyes. "I'm not authorized to *tell* anyone to get out of town, Nudger. I'm not the sheriff and this isn't Dodge City."

"I'm glad you realize that," Nudger told him, "because I can't leave yet. I've got business here."

"I know about your business."

"Did David Collins send you to talk to me?"

Marrivale had a good face for policework; there was only the slightest change of expression. "We can let that question go by," he said, "and I'll ask you one. Why did Fat Jack McGee hire you?"

"Have you asked him?"

"No."

"He'd rather I kept his reasons confidential," Nudger said.

"You don't have a Louisiana P.I. license," Marrivale pointed out.

Nudger smiled. "I know. Nothing to be revoked."

"There are consequences a lot more serious than having your investigator's license pulled, Nudger. Mr. Collins would prefer that you stay away from Ineida Mann."

"You mean Ineida Collins."

"I mean what I say."

"David Collins already had someone deliver that message to me."

"It's not a message from anyone but me," Marrivale said. "I'm telling you this because I'm concerned about your safety while you're within my jurisdiction. It's part of my job."

Nudger kept a straight face, got up and walked to the door, and opened it. He said, "I appreciate your concern, Captain. Right now I've got things to do."

Marrivale smiled with his mean little mouth. He didn't seem rattled by Nudger's impolite invitation to leave; he'd said what needed saying. He got up out of the armchair and adjusted his suit. Nudger noticed that the suit hung on him just right and must have been tailored and expensive. No cop's salary, J. C. Penney wardrobe for Marrivale.

As he walked past Nudger, Marrivale paused and said, "It'd behoove you to learn to discern friend from enemy, Nudger." He went out and trod lightly down the hall toward the elevators, not looking back.

Nudger shut and locked the door. Then he went over to the bed, removed his shoes, and stretched out on his back on the mattress, his fingers laced behind his head. He studied the faint water stains on the ceiling in the corner above him. They were covered by a thin film of mold. That reminded Nudger of the bayou.

He had to admit that Marrivale had left him with solid parting advice.

Though plenty of interested parties had warned Nudger to stay away from Ineida Collins, everyone seemed to have neglected to tell him to give a wide berth to Willy Hollister. And after breakfast, it was Hollister who claimed Nudger's interest.

Hollister lived on St. Francois, within a few blocks of Ineida Collins' apartment. Their apartments were similar. Hollister's was the end unit of a low tan stucco building that sat almost flush with the sidewalk. What yard there was had to be in the rear. Through the low branches of a huge magnolia tree, Nudger saw some of the raw cedar fencing that sectioned the back premises into private courtyards.

Hollister might be home, sleeping after his late-night gig at Fat Jack's. But whether he was home or not, Nudger decided that his next move would be to knock on Hollister's door.

He rapped on the wooden door three times, casually leaned toward it and listened. He heard no sound from inside. No one in the street seemed to be paying much attention to him, so after a few minutes Nudger idly gave the doorknob a twist.

It rotated all the way, clicked. The door opened about six inches. Nudger pushed the door open farther and stepped quietly inside.

The apartment no doubt came furnished. The furniture was old but not too worn; some of it probably had antique value. The floor was dull hardwood where it showed around the borders of a faded blue carpet. From where he stood, Nudger could see into the bedroom. The bed was unmade but empty.

The living room was dim. The wooden shutters on its windows were closed, allowing slanted light to come in through narrow slits. Most of the illumination in the room came from the bedroom and a short hall that led to a bathroom, then to a small kitchen and sliding glass doors that opened to the courtyard.

To make sure he was alone, Nudger called, "Mr. Hollister? Avon lady!"

No answer. Fine.

Nudger looked around the living room for a few minutes, examining the contents of drawers, picking up some sealed mail that turned out to be an insurance pitch and a utility bill.

He had just entered the bedroom when he heard a sound from outside the curtained window, open about six inches. It was a dull thunking sound that Nudger thought he recognized. He went to the window, parted the breeze-swayed gauzy white curtains, and bent low to peer outside.

The window looked out on the courtyard. What Nudger saw confirmed his guess about the sound. A shovel knifing into soft earth. Willy Hollister was in the courtyard garden, digging. Nudger crouched down so he could see better.

Hollister was planting rosebushes. They were young plants, but they already had red and white roses on them. Hollister had started on the left with the red roses and was alternating colors. He was planting half a dozen bushes and was working on the fifth plant, which lay with its roots wrapped in burlap beside the waiting, freshly dug hole.

Hollister was on both knees on the ground, using his hands to scoop some dirt back into the hole. He was forming a small dome over which to spread the rosebush's soon-to-be-exposed roots. He knew how to plant rosebushes, all right, and he was trying to ensure that these would live.

Nudger's stomach went into a series of spasms as Hollister stood and glanced at the apartment as if he had sensed someone's presence. He drew one of the rolled-up sleeves of his white dress shirt across his perspiring forehead. For a few seconds he seemed to debate about whether to return to the apartment. Then he turned, picked up the shovel, and began digging the sixth and final hole.

Letting out a long breath, Nudger drew back from the open window and stood up straight. He'd go out by the front door and then walk around to the courtyard and call Hollister's name, as if he'd just arrived. He wanted to get Hollister's own version of his past.

As Nudger was leaving the bedroom, he noticed a stack of pale blue envelopes on the dresser, beside a comb and brush set monogrammed with Hollister's initials. The envelopes were held together by a fat rubber band. Nudger saw Hollister's address, saw the Beulah Street return address penned neatly in black ink in a corner of the top envelope. He paused for just a few seconds, picked up the envelopes, and slipped them into his pocket. Then he left Hollister's apartment the same way he'd entered.

There was no point in talking to Hollister now. It would be foolish to place himself in the apartment at the approximate time of the disappearance of the stack of letters written by Ineida Collins.

Nudger walked up St. Francois for several blocks, then took a cab to his hotel. Though the morning hadn't yet heated up, the cab's air conditioner was on high and the interior was near freezing. The letters seemed to grow heavier and heavier in Nudger's jacket pocket, and to glow with a kind of warmth that gave no comfort.

Nudger had room service bring up a plain omelet and a glass of milk. He sat with his early lunch, his customary meal (it had a soothing effect on a nervous stomach), at the desk in his hotel room and ate slowly as he read Ineida Collins' letters to Hollister. He understood now why they had felt warm in his pocket. The love affair was, from Ineida's point of view at least, as soaring and serious as such an affair can get. Nudger felt cheapened by his crass invasion of Ineida's privacy. These were thoughts meant to be shared by no one but the two of them, thoughts not meant to be tramped through by a middle-aged detective not under the spell of love.

On the other hand, Nudger told himself, there was no way for him to know what the letters contained *until* he read them and determined that he shouldn't have. This was the sort of professional quandary he got himself into frequently but never got used to.

The last letter, the one with the latest postmark, was the most revealing and made the tacky side of Nudger's profession seem worthwhile. Ineida Collins was planning to run away with Willy Hollister; he had told her he loved her and that they would be married. Then, after the fact, they would return to New Orleans and inform friends and relatives of the blessed union. It all seemed quaint, Nudger thought, and not very believable unless you happened to be twenty-three and love-struck and had lived Ineida Collins's sheltered existence.

Ineida also referred in the last letter to something important she had to tell Hollister. Nudger could guess what that important bit of information was. That she was Ineida Collins and she was David Collins' daughter and she was rich, and that she was oh so glad that Hollister hadn't known about her until that moment. Because that meant he wanted her for her own true self alone. Ah, love! It made Nudger's business go round.

Nudger refolded the letter, replaced it in its envelope, and dropped it onto the desk. He tried to finish his omelet but couldn't. He wasn't really hungry, and his stomach had reached a tolerable level of comfort. He knew it was time to report to Fat Jack. After all, the man had hired him to uncover information, but not so Nudger would keep it to himself.

Nudger slid the rubber band back around the stack of letters, snapped it, and stood up. He considered having the letters placed in the hotel safe, but the security of any hotel safe was questionable. A paper napkin bearing the hotel logo lay next to his half-eaten omelet. He wrapped the envelopes in the napkin and dropped the bundle in the wastebasket by the desk. The maid wasn't due back in the room until tomorrow morning, and it wasn't likely that anyone would think Nudger would throw away such important letters. And the sort of person who would bother to search a wastebasket would search everywhere else and find the letters anyway.

He placed the tray with his dishes on it in the hall outside his door, hung the "Do Not Disturb" sign on the knob, and left to see Fat Jack McGee.

They told Nudger at the club that Fat Jack was out. Nobody was sure when he'd be back; he might not return until this evening when business started picking up, or he might have just strolled over to the Magnolia Blossom for a croissant and coffee and would be back any minute.

Nudger sat at the end of the bar, nursing a beer he didn't really want, and waited.

After an hour, the bartender began blatantly staring at him from time to time. Mid-afternoon or not, Nudger was occupying a bar stool and had an obligation. And maybe the man was right. Nudger was about to give in to the weighty responsibility of earning his

place at the bar by ordering another drink he didn't want when Fat
Jack appeared through the dimness like a light-footed, obese spirit
in a white vested suit.

He saw Nudger, smiled his fat man's beaming smile, and veered
toward him, diamond rings and gold jewelry flashing fire beneath
pale coat sleeves. There was even a large diamond stickpin in his
bib-like tie. He was a vision of sartorial immensity.

"We need to talk," Nudger told him.

"That's easy enough," Fat Jack said. "My office, hey?" He led
the way, making Nudger feel somewhat like a pilot fish trailing a
whale.

When they were settled in Fat Jack's office, Nudger said, "I came
across some letters that Ineida wrote to Hollister. She and Hollister
plan to run away together, get married."

Fat Jack raised his eyebrows so high Nudger was afraid they might
become detached. "Hollister ain't the marrying kind, Nudger."

"What kind is he?"

"I don't want to answer that."

"Maybe Ineida and Hollister will elope and live happily—"

"Stop!" Fat Jack interrupted him. He leaned forward, wide forehead glistening. "When are they planning on leaving?"

"I don't know. The letter didn't say."

"You gotta find out, Nudger!"

"I could ask. But Captain Marrivale wouldn't approve."

"Marrivale has talked with you?"

"In my hotel room. He assured me he had my best interest at
heart."

Fat Jack appeared thoughtful. He swiveled in his chair and
switched on the auxiliary window air conditioner. Its breeze stirred
the papers on the desk, ruffled Fat Jack's graying, gingery hair.

The telephone rang. Fat Jack picked it up, identified himself. His
face went as white as his suit. "Yes, sir," he said. His jowls began
to quiver; loose flesh beneath his left eye started to dance. Nudger
was getting nervous just looking at him. "You can't mean it," Fat
Jack said. "Hey, maybe it's a joke. Okay, it ain't a joke." He listened a while longer and then said, "Yes, sir," again and hung

up. He didn't say anything else for a long time. Nudger didn't say anything either.

Fat Jack spoke first. "That was David Collins. Ineida's gone. Not home, bed hasn't been slept in."

"Then she and Hollister have left as they planned."

"You mean as Hollister planned. Collins got a note in the mail."

"Note?" Nudger asked. His stomach did a flip; it was way ahead of his brain, reacting to a suspicion not yet fully formed.

"A ransom note," Fat Jack confirmed. "Unsigned, in cutout newspaper words. Collins said Marrivale is on his way over here now to talk to me about Hollister. Hollister's disappeared, too. And his clothes are missing from his closet." Fat Jack's little pink eyes were bulging in his blanched face. "I better not tell Marrivale about the letters."

"Not unless he asks," Nudger said. "And he won't." He stood up.

"Where are you going?"

"I'm leaving," Nudger said, "before Marrivale gets here. There's no sense in making this easy for him."

"Or difficult for you."

"It works out that way, for a change."

Fat Jack nodded, his eyes unfocused yet thoughtful, already rehearsing in his mind the lines he would use on Marrivale. He wasn't a man to bow easily or gracefully to trouble, and he had seen plenty of trouble in his life. He knew a multitude of moves and would use them all.

He didn't seem to notice when Nudger left.

Hollister's apartment was shuttered, and the day's mail delivery sprouted like a white bouquet from the mailbox next to his door. Nudger doubted that David Collins had officially notified the police; his first, his safest, step would be to seek the personal help of Captain Marrivale, who was probably on the Collins payroll already. So it was unlikely that Hollister's apartment was under surveillance, unless by Frick and Frack, who, like Marrivale, probably knew about Ineida's disappearance.

Nudger walked unhesitatingly up to the front door and tried the knob. The door was locked this time. He walked around the corner, toward the back of the building, and unhitched the loop of rope that held shut the high wooden gate to the courtyard.

In the privacy of the fenced courtyard, Nudger quickly forced the sliding glass doors and entered Hollister's apartment.

The place seemed almost exactly as Nudger had left it earlier that day. The matched comb and brush set was still on the dresser, though in a different position. Nudger checked the dresser drawers. They held only a few pairs of undershorts, a wadded dirty shirt, and some socks with holes in the toes. He crossed the bedroom and opened the closet door. The closet's blank back wall stared out at him. Empty. The apartment's kitchen was only lightly stocked with food; the refrigerator held a stick of butter, half a gallon of milk, various half-used condiments, and three cans of beer. It was dirty and needed defrosting. Hollister had been a lousy housekeeper.

The rest of the apartment seemed oddly quiet and in vague disorder, as if getting used to its new state of vacancy. There was definitely a deserted air about the place that suggested its occupant had shunned it and left in a hurry.

Nudger decided that there was nothing to learn here. No matchbooks with messages written inside them, no hastily scrawled, forgotten addresses or revealing ticket stubs. He never got the help that fictional detectives got—well, almost never—though it was always worth seeking.

As he was about to open the courtyard gate and step back into the street. Nudger paused. He stood still, feeling a cold stab of apprehension, of dread knowledge, in the pit of his stomach.

He was staring at the rosebushes that Hollister had planted that morning. At the end of the garden were two newly planted bushes bearing red rosebuds. Hollister hadn't planted them that way. He had alternated the bushes by color, one red one white. Their order now was white, red, white, white, red, red.

Which meant that the bushes had been dug up. Replanted.

Nudger walked to the row of rosebushes. The earth around them was loose, as it had been earlier, but now it seemed more sloppily spread about, and one of the bushes was leaning at an angle. Not the work of a methodical gardener; more the work of someone in a hurry.

As he backed away from the freshly turned soil, Nudger's legs came in contact with a small wrought iron bench. He sat down. He thought for a while, oblivious of the warm sunshine, the colorful geraniums and bougainvillea. He became aware of the frantic chirping of birds on their life-long hunt for sustenance, of the soft yet vibrant buzzing of insects. Sounds of life, sounds of death. He stood up and got out of there fast, his stomach churning.

When he returned to his hotel room, Nudger found on the floor by the desk the napkin that had been wadded in the bottom of the wastebasket. He checked the wastebasket, but it was only a gesture to confirm what he already knew. The letters that Ineida Collins had written to Willy Hollister were gone.

Fat Jack was in his office. Marrivale had come and gone hours ago.

Nudger sat down across the desk from Fat Jack and looked appraisingly at the harried club owner. Fat Jack appeared wrung out by worry. The Marrivale visit had taken a lot out of him. Or maybe he'd had another conversation with David Collins. Whatever his problems, Nudger knew that, to paraphrase the great Al Jolson, Fat Jack hadn't seen nothin' yet.

"David Collins just phoned," Fat Jack said. He was visibly uncomfortable, a veritable Niagara of nervous perspiration. "He got a call from the kidnappers. They want half a million in cash by tomorrow night, or Ineida starts being delivered in the mail piece by piece."

Nudger wasn't surprised. He knew where the phone call had originated.

"When I was looking into Hollister's past," he said to Fat Jack, "I happened to discover something that seemed ordinary enough then, but now has gotten kind of interesting." He watched the perspiration flow down Fat Jack's wide forehead.

"So I'm interested," Fat Jack said irritably. He reached behind him and slapped at the air conditioner, as if to coax more cold air despite the frigid thermostat setting.

"There's something about being a fat man, a man as large as you.

After a while he takes his size for granted, accepts it as a normal fact of his life. But other people don't. A really fat man is more memorable than he realizes, especially if he's called Fat Jack.''

Fat Jack drew his head back into fleshy folds and shot a tortured, wary look at Nudger. "Hey, what are you talking toward, old sleuth?''

"You had a series of failed clubs in the cities where Willy Hollister played his music, and you were there at the times when Hollister's women disappeared.''

"That ain't unusual, Nudger. Jazz is a tight little world.''

"I said people remember you,'' Nudger told him. "And they remember you knowing Willy Hollister. But you told me you saw him for the first time when he came here to play in your club. And when I went to see Ineida for the first time, she knew my name. She bought the idea that I was a magazine writer; it fell right into place and it took her a while to get uncooperative. Then she assumed I was working for her father—as you knew she would.''

Fat Jack stood halfway up, then decided he hadn't the energy for the total effort and sat back down in his groaning chair. "You missed a beat, Nudger. Are you saying I'm in on this kidnapping with Hollister? If that's true, why would I have hired you?''

"You needed someone like me to substantiate Hollister's involvement with Ineida, to find out about Hollister's missing women. It would help you to set him up. You knew him better than you pretended. You knew that he murdered those three women to add some insane, tragic dimension to his music—the sound that made him great. You knew what he had planned for Ineida.''

"He didn't even know who she really was!'' Fat Jack sputtered.

"But you knew from the time you hired her that she was David Collins' daughter. You schemed from the beginning to use Hollister as the fall guy in your kidnapping plan.''

"Hollister is a killer—you said so yourself. I wouldn't want to get involved in any kind of scam with him.''

"He didn't know you were involved,'' Nudger explained. "When you'd used me to make it clear that Hollister was the natural suspect, you kidnapped Ineida and demanded the ransom, figuring Hollister's past and his disappearance would divert the law's attention away from you.''

Fat Jack's wide face was a study in agitation, but it was relatively calm compared to what must have been going on inside his head. His body was squirming uncontrollably, and the pain in his eyes was difficult to look into. He didn't want to ask the question, but he had to and he knew it, "If all this is true," he moaned, "where is Hollister?''

"I did a little digging in his garden,'' Nudger said. "He's under his roses, where he thought Ineida was going to wind up, but where you had space for him reserved all along.''

Fat Jack's head dropped. His suit suddenly seemed to get two sizes too large. As his body trembled, tears joined the perspiration on his quivering cheeks. "When did you know?'' he asked.

"When I got back to my hotel and found the letters from Ineida to Hollister missing. You were the only one other than myself who knew about them.'' Nudger leaned over the desk to look Fat Jack in the eye. "Where is Ineida?'' he asked.

"She's still alive,'' was Fat Jack's only answer. Crushed as he was, he was still too wily to reveal his hole card. It was as if his fat were a kind of rubber, lending inexhaustible resilience to body and mind.

"It's negotiation time,'' Nudger told him, "and we don't have very long to reach an agreement. While we're sitting here talking, the police are digging in the dirt I replaced in Hollister's garden.''

"You called them?''

"I did. But right now, they expect to find Ineida. When they find Hollister, they'll put all the pieces together the way I did and get the same puzzle picture of you.''

Fat Jack nodded sadly, seeing the truth in that prognosis. "So what's your proposition?''

"You release Ineida, and I keep quiet until tomorrow morning. That'll give you a reasonable head start on the law. The police don't know who phoned them about the body in Hollister's garden, so I can stall them for at least that long without arousing suspicion.''

Fat Jack didn't deliberate for more than a few seconds. He nodded again, then stood up, supporting his ponderous weight with both hands on the desk. "What about money?" he whined. "I can't run far without money."

"I've got nothing to lend you," Nudger said. "Not even the fee I'm not going to get from you."

"All right," Fat Jack sighed.

"I'm going to phone David Collins in one hour," Nudger told him. "If Ineida isn't there, I'll put down the receiver and dial the number of the New Orleans police department."

"She'll be there," Fat Jack said. He tucked in his sweat-plastered shirt beneath his huge stomach paunch, buttoned his suit coat, and without a backward glance at Nudger glided majestically from the room. He would have his old jaunty stride back in no time.

Nudger glanced at his watch. He sipped Fat Jack's best whisky from the club's private stock while he waited for an hour to pass. Then he phoned David Collins, and from the tone of Collins' voice he guessed the answer to his question even before he asked it.

Ineida was home.

When Nudger answered the knock on his hotel room door early the next morning, he wasn't really surprised to find Frick and Frack looming in the hall. They pushed into the room without being invited. There was a sneer on Frick's pockmarked face. Frack gave his boxer's nifty little shuffle and stood between Nudger and the door, smiling politely.

"We brought you something from Mr. Collins," Frick said, reaching into an inside pocket of his pale green sport jacket. It just about matched Nudger's complexion.

All Frick brought out, though, was an envelope. Nudger was surprised to see that his hands were steady as he opened it.

The envelope contained an airline ticket for a noon flight to St. Louis.

"You did okay, my friend," Frick said. "You did what was right for Ineida. Mr Collins appreciates that."

"What about Fat Jack?" Nudger asked. Frack's polite smile changed subtly. It became a dreamy, unpleasant sort of smile.

"Where Fat Jack is now," Frack said, "most of his friends are alligators."

"After Fat Jack talked to you," said Frick, "he went to Mr. Collins. He couldn't make himself walk out on all that possible money; some guys just have to play all their cards. He told Mr. Collins that for a certain amount of cash he would reveal Ineida's whereabouts, but it all had to be done in a hurry." Now Frick also smiled. "He revealed her whereabouts in a hurry, all right, and for free. In fact, he kept talking till nobody was listening, till he couldn't talk any more."

Nudger swallowed dryly. He forgot about breakfast. Fat Jack had been a bad businessman to the end, dealing in desperation instead of distance. Maybe he'd had too much of the easy life; maybe he couldn't picture going on without it. That was no problem for him now.

When Nudger got home, he found a flat, padded package with a New Orleans postmark waiting for him. He placed it on his desk and cautiously opened it. The package contained two items: A check from David Collins made out to Nudger for more than twice the amount of Fat Jack's uncollectable fee. And an old jazz record in its original wrapper, a fifties rendition of "You Got the Reach but Not the Grasp."

It featured Fat Jack McGee on clarinet.

JUST LIKE A HOG

by BRYCE WALTON

Knowing flies, and having patience, Sheriff Gil Mashburn waited and watched the big fellow buzzing and circling to its inevitable fate. He sat with his feet on the corner of the rolltop desk, his sweat-soaked shirt open down to his web belt and the electric fan cooling his belly.

Mashburn was moved to philosophizing about the fly. Everything ought to stay where it was born to be and not go horsing around in strange territory. That fly would probably have lived out its natural life if it had stayed outside the jail and been satisfied with old lady Fenwick's garbage can. Just like that big wild McClinton kid caged up back there, that boy ought to have stayed on the other side of the mangrove swamp under the ridge where he belonged.

With astonishing quickness for a fat man, and with no greater expenditure of effort than a forearm flick, Mashburn reduced the fly to a bloody blot on a rolled-up copy of the *Louisiana Globe.* Then he sighed to his feet, got the pint bottle of Old Thompson whisky from the desk drawer and ambled out of his office and back along the corridor of the city jail.

They ought to keep those swamp boys at home, he thought. They ought to educate them before sending them over into town, or make them stay on a reservation like Indians. Still, he felt kindly toward the McClinton kid. Having had him in that cell for a time, he'd come

159

to know him. The boy had sure got a bum break. Only eighteen, and newly wed, married only one day, then coming over into Riverdale and getting all liquored up and going wild in Harry's Tavern. Tore the place up and pretty near killed a few men before they beat him down with a sawed-off billiard cue. Not surprising that Braymer, who had a badly busted head, was preferring charges against the kid.

"It wasn't just the likker," Braymer had said in coming to in the hospital. "That crazy fool only had a couple shots. Sure we was kidding him a little, but then he had a couple of shots and went plumb crazy, saying he was as good a man as all of us together. If he hadn't been stopped, he'd a killed me. He wanted to kill me. It was all over his face. He's a luny nut and it's dangerous to let him run around loose."

Well, now, I don't go along with that, Mashburn thought. McClinton was wild, young, and too big—big as a bull. Boy like that just don't know his own strength, that's all. On top of that, just turned eighteen, only married one day, strutting into town to feel his oats. It all panned out. Not only that, but McClinton had never been over into town more than a few times in his life, not by himself.

McClinton, wearing a pair of faded Levis, a torn shirt speckled with dried blood, was looking out the barred window.

"McClinton," Mashburn said. "Hey, boy."

McClinton didn't turn. His huge shoulders rose and fell. One hand gripped the bar.

"Let's be sociable now, boy," Mashburn said. McClinton didn't move. "Braymer's coming around. He's a little peeved, but he'll get over it. He'll cool off. They got to prove you broke his head with malicious intent, and they ain't going to be able to prove that. It just ain't so and I know it and everybody knows it. You got to make the best out of just having to stay in here for a spell, that's all. So let's be friendly about it. I didn't put you in here, boy. And if it was up to me, I'd sent you home a week ago. Let's be friends now. How about it?"

McClinton half turned. A gash showed on the side of his head. His left eye was puffed a little. His face was ridged with deep thick bone; his eyes were light blue; his hair was black and curling on the back of his thick neck. He had the kind of loose shyness you associate with children.

"I got to get back home," he said softly.

"I know that. But you got to stay here a spell yet."

"I can't," McClinton said with timid stubbornness.

"You're worried about that gal of yours, I know that, boy."

McClinton sat down on the iron cot, and put his hands between his knees and looked steadily up at Mashburn. Then he whispered, "She's only sixteen. She don't know any better. Listen—she ain't going to write me no more."

"You got two letters. You'll get another one any day now."

"Nope, she ain't going to write me no more."

"Why not?"

"I just know," McClinton said. His neck pulsed, and a drop of sweat ran down the side of his nose. "She won't write. She ain't waitin' for me to come back." Anguish was tight in his throat. "I could tell by the way she wrote in that last letter. It was cold all through. I know. She ain't waitin' any more for me."

"You don't know that, boy. You're jumping to conclusions."

"No, I ain't. She ain't waitin'. I been thinkin' and I know who she's making out with, too. Fella up there—Herb Lathrop. Couldn't be nobody else but Herb."

Mashburn put the bottle through the bars. "Here, boy, this ain't regular, but we ought to have a little drink to clear the air."

McClinton's head jerked up. He wiped at his mouth with the back of his hand. He started to get up, then shoved back until his shoulders pressed into the wall.

"Come on, McClinton. Take a little pressure off."

"No," McClinton ran his tongue over his lips. "Better not."

"It ain't polite to refuse a friendly drink, 'specially with your jailor." Mashburn laughed.

"I ought not. Pa told me not to touch it. He said—he's always told me someday I'd get into bad trouble. Always said I'd have to watch myself or I'd end up hangin' for killin' somebody. He said I got it from Ma's side of the family 'cause she was a Larrimer. Last year I took a little nip of corn and Pa almost killed me with a harness strap. He was right. See what happened to me?"

"Boy, you're just big, that's all. Big and strong as a bull. Any man's liable to go a little wild, and when you get that way, you just naturally do it big."

"Nope, Pa told me, but I didn't pay him no account. He trusted me. I got married and Pa figured I was man enough to come into town by myself and get the axle grease and get the skinnin' knives sharpened up. But I wasn't. I've learned my lesson, though. That's why I got to get back and make it up to Pa. And I got to take care of Lucie."

He stood up quickly. "It's Herb Lathrop," he said. He looked out the window. "I figured out it's got to be Herb gettin' to her."

"You got to calm down, boy. A fella's right to show respect to his pa. But seems to me your pa's been pushing this thing too hard. Making too much out of it. Let's have a friendly drink or two now and let's see just how crazy and wild you are. You're in a cell. You can't go crazy and murder anybody, can you?"

McClinton nodded slowly.

"We got to prove your old man's been making a mountain out of a molehill. You got to have faith in yourself. You can't go around feeling you got this crazy murderer holing up inside. You got to prove you got control over yourself and can take your likker. You got to feel you can come over into town by yourself."

McClinton's face was wet and the fine dark fuzz glistened on his jaw. Mashburn shoved the bottle at him. McClinton took a quick swallow, handed back the bottle to Mashburn, who took a little swig for himself. McClinton wiped his mouth, took a long slow step back from the door. His shoulders weaved heavily.

"There, boy, see how it relaxes. We're going to have a friendly talk about things, and you'll see you ain't such a hellion after all." Mashburn paused. "Not unless you want to be."

"I feel pretty good," McClinton said, staring at the bottle. "But I got to get home. I got another reason to get home. My pa'll think I'm tryin' to get out of helpin' butcher."

"That ain't true, and you got to know it and not be scared."

"Pa won't ask anybody else to come in and help butcher them hogs. He'll be having to do it all by himself." McClinton jumped toward the door. "You still got them skinnin' knives?"

"They're in the desk drawer out there," Mashburn said. "All sharpened up, but you're not going to be home for any butchering. Your pa wants you to be on your own, don't he, otherwise, why'd he send you over into town by yourself to get the knives sharpened up?"

McClinton pulled the bottle back into the cell and drank half the contents. A tremor ran through his body. He pushed the bottle back toward Mashburn. "I got to get home now. Herb Lathrop. Couldn't be nobody else. Lives just down the road a piece. He could come up there, crawl through the fence, go over the creek, and see Lucie without nobody up in the big house knowin' a thing. She wouldn't even call out, 'cause she's too little an' scared. My pa built our house for us, right in back of the home place, right next to the smokehouse."

Mashburn reached for the bottle. He cried out hoarsely as he saw his arm bend suddenly and sharply the wrong way and felt something ripping and burning in his elbow.

"McClinton—" Mashburn said. "Boy—" His body smashed against the bars and his teeth ground into metal. He tried to breathe. He tried to get his mouth open. A throbbing dark pressure beat at his ears. He heard the keys jangling far away. It was like it was Christmas again and he was a kid waiting upstairs, listening to the bells tinkling on the hanging stockings.

He was falling, fighting not to fall, rolling down damp stairs in the dark, and he thought he was having that old dream of his again, that one where he was trapped in a storm cellar under the house and the tornado came over and the rocks fell on him, stifling the life out.

He woke groaning and feeling like one solid bruise all over. He sat up despite Jim Saunders' protests. Doc Martin was standing there.

"Easy, Gil," Saunders said. His Adam's apple bobbed like the cork on a perch line and he pushed his greasy felt hat to the back of his small bony head. "Doc says you got torn ligaments and maybe splintered bone."

"That's right," Doc Martin said. "Maybe internal injuries, too. How you feel inside?"

Mashburn hurt inside, but then he hurt all over. Just bruised, that was all, run over by a light truck. His arm was in a sling. Pain throbbed up into his head. He pushed Martin to one side and went into his office. The fifth of rye was gone from the left-hand bottom drawer. He sat down in his swivel chair and fought away a spell of dizziness.

"Where's McClinton now?" he asked.

"Off in the mangrove swamp," Saunders said. "He took your Olds and ditched it near the Clam Shack on Bayou Road and took to the boondocks."

"He knows the swamp better'n any of us," Mashburn said. "Those boys trap in there all the time."

"I deputized some boys," Saunders said eagerly. "And Brigger's got his hound dogs out there."

"Goddamn it, Saunders. I don't like puttin' dogs on a man."

"Braymer might have a setback and die," Saunders said. "He's got a busted head. And that means we're after a murderer."

"He ain't a murderer yet," Mashburn said. "Chasin' that boy through the swamp with dogs. God a'mighty. Anyway, we'd never catch up to him in there before he—" Mashburn turned back toward his desk.

"Before what?" Saunders said, leaning forward and nervously fingering his pocket knife. Mashburn saw the eager glint in his eyes. If Saunders knew the kid was hopped up and wanting to kill, he'd get the hunting and killing fever himself. He'd get the vigilantes out, get them riled up with free liquor. Maybe McClinton was just plain mean, but Mashburn still didn't believe it. He felt responsible for what had happened now, and for what might happen. Mashburn figured he could get to the Lathrop place by car in plenty of time to head off McClinton, who had to cross the mangrove swamp. That swamp was mighty terrible even for a man who knew it. Moccasins, bull gators, mosquitoes, and the leeches were the worst things of all. Saunders opened the desk's bottom drawer and looked in. "Guess that boy'll be likkered up fit to kill by this time. He took off with your likker, didn't he, Sheriff?"

"According to Braymer, that boy and a bottle ain't such a good combination."

"Yeah," Mashburn said. "His pa taught him all about that." Then he slapped the desk with his flat left hand. "Well, what you standing there for? Get out there and follow Brigger and his yapping dogs!"

Saunders said, "Wouldn't that be a waste of time? Why not head right for the McClinton place by road? Ain't that where the kid's heading?"

Mashburn was on his feet. "McClinton's not an idiot. He knows we figure he'll head straight for home, don't he? He'll lay low in the swamp, won't he? Hell, any animal would be that smart. He'll hide in the swamp. A boy like that could hole up in there for months."

Saunders shrugged and said pointedly, "You're *still* the sheriff."

"That's right," Mashburn said. "And I'll be sheriff after the coming elections."

"Me, I'm no prophet," Saunders said. He intended to be sheriff himself. He went out into the sticky heat and across the weed-grown lot toward his station wagon.

Mashburn studied the gun rack. No guns missing. He jerked open the right-hand bottom drawer. The skinning knives were gone.

"You got any cases pending?" Mashburn asked the doctor.

"Mrs. Johnson's complaining of brain fever again," Martin said. "But then she's always been crazy."

"You can drive me around the mangroves to the McClinton place?"

"I sure can do that little thing, Sheriff. Only my Dodge needs a new transmission and we got to be careful." He opened the door and Mashburn started out. "That McClinton's dangerous, Gil."

"Sure, sure. Anybody's dangerous if you put on enough pressure."

"But some are more dangerous than others," the gaunt, pale-faced doctor said calmly. "Gil, why didn't you take up preaching instead of being a sheriff?"

"I'll tell you why," Mashburn said as he went out. "Preaching never stopped anybody from going off the deep end, not to my knowledge."

Doc Martin drove his mud-splattered Dodge down Main and turned toward Bayou Road. Saunders came out of Harry's Tavern and watched them leave town.

*   *   *

The road was a bog. They lost three hours when the Dodge slid into a ditch near the slew. The thick slewgrass made it impossible to pull themselves out. They walked clear over to the Clam Shack, a dilapidated tavern, for help. It was an unpainted cypress-slabbed hut patched with driftwood and surrounded by a dripping forest of cypress, thick-trunked bougainvillea vines, and mangroves, with the path approaching it heaped with oyster and clam shells. The owner was growling because there weren't any customers. Everybody and his uncle was out splashing through the swamp hunting down that crazy McClinton kid. But a fellow named Mansell was there and he had a jeep. He pulled the Dodge back onto the road and they drove on into a gray dripping twilight toward the other side of the swamp. The road was bad. Martin had spent a lifetime driving through that country, but he had to take it slow.

An impatience that was nearly panic took hold of Mashburn. He kept thinking of McClinton all alone, fighting through the mangrove swamp with the moccasins and spiders, the leeches and gators, and that bottle of damned hootch. And those hungry-eager hounds baying behind him. It was my fault, Mashburn kept saying to himself. I was a sucker, but it was all my fault.

"McClinton ought not to have sent the boy over into town by himself," Mashburn said.

"He had to come over sometime," Martin said. "He's eighteen and a married man."

"But there are special circumstances here," Mashburn said gloomily. "For some reason McClinton built it into his kid that he was a killer. Nobody's born a killer. Why'd the old man do that?"

"Wouldn't know."

"You ever run into these McClintons?"

"No, never did. But I can tell you one thing. Some of these people have never been enlightened by higher education, Gil. They even believe in hexes and the evil eye. Who knows what Mr. McClinton believes, and whatever he believes, his kid's had a lifetime dose of it."

"Yeah, I know," Mashburn said. "For God's sake, push this thing a little, can't you, doc?"

"Nope. If we slipped off the road here, they'd be using grappling hooks to get us out—if they ever found us."

They had entered a thick, darkening forest of jackpines where the damp sultry air smelled of turpentine and the ground was a twisted body of mangroves with roots like swarms of snakes. They swung into the swamp, which was like moving into a green tunnel, and the Dodge was drenched with a bright rain of dew.

"End of the line," Martin said and pulled to a stop.

Mashburn got out and stood in mud and rotting grass. Odd lights flickered in the shadows. Dragonflies quivered and fireflies danced. Big black mosquitoes droned hungrily. Mashburn started along the path that led, at least half a mile, to the Lathrop place. The McClinton place, he knew, was a little way on the other side. A bull gator roared nearby. Mashburn felt a kind of comfort in hearing Martin sloshing along behind him.

They walked past jackstraw piles of abandoned cypress logs and skirted the stinking river, choked with bonnets and purple water hyacinth. They approached the Lathrop place, like an old swamper's bleached cabin half in the shadows, its palm-thatched roof shining. Yellowish smoke rose spiral-like from the chimney.

An old lady was sitting on the sagging porch, with a palmetto fan held halfway to her face. She sat like she was dead.

Tensely, Mashburn moved silently through scraggly rose bushes and crepe myrtle and past an old wagon falling apart. The shack had been put together a long time back with green lumber scraps that had warped, and the holes patched with flattened-out tin cans. Gnats and mosquitoes crawled over Mashburn as he stepped up onto the porch. He stopped. His breath sucked in. The old lady didn't move. Her eyes stared out of a face that seemed frozen in preparation for a scream. The neck was rigid and her eyes bulged.

Mashburn noticed that the screen door was torn half off its hinges. He went inside. The dimly lit room smelled like dead flowers, wilted roses. Sickness swirled in Mashburn's stomach and he backed into Martin as he stumbled back onto the porch.

"Too late?" Martin asked softly.

"I don't know," Mashburn said. "It's the Lathrop boy. Better take care of him."

Martin went in. "He's still alive. But he looks as if he'd been dropped in a concrete mixer."

Mashburn forced his way back inside. Flies buzzed around the Lathrop boy's head, where he lay in a welter of blood half under a broken table.

"I wouldn't touch his Lucie," the whisper came out of the shadows. "He's crazy—crazy in the head—Lucie—I wouldn't touch his Lucie—with a ten foot pole—I wouldn't—"

"Don't let him die," Mashburn whispered, but he was beginning to feel that dull gray hopelessness. What could you do, what could you do about it all?

"I'll do my best," Martin said. "But listen here now, Gil. The world's too big for one man to do anything about very much and this thing—"

Mashburn started back out onto the porch. Martin called out, "Better take this." He stood in the doorway holding a .38 caliber revolver.

Mashburn stared at it, then took it and dropped it into his corduroy jacket pocket. "I didn't give you a permit to carry that," he said, but he wasn't concentrating on what he was saying.

Martin was back inside and Mashburn heard a long whining sound like a hurt dog come from where the Lathrop boy lay.

He ran down the steps, forgetting his own throbbing pains. The old lady still sat frozen and staring as if she had been paralyzed by a snake.

There was no light in the bigger house set in among the cypress trees and the dripping shawls of Spanish moss. A yellow light shone in the window of the smaller, two room shack old man McClinton had built for his son and his new daughter-in-law.

The .38 felt awkward in Mashburn's left hand as he approached the lighted window and the partly opened door. A creek ran beside the shack. Water shadows snaked up the rotted column of a log. Copper waterbugs swung on spider web trapezes, and fungus the size of a fist blossomed from decayed wood.

Hens clicked from the henyard. And Mashburn heard the whir of an owl catching mice in the barn. And there, on the other side, he saw the singletrees, hanging on the cypress branches, that they hung

the hogs on to cut at pig-killing time. His stomach curled as he saw
the big red and white carcasses hanging there in the twilight. He'd
seen them butcher hogs once. Hook the tendons of the pig's hind
legs over the ends of the singletrees and hang it up by a rope through
the ring, then gut it and flay it down to the last leg, working, snicking
away with the knife through the fat, and tugging down the heavy
hide with the other hand. The kid had been too late to help.

Mashburn looked in through the lighted window. Sick rage seized
him, rendered him incapable of movement as he crouched there looking and listening. He knew at a glance what the McClinton boy had
come home to.

The girl lying on the cot, its cover soiled and disordered. Old man
McClinton, looking bigger than his kid, but going to fat, gray hair
at the V of his shirt, his neck a brownish red and running sweat. He
stood beside the cot, and looked at his kid, who seemed to be nailed
to the floor and trying to move toward the cot.

That was why the old man had sent his kid across into town by
himself, and why he hadn't even come to the jail to see him. The
kid had known what was happening all right, only he could hardly
have guessed who had beaten his time with Lucie.

"How could I tell you?" the girl kept whispering like a frightened
child to her husband. "How could I tell you—?"

The McClinton boy stood bent forward, his body covered with
slimy mud and leeches clinging to his arms. He was trying to move,
move toward the looming figure of his father.

"Wait now, wait boy," old man McClinton was saying in a kind
of croon. "You got to be careful." His voice got higher. "You got
to keep that thing inside, boy, or you'll kill somebody sure as the
devil. Now, boy, you listen to me, you got—"

"McClinton!" Mashburn yelled. He kicked in through the door
and leveled the revolver into the room. The kid leaped massively as
though shot forward, and the lamp smashed into the wall and a few
flames ate at the floor and then went out.

A heaving and grunting, a ripping and pounding, broke loose cra-
zily in the dark. Wood smashed. Just as Mashburn tried to get out
the door, it was as if a two by four landed on his neck. The revolver
flew from his hand. He was on his knees crawling, agony in his torn

arm like a dark tide, crawling and calling out to McClinton, trying to stop him.

He tried to stop the kid all right. No one ever could say that Mashburn didn't try to stop the kid from dragging the inert body of his old man across the ground toward the cypress trees, and past the big iron barrel where the hogs were dropped into boiling water to scald, and to the singletrees where they were hung up.

He didn't see Saunders when he came out of the swamp across the road and he didn't hear the rifle crack twice, nor see the kid running and falling into the creek.

They told Mashburn about that later. And for days, weeks, he kept trying to drive from his mind the image of a body hanging among the other carcasses, naked and fat and white just like a hog.

He didn't run for reelection that fall. And when Doc Martin came to see him, Mashburn—sitting on the swing on the front porch—explained how he was considering taking up preaching.

"You got to try to stop things," he said. "Because once they get rolling, it's not easy to stop them from going on to the end."

JAMBALAYA

by *DOUGLAS CRAIG*

Vince Savoy is going to the chair this morning at Angola. That's the way it's got to be, Vince being what he is—an ex-trooper who went bad and brought shame on us all.

I'm no kin to Vince Savoy and I keep telling myself that I've no more pity for him than I'd feel for a mad dog loose in a schoolyard. And yet, while I sit here waiting for the dawn light to come crawling over the marshes, I'm plagued by the thought that there's somebody else who ought to be going with him. Me.

We grew up together in the bayous of Louisiana, in the shadow of oak and cypress that drip long gray moss like the tears of the dead. We rassled gators and dodged quicksands together, baying the moon on white nights. Girls were no problem between us in those days, and we got a big laugh out of it when they passed us up for some type in a tin hat, a *texien* from the oil rigs in the Gulf, or a well-heeled tripper from up north. Women, Vince used to say, brought trouble on nobody but themselves.

There were a couple of exceptions though, and the main one was Clo Ronsard. We'd have died for her any time, either one of us. But as things worked out it was worse than that. When I think of the years stretching out ahead of me now, I get sick.

My name is Mike Logan and I'm a trooper myself. What's more,

I'm married to a girl that's too good for me. Her name is Felice. No kids yet, maybe never. That's not for me to say now.

It never crossed my mind that Felice would get hurt by anything I ever did. But I think she knew what was wrong with me, long before I was assigned to the Savoy case.

The first hint I had of it was that same night, when it struck me for the first time since my marriage that I didn't feel like going home. I hung around headquarters until everybody else was gone and then I went over to Ti'Jean's bar and leaned on that for a while. I didn't get drunk. It just seemed all of a sudden as if life was pretty raw, and I put away a few cherry flips with a bourbon base to kind of improve matters.

But it didn't work. I was in a bad situation, and I knew it.

Vince had dropped out of sight all of a sudden like a gator into its hole, and headquarters picked on me to pole him out. I squawked bloody murder, but it stuck and they detailed Dubois to help me, which was no help at all. Dubois is a good kid, you understand, but heavy footed, the kind you don't trust in the swamps with those size sixteens of his. When he lifts one up, the other only sinks in deeper.

But my main problem was Clo. To get any kind of line on Vince I'd have to keep an eye on her day and night, and I wasn't sure how that would work out. Not sure at all.

I was well stirred up by the time I stomped out of Ti'Jean's place and up along the bayou to my own house, pulling up short at the foot of the steps to draw a deep breath. Then I went on up and the good smell of simmering gumbo came out to greet me and I felt like a dog.

"Felice—?" I said, "Felice—?"

She came out of the kitchen quickly and quietly, wiping her hands on her pink apron, and held up her cheek for me to kiss, a cool, smooth cheek that smelled of rosewater. Homemade rosewater, at that. Her eyes were smiling, but she shoved me away gently and said, "You're late, Mike. You must be hungry. Will you eat right now, or would you like a shower first?"

"Shower," I grunted, holding my breath so the blast of bourbon wouldn't drown out the rosewater. I pulled out my gun and parked it on the shelf behind the clock, as usual. "Tough day," I told her,

heading for the bedroom door with my shirt half off before I got
there. "They've put me on the Savoy case—what d'you think of
that?" And then, before she could speak, I whirled around and saw
the sudden shocked paleness of her face. "Don't tell me!" I yipped.
"I don't want to hear!"

She didn't have to tell me. I could hear the words inside my skull
under the roar of the shower in the old tin tub . . . *but Mike, you
can't—Vince is your friend . . . and what about Clo?*

Sure, what about Clo? I wanted to know myself. There was a
rumor that she'd left Vince. Did that mean she was through with
him now, for keeps?

I wasn't proud of the notion. Not just because Vince had been my
friend a long time ago—hell, he was nobody's friend these days!
And it wasn't only on account of my wife. The thought of Clo was
like a fresh wound, the pain of it banked down under the jab of a
needle—then wham! It busts loose before you even get to the dressing station. That happened to me in Korea.

I tried to stare myself down in the wavy old mirror over the
washbasin, but it wasn't easy. I dug out a clean shirt and buttoned
it slowly, looking around the shabby little room that Felice had tried
to fix up with bright curtains and a bedspread to match and odd bits
of furniture that didn't. Shabby was the word, all right. It was a safe
bet that Vince Savoy had done better by his woman. But maybe she
didn't care where she slept, as long as—

"Mike, are you coming?" Felice called out from the kitchen.

The tone of her voice made me prick up my ears. It sounded
different. I remembered suddenly that she never had much to say
about the Savoys, one way or another, since they got married, except
once. Just once, when she turned to me in the night with a queer
little sob and said, "Mike—wait—there's something I want to ask
you. Mike—are you still in love with Clo?"

That knocked the breath out of me, but I said something fast and
convincing like, "Hell, no—what ever gave you such a crazy idea?"

But she didn't say. Felice is the only woman I ever knew who
never had much to say about anything. It could be restful, if you
didn't start wondering what was going on inside her head.

"Coming," I called back, and a minute later I was digging into a dish of gumbo while she brought the coffee pot and a crusty hunk of bread with garlic butter that she'd been keeping hot in the oven. A meal for a king, as usual. "Great stuff, honey," I mumbled. "You never lose the touch."

"As a matter of fact," Felice said coolly, "it isn't very good tonight. Dubois was here a while ago and I gave him a plate, but he left half of it."

I quit eating. "Dubois?" I said. "What did *he* want?"

"You," said Felice. "He said he'd be back after supper." Her voice had a catch in it.

"Is that all?" I snapped suspiciously. "Did he say anything else?"

She thought about that for a second. "If you mean, did he tell me anything he shouldn't, no," she said. "I think you're too hard on Dubois, Mike. He's young, but he's a good policeman, too."

"Did he—" I was going to ask her if he'd said anything about the Savoy case but I shoved back my plate, instead, and reached for a cup of coffee.

"You see?" Felice said sadly. "It isn't very good. I'm sorry, Mike. I think I'll go and lie down for a little before I wash up. I have a small headache."

"You're not sick?" I asked quickly, but she'd slipped into the bedroom, closing the door behind her.

It's Clo, I thought. She's heard something about Clo. That dumb ape of a Dubois! But it didn't have to be Dubois. Everybody up and down the bayou knew that the four of us had grown up together, but that things had changed between us. That was enough for the busy-bodies with the knack of putting two and two together and making five out of it.

Vince and I had married the Ronsard girls, Clothilde and Felice. They were cousins, no kin to either Vince or me, and that's something in our part of the country.

There's no use denying that I'd been in love with Clo as far back as I can remember. But Vince was more her type. She saw him as some kind of hero, like the great old pirate, Jean Lafitte, whose raiding crews used to roam the Gulf, sacking and burning as they went.

Felice was different, the gentle kind, blond as an angel. She thought the old time pirates were very bloody and sad, poor fellows. What were they, after all, but criminals and lost souls? But you could see the hero worship in Clo's big dark eyes when she looked at Vince. I used to wonder what went on behind those eyes that had come down to her through a long line of Cajun grandmothers, blazing and sultry by turns, loaded with dreams that she kept to herself.

But I could never see myself in any of those dreams, and Vince was my friend. So I married Felice. I got the best girl in the world, bar none. But Vince got the girl we'd both wanted from the time we found out what wanting was.

Felice and I settled down in a comfortable old house close enough to headquarters for me to report in any kind of weather, because we have some fast winds down here in the hurricane season. And we were happy. Maybe it wasn't all fire and honey, as the old folks say, but it was good, even when Felice held back a little. She felt that married love had a good deal of sinfulness in it, and that kind of put the damper on sometimes.

I hate to admit it, but I used to ask myself sometimes if a man didn't make a mistake to marry a woman who was so damned *good*. If only she'd leave off braiding her pretty hair into two tight pigtails every night, and maybe sew a bit of ribbon and lacy stuff into her nightgown. But what kind of animal would want to change a good wife into something that was half hussy?

Vince wouldn't settle for a quiet life, no matter how you sliced it. He transferred to one of the new oil and shrimp towns on the Gulf, where things weren't so tame. Clo had the same streak of wildness in her, I guess. She was crazy for the change.

They bought a modern, ranch-type house, all brick and glass, with a TV aerial as tall as an oil derrick, and an outside freezer that packed the kind of food they liked to eat these days. That freezer really tore it for the folks back home on the bayou, the old time *habitants* who still eat better than any other people in the world, and know it.

There was an ugly rumor that Clo Savoy wouldn't even cook for her husband. Least of all the gumbo and jambalaya that no real man could live without. And her coffee—! It was only a pinch of brown powder that melted away at the touch of hot water. Where were the grounds? The dark, rich, useful grounds that held up the pot on the back of the stove from one day to the next?

Most of it was woman-talk that Felice picked up when she went visiting up and down the bayou, but I kept half an ear cocked, just in case. God forgive me, I was listening for worse, for some hint that the Savoys weren't getting along nearly as well as they might.

After awhile, though, there was another kind of buzz down at headquarters and I gave both ears to that one.

Vince had always been wild, with a sort of blind courage that drove him into every clip joint and dope den along the coast, and more times than not he got the man he was after. He barged deep into the marshlands on the trail of smugglers and hijackers that lived off the muskrat trappers and raided the payboats that were heavy with dough in a good season.

The trouble was that Vince was a smart money man himself, and they don't last. He started out on the force in a blaze of fireworks, but the show winked out in a smelly smudge of damp powder.

That's when the bad breaks began. And it wasn't the sweating taxpayer who squawked about Vince to headquarters—it was the crooks.

The first time it was a payroll job. Somebody knocked off an elderly Chinese who made a fortune drying shrimp in the old fashioned Cantonese way. He couldn't add up to ten without one of those rattling bead counters they call an abacus, and he still paid off his help in silver dollars, the way his grandpa used to do.

One payday somebody plugged him in the back of the head and took off with the cash. We never found out for sure who actually pulled the job or how he got rid of the proceeds. Our real headache was who thought it up? The brains behind it, so to speak.

Of course, there weren't any. We tried it for size on all the "known criminals" in the parish, but all we pulled in was a mess of hurt feelings. Nobody, but nobody, was going to own up to a corny, hamstrung job like that! Some of the biggest thugs in three states were so shocked and embarrassed professionally that they were ready to tell what they knew. It made quite a story. So simple.

A state trooper had planned this one, they told us. An "amachoor,'' what else? His name? Sure, sure—his name was Vince Savoy.

It was the laugh of the year, that picture of Vince staggering around under a load of hot silver dollars. He laughed himself when he was called down to headquarters for routine questioning. ''Crazy, man—crazy!''

But it started me wondering. The Savoys were living high off the hog these days, and his pay was the same as my own. How did he do it?

A wealthy shipbuilder was the next to go. No silver cartwheels this time, just green paper currency, although some of it might be hard to pass. The man had been shot in the back and had fallen forward across his pay table. The stuff must have been soaked with his blood. Nobody tried to pin this on Vince, but the Savoys came out with a fancy car as long as a deep-sea lugger, and I stopped wondering. I knew.

The big surprise came when Vince quit the force of his own accord. The whisper got around that he'd rigged himself up a neat little syndicate, a protection racket based on all he'd discovered while he was in uniform. The slimy roots of it reached up from the muck at the bottom to the top where the politics grow.

Vince was playing pirates for real now, I thought that night, as I paced up and down in front of my house, waiting for Dubois. I wondered how Clo was taking it.

A voice came to me through the half-dark, along with the crunch of heavy boots. ''Logan?'' This would be Dubois turning up after supper, as promised. ''Sorry if I kept you waiting.''

''Think nothing of it,'' I said. ''Maybe we could stroll over to Ti'Jean's for a couple of beers.'' And then, when we were out of range of the bedroom window, I let him have it. ''What the hell did you say to my wife?''

''So help me, nothin'!'' Dubois yelped like a kicked pup. ''I just asked her if she'd seen Clo Savoy since she got back to the bayou—''

''You did, did you?'' I snapped. My tongue was thick in my mouth. Clo—back on the bayou with the old folks on their camp boat. Clo skinning muskrats and running the bloody pelts through a wringer, the way she had to when she was a kid. What kind of life was that? In spite of myself, I said gruffly, "What did she say? Felice, I mean."

"Nothin'," Dubois said glumly.

I laughed. "That sounds about right," I said, but when we got to Ti'Jean's place I was still sweating.

Dubois chattered along for a while over his beer, but I didn't pay him much mind until I heard that name again and I snapped at it. "What's that about Savoy? If you've got any fresh dope, spill it!"

He shook his head. "It's all just say-so. You know."

It was never any more than that. Nobody had ever pinned anything on Vince, and maybe we never would. It wasn't even our job to pick him up unless we caught him standing over a body with a gun in his fist. Knowing Vince, that didn't seem likely. I said so, and Dubois tried to look tough, flattered to be talked to like a grown-up policeman. It was pretty funny and I was trying to wipe a sour grin off my face when he let drop something that hit a nerve.

"That gal of his," Dubois said, looking wise. "She's mad like hell at him. Maybe she'd talk."

"Clo?" I said. "You're crazy. She'd feed herself to the sharks first!"

"Not her—not Mrs. Savoy!" Dubois cut in. He was shocked. "The other one. That doll he took up with after his wife left him."

There was a queer lurch inside me. Another woman, eh? I'd never heard a breath about another woman. "I don't believe it," I said. "Whoever she is, she's lying."

"He's been seen with her a couple of times," Dubois said hopefully. "But it wasn't long before he gave her the air."

I whistled. That made sense. No other woman could get Clo off his mind. Nobody but Clo could do that. I knew. . . . But this briefing was getting out of hand. I was supposed to be filling in a rookie on a tough new case, and here I was with my head stuck through a sheet while he fired coconuts at me.

"Okay," I said, tossing a bill on the bar. "Let's pack it in for tonight. See you in the morning."

"Well, th-thanks—" Dubois mumbled, blinking, and I clapped him on the shoulder, sorry for catching him off balance. "You'll rack up a medal for this job, kid,'' I told him. And with that I headed home by myself, thinking sixteen to the dozen. Another woman! Well, well, well. . . .

I wasn't drunk, but I wasn't sober either. I stumbled on the front steps and barged in with a heavier tread than I meant to. I'd forgotten Felice had a headache. But there she was, sitting in her own chair under the lamp, with a pile of mending beside her. She was sewing buttons on a shirt.

I stopped short. My gun was lying on the table next to her.

She looked up at me and bit off a thread. "I think you ought to be more careful, Mike," she said quietly. "You keep forgetting your gun."

That was all, and God knows it wasn't much. I'd always been careless about my gun, and there was more than one crook from the waterprairies who would have jumped at the chance to pick me off unarmed. Felice had a right to be worried, but tonight I took it as a personal insult.

"When I need your advice, I'll ask for it!" I yelled. "And as for that shirt, it's old enough to throw away—I won't wear it!"

She didn't answer. Her face was still pale but while she put the needle through the hole of a button there was the ghost of a smile on her lips. It took some of the fight out of me. I sat down and started to take off my shoes.

"Well, say something," I growled. "Tell me I'm drunk. Tell me I'm some trooper to be running around in the dark without my gun. Tell me you curse the day you married me—"

"All that?" she asked, the needle flashing into a new hole. "It doesn't sound much like me, does it? Besides, it's none of it true."

I kicked my shoes across the room and rested my head on my fists. I knew I ought to come up with some kind of apology for my rough talk, but I didn't feel like it. I felt like staying mad.

"Mike," Felice said softly.

"Yeah?"

"It's Clo, isn't it? It always has been. Oh, Mike, why did you marry me? It must have been hard—hard for you, I mean."

"Woman," I said, when I could speak at all. "You are out of your mind."

But she shook her head. "You know I'm not," she told me.

I opened my mouth to say something, but she beat me to it. "I don't suppose it's ever occurred to you that I might get tired of playing second fiddle—oh, not to anybody else! Not even Clo. Just to some crazy dream that never had an earthly chance of coming true!"

If there was an answer to that, I didn't know what it was. But I tried. "Since you're talking about Clo," I said, "it's true that I had a bad case on her once—puppy love, I guess you'd call it. But that's long over."

Felice laughed, a thin, silvery sound like ice in a glass. "Oh, Mike, you do try so hard! You're so honest—*policeman* honest—in all the things that don't count! Goodnight, Mike, I'm going to bed."

She stood up and reached for my gun. I suppose she was going to put it back behind the clock, but I jumped.

"Lay off that!" I barked. "You could hurt yourself with that thing!"

Felice gave it to me, but after she'd gone into the bedroom I sat there holding it, my hand slippery with sweat. I'd better find another place for it, someplace she didn't even know about. If she got hurt, I'd never forgive myself—never. I ended up by putting it on a shelf in the china closet, behind the wedding plates we never used, and turned the key in the lock of the glass door.

I was too stirred up to feel like sleeping, so I went out on the *galerie* and smoked a while, looking up and down the bayou where the lights were winking out one by one. Clo was up there somewhere, living on the campboat with the old people, the way she did when we were kids.

I strolled along the old footpath that was seldom used these days. There was a new paved road lying behind the houses, running all the way from the Gulf. You could make time on that road with a motorcycle or a squad car, but it was just as useful for a fast getaway—

That's what I was thinking when I saw the headlights of a big car that came roaring down toward the coast. I was surprised when it pulled up short and a voice came to me from between two old Cajun houses that were pretty much like my own.

" 'Allo, you there—Mike! Mike Logan!"

All the blood in me turned cool and slow, sluggish as the dark stream of the bayou beside me. I'd known it all my life, that voice. It belonged to Vince Savoy.

"'Allo yourself," I said. I didn't have to yell because there he was already, out of the car and coming towards me, tall and thin and swaggering, like the great old pirate Jean Lafitte himself. It was the first I'd seen him in a couple of years.

We didn't shake hands, and somehow that bothered me. There was a little matter of mayhem and murder, sure, and me assigned to tail him from here to hell and back, on account of I was a trooper and he was a crook—but for some reason that didn't stack up very high at the moment. Damn it, I was glad to see him! Still and all, I didn't hold out my hand, and neither did he. Presently the feeling flickered out between us like a tallow candle at the grave of something dead and gone.

"Are you lookin' for me, Mike?" Vince said. His voice sounded light and kind of jeering, like a mockingbird.

"I'm lookin' for you, all right," I said. "But it don't do me much good at the moment. As you very well know."

He laughed. "Man, don't I just! Would I be here if I had fresh blood on my hands?"

"Probably not," I said. "But keep lookin' over your shoulder, boy. I'll be there some day, right behind you."

I couldn't see his face, only the gleam of his strange, light-colored eyes. Maybe he was smiling, but I couldn't prove that either. "Thanks for the tip, Mike. I'll bear it in mind. Where are you headin'?"

"I'm not," I told him. "Just ramblin' along, lookin' around."

But he seemed to want to toss the ball back and forth, just for kicks. "An evenin' stroll, eh?" Vince said. "For instance, you didn't know that Clo's folks have got their campboat tied up a short piece from here, up the bayou?"

"What's it to me? I've got nothin' on her either."

"That's right, you haven't," he said thoughtfully. "They've worked her over at headquarters already. I guess you know that."

"Well, you guess wrong," I snapped. I was getting mad now.

"They'd no business doing that. What's she got to do with the crazy way you act?"

"Not a thing," Vince told me smoothly. "They found that out. She made like them three monkeys—no talk, no hear, no see. You know Clo."

"How is Clo?" I said, to be saying something. And there was a long silence between us, heavy as lead.

"I wouldn't know," he said finally. "She won't talk to me. So long, Mike—see you around." And he was heading back to his car before I could speak again. I stood there staring after him and the haze of light and dust that kept getting smaller as he burned up the new road at ninety or more. The fool thought came into my head that it would be tough luck if he got pulled in for speeding. Then my mind switched back to Clo.

So she wouldn't talk to him. But why would he tell *me* that?

The answer was right there. I couldn't miss it. The four of us had grown up together, he and I, and Clo and Felice. It wouldn't have crossed his mind to lie to me about a personal matter like that. He still believed I was his friend. It doesn't make me feel any better, let me tell you that.

They say there's nothing like an uneasy conscience to turn a man uglier than he is already. I was sure in no mood to go home. I felt stubborn, mean, and I started walking again, only this time I knew where I was going. I'd been assigned to the Savoy case, hadn't I? That meant keeping tabs on the two of them, didn't it? Okay. That's what I was doing.

The old campboat was tied up under a tent of long gray moss that hung down from a big, black cypress. I was standing in the shadow of it when I saw her come out of the deckhouse and look towards me, shielding her eyes against the glare of the deck light.

"Who's there?" she asked sharply.

I went forward, afraid of the change I'd see in her. She was wearing a green dress cinched in at the waist and a flowery apron over it. Her figure was a little fuller, that's all. Maybe richer is a better word. Her dark hair lifted in the light breeze and blew across her forehead just the way it used to, and her feet were bare.

"Mike!" she cried, and she sounded glad. "Oh, Mike, it's been such a long time!'' She ran to me as I stepped over the low deckrail, but not all the way. I saw the quick color whip into her face as she checked herself. "I came close to hugging you," she told me, smiling. "But that would never do. What would Felice say?"

"Likewise Vince," I said, and the tone of it was none too pleasant. "How're things with you, Clo?"

"As if you didn't know," she said. Her face changed. A look of sadness came over it. "You won't ask me any questions, will you, Mike? They tried that at headquarters. It didn't work."

"I'm off duty," I said. There was no such thing as being off duty on a case like this, and she knew it, but she let it go by.

"Will you take some coffee, Mike? For old times' sake? The old folks have gone to church, so I'm alone."

"Just a drop, maybe," I said. "Then I'll be on my way."

Well, the busybodies had lied about her coffee. It was hot and strong enough to stand alone. I tossed it off, knowing I'd best get out of there fast. The crazy dream Felice had been talking about wasn't just a dream any more. Clo was near enough now for me to feel the warmth of her and the darkness around us rocked with the sweet smell of oleander. Not far off a bull gator bellowed and threshed in the slow water, sending a little scurry of ripples along the side of the boat. Clo shivered, wrapping her arms about herself like a kid that feels cold or scared.

"You know, I'd forgotten—" Clo said softly. "I'd forgotten it was so beautiful back here—and so *awful*—"

She was scared! It was a real shock to me. I'd seen her mad when we were kids, spitting mad and ready to take out her spite on anybody, the same as Vince. But I'd never seen a look of fear on her face before.

I was so close to reaching for her that I took a step back and hit the deckhouse wall. A kind of rank bitterness welled up in me. "You like it better in Roux City with the neon signs and the jukeboxes, eh?" I said. "Well, why don't you go back to him? You won't be seeing much of him when he starts doing time."

"Mike, don't *talk* like that!"

"Like what? I'm up to the nose myself with muskrats and mosquitoes. Maybe I'll give the job a heave and stake myself to a lugger

and a stretch of clean salt water. I always thought I had the makings
of a jumbo man—"

"Stop—please . . . stop!" She grabbed my arm hard and her small
fingers felt like the claws of a bird. "That's the way *he* used to talk!
And where did it get us? You and Felice would end up the way
we—we—" Her voice broke in a dry little sob. "He's changed so,
Mike. You've no idea! But you don't just stop loving people."

"That's a fact," I said. Before I knew it my arm went around
her, pulling her close to me, and she buried her face in my shoulder
and cried and cried. So help me, there was nothing worse in me at
that moment than pity for her.

Finally she pulled away, lifting her apron to mop up the tears.
"I'll never go back to him, Mike. But I left everything behind me,
all my clothes, everything—" her voice trailed off and I knew that
she was thinking about her things too. Women are funny. Even Felice, with that old shirt she kept mending and never could bring
herself to throw away.

"Well," I said. "I'll be on my way."

"Don't get mad, Mike," Clo said, very low. "You're sore and
unhappy, I know. Honest, I *know*. There's never been anybody but
Vince for me, but if there was, if there ever could be. . . ." She
stopped.

That was more than I could take.

I grabbed her by the shoulders and shook her until her head fell
back and she set her teeth in her lip to keep from crying out. "You
can't devil me like that! If it was anybody but him, who would
it be—who?"

The answer was so soft I hardly caught it. "You, Mike—you."

I let go of her. I knew I'd go crazy if I didn't. But I was past being
polite, or even careful. "Suppose he two-timed you? What then?"

She looked as if I'd run a knife into her. "He'd better not," she
said quietly. "I'd cut his heart out. The same as he would mine."

I cursed myself for a dumb ox. I'd come close to telling her about
the other woman. I was getting as bad as Dubois. But there was one
more thing to be said, so I said it. "If I can pin anything on him,
Clo, I'll pick him up. But I won't hurt him—not if I can help it."

She nodded without saying anything, and I climbed over the side of the campboat, stepping carefully over the wet mud so I wouldn't sprawl on my face in front of her.

Then I went on home.

After that night I tried to put Clo out of my mind for good. But she was in my blood. It was worst of all when I was with Felice. There was kind of a wall between us, and it shamed me to find I couldn't beat it.

You don't just stop loving people, Clo had said. That's the truth. But there was more to it than that. You don't lie to somebody you love, either, and I loved my wife.

I tried to make it up to her in little ways, like the bunch of store-bought roses I had sent from town for her birthday, and the king-size box of pralines I had shipped over from N.O., and I talked her into spending a few extra bucks on something new and pretty to wear. But I couldn't forget what she'd said that night about "all the things that don't count," and the hurt was there in her eyes, no matter how hard she tried to hide it.

Meanwhile, Vince kept himself out of sight. He didn't need to, as far as headquarters was concerned. He wasn't even on the "wanted" list. But I was curious. Then the word got around that he'd left the parish altogether and I figured he had some big job lined up and wanted to be far, far away when they pulled it off. As it turned out, I was right. Vince had a good organization.

It was Dubois who picked up the information that Vince was having himself a time in New Orleans, and that he had taken a woman along with him. No, not Clo. The other one.

"You can't pick him up for that," I said.

"Maybe not, but she's madder than a wet hen," Dubois told me, happy to be in the know. "Savoy gave her the air again. That's twice, now. She's ready to talk."

"Don't make me laugh," I said, burying my nose in a pint of beer. "If that baby had anything on Vince, he wouldn't let her out of his sight."

But Dubois had dreamed up a different angle. "This doll wants to be friendly," he explained. "If anything breaks, she'd be on the side of the law."

"That's the place to be," I said. "Is something going to break?"

"There's one person who might know." Dubois leaned across the bar and scooped himself a handful of boiled shrimp, feeding them into his face slowly, one by one. It made me feel kind of sick.

"Okay," I asked. "Who?"

"Mrs. Savoy," he said, grinning.

I had to hold down my right fist hard to keep from pasting him one. "I told you before, she won't squawk." But Dubois continued.

"Not even if this other dame gets to her with a lot of stuff about Savoy, personal stuff that only another woman would know?"

"You slimy slug," I said to my trusty sidekick. "You dirty—"

"Hold it!" Dubois gulped down the last shrimp and backed away from me. "This doll hit town an hour ago and I just got through dropping her at the campboat to pay a call on Savoy's wife. What's the harm in that?"

I shoved past him and headed home, sick as a pup. But I still didn't believe it would work. Clo wouldn't talk—I'd have bet my soul on it. She'd find some other way to get even, maybe, but not that!

When I got home I found the place a litter of boxes and white tissue paper and Felice trying on the new stuff she'd bought on a shopping trip to town that afternoon. It looked as if she'd bought out a store, and I almost said so, habit being what it is.

Her eyes were bright and her cheeks pink with excitement as she held the things up in front of her, showing them off to me. There was a real pretty dress with bright flowers all over it, and a yellow one with a big skirt that stood out like a dancing girl's, and she'd had something done to her hair. It was shorter and curled around her face. She'd bought shoes, and a lot of underwear, some plain, some kind of lacy. I stood there gawking while I felt my face get red and the queer, sick feeling grew in the pit of my stomach. I remembered the times I'd wished she'd do something like this—fix herself up a little, make like life was more worth living—I don't know how to say it even now.

The thing was, it was too late! She looked pretty as a valentine, but nothing stirred in me. Nothing. And she knew it. I suppose a woman always does.

I saw the color drain out of her face and she started folding the things up and tucking them away in the tissue paper without looking at me. "Silly—silly—" I heard her whisper to herself, as if I weren't even there, and then she went off into the bedroom and put the boxes away on a high shelf in the closet.

"Aren't you going to wear them?" I said gruffly. "Honey—?"

But the bedroom door banged in my face and presently I heard the creak of bedsprings and the muffled sound of her sobbing. But I didn't go and try to comfort her. I knew I'd make a mess of it. Instead I went into the kitchen and broke out the bottle of bourbon we kept for company and went to work on that, cussin' myself.

That was a long night. I stayed out on the *galerie*, smoking, my head thick with drink and disgust with myself and with Dubois, wondering what had happened on the campboat between Clo and that other woman of Savoy's. I wouldn't have put it past Clo to kill her if the notion took her. Even that didn't seem as bad as Clo there facing up to scolding chatter of the old folks, Clo with her pride smashed, living out her days in the ruins of it. . . . But there didn't seem to be any police action indicated that night, so I finished the bottle.

Next day headquarters filled me in. Dubois had picked up Savoy's ex-doll, crying, but all in one piece, when Clo put her off the camp-boat. She was having second thoughts and now she wanted protective custody. She didn't say whether she was scared of Vince or Clo, but we obliged by locking her up. It brightened up the old jailhouse a good deal for a few days. Then we forgot about her.

The fuse had been lit for the biggest bank robbery the state had ever seen, and it blew up right in our faces, vault and all, netting close to two hundred grand. As usual, there wasn't a jot of evidence to connect it with Vince Savoy.

Two cashiers were killed, both women. Likewise the president of the bank, who was seventy-one, and his favorite grandson, aged nine, who was playing checkers with grandpa in the private office at the time. All four were tossed through the plate glass window into the street. It looked like a massacre, which it was.

We were all put to work on it, every trooper that wasn't nailed down, and pretty soon the F.B.I. came swarming in, with press, radio, and TV right on their tail.

We put Savoy's ex-dollie over the hurdles once more, but she was a complete washout and we let her go, limp as a dishrag and still whimpering for police protection.

Then it was Clo's turn again. We still didn't have anything on her, or Vince, and when we asked her to stop by headquarters for a small chat, she came.

It was the same old story. Nothing. But when I saw her coming out afterward her face told me that she might know plenty. Horror and despair were cut deeply into it, and the look in those great, dark Cajun eyes was a look out of hell.

She went past me without a word.

I could be wrong, I thought. Maybe it was the mark that woman left on her, with her dirty tales about Vince. Maybe the bank job was as much of a surprise to Clo as it was to the bank. But something made me go after her.

The street was shaded by big trees and when she moved from one black shadow to the next it looked as if she'd gone underground. I walked faster and caught up with her.

"What do you want, Mike?" she asked, not even turning her head.

"Mostly I want you to know I had no part in that lousy deal."

She pulled away from the hand I laid on her arm, but not before I felt the chill of her flesh. "That woman? No, Mike, I know you didn't."

Then suddenly she started running. I never knew a girl who could move so fast. She always could when she was a skinny little kid, high-stepping it through the marshes like a heron. Where was she heading now?

Dubois pulled up alongside me in his old jalopy and I got in. "You want us to chase her?" Dubois asked me, every inch the trooper.

"You try that," I said, "and I'll kick your brains out. Run me home."

I felt in my bones that Vince Savoy was the one we wanted, but there wasn't a crack in the big silence that wrapped up his whole organization. I kept thinking he'd come back and answer the headquarters call for routine questioning, the way he had in that silver payroll job a long time ago. Having been a trooper himself, he knew all the right answers, and it sure would look better for him if he showed up of his own accord. But he didn't.

Meanwhile the public was getting pretty wrought up about the kid who'd died. They wanted some kind of police action, any kind, but fast.

It felt like a storm building up. You can smell it and feel it and see it in the queer light over everything, but you never know how bad it's going to be until it hits, and then maybe it's too late. That's how things were the night I got the call from Roux City.

There was a strong wind brewing in the Gulf, driving inland in gusts that churned up the sluggish water of the bayou, but it didn't budge the heavy heat that hung over everything like steam.

Felice had a lot of nice cold stuff ready for the table, nothing hot except the coffee. We were in the middle of supper when the phone rang. "I'll get it—" Felice said. But after she did her voice turned cold as the food on the plates. "It's Clo, Mike."

It was Clo all right, her voice thick and queerly choked. "Mike, I'm back in the house in Roux City."

"That's nice," I said sarcastically. "That's dandy. Am I the first to know?"

"No—no—it's not what you think—" She was close to crying. "I only came back to get some of my things. There's nobody here but me. I've got to see you, Mike—now, tonight! Please, please . . ."

"Okay," I said. "I'll be there." I hung up and turned to find Felice standing close by, her eyes dark with hurt and something that looked like fear.

"You're not going?" she whispered. "What right does she have to call you like that? Don't go, Mike."

"It's my job," I said flatly. "You know that."

"*Clo?* Clo's part of your job?"

"You know she is! You married a trooper," I reminded her.

Felice called something after me, but I didn't hear what it was as I took the front steps three at a time on my way to headquarters to connect with a motorcycle, and less than an hour later I rolled into Roux City on the tail end of a rain squall that flooded the streets.

I found the address of the Savoy house in my notebook. I'd put a red ring around it the day I got my assignment and now the ink ran under the rain, leaving a red smear on the page and on my fingers.

The house stood out from the junk heaps around it like a dimestore diamond in a can of bait. Too flashy for my taste, but it wasn't my house. I ran the bike around to the side and parked it behind some bushes. Then I went to the front door and rang the bell.

That's when I got my first jolt. My hand went back to where my gun ought to be, and wasn't. It flashed over me that that's what Felice had called after me when I left. I'd forgotten it again. I'm one fine trooper.

The door opened and Clo stood there. "You got here fast, Mike."

"That's what you wanted," I said, looking around. It was quite a place. Better furniture than I ever saw outside of a catalogue; lamps and bright colored rugs and drapes that hung all the way down to the floor. I whistled. "Say, this is something."

She nodded. "Vince likes to live good. I used to, too, when I thought it was on the up and up."

"Come off it," I said. "Don't tell me you thought he struck oil?"

I was looking her over now, thinking she was like one of those movie queens that look as if they don't care if they get caught in the rain. She had on a little short black dress with no sleeves to it, and no makeup. Her hair was slicked back, showing every line and bone of her face, dead white, the eyes half shut and the mouth narrowed down to a thin line. She didn't seem like the girl on the campboat with dark hair blowing in the wind. This was somebody strange. She looked as if she'd just been pulled out of the river.

"You need a drink," she said, quietly. "It's still bourbon, isn't it?"

"Thanks." I took the drink she held out to me. "Why did you want to see me?"

She curled up on the big sofa, her long legs drawn up under her. "Sit down, Mike—no, here beside me—that's better—" And then, "This is your big break, Mike. I'm telling all I know."

"You're lyin'," I said. "This is some kind of runaround."

She shook her head slowly. "No. You still haven't got anything on him, I know that. But you will have when I tell you what I know."

I stared at her. No shame, nothing but a kind of frozen pain.

"Why the switch?" I asked her finally. "When they had you down at headquarters, you wouldn't talk. I don't get it."

She had her hands twisted together in her lap, tight enough to hurt, and her eyes kind of veered off mine for a second. "That child—that little boy in the bank—Vince shouldn't have let that happen."

So that was it. Or was it?

"Who says he did?" I said carefully.

"He planned that bank job," she told me. "He worked on it for months. I thought it was just another of his crazy schemes. Vince always has to have something cooking . . ." She stopped.

There was that look again, the one I'd seen on her when she came out of headquarters. That look of the damned.

"You're sure that's what's eatin' you?" I asked her. It wasn't nice, but I had to know. "You're sure it's the bank job that's botherin' you and not that other doll he's been carryin' on with?"

"I—I don't know what you mean." It was hardly a whisper, hardly a sound at all.

"I think you do. You told me that night on the campboat that you'd cut his heart out if he two-timed you. That's what you're doin'. And you know what he'll do to you if you rat on him."

"Why shouldn't I?" she cried out. "He killed everything I ever felt for him. *Why shouldn't I?*"

"Take it easy," I said, putting my big paw over her locked fingers, trying to warm the ice out of them. "You don't have to be the one to sell him out. Some day we'll catch him dropping slugs in a pay phone and that'll be it. We can't miss."

"You can—you can!" she almost screamed at me. "While you're playing cops and robbers, he'll do something worse!"

"Okay, okay, take it easy."

She sat quiet for a long minute, that look frozen on her face, while a dull ugly anger rose up in me and I choked on it. I thought, it's still Vince, Vince, Vince—!

When she started talking again I was slow to tune in.

"—I guess you're right, Mike. I can't do it, after all. I thought I could when I phoned you, but now it's all died out inside me. I'm glad you came, though. I did want to see you again, just one more time.''

She leaned back against the cushions, looking at me with those big dark eyes, and the hard whiteness of her face seemed to soften a little. There was a kind of sweetness about her now. Maybe it was remembering old times, I don't know. But it took the breath out of me. When she held out both hands to me I thought for a flash that maybe I had it doped right, that she felt the same about me as I had about her, for half of our lives.

Her hands were still cold and shaking when I took them, but not for long. She came into my arms with a sob, like a tired kid coming home, and the warmth and sweetness of her overwhelmed me. I couldn't have stopped myself if I'd tried, and nobody could have stopped me.

What happened between us in that fine flashy house of Savoy's that night was like the old dream come true. We didn't stay there in the living room long. I lifted her up and carried her into a big dim bedroom next to it, and once, when she turned her face away from mine for a moment, wondered if she was remembering him. But it was too late then.

It wasn't long before Clo fell asleep. She lay curled up on the big bed like a ten-year-old, with one hand under her cheek and her dark hair spread out on the pillow. I didn't remember any crying, but there were tears on her cheeks.

I pulled the silk spread partly over her before I went into the bathroom, leaving the door open a crack.

I heard Vince when he set his key in the front door and the slam of it after him. Queer as it seems, at a time like that, my first thought was that he'd played it smart—he'd come back for questioning.

He came straight through to the bedroom, shoving his keys back into his pocket. Then he saw Clo and stopped short.

It was plain that the last thing on earth he expected was seeing her there. At first he looked surprised and glad, but then his face turned dark. It's hard to put it, but the place wasn't neat—the way it would have been if she'd been alone. He knew.

Vince's right hand slid back to his gun just as I swung open the bathroom door and came out. He rocked back a step and swung the

gun around to cover me. "So it's you! Stay where you are, Mike!"
He nodded towards the bed. "Who was with her?"

"Me," I said.

I was watching him close and I saw what was in his mind. I dived
into him. There was that one lunge and a jab or two before we
locked, but it wasn't me he wanted. He was holding his gun arm
free, but not for me. The gun exploded and we both stood there
staring at what he'd done. She never even woke up.

The room started swinging around me and there was a thick, roaring noise inside my head. When I could speak, I said, "Okay, Vince.
It's my turn. Get it over."

He laughed. If you could call it a laugh. It was more like the snarl
of a dog that's been kicked in the belly. He was kind of bent over,
looking up at me out of the tops of his eyes, and I saw then that he
was gone—all gone. The craziness that used to come and go in those
queer light eyes of his had moved in to stay.

"There's no hurry about you, Mike. I'd as soon see you sweat
a while."

He went over to the bed and pulled up the spread to cover the
horror and ruin of Clo's face. As he did, I dived again. This time
the gun fell to the floor at my feet. When I picked it up, all the fight
went out of him. It must have been some kind of reflex. He shook
his head a couple of times, as if it needed that to clear it.

"Man, oh man," Vince said, "I wouldn't want to be in your
shoes. No, sirree. You've got to go on living—maybe for a long,
long time."

I motioned him into the front room and called headquarters.

When I put down the phone Vince asked me for a smoke. I shook
a couple loose in the pack and he broke out a fancy lighter, gold.
We sat there smoking until we heard the screech of the sirens.

Later, when they had him booked, I asked him if he wanted anything and he said, "Hell, no. Not any more."

"You could put up an argument," I said. "The unwritten law, all
that stuff. I wouldn't contest it."

He even smiled a little. "Thanks just as much, Mike. Say hello
to Felice." He turned his back to me. But when I was leaving he
swung around on his heels and stopped me. "Don't get the notion

Clo was in love with you," he snarled. "There was another dame and Clo found out about her. It was a spite job! You hear me? A spite job!"

"Sure," I said. If it made him feel any better to think that, okay. Me, I wasn't so sure.

At the trial Vince clammed up completely. He wouldn't tell them anything they wanted to know about his organization, but it will come out sooner or later. Without him it will fall apart, and a few prominent citizens are going to start doing time along with the hoods. It's just a question of when.

He wouldn't defend himself against the murder charge either. He said he killed her, that's all. He wouldn't say why. Vince wasn't the kind of man to tell the world his wife had cheated on him. He left that job to me.

It was in my official report, all of it. What else could I do from inside a uniform? I'm a policeman.

They grilled me for three days in the back room at headquarters, hoping against hope that there was some terrible mistake. But when all was said and done, I was the fair-haired trooper who'd picked up Vince Savoy on a charge that would stick. They settled on some kind of disciplinary action "to be determined later."

What worried me sick was Felice. She'd stuck by me through it all, tight-lipped and dry-eyed. But she never said a word. Felice isn't much of a talker.

The old dream died with Clo, the "crazy dream that never had an earthly chance of coming true." It's my job now to make up to Felice for the hurt I've given her, to prove I love her in the ways that count.

THE THEFT OF THE BALD MAN'S COMB

by EDWARD D. HOCH

It had been more than a year since Nick Velvet's last encounter with Sandra Paris, a thief whom some found more audacious than Nick himself. Using the name of the White Queen, and the Wonderland motto *Impossible things before breakfast*, she had carved a niche for herself in the world of bizarre crime. The rivalry between Sandra Paris and Nick had settled down to an amiable understanding, with a conscious effort to avoid each other's territory. Thus it was a bit of a surprise when she invited him to join her for breakfast at the Waffle House on Route 22.

"Good morning, Sandra," Nick greeted her, sliding into the red plastic booth. "You're looking as charming as ever."

She smiled in return. "A compliment, this early in the morning!"

"That's when you're at your best, isn't it? Before breakfast?" He glanced at the menu and then tossed it aside. "What've you been doing with yourself? I haven't seen any mention in the papers lately."

"In our profession we work best without publicity. You know that, Nick." They ordered breakfast from a pert waitress and over orange juice she continued, "I want to hire you for a job."

"That's a bit unusual, isn't it? After you called me in on that museum business—"

"This is different. A woman has approached me with a very good

195

offer. I find I cannot fulfill the commission, yet I hate to turn down the money and admit to failure.''

"Suppose you tell me the whole story, Sandra, from the beginning.''

"This is in a southern state, back in the hills. You'll get the exact location if you agree to take on the assignment. The woman who contacted me hired me to steal a comb—''

"Something valuable?''

"No, just an ordinary pocket comb that a man carries around with him.''

"Who is the man?''

"His name is Willie Franklin. He and his two brothers live in the remotest part of the hill country. He rarely ventures into town at all. Some say he operates a still and that's why he stays out of sight.''

"Do they have illegal stills these days? It sounds like something from thirty or forty years ago.''

"Whatever he's doing, he stays out of sight. He and his brothers are said to live in an abandoned water mill on the Casaqueek River. I drove down there last week, Nick.'' She leaned forward across the table, more lovely and intense than he'd ever seen her before. "That's a man's country. The women—well, maybe they're not barefoot and pregnant but they might as well be. As soon as I drove into town the word was all over the county. I went up to the mill to look around early one morning—''

"Before breakfast.''

"Sure, before breakfast! All I got for my trouble was a couple of rifle shots that came so close I could feel the breeze. Back in town someone let the air out of my tires, and the next morning I found a dead dog in the backseat of my car. That was enough for me!''

"So you want to subcontract the job.''

"I never thought I'd say this, Nick, but it takes a man. There's no way I could pull it off, even if I went down there wearing a beard and a peg leg.''

"How much?''

"Your regular fee.''

"How much are *you* getting, Sandra?''

She pressed her lips together. "Fifty,'' she said quietly.

"I'll take forty.''

"What? Your usual fee is only—"

"You need me, don't you?"

"I need you," she admitted. "Forty it is."

"Now tell me about the man with the comb. What's he look like?"

"Willie Franklin. He's the oldest of the brothers. All I saw was a group photo of the boys taken at their mother's seventieth birthday party last year. I have it here."

She passed Nick a color snapshot of three men in patterned shirts and jeans, squinting into the sun. The one in the middle was completely bald, with no facial hair. The one on the right wore a neatly trimmed mustache, while the other had a full beard that obscured much of his face. "The bearded one is the youngest," Sandra explained. "He's Jud Franklin, in his late twenties. On the right is Jessie. He's maybe thirty-five. Willie is in the middle."

"The bald one?" Nick asked incredulously.

Sandra Paris sighed. "That's right. I want you to steal a comb from a bald man."

Two days later Nick Velvet flew south to the Casaqueek Hills, renting a car at the airport for the final portion of the journey. He'd considered making the entire trip by car, but decided his New York license plates would attract too much attention in the southern hill country.

West Alum, the place he sought, was little more than a crossroads by the Casaqueek River, with a bar, a general store, a volunteer fire company, and a small church occupying the four corners. Nick assumed there'd been an East Alum at one time across the rickety wooden bridge, but there was no sign of it now. He parked in the cinder lot next to the bar and went inside. It was as good a place to start as any.

The bartender was a middle-aged man named André whom Nick suspected might have drifted up to West Alum from the Cajun country to the south. "Just passing through?" he asked, setting a glass and a bottle of beer in front of Nick.

"Looking for the Franklin family, actually. Drove over from the state capital to settle an insurance claim they've had outstanding."

"The old lady lives up the Post Road. Take the first right over the bridge. It's on the left, about a half-mile up the road."

"Are the sons up there too?"

"Sometimes. Mostly not. They're up in the hills somewhere. The old lady has a black handyman stays with her."

"Mr. Franklin is deceased?"

"Died of cancer a long time ago."

Nick finished his beer and went back to the car. Down the road a bit he could see the sign for the motel where Sandra Paris had stayed. At the risk of getting a dead dog in his car too, he drove down and took a room for the night. Then he returned to the bridge and headed up to the Franklin place.

It proved to be a few acres on the side of a hill, with a tethered German shepherd that started growling as soon as he pulled up in front of the farmhouse. A short white-haired woman came to the door and called him off, then asked Nick, "What you want?"

"I'm looking for a . . . Willie Franklin," Nick told her, pretending to consult some papers from a briefcase he was carrying. "It's about an insurance claim."

"That's my son Willie. My oldest. Don't know anything about no insurance claim, though."

"Mrs. Franklin—"

"I'm Cassy. Everyone calls me Cassy." She smiled when she said it, and he could see the remnants of beauty there, even at the age of seventy-one.

"Well, Cassy, is your son at home?"

"Willie don't live here. He has a place over the hill with his brothers."

"Could you give me directions?"

"He's not friendly toward visitors. I never been there myself."

"He'll be friendly toward me. I have a check covering storm damage to his mill."

"Damage to the mill?" She frowned at that, trying to understand. "He never mentioned anything to me." A strand of white hair drifted over her face and she pushed it away.

"It was fairly minor. He probably didn't want to bother you. Is this mill on your property?"

"No, it's"—she waved her hand toward the crest of the hill—
"over there someplace."

"You see, I need his signature before I can deliver the check.
That's why I couldn't simply mail it."

"Maybe Gus can help you," she suggested, waving toward a tall
black man who'd just appeared around the corner of the house. "Gus,
this gentleman is looking for Willie. See if you can help him. I have
to take Lucky inside."

Gus's hair was almost as white as hers, though Nick judged his
age to be no more than sixty. His skin was relatively light, but the
hair, lips, and general features left no doubt as to his race. He appeared to have spent a lifetime working outdoors. "What can I do
for you?" he asked.

"I'm Nicholas, from State Liability and Life Insurance. I have a
check for Willie Franklin, but I need his signature. Could you show
me the way to his place?"

"The boys don't like visitors."

"Oh, they'll like me!"

Gus thought about that. "They've been known to shoot at
strangers."

"Not if you're along." He reached for his wallet. "Look, I'm so
anxious to get this matter settled that it's worth ten bucks if you can
take me up there."

He shrugged. "I'll take you. Leave the car here. The shortest way
is up over the hill."

Nick locked the car and set off on foot with the tall black man,
climbing up hill to a point where they could gaze on the meander-
ing route of the river through two counties. "It's quite a sight,"
Nick said.

"It's nice like this in the spring, with all the new growth on
the trees."

"You've probably seen a lot of springs here."

Gus turned to him. "Been with Mr. and Mrs. Franklin most of
my life. They only had the one child when I came."

"What happened to Mr. Franklin?"

"Died of cancer about fifteen years back. She's been alone since
then. I do what I can, but the boys don't help much."

"She never had a daughter?"

The black man shook his head. "There was another son, Tom, but he took off when he was seventeen. Went out west somewhere, I hear."

"When was that?"

"Twelve years, maybe. He's between Jessie and Jud in age. Yeah, I've seen them all."

"But the boys don't come home much anymore."

"They like livin' up at the old mill. Willie and his mother don't get along, and none of them ever got married."

"It happens in the best of families."

They hiked a bit farther in silence, until another bend in the river became visible far below. "There it is," Gus said, pointing a bony finger. Nick could see a large building constructed of brown timbers, set at the edge of the water. The window frames were painted white and an unmoving mill wheel was orange. Though the building belonged to another era, some effort had been made to brighten it up. As they started down the hill through a stand of trees, Nick glimpsed a figure moving out the door of the mill. Almost at once they heard the crack of a rifle being fired.

Nick dropped to the ground but Gus merely laughed. "You're not used to country ways. If he was shootin' at us he'd have come a lot closer than that. It was just a warning because he don't know who we are."

He went out to the edge of the trees, shouting and waving his hands. Nick could see the bearded man with the rifle now—that would be Jud, the youngest—putting down his weapon and going back inside. If they weren't to be shot, they weren't exactly being greeted, either.

It took them another ten minutes to make their way down the steep hillside to the mill. Up close the building was more dilapidated than Nick had thought earlier. Even the bright paint around the windows was chipped and peeling.

Two of the brothers came out to greet them. Jud reclaimed the rifle he had leaned against the wall, but said nothing. The other, with a mustache and bright blue eyes like his mother, asked, "Who's this you've brought us, Gus?"

"He's an insurance man with a check for Willie. For damage to the mill."

The brothers exchanged puzzled looks. "There's no damage to the mill."

"Storm damage," Nick added quickly. "A claim was filed. Perhaps your mother filed it and doesn't remember. I'm Mr. Nicholas from State Liability and Life—"

"See if Willie knows about this," Jessie told his younger brother. Jud went off, taking the rifle with him.

Gus was shifting uneasily from one foot to the other. "I gotta get back to your mom," he told Jessie. "She'll wonder where I am."

Jessie turned his pale blue eyes toward Nick. "Can you find your way back, Mr. Nicholas?"

"I think so."

"Go ahead then, Gus. We'll see you around."

As the black man started doggedly up the hill, Jessie smiled. "Moves damn well for his age. Gettin' toward seventy, Gus is."

"He looks younger."

"Handsome man in his day. We always thought he was on the run from something, else why spend his life up here?"

"It's nice country," Nick observed. There was a slight odor in the air that he couldn't quite place. He wondered what an illegal still smelled like.

Jud came back then, still carrying the rifle. "He don't know anything about insurance, and there hasn't been any damage. He says it's a mistake."

Nick took the check from his briefcase. "Here it is, all signed and legal. Three hundred and fifty-four dollars in full payment of the claim. All I need is his signature."

Jessie reached out his hand. "I'll take that up to Willie and get him to sign for it. He can't leave his job right now."

"What's he doing that's so important?"

"Business. We all have our business, don't we?"

"I'm sorry, but the release has to be signed in my presence. I have to verify his signature."

They seemed to have reached an impasse. The brothers stepped inside the door and did some whispering. Finally the older one, Jessie, came out and said, "Follow me."

Nick entered the building, with the younger brother bringing up the rear. The main floor of the mill had been converted into reasonably comfortable living quarters, with a television set and a rack of rifles and shotguns for hunting. The windows overlooked the river, with a convenient kitchen and dining area at the other end of the big room. There was no indication of any female presence.

Jessie led the way up an open wooden stairway to the second floor. Nick could see doorways to separate bedrooms and a bath that occupied one side of the building. The other side was occupied by some sort of large storeroom, and Nick caught only a glimpse of it as Jessie opened the door. "Willie, you got a second?"

A beefy bald man came out to join them. He glanced at Nick with something close to contempt. "Why'd you bring him up here?"

"He has to see you sign for the check. He just wouldn't go away."

The big man grunted and extended his hand. "Willie Franklin. You got business with me?"

Nick shook hands and extended a business card. "A claim was filed for storm damage—"

"There's no damage."

"Perhaps your mother filed it and forgot."

"This ain't her property."

"Look, I just need your signature and the money's yours. I want to be on my way."

Nick guessed the bald man to be around forty, though his size and baldness added years. He took the check and the release form and studied them carefully. Nick didn't believe in cheating people while he was robbing them. The check was drawn on an account that had exactly three hundred and fifty-four dollars in it.

"We'll have to ask Mom about it," Jessie suggested.

Willie Franklin's face broadened into a smile. "Hell, can't look a gift horse in the mouth, as they say. Who's got a pen?" Nick purposely refrained from offering his own, and Willie finally reached into his pocket. He was wearing an old pair of army fatigue pants with the deep patch pockets and his meaty hand came out like a claw machine holding a number of objects. Nick caught a quick glimpse of a small black pocket comb before it dropped back out of sight. Franklin held a cheap ballpoint, with which he carefully signed his name. "That satisfy you?"

"Fine, fine." Nick handed over the check. "I'll be on my way, then."

"Not so fast," Jud said. "How do we know he's not a cop, come to look over the place?"

Willie Franklin frowned. "Sheriff Garvey's got no reason to bug us."

"I'm just an insurance man," Nick tried to reassure them. "If you fellows are making a little home brew on the side, it's nothing to me."

They all laughed at that and Willie waved his hand. "Go on, get out. Don't try to come back, though. We keep watch day and night. Hate to mistake you for a deer."

As Nick clambered over the rough terrain on his way back to Cassy Franklin's house, he heard the crack of a shot and the snipping of branches far overhead. The bullet hadn't been meant to hit him. It was just the good old boys sending him on his way.

The first thing Nick did upon reaching his motel was to phone Sandra Paris back in New York. When her voice came on the line he said, "I'm having difficulties. Nothing serious, but it would help a great deal if I could speak with the woman who hired you."

"Why is that necessary?"

"I went over to the mill today. The experience was about as you described it. Those boys are fast with a gun, and I'd like to know how serious they are."

"I got the impression from my client that they're damned serious. That's why I backed off. You know it takes more than a gun to scare me off, Nick, but I guess I operate better in an urban atmosphere."

"Can you give me her number?"

"Not without her permission."

"Get it and call me back." He gave her the phone number of the motel.

In less than ten minutes she was on the line with the answer. "The woman's name is Dusty Wayne. She sings country and western songs at a bar over in Gunnerville. That's about twenty miles away. You can see her there tonight, any time after eight. I described you as an attractive older man.'' He could detect the trace of humor in her voice.

"Thanks," he said dryly.

"Don't mention it. The name of the bar is Hardy's. It's right on the main road. You can't miss it."

"I'll be in touch," he promised.

That evening Nick found the town of Gunnerville without difficulty. Hardy's proved to be more of an old-fashioned roadhouse than a bar, with a large parking lot and flashing neon signs on all sides. The lot was about half full, which struck him as a fairly good crowd for a weeknight.

Inside there were little tables and a dance floor, but Nick ordered a beer and stood at the bar, listening to the sweet-voiced country singer who wore fringed buckskin and strummed her guitar like someone left over from the sixties. He sent a note to her via one of the waiters and presently she took a break, resting the guitar atop the stool she'd used while singing.

She came up to him and asked, "You're Nick Velvet?"

"That's right."

"I'm Dusty Wayne." Up close she was attractive in a tomboyish way, probably in her mid-thirties, with black bangs that reached almost to her eyelids. The buckskin pants fit with just the right degree of snugness.

"I enjoyed your songs. They reminded me of Loretta Lynn."

"Thank you." Dimples appeared as she gave him a slow smile. "Sandra said you were nice."

"How did you come to know her?"

"That goes way back to our school days. We were classmates at college for a year, but I dropped out and went on the road with my guitar."

"You know what I'm here for."

She glanced sideways at the bartender. "Let's get a table where we can talk privately." Nick followed her to one against the far wall. She sat down and lit a cigarette apologetically. "I was off these things until I heard about that damn comb."

"Tell me about it. Why is it so valuable to you?"

"I won't know if it's valuable at all till I see it. Back when I first started singing I fell in love with one of the Franklin boys—Tom Franklin. He was six years younger than me, just seventeen, but he was the best-looking of them all. Very dark, with curly black hair and eyes that could look into your soul. We were going to run off together and travel around the country singing country music. Then one day he just . . . disappeared. His brother Willie told me he ran away, went out west."

"What about the comb?"

"I'm getting to it. Tom was always fussing with his hair. I think he wanted to look like Elvis, but his hair was too curly for that. Anyway, I gave him a comb that he always carried, with his initials on it, T.F. He treated it like some sort of lucky charm. He never went anywhere without it, and he certainly wouldn't have gone out west without it. He might have left me, but he'd never leave that comb. A couple of months back someone from West Alum told me they ran into Willie Franklin at a pharmaceutical supply house over in Casper Hill and he had a comb in his pocket. He dropped it when he was getting out some money."

"That's true," Nick confirmed. "I saw it too."

"My friend thought it was funny for a bald man like Willie Franklin to need a comb, and I thought it was funny too." She took another drag on the cigarette. "Then I got to thinking about Tom one night, and about his comb. I never really believed that he just ran away twelve years ago, without even a word or a note to me."

"What do you think happened?"

Dusty Wayne took a deep breath. "I think his brother might have killed him and buried the body somewhere. There was always bad blood between them. I'll probably never be able to prove it now, but I just want to know. If he's carrying Tom's comb around, that'll be proof enough for me."

"You're paying a great deal of money to find out."

"I've done well on a couple of CDs, and I've appeared in Nashville a few times. I'm married now, but sometimes I still dream of Tom Franklin and what happened to him. I want to know the truth. It's worth that much to find out."

"I'll do what I can," Nick promised.

*   *   *

The next morning Nick drove a few miles upriver from West Alum and rented a rowboat, speaking vaguely about doing some fishing. He went out in the gently flowing Casaqueek, getting the feel of the current, and finally rowed to shore about a mile up from the old mill. Approaching the place by night might be dangerous. He wasn't a woodsman but he'd read enough to know that the mere breaking of a twig could be fatal in the dark with an armed man nearby. An arrival by water should be safer.

He had some other tasks that day. First he found an almanac at the county library and checked out the time for the rising of the moon. Happily it was only in its first quarter and shouldn't give too much light. Then he went searching for a stray cat. He'd noticed a couple on the prowl around the town, and before too long he managed to entice one to him with some catnip purchased at the store near the library.

Just before midnight he set off in his rowboat with the cat in a convenient bag. He kept the boat toward shore, avoiding the more visible center of the river. Before long the mill came into sight, but he saw that there was still a light burning downstairs. He couldn't be sure if they left it on every night or if it was a sign that someone was still up and about. Nick grounded the rowboat in the shadows near the mill wheel and waited.

He was rewarded about fifteen minutes later when Jud Franklin strolled to the door and stared out at the night. He had a beer bottle in one hand and drained it as Nick watched. Then he closed the door and turned out the light. Presently a light went on in one of the upstairs bedrooms, stayed lit for about ten minutes, and then was extinguished. Nick waited another half-hour before he left the rowboat carrying his bagged cat.

He had no trouble with the door, entering silently and closing it behind him. Remembering the downstairs room as well as he could, he crossed to a table and picked up a lamp, then thought better of it and chose an empty beer bottle instead. He carried bottle and sack silently up the staircase to the second floor. "Now you come out, kitty," he whispered, leaning over the staircase to drop the cat onto a main-floor sofa some eight feet below. He followed it with the beer bottle, but this landed on the bare floor, shattering with a satisfying crash.

Nick ran quickly into the workroom where Willie had been and hid behind the door. Already he could hear the Franklin brothers shouting and jumping out of bed. "What was it?" one of them called out. "Get your gun!"

They ran to the top of the stairs and flipped a switch, lighting the main floor. Willie, his bald head gleaming, grabbed the rifle from his brother and led the way. As soon as they were all downstairs, Nick left his hiding place and hurried silently into the nearest bedroom. He was pretty certain it was the one from which Willie had emerged, and a sweep of his tiny flashlight across the nightstand next to the bed proved he was correct. There was the comb, along with coins, a pocket knife, and a handkerchief. He turned it over and saw the initials: T. F.

"A cat!" someone downstairs exploded. "It's a damned cat!"

"Jud, you were the last one up. Did you let a cat in?"

"There was no cat here when I went to bed," Jud insisted.

"Well, he's here now. Toss him outside or I'll put a bullet in him." Nick could recognize Willie's voice now, ordering his brothers about. He stayed in his hiding place, reasonably certain that if they decided on a search it wouldn't include the upper floor.

Presently the cat was exiled to the outer darkness and the brothers came upstairs to bed. "I still say I didn't let the damned cat in!" Jud insisted.

After a time they settled down, but Nick remained where he was for another thirty minutes. When he finally tiptoed across the floor to the stairs, something on the bottom of his sneakers made a scraping sound. He pried it off and dropped it in his pocket, but Jessie Franklin had heard something. "That you, Jud?"

From the next room Willie shouted, "Shut up, damn it! I'm trying to sleep."

"I think somebody's out there, Willie."

Nick heard the bed squeak and knew he had to hurry. He went down the stairs and out the door, just as the light went on. Slipping down the riverbank toward his hidden boat, he saw Willie outlined in the lighted doorway as Jud had been earlier. "He got away," Jessie said.

"It don't matter," Willie's voice spoke calmly. "I know who it was. He'll be dead by morning."

Nick returned the rented boat in the morning and then phoned Sandra Paris. "How'd you make out?" she asked.

"You owe me forty."

"Good. I'll fly down and you can meet me at the airport in Atlanta. You'll get paid and I'll continue on my way to make delivery to Dusty."

"Sounds agreeable to me. Name the time."

"I'll check the flights. Call me back in two hours and I'll let you know. It'll be either late this evening or tomorrow morning."

Nick was just leaving the phone booth when a sheriff's car pulled up next to his. "Mr. Nicholas?" the deputy asked as he slipped out from behind the wheel.

Nick had a sinking feeling in his stomach. If they knew the name he was using, it meant they wanted him for something. "That's me."

"You were at the Franklin home day before yesterday?"

"That's right. I went there to settle a claim—"

"Come along with me, sir. The sheriff would like to speak with you."

"What about?"

"There's been a killing. Black man named Gus Adams who worked for Mrs. Franklin."

On the way to the sheriff's office, following the deputy's car, all Nick could think of was that Willie hadn't known who it was after all.

The sheriff was a small man who spoke in a soft voice and seemed completely out of place in West Alum and the Casaqueek Hills. His name was Garvey and his first statement was, "Mr. Nicholas, I find no record of the State Casualty and Life Insurance Company. Isn't that the name of your employer?"

"It is indeed. They sometimes do business under the names of subsidiaries."

The sheriff grunted. "Mrs. Franklin says you came to her place on Tuesday with a check for her son."

"That's correct."

"And Gus Adams took you to the mill where her three sons live."

"That's right. I only knew him as Gus."

"Too bad you didn't know him better. He was a fine man, much liked around these parts."

"He seemed friendly enough."

"Someone killed him this morning."

"That's what your deputy said."

Sheriff Garvey leaned back in his chair. "Shot him with a rifle through the window of his cabin on the Franklin place. Killed him at the kitchen table. Any idea who could have done it, Mr. Nicholas?"

"None. What would I know about it?"

"A man like Gus don't make many enemies. Hell, he was almost seventy years old."

"Maybe he was killed accidentally by a hunter," Nick suggested.

"It's not hunting season. Did he say anything to you about any threats to his life?"

"He wouldn't be likely to talk to a stranger about it."

The sheriff played with a pencil and studied Nick carefully before speaking. "I think you'd better stay around here for a day or so till I can check on you."

"I'll certainly want to pay my respects to the Franklins before I leave." As Nick stood up another thought came to him. "When I was out at that old mill it looked like the Franklin boys were doing something illegal, maybe operating a still."

Sheriff Garvey chuckled. "That's Willie's idea of humor. I went out and took a look once, but there's no still. He's got a couple of old lab machines of some sort, but there's no moonshine in sight."

Nick hadn't noticed the humorous side of the bald man in their brief meeting, but he let that pass. "I'll be around if you want me," he said, trying to sound sincere.

There were several cars parked in front of the Franklin home when he paid a visit after lunch. Inside, Cassy Franklin was in a state of near collapse, being tended to by neighbors and friends. Her three sons were nowhere in evidence. "Mr. Nicholas," she said, recognizing him at once.

"I was still in the area when I heard about your tragedy," he said. "Gus was a real gentleman. I'm sorry his life ended in such a terrible way."

"He worked for me nearly forty years," she said. "Don't know what I'll do without him."

"When is the funeral?"

"Saturday. He'll be laid out tomorrow at the funeral parlor in town."

"I'll try to come by if I'm still in the area." That was the least he could do for the man who had died in his place.

He went back to the phone booth by the gas station that he'd used before. It was probably the only phone booth in the county. Back in New York, Sandra Paris was waiting for his call. "It's been more than two hours, Nick. Closer to three."

"I'm sorry, there's been a complication here. A man was killed and in a way I'm partly responsible. They thought he broke in and stole the comb."

"Why is that?"

"I don't know," Nick admitted. "But I should stay around till tomorrow, anyway, if only to keep the sheriff happy."

"Don't get arrested, Nick. I can't be springing you from jail again."

"I'll be careful."

"I'd better phone Dusty and tell her what's happened. Who was it got killed?"

"An old black man named Gus Adams who worked for Mrs. Franklin."

"You think the sons did it?"

"One son—Willie. Damned if I can prove it, though."

"Be careful," she said again as she hung up.

Nick left the booth again and headed for his car. This time, happily, there was no sheriff's car waiting. He put his hand in his jacket pocket, reaching for his keys, and felt a little piece of something. It was a flattened gelatin capsule of the sort used for medication. He remembered prying it from his sneaker in the dark the previous night. He remembered something else too. A friend of Dusty Wayne's had run into Willie Franklin at a pharmaceutical supply house.

Nick decided it was time he paid a return visit to Sheriff Garvey.

*   *   *

The sheriff needed some convincing. He listened to Nick's story and shook his head. "You may be right about Willie Franklin, Mr. Nicholas, but I need some evidence to arrest him."

"Then arrest his brothers. Bring them in and see if they'll talk."

"On what charges?"

Nick sighed, feeling frustrated by his attempt to work within the law. "Look, Sheriff, Willie may not have an illegal still up at that old mill, but he's got something illegal. Why else do they take shots at people who approach too closely. He's filling these capsules with an illegal substance, a drug of some kind."

"Prove it and I'll have them locked up within an hour."

"I'd prove it if I could get back inside that mill."

The sheriff smiled at him. "Right this minute all three of the Franklin boys are at their mother's house."

Nick Velvet returned the smile. They understood each other.

The mill was quiet when he reached it a half-hour later. The door was even easier to open by daylight, and he wasted no time. He took samples of all the capsules he could find, along with loose powder that was in barrels labeled *flour*. When he left he went along the riverbank, careful not to encounter the brothers on their way back.

Sheriff Garvey studied the samples that Nick delivered to him late that afternoon. "The state police can analyze these for me overnight if I put a rush on it."

Nick smiled. "You don't like the Franklin boys any better than I do."

"Maybe even less, Mr. Nicholas."

Nick went back to his motel and found a visitor waiting in the parking lot. It was Dusty Wayne, sitting behind the wheel of her little sports car. "I'll bet you're looking for me," he said, leaning in the open window on the passenger side.

"Get in. We have to talk."

Nick slid in beside her. "You've talked to Sandra?"

She nodded. "That's why I'm here. Do you have the comb with you?"

He showed it to her. She took it, barely able to breathe, and turned it over in her hands. He saw a tear start to run down her cheek. "That's it?" he asked, knowing the answer.

"That's it. Tom's own brother killed him."

"But why? A man killing his brother—"

"It's been happening a long time, Mr. Velvet. Let me tell you about Cain and Abel sometime."

"He might have dropped the comb, or given it to Willie when he left."

"No. This was the first gift I ever gave him. He'd have kept it. He might have thrown it away at thirty-five, but not at seventeen."

"I have an appointment with the sheriff in the morning. Come there with me."

"Nobody listened to me before."

"I think they will now."

They were at the sheriff's office before nine. He shook hands with Dusty Wayne and pulled out a chair for her. "A pleasure to meet you, Miss Wayne. I like your music."

"Thank you!" She gave him a broad but brief smile. "I wish we were meeting under more pleasant circumstances."

His gaze shifted to Nick. "You're a bit early, Mr. Nicholas. The state police haven't phoned in with the lab report yet."

"Can't you call them?"

"I suppose so," he agreed, reaching for the phone. After a few moments' wait he was connected to someone in the lab, and made several quick notes as they conversed. When he finally hung up he was smiling.

"An illegal drug of some sort," Nick guessed.

Sheriff Garvey shook his head. "No, it's quite legal. A common, though expensive, prescription heart medication."

"What?"

The sheriff smiled at Nick's surprise. "But it's been cut to fifty percent of its normal strength with flour—the flour from that barrel you sampled. Willie and his brothers are doctoring prescription drugs, repackaging them in their own capsules, and selling them at a big profit."

"Isn't that dangerous to the user?"

"Damn right it's dangerous! In some cases it could kill them."

"What are you going to do?"

"The state police want to move in today. We can't admit that you broke into the place to get the evidence, so they'll request a search warrant for an illegal still. We have to shut down their operation and discover whether they were selling the stuff in large lots or to individual pharmacies."

"Try to question Jud and Jessie separately," Dusty suggested. "Offer them a plea bargain if they tell you about the murders."

"Young lady, I don't need instructions from you." He narrowed his eyes. "What murders? Gus Adams and who else?"

"Their brother Tom. He disappeared twelve years ago. He was supposed to have run away but I never believed it."

As it turned out, Willie Franklin was not at the mill when the state police moved in. Jud and Jessie denied everything, but it was immediately obvious they weren't about to take the fall for Willie. By late afternoon they'd both signed statements implicating Willie in the shooting of Gus Adams.

Nick listened as Jud's confession was tape-recorded.

"Why did your brother want Gus dead?"

"He thought Gus had broken into the mill and stolen a comb."

"What comb?"

"It belonged to our brother Tom. Willie kept it, carried it with him all the time. Crazy thing to do."

"What happened to Tom?"

"Willie killed him a long time ago. Twelve years ago."

"Do you expect us to believe that?"

"I can show you where he buried the body. You'll find it in the riverbank just behind the mill wheel—what's left of it."

"Where's Willie now?"

"Gone to the pharmaceutical house for supplies. He'll be at the funeral parlor tonight."

Listening to the confession with Nick, Sheriff Garvey nodded. "We'll take him there," he said.

Nick phoned Sandra Paris and told her he'd delivered the comb to Dusty. "She's pleased. The local police are wrapping it up tonight."

"Good! I've made arrangements with her about the money. She'll pay me with a draft and I'll pay you."

"I only want my usual twenty-five. Give her back the rest."

"What's this—a charity case?"

"She was paying the money for love—love of a kid who's been dead twelve years."

"Suit yourself, Nick."

They drove to the funeral parlor just as it was opening for the evening. Gus Adams didn't have any family; Cassy Franklin was the closest thing to it. She stood by the open casket, greeting everyone who came to pay their respects. He knew she hadn't been told about the arrest of Jud and Jessie.

Willie Franklin was seated in a far corner of the room. He got up when he recognized Nick and started toward him. Then he got another surprise as Dusty Wayne entered, wearing a plain black dress.

"Hello, Willie," she said.

"What—? Dusty, is that you? It's been a long time." The top of his head was growing moist with sweat.

It was Sheriff Garvey who spoke the words. "Willie, I'm going to have to arrest you on suspicion of murder."

"Murder? What murder?"

"Two, actually. Gus Adams and your brother Tom."

He tried to break through them then, heading for the door or perhaps just away from the casket behind him. The state police had him before he got more than a few feet, and his hands were quickly cuffed. Nick hoped his mother hadn't noticed the brief scuffle.

It was Nick who said to him, as he was being led away, "Willie, we know about Gus, but why did you kill your brother?"

He stared at Nick as if seeing him for the first time. Perhaps he thought Nick was a state cop too, and was cursing his brothers for ever letting him into the mill.

But he turned and looked back at the black man in his coffin, and in that instant Nick remembered the descriptions he'd heard of Tom Franklin—the dark complexion, the curly black hair. "He was seventeen years old," Willie said quietly. "He was starting to look too much like his father."

THE SECRET

by FLORENCE V. MAYBERRY

G randma said, "Time to get the milk, Sary."
I was glad it was time because then I could visit with Miss Abbie and the girls. This took a while. Sit in one of the cane-bottomed kitchen chairs, eat a cookie and watch the fluttering hands of Mable and Roxy, try to guess what they said before Miss Abbie translated for me. Mable and Roxy were deaf-and-dumb. Dumb of voice, not of mind, because Miss Abbie declared they were smart as tacks even if they hadn't had much school learning. She should know because she was their older sister and had been with them all their lives. Brightest little things you ever saw, she said, those twin baby girls, keeping an eye on everything from their crib, walked early, figured they'd talk early too. Only they didn't, beyond a queer baby gurgle deep in their throats. They could hear the loudest sounds, like a thunder clap, because they'd whirl their heads toward it. But any noise that didn't shake the house they'd pay no mind to. So you had to look right at them and move your lips slow, or use deaf-and-dumb talk with your hands like Miss Abbie did.

Grandma handed me the tin milk bucket and I walked barefooted down the grassy middle of the road to the house of Miss Abbie and the girls, avoiding the dusty ruts made by wagons and buggies. Nobody in our Missouri town had an automobile, danged things good for nothing but to scare horses. It was midsummer, hot but pleasant

215

in early mornings and late afternoons because our town was in the Ozark Mountains in a high, rolling valley. On one side of the road, just beyond our house, was the woods where in spring I could find violets peeking through dead leaves packed by winter snows. Splitting the woods into two unequal parts, the larger part on the far side, ran the creek, arched over by joined tree branches. On the creek's near side was the pasture where Mable and Roxy let their two cows feed. On the creek's far side was a scrub pasture not fit for grazing. Gypsies and other folks traveling by covered wagon sometimes used it for a camping ground.

When I reached the yard of Miss Abbie and the girls, Roxy was walking to the house with her milk pail, leaning one-sided to balance its weight. She waved, her mouth spread in a laugh, and jabbed her finger excitedly toward the little barn where she and Mable did the milking. This meant she had won. Every night she and Mable raced to see who could milk the fastest; they each did a cow, everything was twin with them.

"Evening, Roxy," I said, my lips making large and slow movements so she could read them.

"Yah-h-h-uh, gugh-gugh, yah-h-uh!" she said. She and Mable always tried to talk to me. I ached inside me when they did but I hated to ask Miss Abbie to have them stop, they were so pleased that I could hear their sounds. When they were together as they did that talking they would bob their heads at each other, grimace with laughter, turn and "Yah-h-h-uh, gugh-gugh, yah-h-uh!" at me again. It sent tingly chills down the back of my legs like when you hear that somebody cut their finger or broke a leg or something.

Mable came jog-trotting out of the barn, gargling and gurgling as she hurried, pointing at her milk pail to show it was fuller than Roxy's, then flying her free hand in deaf-and-dumb words at Roxy. Roxy's hand danced in answer and they both strangled out their laughter.

Miss Abbie came out on the back porch. "Evening, Sary ... been expecting you. The girls thought you might be a little early so's you could watch them milk."

They were always wanting me to do that. Once, for manner's sake, I did, but afterwards I didn't drink milk for days; it was the first time

I had really thought about how milk came out. So now I managed to come a little late.

The girls carried their milk pails down cellar beneath their house where big shallow pans were set out to hold the milk for cooling. "Come set a while," Miss Abbie said, taking my bucket. "The morning's milking is up here ready for you, nice and cool. Help yourself to a cookie from that crock on the table. The girls just baked them. They'll be up directly to visit with you. Your Grandma won't mind you waiting a bit, will she?"

I shook my head. Grandma never minded about me eating between meals, or waiting extra, or anything much I wanted to do. I was their orphaned baby girl, a skinny little kid she and Grandpa had had a time raising up to the age of seven. Or so they said. Actually I felt fine, just skinny.

I hurried to eat the cookie before Roxy got to the kitchen and did her trick. For reasons known only to herself, she thought letting her false teeth click together outside her mouth in a terrifying skeleton grin amused me. She did it at least once every time I came, followed by throwing back her head in a gargly laugh and gleefully patting her round stomach. She did it so often that finally the teeth loosened and sometimes dropped out when she didn't want them to. Like once in church when she was pretending to sing. Embarrassed her so, she ran out of church crying.

Except for their brown eyes, Mable and Roxy didn't look alike. Roxy was round, plump, and flouncy. A strong girl but always had poor teeth, Miss Abbie said. Probably from too much sucking on sugar lumps and eating sweets, young'un or grown, ruined her teeth and put weight on her. Mable was tall and slim with honey-blond hair. It really looked pretty with those brown eyes. Kept her own teeth, white as snow, too. Although the twins were in their thirties and should have seemed old to a child of seven, they didn't. Everybody called them the deaf-and-dumb girls and that's how I thought of them. As girls.

Roxy's cheeks were full and rosy, her dark brown hair kept in a knot on top of her head, her neck smooth and white. "It's a shame Roxy's deaf-and-dumb," Grandma sometimes said. "Strong, handy girl like that. Not exactly pretty, but right good-looking. And Mable, with a little fixing she'd be a beauty. I feel real bad those two girls have to end up old maids.''

Grandpa would crinkle his brows, shake his head, and say, ''Maybe won't need to, got to be men around would count it a blessing to have a deaf-and-dumb woman in the house.'' Then laugh when Grandma stomped her foot at him.

Mable for sure was the pretty one of the two. Wore her blonde hair in a braid like a crown around her head and looked like the Virgin Mary in the stained-glass window in our church. ''Mable's a mite thin, though,'' decided Grandma, who was even plumper than Roxy. ''And you watch it, Missy, or you'll end up the same way if you don't eat your vittles.'' Which did nothing to encourage my appetite. I wished I could end up looking like Mable.

When they had the milk in pans, the girls came up to the kitchen, Roxy's head peeking mischievously at me around the taller Mable. I stiffened as she opened her mouth, pushed out her teeth with her tongue, and clacked them at me. It made me afraid that next thing her eyes might pop from their sockets, her arms and legs fly off like a doll coming to pieces. I covered my eyes with my fingers, peeking through to see when she came together again. That was part of the game for Roxy. She popped her teeth inside and both girls laughed, gurgles bubbling in their barren throats.

Then Mable put her finger against her mouth in a hush gesture, a signal for me to stay put. ''She has a surprise for you,'' Miss Abbie said. ''Been working on it for days.''

Mable left the kitchen and Roxy came and sat before me. The girls never sat beside me, always in front so they could watch what I said. Mable returned, one hand behind her back, the other fluttering at Miss Abbie. ''She wants you to shut your eyes,'' Miss Abbie said. I did, felt Mable move close and a featherweight object fall on my lap. ''Now look,'' Miss Abbie said.

I opened my eyes. On my lap was a tiny dress made of sprigged calico, a ribbon sash around its waist. I sprang up, holding the little dress before me, hopping in delight. It was the size of my china-headed doll, the one my mother had played with when she was a little girl. I ran to Mable and hugged my face against her flat stomach.

When I looked up she was crying, tears dripping down her cheeks. I turned to Miss Abbie, frightened. "What did I do?"

"Nothing but be happy like Mable hoped. She's crying because she's so glad you like it."

Mable's hands clenched and spread, making signs at her older sister. "She's saying, she wishes she had a little girl just like you."

"Why doesn't she get one then?"

Miss Abbie's hands moved, and the twins doubled over with soundless laughter. Along with Mable's tear-streaked cheeks and the doubling up, it looked peculiar, like they had stomachaches. It didn't seem to me I had said anything funny, but Roxy was so tickled she clacked out her teeth at me again. With her teeth grinning in front of her mouth, she handed me the cookie plate, motioning for me to take another. I didn't want to, but I did. Good manners make you never let on to a deaf-and-dumb girl you love that she makes you sick.

"Has the Gypsy tinkerman come to your place yet?" Miss Abbie asked. I shook my head. "Well, reckon he hasn't had time to get around, not been here either, even though he's camped right beside us. I got a kettle needs mending, maybe he'll come around tomorrow."

I almost choked on the cookie, I was so excited. "Oh, Miss Abbie, please let Roxy and Mable take me to see the Gypsies! Grandma won't ever let me go alone."

"Don't think that would be right. There's no women along with this Gypsy wagon, just two lone men," Miss Abbie said doubtfully. "Just an old man and a young one, maybe his son, look alike."

"Oh please, Miss Abbie! I've never ever visited a Gypsy camp. Roxy's big and strong, she can take care of Mable and me. Please!"

Miss Abbie looked uncertain, made deaf-and-dumb talk to the girls. They clapped their hands, excited as I was. Three pairs of hands danced in the air, and at last the girls motioned for me to follow them.

Miss Abbie trailed after us and we all passed through the cow lot, into the side pasture that led to the creek.

Across the creek a dark-skinned old man with white hair to his shoulders sat on a box beside the covered wagon watching a younger man stir something over a cookfire. Even though the second man was younger, to me he looked pretty old too, almost as old as Miss Abbie, who was forty-some. That man raised his face, saw us across the creek, and nodded his head in greeting. A big man, his arms heavy-muscled.

Miss Abbie nodded back, curt and quick, but Roxy and Mable were all smiles, nodding and waving. "Head for the house, Sary!" Miss Abbie ordered, soft but sharp. She yanked the girls around and shoved them toward the cow barn. "Never should've come, never should've come!" She kept muttering. "Run get your milk, Sary, and hike for home before your grandma gets anxious."

When we reached the back steps of their house, Mable turned fiercely on Miss Abbie, clenched her hands, stomped up and down, had a regular tantrum, her pretty face squeezed up and tears running down her cheeks. Roxy threw her arms around her twin and grunted at Miss Abbie like an angry little pig.

Miss Abbie looked flabbergasted. Her hands flashed before the girls, theirs answered back. "What on earth's got into these girls, wanting to hang around staring at that camp!" Miss Abbie wasn't really talking to me, just letting out her shock. "Waving, acting so tickled! Those men could take them wrong. I knew I shouldn'ta let you children go down there, it ain't ladylike."

That's how she felt about Roxy and Mable, like they were her children.

I scampered toward home, leaving Mable still snubbing Miss Abbie and Roxy sassing her with her hands.

As I sat on our front porch with Grandma that night, I saw the Gypsy campfire still burning. The sound of a mouth organ drifted to us, mingled with night sounds of a bird's sleepy twitter, frogs croaking, insects singing. Fireflies danced around our yard as the music switched from fast and bouncy to soft and sweet, dreamy and sad, back to bouncy. I got off Grandma's lap and whirled in the moonlight with the fireflies.

"Careful, or you'll be getting yourself with the moon madness," Grandma said, her voice easy and comfortable. It was just something to say because the night was so pretty.

After I went to bed I lay across its foot, my face by the window with the moonlight shining full on it. I wished I could catch the moon madness. Then I would be crazy enough to creep out of the house, run down the lane, cross the pasture, wade the creek, and sit beside the Gypsy fire and its music. When I fell asleep I dreamed I did.

Next afternoon when I went for the milk Roxy was still mad at Miss Abbie. Pouting, wouldn't make her fingers say anything. "I caught her down by the creek today after she let the cows into the pasture," Miss Abbie explained testily. "Just acting the fool, waving at that Gypsy man, so I sent her hiking home. So now she's stuffed up in a sulky fit."

Mable was acting strange too, broody, no fun at all. Quick as I could, I took my pail and started home.

But Roxy skittered between me and the back screen door, and clacked her teeth at me. A smile like that is pretty terrible, but I knew what she meant. She was sorry about being unfriendly. She took my milk pail, motioning she would carry it for me.

Once we were out of sight of the house she bent down with her finger to her lips, shaking her head back and forth. Sh-h-h-h, she meant. She pointed toward the pasture and the creek. Smoke from the Gypsy fire rose in a graceful frond, seeming to bear with it the lively sound of the mouth organ. Not that Roxy could hear the music, but she could see the younger man with the instrument at his mouth as he sat on a stack of firewood beside the fire. Maybe her skin felt the music.

She jabbed her finger toward the camp, pointed at herself, then at me, again at the camp.

I shook my head no, pointed toward my house, then toward where Miss Abbie was. Moved my mouth in a lip message, "Grandma— Miss Abbie—they won't let us go over there."

Her head bounced yes-yes-yes defiantly, and she pulled me behind the stable. Took a stub pencil and a piece of paper out of her apron pocket. "Tonight we go," she wrote. "Abbie sleep. Granma sleep. Mable sleep. Roxy Sary go jipsy have fun."

I shook my head.

Roxy stamped first one foot, then the other, hard. She wrote again: "I go my self alone."

Roxy was a grown woman and I was only seven. But she was deaf-and-dumb and everybody knew those girls had to be looked after, that's why Miss Abbie never married, gave her life to them. So what else could I do? A deaf-and-dumb girl shouldn't go traipsing out alone at night, maybe fall in the creek and drown, not being able to call for help.

Besides, I wanted to go.

"All right," I mouthed. "I go too."

Roxy whirled in a clumsy dance of pleasure. Then wrote with her stub pencil, "Tonight cum barn I here."

I nodded, ran for home as though the devil was after me. Quivered inside all through supper, knowing the devil would surely be waiting for me at the Gypsy camp, pitchfork and all, because of the sneakiness I was helping Roxy carry out.

"Think I'll set on the porch a while," Grandma said after supper. "Want me to sing to you?"

"Hunh-uh. I'm too sleepy."

"Mite sleepy myself," Grandma said. "I'll not set out long, just enough to settle the day. You run along to bed."

I lay in bed tight as a string in a hard knot, listening to the creak-creak of Grandma's cane rocker. Heard the far-off music of the mouth organ and Grandma begin to hum with it.

At last the creaking stopped and Grandma's solid steps crossed through the sitting room into the kitchen. The tin dipper clinked against the water bucket. She went into her bedroom and after a bit the bedsprings squeaked under her weight.

When her lighter snore joined Grandpa's I slipped off my nightgown, pulled on my dress, tiptoed away from the bed. Turned back, fluffed the quilt over my pillow so it looked like someone was in bed.

Out on the porch, Nervy, our big black tomcat, meowed and rubbed against my leg. I picked him up, stroked him to make him hush for fear Grandma would hear and get up to let him inside. I tiptoed into the shadows beside the porch, heart pounding, listening for Grandma's footsteps. When none came I ran from the yard, down the lane, toward the cow barn. Halfway there I realized I still had Nervy in my arms, dropped him, and ran on.

Roxy appeared so suddenly out of the barn that I had to stifle a squeal of fright. She began strangling with deaf-and-dumb sounds and I hushed her with my finger against her lips. Her head bobbed in agreement, she took my hand and led me to the pasture.

Both men were sitting beside their campfire but the old one looked asleep, his head drooped almost to his knees. As we hesitated, watching, he jerked and swayed, raised his head, dropped it again. Roxy pulled me forward until we stood opposite the campfire. The men, one nodding and the other busy with his mouth organ, didn't see us. Then the old one staggered to his feet, rubbed his back, went to the covered wagon, and climbed in.

The younger man put down his mouth organ to stir the fire, looked up, and saw us staring at him. He stood up and walked to the creek bank. Somehow, that close, he stopped looking like a foreign stranger but just a plain man, like he'd come in from just some other town. "Howdy!" he called. "Come on over and visit a while. Evening's nice."

Roxy stood there, grinning, too far away to read his lips. I said, "She's deaf-and-dumb, she can't hear you."

He beckoned, smiling, pointing to the boxes set beside the fire. Roxy took a step forward, stopped bashfully. He beckoned again— another step, beckon, step, until she reached the water's edge. Then shook her head, pointed to her shoes, pointed at the water. I moved close to her, uncertain, ready to run back to the barn, felt the tremble in her body. The big man bent down, unlaced his shoes, kicked them off his unsocked feet, rolled up his pants legs. Then he waded calf-high across the creek, swung Roxy over his shoulder like a sack of potatoes, and carried her to the campfire. He turned and came back towards me.

I ran backwards toward the barn, tripped, fell, scrambled up like a terrified little animal. The man stood, hands on hips. "Don't be afeered, I'll carry you acrost."

I shook my head. He shrugged, waded back. I stood, watching to see that nothing happened to Roxy.

The firelight revealed a big happy grin on Roxy's face. She looked up at the man, pointed at her throat, shook her head; pointed at her ears, shook her head. Opened her mouth, went, "Aanh-aanh, aanh!" The man nodded, patted her back, urged her to sit down on a box, and sat on another beside her. He picked up his mouth organ, blew high piercing notes, dropped the organ, made signs meaning could she hear that. Roxy nodded, lying probably. Or maybe she did, the sound was so high pitched, because she kept nodding as he played. The man suddenly stood up, playing the organ with one hand, pulling Roxy to her feet with the other, swaying with the music, Roxy lumbering after him, hopping up and down, a look of unutterable joy on her face. She let go his hand, stomped her feet up and down in time with some awkward tune inside herself. It was like a show, the fire for footlights, the man and his music the orchestra, Roxy the dancer. I sat down to watch.

When I awoke, shivering on the damp rough pasture grass, the moon was still high. But the fire had burned to embers and the two figures were shadows leaning against each other.

I walked to the creek bank, motioned at Roxy. She jumped up, hurried to the creek, lifted her skirt like she was going to walk into the water with her shoes on. But the big man swung her to his shoulder and toted her across. When he set her beside me she was breathing hard and fast, gurgling in her throat. It maybe would have been a giggle if she hadn't been deaf-and-dumb.

Roxy walked me up to our gate and I skittered inside the house and into bed with my clothes still on. Listened for a sound from Grandma. Nothing but snores. Took off my clothes, found my nightgown, got into bed and fell down a tunnel of sleep.

Next afternoon I played like I had a stomachache and Grandpa went for the milk. I was afraid to face Roxy for fear one of us might let on to Miss Abbie we'd been up to something. Grandma gave me peppermint tea and sent me to bed early. I didn't mind, I was sleepy.

I stirred awake to the striking of our big old wall clock, counted ten. I crept out of bed, padded through a path of moonlight to the window that faced the pastures and the creek.

The tinkerman's campfire still burned, but I heard no music. This time I didn't bother to dress but slipped outdoors in my nightgown, ran barefooted through the damp grass growing between the wagon ruts, and across the cow paddock. I hid behind a clump of elderberry at the corner of the cow barn and watched what was happening across the creek.

I blinked my eyes, afraid I was still sleepy and not seeing right. But what I saw stayed the same. The tinkerman had his arms around Roxy and was kissing her right on the mouth. My cheeks burned with shame for her. Not even my Grandma and Grandpa did that and they had been married forty-two years.

I slipped back, close beside the barn, ran up the road to our house, got into bed, couldn't sleep. Next day I was really sick, no pretend about it, and had to take some of Grandma's bitter patent medicine along with more peppermint tea.

It was two or three days before I felt like going for the milk again. I thought maybe Roxy would look sick too. She didn't. Her face was all shiny and her eyes sparkled like she might be watching a merry-go-round go round and round and she was fixing to get on it. It made me feel lots better. Maybe being kissed wasn't so bad after all.

Still, I wasn't sure I wanted to see any more of that kissing. For a whole week I didn't slip over to the pasture and creek in the nighttime. But I could hear the music from our front porch, see the dancing flames of the fire. It made me restless, and I argued with myself about it. Surely by this time Roxy and the tinkerman would be tired of kissing. So finally one night I crept out and hid again behind the elderberry bush.

Was I ever surprised! This time three figures sat beside the fire. Roxy, the big tinkerman. And Mable. The old man wasn't there. The three of them had their backs turned toward me and the creek, and the tinkerman was making shadow pictures against the white canvas top of the covered wagon with his hands and the firelight. He made a dog chase a rabbit, the dog's mouth snapping in fierce bites, the rabbit's ears going up and down. Then he made a man run, with a gun on his shoulder. The man vanished and a monkey climbed up and down the canvas.

The twins clapped their hands and Roxy jumped up to dance along with the shadow monkey, up and down, bouncy-bouncy. The tinkerman caught her hands and they danced around the fire while Mable clapped for them.

Then it happened. Not for fun, not to tease anybody. Caused by the bouncing, up and down, fast, fast. Roxy's teeth popped outside her mouth in a horrid skeleton grin at the tinkerman and he froze in his tracks. She shoved her teeth inside her mouth and ran to the creek, jumped into the water shoes and all, ran past me and the elderberry bush and around the barn.

With a detached smile, Mable watched the awkward, bulky figure of her sister vanish. Then she looked up at the tinkerman, her cheeks bright with reflected firelight. Her blond head ducked bashfully as the man sat beside her and took her hand in his. For a long time neither moved, so long that my eyes turned dry and scratchy like itchy marbles. I blinked to keep them open, started to edge backwards toward the road and home. Stopped, horrified. Because now the tinkerman was carrying on with Mable just like he had with Roxy. Kissing her.

Like I said, everything was twin with Roxy and Mable. So now, Mable was kissing him back.

I darted into the shadow of the barn, bent low, and took off. As I slipped past the paddock fence I saw Roxy leaning over its corner, oblivious of me, staring at the pair across the creek.

It gave me nightmares. All night I seemed to be running barely ahead of snapping teeth that were trying to kiss me.

Next day Grandma told Grandpa that those tinkermen seemed to be hanging around a mighty long time, who'd think there would be that much in town to mend, wonder if they were fixing to settle down here and stay.

Later in the day I asked Grandma, "Do deaf-and-dumb ladies get married?"

"Land's sake, what put that idea in your head?"

"Well, all grown-up ladies can get married, can't they, they don't have to end up old maids like you said the girls would, do they?"

"I wouldn't trouble myself over things like that at your age."

"Well, do they?"

She never answered me. Just said, "Now mind, when you go for the milk don't you be asking questions like that, those girls can read lips. Hurt their feelings."

When the girls came in from milking that evening I looked close at Mable to see if she acted shiny like Roxy had after kissing the tinkerman. And she did, only dreamier, a smile slipping in and out on her face.

Roxy wasn't smiling. Her full lips were bit tight, her eyes flat and still. I sat at the kitchen table, a cookie in my hand, tensed for when she would play her game and drop her teeth at me. She didn't. For the very first time I wanted her to, and motioned at my mouth, pointing at hers. She shook her head.

"I think maybe Roxy's coming down with something," Miss Abbie fretted. "She's always so full of fun, but today she won't talk, even acts like she's mad at Mable. Deliberately shoved her so's Mable's pail slopped milk all down her apron. Then tried to slap her like it was Mable's fault. And all the time Mable smiling sweet as an angel, like she understood Roxy wasn't herself. I thought maybe Roxy had a warm weather fever, but her cheeks were cool."

Tinkerman's kisses, that's what. I might have been only seven but I could figure that out. Only I wasn't about to tell Miss Abbie and get us all in trouble. Roxy was mad because her teeth dropped out in front of the tinkerman, and afterwards he kissed Mable instead of her. I felt real bad because it was the first time that everything wasn't twins with them. I felt so bad I told myself never to go near the tinkerman's camp anymore.

But in about a week curiosity got the best of me.

That night Grandma felt like singing all her old songs to me. Usually I loved her mournful singing of "The Drunkard's Lone Child," "The Little Brown Church in the Vale," and the sad ballad about the girl who hanged herself because a man married somebody else. But not on this night with the tinkerman's fire flickering down in the pasture and maybe both the girls already sneaking over to it. Which would he kiss tonight? Maybe both.

I played like I fell asleep against the porch post. And then I did. Grandma shook me awake, led me inside, and helped me undress. But the nap had taken the sleep out of me and now I was wide awake, tensed up to hear Grandma settle in bed and start her snoring.

The moon had changed and the night was dark when I left our yard. Instead of going to the barn I cut across the back end of the pasture, headed for a lone fence post which speared through a tangle of wild grape near the creek bank, the rest of the fence rotted and vanished long ago. I crept behind the tangle.

Down by the cow barn I saw first one shadow, then a second slip past its dark outlines. The first shadow reached the creek's bank. The second hung back, its stocky outlines telling me it was Roxy. The big tinkerman left the fire, walked to his side of the creek, beckoned. Mable quickly knelt, took off her shoes, raised her skirt, dipped her bare feet in the water. She waded quickly across and stood beside the fire, skirt still held high, her white legs gleaming in the firelight.

Roxy waited, hesitant, staring at them.

In the flickering light and shadow of the fire, the tinkerman moved close to Mable, bent his head, put his hands on her shoulders. This galvanized Roxy into action. She bent over, began unlacing her shoes. The tinkerman looked over at her, suddenly lifted Mable in his arms, took long, fast steps with her toward the dark clump of woods that bordered the pasture.

Roxy, with her head bent down, fooling with her shoes, hadn't seen them leave. Her head still bent, she picked a careful way through the water. When she reached the fire, she stamped her feet, tossed up her head. And saw she was alone. Swung around, her head twisting and turning, fighting the darkness. At the last moment she saw the shadow-blurred figure of the tinkerman with Mable in his arms vanish into the impenetrable darkness of the woods.

Her enraged gargle rose up and down as she plunged after them, across the pasture, toward the woods. Then was absorbed into its blackness.

Roxy had been so loud that I feared Miss Abbie would hear and come running. Then the heavy thrashing and grunting sounds that came out of the stand of oak and black walnut trees took my mind clean off Miss Abbie or anything but those girls alone with the tinkerman. Was he killing them? Should I scream for Grandpa? Get my bottom blistered?

I ran along the creek to the woods, splashed knee-high through the water to the opposite bank. As I clambered up its slippery side the tinkerman bumped into me, backing out of the trees. He stared down at me, turned, and ran to his camp.

The violent thrashing inside the woods continued, twigs snapping, a heavy object falling, a pounding on the earth.

I hurried toward the sounds, bushes scratching and snagging me. Two flailing shadows, more sensed than seen, rolled and tumbled, in company with the crackling of snapping twigs and enraged grunting, at the foot of a big tree. I grabbed at one of the shadows. Felt the cloth of its dress yank free and the brush of its kicking feet. Desperately I felt around for a broken-off branch, found it, switched at the shadows. Hopeless. I tossed the little stick into the tangled bodies, turned, and ran for help.

I beat on Miss Abbie's back screen, yelling, "Hurry, hurry! The girls are killing each other!"

It seemed forever before she appeared on the back porch, stumbling with sleep. "Hurry, Miss Abbie! Roxy 'n Mable—they're out in the woods killing each other!"

She ran from the house, through the cow lot and the pasture, her white nightgown flapping, me at her heels. I took a quick look at the tinker camp. The old man was up, hurrying with the tinkerman to hitch up their horses.

As Miss Abbie and I neared the woods I could hear that the heavy thrashing had become a heavy thud, measured and steady. Miss Abbie plunged into the dark, following the sound. I could feel her body pull, slap, and at last fling the broader, chunkier shadow aside from the slimmer one lying on the ground. That broader shadow fell against me, tumbled to the ground. A grey film of light that sifted through tree branches revealed Roxy's teeth dangling palely across her mouth.

Miss Abbie shook the shadow still on the ground, half crying, half moaning, "Mable baby, wake up, dear God, oh, Mable! It's Abbie, wake up!"

No sound came from Mable. Miss Abbie stopped shaking her, sobbed, "She's killed her! Roxy's killed her own sister!"

In the distance wagon wheels creaked as they bumped unevenly across the pasture and onto the road.

Miss Abbie stood up, grabbed Roxy, yanked her over to Mable. Together they lifted the sagging body and staggered with it across the creek, me behind them. At the house they laid Mable on the porch until Miss Abbie could light the oil lamp, then carried her to her cot.

Mable's forehead was gashed, her face blood-streaked. Beneath that red rivulet she was still and white, eyes closed. Miss Abbie's hands waggled furiously in deaf-and-dumb talk and Roxy, her eyes large and frightened, ran to the kitchen, returned with a pan of water. She looked awful. Her teeth had fallen out somewhere in the woods or creek and her face had collapsed, as though she were swallowing herself to escape the terrible thing she had done.

"Run for your grandpa, Sary, have him fetch the doctor," Miss Abbie ordered. I ran.

You can imagine that our town did a lot of talking about what happened that night. Trying to figure out why Roxy had half killed Mable, pounding her head with a rock. Everybody kept at me, asking did I know what started such a ruckus and what on earth had made me get up in the night to catch those girls at it. And why ever were they out in the woods anyway.

Even at seven years old, maybe even especially at seven, you know when things ought to be a secret. So I said I'd heard our cat meowing, got up to let him in, and then heard the racket in the woods.

"Mighty odd those tinkermen packed up and left that same night," Grandma mused. "What in the name of sense would those girls be fighting over? Sure you don't know anything more about it, Sary?"

I shook my head.

When Mable got well she and Roxy didn't act like twins anymore, wouldn't even talk to each other except indirectly through Miss Abbie. Roxy never dropped her teeth at me either, because she never could find them even though she scrounged through the leaves in the woods and waded up and down the creek bed days on end looking for them. A heavy rain had fallen after that fight and the creek was running full, no telling where the teeth traveled.

Actually the only time those girls ever seemed happy anymore was when they played with the baby. Loved that baby together like they always had loved everything together before the fight. Certainly was lucky Miss Abbie had found that baby on their front doorstep one early morning and they decided to keep it. I don't see why whoever gave that baby away couldn't have just walked up the road a piece and left it at Grandma and Grandpa's house so it could be orphans with me; I needed somebody to play with. So cute, too, big black eyes, dark curly hair, a little boy kicking and gurgling if you tickled his stomach. "Brightest little thing, watches every move any of us make," Miss Abbie bragged. "And already spoiled rotten from all the attention he gets. I have to time those girls so's one don't hold him a minute more'n the other. I'll not stand any more squabbling around here."

"Whose baby is it?" I asked Miss Abbie one day when the girls had the baby outside in the yard for a breath of fresh air.

"The Lord's," she said.

"Well, why'd He pick your house to leave it? He could've sent it to our house just as well, couldn't He?"

She thought a minute, then said, "I reckon not. You see, the Lord's ways are His, real special, and we never figure out exactly where they're headed, or why. It's kind of a secret, the Lord's secret."

"I love secrets," I said. "They're fun. Especially when they're about presents. Do you suppose that's why the Lord sent the baby here, giving you him as a present so Roxy and Mable would make up?"

Miss Abbie took kind of a deep breath, turned to look out the window at the girls sitting on a blanket in the yard, the baby between them. "Maybe so," she agreed. "Anyway, it's working."

THE FAMILY ROSE
by *CHARLOTTE HINGER*

Maybelle Rose's eyes swept across the girl with contempt, but she reached for the autograph book and signed it with a quick flourish. The fan was a ratty little thing, wearing a faded jean jacket and a gauze blouse tucked into a three-tiered calico skirt. Her long blond hair crinkled down her back and she had puppy-trust blue eyes. Clearly nobody.

But on the other hand, they weren't exactly lined up at her concerts nowadays. Tiredly, Maybelle tried to remember just when was the last time a real somebody had asked for her autograph. It was what came from being the opening act for newer, brighter stars with brassier sounds.

"You don't know how much this means to me," the girl said fervently. "I've loved the Family Rose all my life. There just ain't no other group like them. And you're my favorite of all."

"What's your name, honey?" asked Maybelle, quickly deciding she'd misjudged her.

"June," she said softly. "June Jones."

"Well, June, let's me and you have a little talk about the Family Rose."

"Oh, I wouldn't feel right," said June reverently, "taking up your time and everything."

"No bother. After all,—if it weren't for our fans! Besides, we're

233

short on help here and I could use a hand in wrestling some of these props back into the van.''

June scurried back and forth looking as if she were trying out for a job at McDonald's, smiling and nodding at Maybelle all the while she packed boxes and cartons and instruments. Maybelle watched, shrewdly evaluating June's tireless energy.

The high lonesome sound of pure bluegrass had its own loyal following, and God knew, not so long ago, ten, well maybe fifteen years, she had been on top and she would be again. At one time, she was one of the high-flying fussed-over members of the Family Rose.

She winced as she recalled the reviewer who had just recently referred to her as the "last rose of summer."

Momma and Maybelle and her two sisters had been like a sweet bouquet of country wildflowers, picking and singing their little hearts out.

"And when I die," Momma'd said, "one of you is going to get the family rose. If one of you is worthy by then."

Every time she'd said this, Maybelle and Lulu and Winona would stare wistfully at Momma's guitar—which had an elaborate cloisonné rose inlaid on the polished mahogany case. It was very old and a wonder of workmanship. It had been made by the husband of the slave woman who gave Momma's great-great-grandmother the medicine bundle, and they could only guess at how the man had managed to bring the tiny lengths of rare woods out of Africa.

The daughters' guitars all looked like hers. It required a trained eye to discern that the woods used to shade the petals on Momma's were cocobolo and purpleheart and teak whereas the girls' were merely mahogany and birch with a smattering of maple.

It was a family ritual for Momma to begin each concert by telling folks the history of the guitar—slyly working in their aristocratic southern background. Then she delicately extended the guitar as if she were inviting them to partake of a sacrament, and Maybelle and Lulu and Winona would walk forward and reverently touch the center of the family rose. Their fans loved the sight of the three lovely daughters paying homage to Momma Rose's abilities.

Momma reminded them often that only one daughter would receive her guitar—the family rose—along with the blessing and the medicine bundle as they had been handed down to her from generations of women.

There were two things Maybelle had wanted more than anything in the world: the family rose—and Momma's medicine bundle.

"You've got a mean streak to you, child," Momma had said once, eyeing Maybelle suspiciously when she urged Momma to choose her inheritor before it was too late. "Don't seem right to give the family rose to the one with the tiniest heart. And as to the medicine bundle! That's to be buried with me. None of you care a fig about being a Wise Woman. It would be misused."

Maybelle's mouth twisted with bitterness as she watched June work. Momma had up and died without naming her successor or writing down her wishes, and Maybelle had them both: the family rose and the medicine bundle. But a lot of good it did her! She had acquired the guitar without the blessing and now she simply could not bring herself to play it.

After all, if she did have a mean streak, she had gotten it from Momma. It would be just like the old witch to curse her from beyond the grave.

But the guitar was there at every concert, propped up on a little stand with a spotlight trained on it. And before she sang she would reverently step forward and touch the center of the family rose and say, "This one's for you, Momma," and the crowd would go crazy.

After Momma died, Maybelle's sisters wanted to break up the act.

"You can't *mean* that," Maybelle had protested. "We're a family group. A tradition."

"Without Momma, we ain't nothing, kiddo," Lulu had said flatly. "Without Momma, we can't even carry a tune."

"She died without passing down the gift," said Winona. "We might as well face it."

"That's not true," stammered Maybelle, "and I'm going to prove it."

Well, she had been ten, maybe fifteen years proving it, and now she had nothing to show for it, except a collection of satiny skirts and blouses and callouses on the tips of her fingers and a few ratty old run-down pitiful fans like this poor pathetic little old June Jones. The girl was a worker though. She could say that for her.

"That's it, kid. Thanks a bunch. Now put Momma's guitar back in the case."

"Oh, I couldn't," June said passionately. "I'm not worthy. I'm just a poor homeless orphan girl without kith or kin. I could never, never bring myself to touch Momma Rose's guitar."

"Well, as I live and breathe," drawled Maybelle, "a true believer. Where you staying, kid?"

"Nowhere," she mumbled. "I'm just kind of hanging around the parks. I'm sorta between jobs right now. I'm not a hooker," she blurted suddenly. "Don't want you to think that."

"It never entered my mind, darlin'. Tell you what, I'm a little down on my luck too, right now. Had a little spat with the boys. They got a little impatient over some money they claimed I owed them. No loyalty from anyone nowadays. I could use a little help setting up and taking things down, so why don't you throw in with me."

June's face lit up like a child's at Christmas.

"Oh, thank you, thank you, thank you. I just want you to know I'll do *anything* for you."

"Except touch Momma's guitar," Maybelle teased lightly.

June lowered her eyes and dug the toe of her old shoe around and around in the dust.

"Ma'am, there's some things I'd rather you didn't tease me about. And the feelings I have for Momma Rose's guitar is one of them. It's kind of like you're making fun of Jesus or something. Growing up in an orphanage was hard. Harder than you'll ever know, and music—especially your family's music—was the only thing that kept me from going crazy."

Maybelle rolled her eyes and examined her nails, but she shut her mouth.

They took off for Nashville, with June driving and Maybelle talking a blue streak as she sipped on a Budweiser.

June worked steadily setting up the stage at a minor open-air concert which Maybelle assured her was not typical of the bookings she ordinarily got, but just one of her little charity obligations she did out of the goodness of her heart.

"You know how to see if everything is hooked up right, kid?"

June nodded. "We had a little group at the orphanage."

"Great. I'll go catch twenty winks. Need my beauty sleep. Then after you sweep everything up, come get me in about an hour—and have some lunch ready."

June nodded and picked up one of the two guitars besides Momma Rose's that they had hooked up to the amps. She strummed the first one, then seeing that all the wires were in working order, she crossed to the second guitar, picked it up, and began to sing.

Maybelle Rose froze in her tracks. Stopped cold dead still. The child had a rare pure voice that sent chills down her spine.

"Stop that caterwauling," she said quickly, needing time to think. "Just strum." She did *not* want anyone else to hear that voice.

"Sorry, ma'am," said June, her voice quivering with shame. "Guess I just got plumb carried away, I miss my old group so much."

"Never mind, darlin'," said Maybelle, "I forgive you. Shucks, child, with a little coaching from me—your voice is untrained, of course—maybe you could sing backup for me."

June paled with wonder and she looked down at her feet.

"That would be my idea of going to heaven. Truly it would, ma'am."

Maybelle switched off the amplifier and asked June to sing "Wildwood Flower." Her eyes misted. The kid had It. That illusive quality that made critics spin circles. It was the sound that had been missing ever since Momma died. In fact, there was a quality of the voice that brought Momma to mind. If she closed her eyes, Maybelle could see Momma Rose standing there.

"Darlin', do you know the words to all the songs I'm going to be singing tonight?"

June nodded.

"I want you to sing right out. Not overpowering, but confident. Understand?"

"Oh yes, ma'am." The girl's eyes shone.

That night, Maybelle sang and swayed and for the first time in two years, she could see the audience responding in kind. They liked her. Liked her a lot. Pity she was just a simple warm-up act instead of getting top billing. Then after two weeks of studying and stewing,

she began fiddling with the sound systems, and in a moment of
superb inspiration she tried switching the mikes and amps and sound
systems around until it sounded as if June's voice was coming from
her mike. And it worked.

By the next stop she had coached June to give the appearance of
just swaying modestly and only moving a little, while she was actually belting out the lead using the whole range of her extraordinary
voice. Maybelle was actually doing the modest backup, but through
hopping, dipping, swaying, and passionately mouthing the words, she
appeared to be the one really singing.

"Guess you know," said Maybelle sullenly, after one concert
when they had been called back for five encores, "that you don't
get to touch the family rose, kid. It's an honor that's reserved for
our family."

"I wouldn't think of it," said June. "I told you that right off."

"Just don't want you getting a swelled head. Forgetting who's the
actual star around here," said Maybelle.

"About that," said June timidly. "Is what we're doing really
right? After all, you're the one all those good folks are paying to
see."

"It's just till I get this little sore throat cleared up, honey," she
said, giving her a comforting little pat. "Don't you *know* the show
must go on? It's done all the time in the business. What would be
wrong would be taking all their money and then not giving them a
show at all."

June brightened, "Yes, I *do* understand. It's going to take a long
time for me to think like a professional, ain't it, Maybelle?"

Suddenly their bookings began to improve. Instead of always being
the opening act, they were asked to be the main show in minor
concerts.

By the time they pulled into Nashville in early April, Maybelle's
headquarters, the old Bide-A-Wee Motel—sitting rooms and a kitch-
enette, let by the day, week, or month—looked like the Helmsley
Palace.

"This is just temporary, darlin'," purred Maybelle, "until things
get better. Gives us a chance to rest our feet and catch our breath."

"It's wonderful," said June. "Truly wonderful."

Maybelle laughed. "After you unload the car and run my bath water, go ahead and take care of the phone calls. Then just scramble me a few eggs and fix a couple of slices of toast for supper. I'm off my feed a little."

After June had wrestled in the equipment, she obediently called Maybelle's answering service. She faithfully recorded each message, taking care to make a little frowny face beside anyone who might be a bill collector, just as Maybelle had taught her.

Of the sixteen phone calls received during the last two weeks, there was only one she could safely bring to Maybelle's attention. June sat respectfully on the edge of the bed, watching the face of the last performing member of the Family Rose as Maybelle returned the call.

Maybelle gasped and tried to control her voice. Dizzily, she replaced the receiver in the cradle and pirouetted across the room.

"This is it, kid, my big break. I've been asked to sing at the Merle Watson Memorial Festival."

"The big one in North Carolina?" squealed June.

"The same! Seems as though old Doc Watson was mighty fond of Momma—and this year he has a hankering to perform with some of the old groups that first gave him a leg up."

"God almighty!"

"It can mean records, bookings, the Grand Ole Opry. Fame, kiddo, fame. And oh, baby, once you've had a taste of it, there ain't nothing else that'll take its place ever again. We've got to be perfect. I want you to practice until you drop."

June started backing away from her.

"No, ma'am. I know my place. I have no business up there singing in front of those folks." She set her lips in a thin line. "It just wouldn't be right."

"You little fool," snapped Maybelle as she reached for June's wrist. Then, seeing the shock on the girl's face, her voice became low and coaxing.

"It's all in your head, darling. You've got to get over this. And you will, by God. I'm going to see to it."

Desperately, she cast about in her mind for what it would take to give the girl confidence. She briefly considered all the contents of the medicine bundle. Then, inspired, she knew what it would take—but it cost Maybelle Rose a whole hunk of pride.

"You're going to touch Momma's guitar."

"Please, don't make me," said June.

"Do it, I said. Right on the rose."

June trembled and uneasily extended her hand toward the mahogany case. When her fingers came in contact with the cloisonné rose, she blanched and withdrew them at once.

"There now," said Maybelle. "It didn't kill you. And you're going to join me in our family ritual. And you're to stop crying and carrying on. Just close your eyes and see Momma giving you permission to be up there on that stage."

The next morning, June's face glowed with wonder.

"Miss Maybelle, it's all right if I sing with you. I've got to tell you. Momma Rose came to me in a dream last night. She was standing before me just as real as life and she talked to me. Talked to me real nice."

"Stop that," shrieked Maybelle, aghast at the child's precarious hold on reality. "Stop that. It was something you ate."

But from that time on, June stepped onto the stage with impeccable carriage and walked easily over to the family rose, and confidently extended her finger toward the center of the flower, murmuring her homage to Momma. Then she turned and smiled brilliantly and blew a kiss at the crowd before she modestly took her place five steps behind Maybelle.

Maybelle began to eye her uneasily. The girl was changing before her very eyes.

The night before the Merle Watson Memorial Concert, they were one of several groups checking their equipment. The patriarch of bluegrass guitar, Doc Watson, blind since childhood, was being led from group to group. He had a legendary sense of sound and had been known to stop a number stone cold dead to holler out instructions to a bewildered technician.

"That bass is too bright, son," he would snap, and listen keenly, with an ear cocked to one side, as minute adjustments were made in the balance of tweeters and woofers. Despite all his efforts to sound gentle, nothing softened his underlying irritability with inept musicians. He simply could not tolerate them. He had an august, dignified, white-headed physical presence, further augmented by the fans' awareness of the pain he had borne throughout his life.

Old now, and mourning the tragic death of his son, Merle Watson, his awesome stature as the World Champion Flat Guitar Picker unsettled many of the musicians who appeared at this star-studded annual memorial concert. Seasoned guitarists dropped their picks and fiddlers' fingers fumbled on the frets. Cloggers stepped on each other's toes and little starlets squeaked on the high notes until the kindly old man settled them down with a tolerant chuckle. Doc Watson had become art, and the epitome of tragedy borne with dignity.

He stopped before June and Maybelle where they were rehearsing on the porch of the cabin. A setting where the lesser solar system of stars performed. He listened keenly, then turned and spoke sharply to his assistant. The man looked blankly at the arrangement of the sound systems. Hastily Maybelle stepped forward.

"As I live and breathe," she gushed, standing directly in front of the grand old man, "I'm Maybelle Rose, sir. And I believe you knew Momma. I'm so proud to meet you. I'm sorry that you've had to listen in before we get things set up right."

"I'd like to meet your backup singer," Doc Watson said quietly.

She studied his face, then spun around and asked June to step forward.

She did, but she could barely blurt out a hello. She dipped her head.

"It's an honor," she murmured.

Doc Watson changed color and he was deathly still.

He knows, Maybelle thought wildly. *He knows.*

He walked off without saying another word to either of them.

Feverishly Maybelle paced the floor that night. The old man knew! His temper was well known. Sickened, she tried to imagine what he would do or say. Would he expose her right off? Ruin her? Her big chance was becoming a living nightmare.

By morning she had made up her mind. Never in a hundred years would she allow June to take her place. Never.

Calmly, she sent a note to Doc Watson's assistant. "Please inform

Doc Watson that my first two songs will introduce my backup singer, June Jones, a young lady of exceptional voice.''

She pulled on her rubber gloves and trembled as she loosened the leather tie on her medicine bundle. The substance she wanted was in a golden locket molded around a tiny vial. Gingerly she unscrewed the stopper and dipped a pin inside. Then she carefully dropped a pinpoint of liquid onto the center of the rose on Momma's guitar.

There were poisons which would have acted faster. But a long, loving, extravagant introduction would set well with Doc Watson. Maybelle savored the idea of folks talking about how generous and unselfish she'd been. Besides, the first song would not show off the spectacular range of June's voice.

"Ready, kid?" asked Maybelle, just before they were ready to go on.

June nodded, her eyes filled with tears.

"I have a surprise for you, Maybelle."

"Well, I have a surprise for you too, kid," said Maybelle coldly.

"But I want to *tell* you something," begged June.

Maybelle brushed past her and walked out of the cabin.

"Come *on,*" she hissed back at June. "My fans are waiting."

"Thank you. Thank you." Maybelle smiled brightly at the applause. "And now, as many of our fans know, before we begin a concert, I always thank Momma Rose. We owe it all to her."

The applause was deafening. She respectfully dipped her head and walked over to Momma's guitar.

"Be with us, Momma," she said slowly. She reached for the rose, but her fingers stopped short by a quarter of an inch.

Then June stepped forward and imitated Maybelle. Her fingers connected, resonating on the soundboard with a soft muffled thump. Then, standing side by side, they gave a slight bow and went to the front and picked up their guitars.

"My little backup singer knows I have a surprise for her, but she doesn't know what," said Maybelle coyly. "As you all know, it has long been the tradition of the Family Rose to support new talent."

She swallowed hard, nearly choking on the words. "And today, making her debut solo performance is my own little ol' backup, June Jones.''

June gasped and stepped forward.

"I can't," she stammered. "I can't possibly."

"I insist," hissed Maybelle. "Give it all you've got."

June stepped forward as if she were waking from a dream. At first she kept her head bowed, then when the warmth of the audience reached her, the rhythm began pulsing through her body. She finished the first song to deafening applause and then started on her second number. The one that would demonstrate her incredible range.

Horrified, Maybelle watched. Her throat constricted in protest. She shouldn't be able to carry on. Now everyone would know it had been June's voice all along. Everyone would know.

June's eyes glittered with excitement and she became lost in the high sweet tones, her fingers flying across the guitar.

Maybelle's heart beat faster and faster. The audience rose to its feet and was swaying—clearly loving, adoring June Jones. Maybelle's blood rushed to her head. It wasn't working. She gave a little squeal before she fell writhing to the floor of the stage.

June got to her first.

"No, no, no," she cried frantically. "Please!" She turned to Doc Watson's assistant, who had rushed onto the stage. "Get an ambulance."

"Maybelle, you're the only family I've got. You're going to be a star." June cradled Maybelle in her arms. Tears streamed down her face.

"Maybelle. Listen to me. I tried to tell you. It's your time. Momma came to me in a dream last night and said so. She told me it was time that you had her guitar. You were playing her guitar, sweet darlin' Maybelle. Momma said it was time to hand you the family rose.''

THE LAST REVIVAL
by CLARK HOWARD

Coy slipped off the side of the empty boxcar an hour after the slow-moving freight train crossed the Arkansas state line. He slid down the cinder-covered embankment to the gully beside the tracks and waited there, hiding in the bushes, until the rest of the train lumbered by and the caboose was well down the tracks. Then he climbed back up the hill and looked around.

In three directions Coy saw nothing but wide vistas of evenly furrowed farmland, broken now and again by a fence or a house, or a stand of trees. In the fourth direction his scrutiny was rewarded by the sight of a blacktop secondary road running perpendicular to the railroad tracks. About half a mile down the road, Coy saw what looked like a small service station. Thinking he might be able to get some food there, he started toward the place. As he walked, his stomach growled furiously.

Coy's last meal had been supper the previous night, five hours before he had dug under the road-gang fence back in Mississippi and headed for the Arkansas line. It was close to one o'clock now, judging from the slant of his shadow, which meant he had been without food for close to twenty hours. He had two dollars and sixty cents left and he wanted to keep as much of it as possible. In Arkansas it took a minimum of a dollar to keep from being a vagrant, but he was going to have to get something to eat soon or he knew he was going to be sick.

It turned out that the service station was also a country grocery store. After looking around inside, Coy finally invested fifty-eight cents in a can of Vienna sausages, a package of crackers, and a cold bottle of orange pop. He had the storekeeper open the can for him and took his food outside where he sat on an empty box to eat. He was sitting there eating when the Revival Bus pulled in for gas a few minutes later and he saw the girl for the first time.

Maybe it was her hair, dark cherry-colored and long, very finely textured, or the wide shoulders that tapered to a waist so trim it seemed incapable of holding her together—or maybe it was the way her uncolored lips parted as she paused for a moment on the raised steps of the bus. Maybe, he told himself, it was just that she was the first woman he had seen up close after seven months of abstinence in the Squires County Prison Camp over in Mississippi. Whatever it was that passed between them when their eyes met and locked for that split instant, one thing was for certain: it was electric and it was mutual. Coy was sure she felt it just as much as he did.

She stepped quickly down and went around to the side toward the restrooms. When she was out of sight, Coy turned his attention to the bus itself. It had seen better days, that was obvious. Coy guessed it was a reconditioned school bus. Through the windows he could see that the rear half of it had been converted into living quarters of some kind. Across the side under the row of windows were painted the words HOLY WORD REVIVAL.

Two men got off while Coy was watching. One of them was a cold-eyed, bitter-faced man, tall and lean as a stick. Despite the heat of the day, he was wearing a black suit and a string tie knotted at the throat. He walked stiffly erect, glancing neither left nor right.

The second man who got off was smaller and crippled. His left foot was clubbed, and he wore a high-laced leather shoe with an enormous heel. Understandably awkward in his gait, he labored along behind the taller man.

After the men had gone inside the store, Coy finished eating and went around to the side of the building where the girl had gone. From his shirt pocket he took out one of two cigarettes that were left in a crumpled pack. He dug his thumbnail into the head of a wooden match and lighted up. He had just thrown the match away and was lounging against an empty oil drum when the girl came back out. Her face was flushed, as if she had just finished splashing cold water on it. She glanced briefly at Coy and started back toward the front of the store.

"Hey," he greeted her quietly as she walked past him.

"Hey yourself," she answered back. She almost paused, then seemed to think better of it. After half a step's hesitation, she kept going.

"Hold on a minute, will you?" Coy said, catching her by the arm. "You're riding that revival bus out there, aren't you?"

"You saw me get off it, didn't you?" she replied. She made no move to take his hand off her arm.

"You reckon I could get a lift to the next town?"

"Not a chance," she said emphatically. "Brother Monroe, he's the preacher, never picks up hitchhikers." She looked down at his hand. "You through with my arm?"

Coy let go and she started to walk away. Before she had gone two steps, she turned back again.

"If you'll give me a puff of that cigarette, I'll tell you how you *might* be able to get yourself a ride," she said.

Coy nodded and held the cigarette up. The girl glanced apprehensively toward the front of the store, then stepped quickly over to him and took a long, deep drag. She stood very close to him, touching his wrist lightly with her fingertips. There was a slight fragrance about her that he found pleasant as she stood there. He saw that she had freckles down the front of her dress where it was unbuttoned at the top.

"That sure tasted good," she said after she exhaled. She swayed slightly. "Wow! When you haven't had a smoke for a week, it really hits you."

Coy took her arm again to steady her. She leaned toward him, smiling almost giddily.

"What about that ride?" he said.

"Okay, listen. You go out and offer to drive the bus for Brother Monroe. You know how to drive, don't you?"

"Sure."

"Good. Brother Monroe doesn't like to drive, says it bothers his back. The other one, Aaron Timm, with the clubfoot, has been doing the driving, but the state troopers fined Brother Monroe for it yesterday outside Little Rock. They said Aaron shouldn't be handling a bus in his condition. So, if you say you'll do all the driving, Brother Monroe just might let you come along."

They both heard the store's screen door slam and the girl quickly pulled away from Coy.

"I've got to go." She hurried back around front.

Coy took another drag on the cigarette, thinking that her lips had just been on it, thinking of the way she smelled and of the freckles that disappeared under the top of her dress. Smiling to himself, he tossed the butt away and walked around to the bus.

The girl was already on board, sitting by one of the open windows. Aaron Timm was waiting at the bus door while Brother Monroe counted out a handful of change to pay for the gas.

" 'Scuse me, Reverend," Coy said when the preacher was finished. "I was wondering if you could let me have a ride into the next town?"

"Don't take hitchhikers," Brother Monroe said gruffly.

"I'd offer to pay if I had any money, sir," Coy said politely. "Sure be glad to work it out, though. I could help with the driving or whatever else there was to do."

"Might not be a bad idea, Brother Monroe," said Aaron Timm. "Them troopers could have sent word ahead to watch for us."

"They might put us in jail next time, Brother Monroe," the girl added from the window.

"Shut up, both of you!" the preacher snapped. "I don't need the likes of you two to do my thinking for me!" He looked Coy up and down. "You a good driver? Careful?"

"Yes, sir," Coy said solemnly.

"All right, get behind the wheel," Monroe ordered. "I'll try you for a mile or two."

"Thank you kindly, Reverend," Coy said. As Brother Monroe turned to board the bus, Coy smiled up at the girl. She smiled back and winked.

*   *   *

The broad, flat farmlands sped by as Coy guided the bus smoothly along the blacktop. In the rear view mirror he could see Aaron Timm curled up asleep on one of the double seats. Brother Monroe, after sitting up front and watching him drive for all of two minutes, had retired to the rear of the bus and drawn the heavy curtain that partitioned off his private quarters. The girl had moved over to a seat on the aisle and propped her knees up on the seat in front of her to read a dogeared movie magazine. Sitting the way she was gave Coy a good view of her legs. For a while he divided his time between watching the road and watching her. After a few miles, the girl's eyes closed and she leaned over in the seat to doze, and Coy could no longer see her.

When there was nothing else on the bus to occupy his mind, Coy fished out the last of his cigarettes and smoked while he drove. He thought of Gaston, the town they were heading for. Roscoe was in Gaston—at least he had been a week ago. Coy had found that out from a new arrival on the road gang who had worked as a cleanup man in the Gaston Pool Parlor for a few days and then had wandered across the state line to Lill, Mississippi, where he had taken a fall for petty theft. He had been given a ninety-day sentence and had arrived at the Squires County Prison Camp that same afternoon. It was two days later that Coy heard him mention a man named Roscoe who was dealing cards in the back room of the Gaston Pool Parlor.

Coy wondered who Roscoe was using for a straight man now. Probably another poor sucker like I was a year ago, he thought. His mind drifted back to the day Roscoe had found him in a cheap Alabama cafe where Coy had been washing dishes for four dollars a day and meals. Roscoe had liked his looks and had taken him out of the joint and taught him how to be a straight man in a poker game. It wasn't really cheating, Roscoe had explained. All a straight man did was help build up the pot whenever his partner gave the high sign that he was taking less than three cards on a draw. It was supposed to be a simple matter of percentages, that was all—nothing crooked about it—except that Roscoe was tilting the odds to about ninety percent in his favor by using marked cards. Then, one night he had left Coy holding the proverbial bag in a roadhouse in Squires County.

Coy flipped his cigarette out the vent window and rubbed the scar that cut an arc around his jawbone. That was from a beer bottle one of the players had broken across his face before they dragged him off to jail. The roadhouse owner who had been running the game was a cousin of the county magistrate, so to console his players who had lost part of their cotton-crop profits, he arranged with the magistrate for Coy to draw a one-year sentence.

On the road gang the men dug irrigation ditches twelve hours a day. Coy got used to it after a few weeks, after his blisters had swollen, broken, bled, and then hardened into calluses; after his shoulders ached some more, then loosened into workable, elastic muscles; and after his stomach stopped revolting against the watery grits and lumpy oatmeal that Squires County fed its convicts. He got used to it, and determined to see it through. A year, the magistrate had said when he railroaded him, so a year Coy would do.

He would have, too, if he hadn't heard where Roscoe was—but thinking about Roscoe had been too much for him. Roscoe wearing fancy silk shirts while Coy wore striped sackcloth; Roscoe eating steak and eggs while Coy ate slop; Roscoe sleeping on a feather mattress in an air-conditioned motel room while Coy spent his nights on a wooden bunk in a sweltering prison barracks. Thinking about all that was just too much. The work grew unbearable, the food became intolerable again, and the nights were dark periods of torture in which Roscoe's smiling face was ever in his mind.

Coy could not take it, so he dug out. At ten o'clock one night he made it through a loose floorboard in the barracks and dug under the barbed-wire fence. He headed west, toward the nearest state line. He walked for nine hours, and at seven o'clock the next morning stole a pair of overalls and a work shirt off some farmer's wash line. After changing clothes, he made it to the nearest highway and got a ride on a vegetable truck. Three towns down the road he earned three dollars unloading the truck at the produce cannery. He bought a pack of cigarettes and immediately hopped a freight out of town. He rode the freight until an hour after it crossed the Arkansas line.

Then he rolled off and walked down to the gas station where the Revival Bus had pulled in.

Now, Coy told himself as he drove, he had two things to accomplish: getting even with Roscoe—and getting away. If they caught him and sent him back to Mississippi, he'd get an additional sentence for his escape: twice the time he'd had left to serve, plus a year. That would be twenty-two months instead of the five he'd had left.

Coy smiled grimly. It was worth taking the chance. Catching up with Roscoe would *make* it worth taking the chance.

He leaned over the wheel and hunched his back to relax. He wished he had another cigarette, but it wouldn't be long now. Up ahead a sign read: GASTON 12.

On a large vacant field just outside the Gaston city limits, Coy took off his shirt and helped Aaron Timm unload the bus. The revival meeting tent, which was tied to the cargo carrier on top, was the first to come off. Then they took down the stacks of folding chairs and a collapsible pulpit which had been carried beneath the folded tent. Last came a small pedal organ that was lashed to the rear luggage rack.

"When do you set everything up?" Coy asked when it was all unloaded and piled in a neat row.

"In the morning," Aaron said, chewing on a toothpick. "I'll raise the tent and set up all the chairs and things right after breakfast. Then in the afternoon I go into town and pass out them handbills over there." He pointed to a cardboard box filled with printed circulars. "The meeting'll be tomorrow evening after the supper hour. Brother Monroe, he'll preach a sermon and play the organ. The girl there, she'll sing hymns. I'll pass the collection plate afterward."

Coy nodded. He glanced over and saw the girl opening up a box of pots and pans next to a portable cookstove she had just set up. The preacher was slumped down in a camp chair under a tree with his eyes closed.

"He sure don't overwork himself, does he?"

"Why should he?" replied Aaron, momentarily angry. "Why should he, when he's got fools like me and the girl to do everything?"

"If you don't like it, why don't you quit?" Coy said. He kept his tone conversational.

"And do what?" Aaron asked with a grunt. "Jobs ain't easy to come by when you got a clubfoot and don't know how to do nothing. And I don't know how to do nothing." His anger passed quickly and he rubbed his hand fondly over the smooth-finished top of the pedal organ. "Except play the organ, that is. I do that real good."

"Thought you said the preacher did the organ-playing."

"He does. But I could, if he'd let me. Play a lot better'n he does, too."

"Why won't he let you?" Coy asked.

Aaron Timm looked down at the ground, embarrassed. "He thinks we make more money when I pass the collection plate. Says people are apt to drop in a little extra when they see me dragging my clubfoot along."

Cory nodded and did not pursue the subject. "Anything else I can help you with," he asked.

"I have to unfold the tent now and spread it out so's it'll be ready to hoist in the morning," Aaron said. "You can lend me a hand with that if you want."

"Sure."

While they worked the big, heavy tent, Coy watched the girl putting canned stew into a cook pot and lighting a fire under it. Her back was to him and when she moved he could see ripples where her leg muscles flexed and loosened. He always had admired a woman with good, strong legs.

"What's her name?" he asked Aaron, bobbing his head toward the girl.

"Willow," said Aaron. "Don't know her last name."

"Where'd she come from?"

"Monroe picked her up a few weeks back when he was in southern Indiana. I think she's a runaway." Aaron chuckled. "Old Monroe, he had it in mind for her to share the back of the bus with him. He ain't had much luck with her, though—she still goes off and sleeps outside by herself."

Coy looked over at Brother Monroe sprawled in the camp chair. "He sure don't fit my idea of a preacher."

"He ain't," Aaron said, grunting again. "Ain't no more a preacher than you are. He just knows how to talk good, is all. Why, when he's behind that pulpit threatening brimstone and eternal damnation, he's as good as any preacher you ever seen, but that's when he's getting ready to pass the plate. After it's over, when all the farmers and their families have gone on home, then he's back to the jug again and thinking about that girl Willow—"

"Likes his liquor, does he," Coy said, more of a statement than a question.

"You bet your boots he does," Aaron told him emphatically. "He'll have me running all over town tomorrow looking for a boot-legger to buy a jug from. This here state's dry, you know—can't sell hard liquor over the counter in Arkansas."

"Yeah. I know." So old hatchet-face is a big fraud, Coy mused. Just a good talker . . .

They finished laying out the tent and went back over to the bus where Coy had hung his shirt.

"Well, I guess I'll be on my way," Coy said. He noticed a pained look come over Aaron's face, as if the little man did not want to see him go.

"If you'll stick around," he said, "I'll see if I can sneak you a bowl of that stew Willow's making."

"Maybe I'll see you later," Coy told him. "Right now I want to go into Gaston."

"Sure," Aaron said, a little downheartedly. "Well, thanks for lending me a hand."

Coy walked on around the bus. When he was out of sight, he paused for a second to steal several of Brother Monroe's handbills from the box he had seen earlier. Then he crossed the field to the highway and started walking into Gaston.

The back room of the Gaston Pool Parlor was filled with the thick closeness of sweat and smoke. A dozen men in overalls and scuffed work shoes stood watching the poker game that was being played on an oilcloth-covered table under a low-hanging light. There were five players in the game, two of them farmers and two others who looked like poolroom bums. The fifth man was Roscoe.

Coy stood well back in the group of spectators, in the shadows so that Roscoe could not see him. Unlike the other onlookers, he was not watching the game itself, not following the cards and bets and raises. He was just watching Roscoe, watching his face and eyes, thinking about how many good meals Roscoe had eaten in the last seven months; how many nights Roscoe had crawled between clean sheets; how many hot baths Roscoe had taken. Unconsciously, as he thought about those things, Coy reached up and rubbed a fingertip along the scar where the beer bottle had broken across his cheek.

Enjoy the game, gambling man, he thought. It's the last one you'll be dealing for a long time.

Coy edged behind the watching men to the back door and slipped out into the alley. He took Brother Monroe's handbills out of his shirt and put them under a trash barrel where he could easily find them again. Then he walked down the alley to the street. It was dark out now and he had to stand under a street light to count his money. He had a dollar bill, a dollar in change, and two cents left over. Taking the two cents out, he wrapped the rest of the money in the empty cigarette package he still had in his shirt pocket. Whistling softly, he walked across the town square and found an all-night cafe with a taxi parked in front of it. The driver was resting his head back against the seat, smoking.

"Evening," Coy said, leaning with one hand on the car roof.

"Evening," the driver replied. He studied Coy thoughtfully.

"Warm tonight," Coy observed.

"A mite," the driver allowed, "for this time of year."

Coy looked back at the square. "Right nice little town you got here."

"Stranger, are you?"

Coy nodded. "Just passing through. Camped 'bout a mile up the highway." He smiled. "Kind of hard on a man in a strange town, not knowing anybody at all. Man don't even know where to buy a jug."

"Can't buy a jug in this state," the driver said. "This here is a dry state."

"Sure," said Coy, "I know about the liquor laws. Know a little about the taxi business, too."

"That so?" The driver's tone was carefully neutral.

"Sure. Used to drive one myself up in Junction City, Kansas. It was dry up there, too, but what we'd do was tell a thirsty man to leave two dollars somewhere—'' Coy looked around and then nodded toward a stack of empty cola cases at the side of the cafe. "Like in that top crate over there. Then we'd tell him to take a walk around the square. Sure enough, when he got back, his two dollars would be gone and there'd be a two-dollar jug of homemade mash there instead.''

"That's right interesting,'' the driver observed.

"Well, one thing about it,'' Coy said, "there wasn't no way for the man doing the selling to get caught.'' He took his hand off the top of the car and stretched. "Well, it's getting late. I reckon I'll walk once around town and then head back out the highway. See you.''

The taxi driver nodded. Coy stepped back onto the sidewalk and sauntered over to the stack of cola cases. He put one foot up on the empty boxes to retie his shoelace, and as he did he slipped the cigarette package of money into the top crate. Then he started around the square, whistling softly again.

When Coy got back to the cafe, the taxi was gone and so was his money, and a corked, unmarked quart bottle of bootleg whisky was in the top crate. Coy slipped the bottle under his shirt and strolled back to the alley behind the poolroom. He set the bottle on the ground behind the trash barrel where he had put Brother Monroe's handbills. Then he sat down across the alley near the back door of the poolroom and leaned up against somebody's fence. He relaxed and looked up at the starry sky.

Waiting there in the dark, Coy thought about the girl, Willow, and how she had touched his hand when she shared his cigarette back at the gas station. He thought about how she had stood close to him and how the sunlight had fallen on the freckles that spread down inside her dress . . .

Closing his eyes, Coy smiled and wondered if she had freckles all over.

Roscoe came out of the poolroom at midnight looking as cool and detached as ever.

Coy's eyes snapped open at once at the sound of the door opening. He tensed and remained perfectly still, looking up from where he was sitting as Roscoe stood in a rectangle of light and slipped the knot of his tie up to the buttoned collar of his silk shirt. After putting on his coat, Roscoe cracked two of his knuckles, stared at the clear night sky for a moment, then stepped into the alley, closing the door behind him. Coy waited until Roscoe walked past him, then he stood up.

"Hello, gambling man," he said softly.

Roscoe whirled around and met Coy's fist, thrown at him with seven months of road-gang strength. It struck him solidly in the mouth, splitting both lips and driving his front teeth inward. Before he could even moan he was struck again, flush in the center of the face, the impact laying waste to the cartilage and bone of his nose. Blows began to rain down on him, ripping his cheek, tearing his ear, fracturing his jawbone. They were hard-knuckled blows that beat a methodical tattoo of pain that quickly began to blacken his consciousness. He slumped against a building as explosions of red flashed under his closed eyelids. Instinctively he raised his arms and sought to shelter his face behind them, but when he did so, he felt his rib cage rocked by the same incessant pounding until momentarily the breath in his lungs deserted him and he choked for air. A final vicious blow dug deeply into his soft stomach and he doubled up and pitched onto his face in the dirt of the alley.

Coy stood over him, his chest heaving, fists aching, upper arms searing with exertion. For the seven months, gambling man, he thought coldly, and for the scar on my face.

Rolling Roscoe onto his back, Coy took the billfold from his inside coat pocket and a half-filled package of cigarettes from his shirt pocket. Then he got the revival handbills from under the nearby trash barrel and spread them loosely under Roscoe's limp arm.

Retrieving the quart of whisky from where he had put it, Coy left the alley and headed out the dark highway. Half a mile outside of town, he left the road and cut over to a stream he had seen earlier. He stretched out on his stomach and soaked both of his hands in the cold, soothing water. When he was sure neither hand was going to swell up, he dried off his hands on his shirttail and went back to the highway.

*   *   *

Brother Monroe was still awake when Coy got back to the camp. He was sitting on his cot in the back of the bus. The blue light of an oil lantern cast heavy shadows around him.

"Reverend," Coy said quietly.

Monroe jumped, startled. "What—who's there?" Then he saw who it was. "What are you doing prowling around here, boy?" he bristled. "What do you want?"

"Didn't aim to disturb you, sir," Coy said. "There's something I need your advice about."

"You must be crazy, boy," Monroe snorted. "It's the middle of the night. Now you get on out of here—"

"But I just wanted to know what to do with this," Coy said, taking the bottle of whisky from under his shirt and holding it so that Monroe could get a good look at it. The hard-eyed old man leaned forward and peered at the bottle. His tongue wet his lips. "The man that owns the poolroom gave it to me for sweeping out his place," Coy said innocently. "It's hard liquor and I don't know what to do with it. Liquor's sinful, ain't it, Reverend?"

"Eh?" Monroe said, his eyes never leaving the bottle. "Sinful? Oh, yes! Yes, indeed, it certainly is sinful."

"I didn't want to throw it away anywhere for fear somebody'd find it and drink it," Coy declared. "And I didn't want to pour it out because it ain't fit to pour on good soil. So I thought I'd ask you about it, sir."

"Best thing you could have done, boy," Monroe said with growing enthusiasm.

"I was thinking maybe you could use it at the revival meeting tomorrow night," Coy said. "Kind of an example against sinful ways. You could just smash it right in front of everybody to show folks how easy it is to put the devil behind them."

"An inspirational idea, my boy!" Monroe beamed. "Might help some poor soul see the light of salvation. I'll do that very thing. Give me the bottle."

Coy handed it to him. Monroe placed it gently on the cot, then got up and put a fatherly hand on Coy's shoulder. He guided him back through the bus to the door.

"You did a good Christian act tonight, my boy, and I'm sure

you'll be amply rewarded for it in the Hereafter. I'll ask you to leave me to my meditation now. Go your way in peace, knowing that you've been of considerable help to a spreader of the true word."

"Thank you, reverend," Coy said humbly.

Coy stepped down out of the bus. Before he had gone three steps, he heard the cork pop. Smiling, he went off to look for Willow and Aaron Timm.

The sheriff was there bright and early the next morning, accompanied by two deputies. Coy, dressed in Brother Monroe's best black suit and a clean white shirt, stepped down from the Revival Bus to meet them.

"Morning," said the sheriff. "You the parson?"

"Yes, I'm Brother Coy." He smiled and turned to Aaron, who was nearby setting pegs for the tent, and Willow, who was getting ready to prepare breakfast. "This is Sister Willow," Coy said. "She sings hymns at our meetings. And this is Brother Aaron Timm, our fine spiritual organist." He folded his hands in front of him. "How may we be of service to you, Sheriff?"

"Sorry to have to trouble you folks, Reverend," the sheriff said, "but we had a little trouble in town last night. Some gambler named Roscoe got beat up and robbed. We found these where it happened—" He held out a handful of revival circulars.

Coy looked at them and sighed heavily. "I was afraid something like this would happen," he said, with a hint of sadness in his voice. "I'll have to accept the blame, Sheriff. Will you come with me, please?"

Coy led the sheriff and his deputies around to the other side of the bus. On a blanket up close to one of the big tires, Monroe was snoring loudly in drunken sleep. He was unshaved, his hair uncombed, and he was wearing the faded work clothes Coy had stolen off the wash line. On the ground beside him was the unlabeled whisky bottle, empty.

"We picked him up yesterday," Coy told the sheriff. "He said he'd been a preacher of the Holy Word himself in years gone by, but had fallen on hard times. I offered to let him come along with our group as a handyman until he could get on his feet again. Last

night after supper I sent him into town to pass out those handbills.
I didn't see him again until this morning." Coy shook his head
slowly. "I had no idea he'd been in any trouble."

The sheriff knelt beside Monroe and went through his pockets. He
found Roscoe's wallet.

"Looks like this is our man, all right. Pick him up and put him
in the car, boys."

"I really don't know what to say, Sheriff," said Coy. "I feel this
whole thing is my fault."

"No cause for you to blame yourself, Reverend," the sheriff said.
"After all, you was just trying to help him."

"Yes, I know, but I have a feeling that the poor soul isn't responsible. All yesterday he kept saying that our little revival group was
just like the one he used to have, and last night he kept referring to
the bus here as *his* bus. It was as though he thought he was the
preacher and we all worked for him."

"Sounds to me like he might be a little touched," said the sheriff,
rubbing his chin thoughtfully. "If he starts that business with me
when he wakes up, I might just send him down to the state hospital
for observation."

"Whatever you think would be best for him, Sheriff. After all,
you're a professional in these matters. Incidentally, how is the man
he beat up?"

"Well, he was worked over pretty good—that old drunk must have
used a club on him. He's in the hospital over at the county seat. I
reckon he'll be all right in time."

"We can give thanks for that much," Coy said reverently.

"Suppose so," the sheriff said indifferently. They walked back
around the bus and the sheriff tipped his hat to Willow. "Well, good
day to you folks."

"Good day, Sheriff."

After the sheriff and his deputies left with Monroe, Coy and Willow and Aaron all looked at each other and smiled triumphantly
in unison.

That night, due to the gossip stemming from Roscoe's beating and
Monroe's arrest, half the townspeople of Gaston turned out to hear

the new circuit preacher, Reverend Coy, deliver an inspired sermon on the evils of drink. After the sermon, Sister Willow sang "Give Me That Old-Time Religion," accompanied on the organ by Brother Aaron Timm. Brother Timm then played a solo medley of hymns while young Reverend Coy himself passed the collection plate.

When Coy returned to the pulpit and handed the money-laden tray to Willow, he noticed that under the tent lights the freckles on her chest seemed to sparkle and glow like the star-sprinkled sky he had looked at while waiting in the alley for Roscoe.

As she took the collection plate from him, Willow squeezed his hand briefly and looked nakedly into his eyes. Coy smiled at her and nodded once.

Being a preacher isn't going to be too bad at all, he thought.

WILLIE'S STORY
by *JERRY F. SKARKY*

It was Sunday morning, Willie's morning to collect cans. He knew which bars and parking lots were worth the gas to drive to, and in The Ville he knew the lots where the kids hung out, even the stretches of bar ditch that were worth the walk and the bend and stoop.

He was still agile for his age, and the early Sunday stillness stirred a nostalgic reverence in his soul. He didn't smash the cans; he didn't like the noise. But the muted clink of the cans in the trash bag his failing ears did enjoy, like distant chimes or tolling bells.

His last stop every Sunday was a bridge over a drainage ditch out on the blacktop half a mile past the city limit sign. Wille had deduced that those kids driving around partying on the country roads would dump their empties on the way back, and the ditch was usually good for at least a couple of empty six-packs. And after the hard rain Wednesday of the previous week, no telling what had caught in the culvert's mouth.

Willie parked his old station wagon past the bridge and walked back, picking up the bad tosses on the way. Weeds had shot up waist high under the bridge, and the high water had matted them with debris, dead vegetation, paper trash, fragments of plastic, oil cans.

Willie looked down at the ditch's upper channel still treacherous with mud. A bright red car whizzed by, a church-dressed white family staring with cranky, fleeting eyes that Willie felt from the back of his head appraising him, categorizing him, dismissing him. A poor old black man collecting cans.

A smile crawled slowly over his face as he peered down, looking for the telltale glint or, better yet, the full brown sack riding the weeds.

He shifted his weight, and sun on aluminum caught his eye from directly below. The sun was high enough now to dazzle. His head moved a fraction reacting to the glare, his eyes squinted, focused on the bottom end of a Silver Bullet. At first he thought the can was partly buried in mud, rich chocolate mud that slowly, numbingly took form and made his heart slap in his chest. Not mud; a leg camouflaged in detritus, a human leg, a brown leg, a girl's brown human leg. And the other leg, disappearing with the rest of her under water-bent weeds.

Still. The legs were still.

As he walked kneeless to his car, and again several minutes later as the car lurched urgently through ascending gears, Willie told himself he had never seen anything as still as those young legs.

"And you last saw Sabrina Thursday evening about nine, you say?"

"No, man, I told you, Wednesday, man."

An hour before it had been "sir"; the boy was getting tired. His lanky frame had slid down in the chair to an angle that couldn't be comfortable. The expressive eyes had lost the glaze of grief and fear.

Detective Lewis Allan made a second check beside the question on his notepad and without moving his head looked again at the loose shirt the boy was wearing, yellow with red and lavender diagonal bars. The shirt irritated him.

"Did you get along with her grandmother, Lenard?" The murdered girl had been left by her mother as an infant. The mother's present whereabouts, unknown. Father, unknown.

The face above the shirt had assumed an air of punk toughness. Without looking at Allan the boy shrugged.

Time to try a little shock therapy.

"Lenard, this is your girlfriend we're talking about. A knife was stuck in her. Not just once, Lenard. Not in her heart, not in her stomach. In a place where some girls her age haven't even been touched." Allan paused to smile at the boy, knowing exactly how chilling the smile would be.

"Somebody was mad at her, Lenard, or crazy. Women sometimes do things to make a man crazy, don't they, Lenard?"

The boy's face had fallen apart feature by feature. Allan rocked gently in his chair and drummed his pen on the edge of his desk. The slow tap of the pen was the only sound in the room.

"What did you do with the knife, son?" Allan asked.

Lenard tried to sit up, but his feet slipped on the tile floor. His eyes bulged desperately, then his hips bucked again as he dug into his pocket.

"Here's my knife, man, you check it out." He started to toss the closed knife, thought better of it, and handed the knife across the desk.

The boy watched with burning eyes while Allan looked at the cheap, cracked plastic on the handle and opened first one, then the other small blades. One of the thumb-grooves was packed with gummy dirt, and Allan cleaned it out with his thumbnail before closing the blades and handing the knife back.

The blade that had mutilated the girl was eight to ten inches long, approximately an inch and a quarter wide. A tiny steel sliver had been found in her pelvic bone, so the knife they were looking for was a butcher knife with a nick in it.

"My granddaddy gave it to me when I was a kid," the boy said, stuffing his knife into a tight pocket.

"Used to have one about like it," Allan said absently. He was telling himself that he still had to treat the boy as a suspect, and his gut wasn't buying it. He made himself look one more time at the boy, at all the emotion wrestling naked under the smooth dark skin.

He sighed, rubbed his face. "I'm sorry, Lenard," he said, including everything in the apology, the girl's death, the interrogation, life itself.

The boy's face registered mistrust. Allan stared at the plaster unicorn on his desk, proudly painted and presented to him by his niece, age nine.

"See, Lenard," he said finally. "It would be a lot easier if you had done it. The boyfriend or the husband is always suspect number one."

The boy licked his lower lip uneasily and nodded.

"Did she tell you she was three months pregnant, Lenard?"

Lenard's head jerked up. He swallowed, his eyes began to fill and he looked down.

"She didn't tell you?"

"No," Lenard said, a sob.

"It was yours?"

The boy lifted his eyebrows, opened his mouth, then nodded.

"I'm sorry, Lenard," Allan said again.

Detective Donahoe elbowed through the door, a cigarette hanging from his mouth, a canned Coke in one hand, a Styrofoam coffee cup in the other. He nudged Lenard's shoulder to get him to notice the Coke. His eyes squinted a question through the cigarette smoke as he handed Allan the coffee.

Allan answered by rubbing his eyes.

Donahoe stubbed out his cigarette in the ashtray on Allan's desk. He lowered his bulk in the room's other chair, crossed his ankles, and folded his arms self-consciously over his belly.

Allan sipped at his coffee. Donahoe had forgotten the cream and sugar. He was about to tell Donahoe to give the boy a ride home when Lenard spoke, his voice thick but under control: "I guess that's why she was going to New Orleans. Have that baby. Sabrina, she private about things like that. Old fashioned like. Most girls, they always bitchin' about periods—"

"When did she tell you this?" Allan asked, writing in his notebook.

"Wednesday night. She waited around like I should talk her out of it. Said she was gonna get a job in New Orleans. I thought she was, you know, jerkin' with me. There's this other chick I been out with, and I thought she . . . I didn't know about the baby. It was just a thing, man, I mean, no promises. . . ."

"Why New Orleans?"

"I don't know. Her grandma used to live there, I think."

"Did she say how she planned to get there?"

The boy sniffed, wiped his nose with his hand. "Bus."

"Did she have the money?"

The boy sniffed again and nodded. Allan offered him a box of tissues. Lenard took one and blew his nose.

"Where'd she get it?"

"She babysit, sometimes she get paid for it. Willie, he pay her to clean his house and feed his rabbits sometimes."

Allan stopped in the middle of a sip. "Willie who?"

"Old Willie Dixon. You know, he found her."

Donahoe and Allan exchanged a look, and Donahoe stood and left the room without saying anything. Allan flipped back a few pages in his notebook. *W.D. said he had seen the girl, didn't know her name.*

"So she knew Willie?" he asked the boy.

"Yeah. Her grandma didn't want her over there, though. She didn't like Willie, I never knew why. Everybody likes Willie. He's always helping kids when they, you know, get in like a hassle. Give people a place to stay. Willie, one time he lent me money for a battery for my car, said he got tired of having to jump me with the cables all the time. I mean, he treated Sabrina good, he ain't a dirty old man or nothing. Sabrina, she called him Uncle Wiggy. He was like a granddaddy to her, you know?"

Uncle Wiggy. Allan held his coffee and rocked thoughtfully.

The cup was empty when Donahoe came back in.

"I sent a couple of uniforms out to pick him up. What do you think, professor?"

Allan had taught sociology for a couple of years while working on a doctorate in criminology. It didn't matter that he had never finished his thesis, that he had moved back to the small-town life of Martin City when his marriage broke up. To the other cops he was "professor," and he would always be "professor," to them a title bestowed partly to honor, however jokingly, to him a reminder of work left unfinished in his life, unfinished and therefore tinged with failure.

He dented the rim of the cup with his thumbnail.

"Well, I ran him," Donahoe said. "Nothing current. Few public drunks, a dropped assault, a DUI that dropped his license for a year." He shrugged. "The assault was kinda interesting. He popped a forty-year-old black male up side the head with the butt of a sawed-off shotgun. Legal length on the gun, it wasn't loaded. Refused to make a statement. Martinez wrote in the report that the younger dude said he didn't know the bitch was a friend of Willie's—that's a quote—and if Willie wouldn't come after him again he wouldn't press charges. This was last summer, by the way, and Willie was only seventy-four.''

"Anything else?''

"Carmella in the office, when I gave her the name, said that Willie was the best old soul in town and I shouldn't be picking on that old man. That's a quote.''

"It's Sunday, you don't have to quote.'' Allan finished circling the rim of the cup with thumbnail creases and set it on his desk.

"Yeah, Larry and I were going fishing. Ten more minutes and you'd never a got me.''

Allan looked at his watch: ten after six.

"We still have time for a Sunday drive.''

The smile wavered on Donahoe's face. "The uniforms—''

"Let's go to Grandma's house,'' Allan said, headed for the door. He wasn't sure, but behind him he thought he heard a moan.

The small house was sided with gray shingles which had darkened at the bottom. Otherwise it was notable mostly in that it sat farther from the street than the other houses on the block. There was no sidewalk, and the sandy path to the front door had been worn down below the grass on either side. The grass had just been cut, and the smell hung sweet and heavy in the warm air. Willie Dixon was loading a dirty red lawnmower in the old Datsun station wagon parked in front.

Donahoe's hand reached inside his jacket as the car settled to a stop. Allan touched his elbow.

"That's a lawnmower, not a machine gun. He mowed the old woman's lawn.''

Allan stepped out of the car while Donahoe pondered the implications. Willie slammed the car door and watched him approach with eyes swollen into glistening slits.

"You do good work, Willie.''

"Suh," Willie said. His forehead creased and one puffy eye bulged open. A hand lifted slowly to tug his ear. "I wasn't sure, you un'stand. She shouldn't have been the girl I knew. No, suh, not like that."

"How's the girl's grandmother taking it?"

"She'll open the door to you, suh, I believe." He shook his head and his smile was painful. "But not to me."

The old man seemed to bend and age as Allan watched; tears glittered and filled and overflowed, and he took a wavering step back against the car. But he smiled and shook his head when Allan took a step forward to steady him. With gnarled dark fingers he tapped his chest.

"The pump," he said. "He pumps hard, but he don't do me no good."

"Can you drive, Willie?"

"Oh, sure. I sit down I be all right."

"We're gonna need your help, so I want you to go home and get some rest, okay?"

Allan felt those eyes studying his face while he wrote on one of his cards, using the car roof as a desk.

"There's probably a couple of officers waiting for you at home, so I want you to give this to them, all right? Will you come to my office in the morning, and get some rest tonight?"

Willie took the card and squinted at it.

"You want me now, I go."

Allan smiled at him and found himself patting his shoulder.

"Tomorrow, Willie."

They smiled at each other for a moment before Willie turned toward the front of the car.

"Whatever I can do," he said over his shoulder. "You know that."

Donahoe had been waiting with folded arms beside the car. He joined Allan as he strolled down the path, apparently deep in thought.

"No physical evidence and you treat our two best suspects like some kind of royalty," he said, his tone lighter than the words.

"Uh-huh," Allan said.

The front door had been opened since their arrival. Through the wooden screen door Allan could hear Mike Wallace on *60 Minutes*. He knocked twice. Mike Wallace faded, and after a few seconds Sabrina's grandmother, Miss Carrie Webster, appeared at the door.

"Hello, ma'am," Allan said, not smiling. "Very sorry to bother you. We have a few questions."

The old woman peered at them each in turn through black-framed glasses with bottom rims that curved to a point at the corners. She unlatched the door and stepped back, jerking her left leg awkwardly.

The credits for *60 Minutes* were running soundlessly on the old black and white portable sitting atop an even older round-tubed console. The divan and two overstuffed chairs were covered with worn bedspreads. The walls were nearly covered with photographs, most unframed, many of the murdered girl, some much older, formal portraits of somber faces. Large color renditions of Jesus dominated two walls.

They stood in the center of the dim room while the old woman moved stiffly around them and sat heavily in the straight-backed rocker, her wide hips bulging over the seat.

"You all may be seated," she said.

The worn carpet gave strangely under his feet, and he realized as he sat down on the sofa that there were two layers of carpet, one over the other. On the coffee table lay a worn leather-bound Bible, its pages thickened at the upper corner from years of thumbing.

Allan looked over the room, intimidated in a way that the homes of the rich had never intimidated him. It was hard for him to imagine a young girl growing up here, but already her death darkened this house, had settled in with a permanence, as if her life and youth and energy had been no more than a temporary interruption. He was ready to leave; if he had been alone, perhaps he would have mumbled an excuse and left.

Donahoe was staring at him.

"Mrs. Webster, when was the last time you saw your granddaughter?"

She looked at the silent television as she answered, her eyes unblinking. "Wednesday."

"She didn't come home Wednesday night?"

The rocking chair began to move an inch or two back and forth. "No."

"Was it unusual for her to stay out all night?"

The old woman's lip trembled. "She was out late nearly every night. I'm an old woman, I can only tell her how to be. I tell her what the Good Book say, and she smile and do what she want."

"But it was unusual she didn't come home?"

"Twice before she gone two nights. An old woman can only worry, and pray."

"Do you know where she was on those occasions, ma'am?"

"She with that boy."

"Lenard?"

Her eyes still on the television, she stopped rocking. "I told her about the wrath of God, I spoke to her of the fires of Hell."

She turned to Allan with eyes filled with some of that fire. She began to rock again, her nostrils flaring, tears rolling down her cheeks.

"God's will be done," she said softly, her eyes softening and turning inward.

Allan took a deep breath and let it out. Donahoe pressed his thumbs together across his belly.

"This is difficult, I'm sorry, but were you aware the girl was . . . in a family way?"

The old woman's eyes squeezed shut and her lips began to move in mumbled prayer.

"I appreciate how painful this is, ma'am. Just one thing more for now. Were you aware that Sabrina did part-time work for Willie Dixon?"

The chair jerked forward as the old woman leaned over it. "That name has been forbidden in this house for more than forty years. You tell me that my flesh and blood took money from that man? No, I will not hear it. I will not hear it."

Later, in the car after they had calmed down the old woman and made their exit, Donahoe told Allan, "If I was that poor girl, I think I'd of got myself pregnant sooner."

Allan had his note pad out and was writing *40 yrs ASK WILLIE*.

When he was finished he reached over and patted Donahoe's belly.

"I think you timed it about right."

* * *

"Coffee, Willie?"

"No, suh, thank you, I had my cup."

Allan was working on his third. It had been one of those nights when the emptiness of his bed had itched against his skin, and sleep had come and gone more than once, leaving prickling after-images and half-memories. Willie looked energized and eager.

"The uniformed officers give you any trouble last night?" he asked the old man.

"No, suh. They was there like you say, and I show them that card, and whoo, they was none too happy, but they leave me be."

Allan picked up a pencil and laced it between his fingers.

"Willie, who do you think killed Sabrina?"

Willie's eyes twitched and refocused on Allan's tie. He spoke slowly, considering every word: "A man can think any thing he wants, suh. Any thing. It don't make it so. But when he goes to open his mouth—now you hear me good. When he goes to open his mouth, he better know what he say be true."

"I hear you, Willie." Allan sighed and drummed his desk. "What if I wasn't a cop?"

Willie smiled. "Then you wouldn't be talking to me now."

Allan laughed. He pushed back his chair and crossed his feet on the corner of his desk.

"How do you want to help me, Willie? You tell me how you want to do it."

"How 'bout I tell you a story," Willie said, leaning forward, elbows on knees, his smile sly and sad.

"A true story?"

"Oh, yessuh, it true. This story I know is true."

His eyebrows raised, Allan nodded.

Willie leaned back and settled himself in the chair.

"Long time ago. Down south. The city of New Orleans, Louisiana. There was this young man, done been in the war and got himself shot up and they send him home, you un'stand. Now you hear me good.

"This young man, he was crazy for some time. The war done that to him, you un'stand? For some time now, he didn't care he was alive or he was dead, and he took to drinking wine, he drinking wine on the streets, you un'stand? He almost died, woulda died too, this woman hadn't took him in.'' He lapsed for a moment, his eyes distant. Allan waited till he roused himself.

''A fine woman. She didn't have to do that, take in no sick man off the street, feed him and nurse with him until he well enough and go out and get drunk again. Then she take him in again. She didn't have to do that, no, suh. And the man, he can't understand it. She don't want him as a woman wants a man, no way. Why did she do it? And he puzzled on it. Then one day when he stone cold sober it came to him, that she not doing it for him, she doing it for Jesus. You hear what I'm saying?''

Outrage had crept into Willie's voice, and Allan nodded uncomfortably, staring at the reminder in his notebook, *40 yrs ASK WILLIE*. He reached for his pen and drew a line through it.

''She do it for Jesus,'' Willie said, shaking his head. ''And what do he do when he figure it out? That's right, he go get drunk, he steal some of her money and he buy a bottle of that cheap wine and he get drunk. But this time he mad drunk, he mean drunk, un'stand? So when he come back home, she there and he drunk . . . he did what he did, he lay with her, you hear what I'm saying to you? All the time she praying . . .''

Tears glittered in Willie's eyes and he sighed and sniffed before he went on.

''He a crazy man then, but when he wake up he know what to do. He try to make it right by her, you un'stand? But she, the woman, it like she take over being crazy from him, you un'stand? She won't talk about it, she begins her praying again, right while he be speaking to her, she be praying. She didn't do nothing but pray, for a while, and for that while he was taking care of her, you un'stand. . . .''

Willie's voice had dropped low, and Allan's mind had jumped ahead, trying to fit it all together. Then Willie stopped talking and stared at him, his eyes haunted.

''She was pregnant, wasn't she?'' Allan said softly.

Willie's eyes jumped with surprise, but he nodded slowly.

''She was that,'' he said.

''That's where the story really begins, doesn't it,'' Allan said.

''Who's to say, suh. Who's to say.''

Allan opened the bottom right drawer of his desk and brought out the nearly-full pint of Wild Turkey. It had been there for six months, a Christmas present from the chief, who hadn't bothered to find out that Allan drank scotch on those rare occasions when he drank at all.

Allan pulled two Styrofoam cups from the stack he kept in the same drawer. He set the cups down and began to pour.

The liquor sloshed the light cup almost off the desk, but before he could grab it, Willie's hand was there to steady it, his quickness astonishing. When the liquor was poured Willie took his hand off the cup and let Allan present it to him. Allan returned the bottle to the drawer.

"That's coffee if anybody asks," he said.

"Mighty fine brew it is, too," Willie answered by way of a toast, raising his cup. He took a good swallow and smacked his lips, beaming.

Allan let him take another sip before prompting. "So she was pregnant. What did you do?"

Willie shook his head, smiling. "I tell you a story. I may be somebody in that story, I may not be, you un'stand."

He twisted sideways in the chair and leaned forward, holding the cup carefully. "Now listen to me good. A man's past is history, a woman's past is hers alone. Do you hear what I'm saying to you?"

"Even when there's a murder involved?"

Willie shrugged, tapped his chest. "I tell you about me, what I believe, what way I live. Not always, but what way I live life now."

Allan nodded and saluted Willie with his cup. "It's your story, Willie. Tell it."

Nodding, Willie cleared his throat, his eyebrows drawing together in thought.

"I got a job," he said. His eyes lifted sheepishly to look at Allan. When Allan didn't react he took a quick sip.

"He got a job. Working in a kitchen. He didn't go getting drunk so much, 'cept maybe on payday, you un'stand? He stay home, he take care of the woman, he work, and she sit around and get big with the baby and she pray all the time. He owe the woman, you un'stand.

"And she has that baby. Prettiest little girl-baby you ever saw. Maybe he didn't love that woman, but he love that baby. And she take good care of that baby. He thought she was getting well.'' He took a sip from his cup and made a face that had nothing to do with the whisky.

"Then one day he come home and the woman and the baby, they gone. The money, they had a little money, it was gone. That little baby, she was just a month old, that woman done take her and run off. Yes," he said, drawing it into a hiss extinguished by a slow sip from the cup. In his eyes Allan saw the man who had wielded the shotgun.

"You know the man have to find that woman. The baby. He have to see the baby all right, you un'stand? And he did. The woman, she have a sister up north. That's where she was, yes, and he follow her and he find her."

"In Martin City."

The old man stared at him without appearing to hear. "That woman, she won't let him have a thing to do with her, not one thing. The sister, maybe she understand. He get a job and he give the sister money. For the baby. And he gamble, the man do that. He drink some too, but he don't drink as much when he gamble as he let on, you see what I'm saying, and he don't lose too much.

"He did himself all right, yes he did. And he did as right by the girl as he could while she growing up. You know he do that. Even when he have children by other women, he did that."

Donahoe opened the door and Allan kept him there with a look.

"You fellas need anything?" he asked around the door. "Coffee?"

Willie grinned and held up his cup. "Mr. Allan here, he done get me some coffee."

Donahoe smiled back and disappeared behind the closing door.

"He your partner, like on TV?" Willie asked.

"Yep. Andy and Barney."

Willie laughed, his eyes showing the whisky. Allan wondered if he had been too generous with it. He resisted the urge to prod the old man, sensing that Willie was feeling his way through the painful history, balanced on the invisible like a blind man on a tightrope. Willie was staring at him, studying, wondering.

"Mr. Allan, I got to ask you something now, and I don't want to get you mad or anything. You un'stand? I mean, now, I know you a policeman, and that's fine. But can you not be a policeman for a few minutes? Can you just be a man listen to another man, hear a man what he say? Can you do that? Then you can be a policeman again all you want?''

"Willie, as far as I'm concerned, you haven't said anything on the record yet.''

"Uh-huh, that's good. I tell you some things now a policeman, he might not understand, but the man would, you hear what I'm saying.''

"Yeah,'' Allan said, realizing that the bottom showed through the liquor in his own cup, which explained that soaring sensation. "Remind me to get drunk with you sometime, Willie.''

"You bet,'' Willie said, his head tilted thoughtfully. "I hate to tell you this next thing, but the man in the story—you know who—he's not around no more. You listen to me good. He die in the doing. He the memory of a man somebody used to be.''

Allan closed one eye, nodded once, opened the eye. Patience, he told himself.

"When the girl grew up, she weren't real pretty,'' Willie went on as though the story had never been interrupted. "And she went long time without a man. Her daddy got to know her some, not as her daddy, as a friend. Someone to listen where her mamma's too busy praying to listen. Then when she did get a man, he were no good. Bad, bad man. And she let him do what he want, she afraid she lose him, you hear how it was?

"Then one day he do her real wrong. He beat on her, tore her up, bad. And she come to me. Not the first time, but this was worst. She never talk right again, you un'stand. So I—her daddy, her daddy, he go find that man, he was a big mean man, and there weren't nothing else to be done or said by then, so that man died. You hear me good now. Right or wrong, that man never beat no woman again.''

Willie sighed, drained his cup, leaned forward to place it on the desk.

"The girl never told she was pregnant. Never said. The thing he handled different if she say. She maybe didn't know. But without no man she went back to her mamma, and her mamma—'' He shook his head and pushed the air with his hand.

"Her mamma's sister say that crazy woman, she preach that poor girl to death. I don't know what the truth be, really. The sister, she say first the girl die giving birth to the child, but why they tell everybody else the girl go and run off? Then the sister, she wasn't right after that. She wouldn't take no money for the baby, she act scared all the time." He tapped his skull. "Her mind start to go. The sister. She walk down the street laughing and talking and she be alone. She pretend to me, me who know, that the girl didn't die she run away. She see me again, she scream, she jump up and down and she run away.

"Then they find her dead one day, froze to death, no coat on. I ask myself, why her mind go? I ask myself, what did happen to the girl? I ask myself, how crazy is that woman? You hear what I'm sayin'?''

Allan took a deep breath and ran both hands through his hair, letting it stay where it stood.

"I hear you, Willie. Number one, we got no proof. Number two, I don't quite understand why you decided to tell me all this. No offense, Willie, I just don't think you've ever given a cop anything but a bunch of jive in your life."

Willie threw his head back laughing and slapped his leg. "Number two, you too right," he said. "I never did. But I getting old, Mr. Allan. The man I tell you about, he deal with things in a different way. I couldn't do that. I not that man any more, I tell you that. A man has to learn as he gets along, Mr. Allan."

"I understand, Willie."

"Yessuh, that's fine. But number one. Big number one. I think I have a way to get you that evidence."

Allan leaned forward in his chair. What the hell, he thought, and opened the bottom right drawer.

By the middle of the afternoon, the effects of the whisky had worn off and Allan was cranky. Willie's plan, which that morning had seemed both appropriate and daring, looked more cop-show melodramatic by the minute. Nothing had gone right.

He had explained the plan to the captain, who had sniffed skepti- cally at his mint-scented breath and asked questions that had nothing to do with anything. But Allan had been glib and eloquent, or so it seemed at the time, and the captain reluctantly gave permission, though he dug out a release form he insisted Willie sign first.

Then Allan's request for the necessary equipment had been put on hold. The equipment had been checked out for an undercover drug job, and although a murder investigation should have priority, shoul- ders had been shrugged.

Even Donahoe had suggested maybe he should sleep on it first. How could that old woman dump the body, professor? Does she own a car? Can she even drive?

Then check on it, Allan had ordered.

Donahoe's face had been carefully neutral when he reported back that Miss Carrie Webster did have a current license and owned a 1971 Mercury Comet.

"Would you like me to find out if she has a membership at a fitness center?" he had asked.

"I'd rather have a search warrant on the car," Allan had answered, his tone conciliatory.

"Professor, listen, has it occurred to you maybe the old dude's handing you a load?"

"Has it occurred to you maybe he isn't?"

Donahoe had sighed wearily and sat down, and that was where they were now, Allan waiting for his wounded brain capillaries to heal, Donahoe agonizing.

"Maybe if Willie signed a statement—"

"No," Allan said.

Donahoe sighed and massaged both his chins. "Then we just don't have anything to justify a search warrant."

"Not yet," Allan admitted. "Let's go talk to Willie."

Pain stabbed his temples when he stood.

Willie's station wagon was parked next to a husky mulberry tree that threatened the porch of the small frame house on the large corner lot. The neighborhood was predominantly white working class, and

Allan wondered what the neighbors thought of the scruffy chickens inside the sagging wire fence.

Willie answered the door shirtless and puffy-eyed but cordial. Inside they found the same sort of furnishings as in Miss Webster's house, down to the televisions stacked one on the other. The house was bachelor neat; grimy handprints on the white woodwork but the ashtrays clean, no litter.

As opposed to Miss Webster's, the house had a bright, comfortable feel to it. When Willie excused himself to put on a shirt, Allan and Donahoe sat on the couch and Donahoe lit a cigarette.

"You see the muscle tone on that old boy?" he asked Allan. "Now there's somebody who could heft a body around."

Allan was afraid Willie would come back carrying a bottle, but he didn't.

"You gentlemen care for some iced tea maybe?" he asked instead.

Allan shook his head. "We've run into some problems, Willie."

Willie's face registered concern. He sat and leaned forward in the bedspread-covered chair, cocking an ear.

"The equipment we need isn't available right now. Be a few days."

Willie looked back and forth between them as if he wasn't sure what this meant. Before Allan could explain further, Donahoe cleared his throat and spoke, his tone official.

"Sir, there's some questions I would like to ask you. First, what makes you think that an old woman like Miss Webster would have the strength to lift the dead weight of a body for the purpose of disposing of it?"

Willie looked at Allan with a hurt expression. Allan gave him an apologetic shrug and a quick wink.

Willie leaned back, fixing Donahoe with one eye. "Miss Carrie? Why, Miss Carrie, she was a butcher during the war. After the war some. She lift a quarter of beef like nothing to it. Miss Carrie, she was a strong woman."

"Then how," Donahoe asked, glancing at Allan, "did you manage to rape her?"

Willie's jaw jutted out. "Rape? Who say a thing like me raping the woman? Weren't no rape. I say I lay with her, I go into her bed drunk—now hear me good. A woman may not want a man, but she weak for the need of one, you hear what I'm saying? Mr. Allan, he understand.''

Allan nodded at Willie and smiled at Donahoe, whose ears blushed a furious pink.

''Okay,'' Donahoe finally said.

Willie gave Allan his wink back.

''One thing bothers me, Willie,'' Allan said. ''How do you plan on getting in to see her? If she won't let you in, it's down the tubes.''

Willie's nostrils flared as he smiled. ''She has to see me if I goes over to evict her.''

''You own her house?''

''Oh, yessuh.''

Allan began to chuckle, as much from the expression on Donahoe's face as anything.

''You own this house, too?'' Donahoe asked, shellshocked.

''A few houses is on land I own,'' Willie said to Allan. ''A business or two. I do all right, I tell you that.''

''Does the Webster woman know you own her house?''

Willie's face clouded. ''The sister tell her, she admit it to me. She knew she not supposed to, supposed to not say nothing. By then, Miss Carrie, she old, she have no other place to go, you un'stand. She had the granddaughter she raising. I don't ask for nothing. I pays the taxes, she just stay there.''

''I don't understand,'' Donahoe said, almost whining. ''Why is a man with all this property out picking up cans?''

''Cans is forty-nine cents a pound,'' Willie said.

Allan bit his lip and looked away.

''The can money, that's the money I play with,'' Willie explained.

''Gamble with, you mean.'' Donahoe could be stubborn.

Willie grinned at him. Donahoe looked at Allan to make sure he wasn't laughing. Allan reached inside his jacket for the liability release and unfolded it.

''Willie, the captain gave me this release for you to sign. It says that if anything happens to you the department and the city won't be responsible. You'll be on your own. So if you're having second thoughts, now's the time to say so.''

"And if I do?"

Allan shrugged. "We bring Carrie Webster in for questioning. I don't want to do that unless you do change your mind because we want her off guard when you go see her. But if we bring her in, we might get her to confess."

Willie snorted. "That woman? You don't get that woman confess nothing."

"That's why we're willing to go along with your idea. As soon as we get the equipment."

Willie nodded, his face drawn. Then his eyes lit up.

"We see what you think," he said.

He sprang to his feet and hurried to the back of the house. Donahoe scooted to the edge of the couch and checked his shoulder holster.

When Willie returned, he sauntered into the room, smiling innocently. He casually took the chair across the small room from the two detectives. Allan noticed the checkbook in his shirt pocket.

"Say something. Say some words," Willie said.

Allan raised his eyebrows at Donahoe and Donahoe growled, "You have the right to remain silent, you have the right—"

"That's good." Willie pulled the hidden object behind the checkbook from his shirt pocket and handed it to Allan. It was a microcassette recorder, the slimmest Allan had ever seen.

"Where did you get this?" Allan asked.

"Radio Shack," Willie said. "Cost nearly a hundred dollars."

Allan pushed the rewind button, stopped it, pushed play.

"—get this? Radio Shack. Cost nearly a hundred dollars."

Allan hit rewind again, this time held it longer.

"—ay something. Say some words." Then barely audible, "You have the right to remain silent . . ."

"Voice activated," Donahoe said.

"Willie, with our equipment, we can monitor you," Allan explained carefully. "We can hear everything going on so if you need help, we can be there. But with this—"

"I be on my own. Yessuh," Willie said. "Miss Carrie don't scare me."

"What're you doing with one of those things?" Donahoe wanted to know.

Willie smiled. "People, sometimes they say an old man forget, sometimes remember wrong. Specially when they money on the line. You hear what I'm saying? Somebody get away with that once, it's all right. After that, they get away with it again, everybody think Willie a fool? Huh-uh, no suh."

Allan looked at Donahoe.

Donahoe blinked at him twice, then said, "Let's go for it."

Allan nodded. Willie reached for the tape recorder.

"I use this, I don't have to sign that thing you said."

Allan hesitated. "Willie, I—"

"You tell your captain I change my mind, you un'stand? I bring this to you when I'm done. This just be me and her. The way it began. Just me and her."

For a few seconds the white cop and the old black man stared at each other, neither smiling. Allan had a vague though strong urge to warn the old man, but he realized there was nothing he could say that the eyes staring at him didn't already understand. He stood, folded the release form, and nodded at the open-mouthed Donahoe.

Willie followed them to the door. On the porch Donahoe said over his shoulder, "Don't forget to rewind that tape. And check the batteries."

The following morning, before he played the tape that Willie had recorded the night before, Allan rewound it, removed it from the machine and examined it. The recording tabs were intact.

To prevent the tape's being recorded over, Allan carefully broke the tabs with a ballpoint. Then he initialed both sides and snapped it back into the recorder. Before he hit the play button, Donahoe burst through the door.

Donahoe's eyes bulged and he was out of breath. "I just heard," he said.

"Sit down and try to breathe through your nose," Allan said.

Donahoe gave him a perfunctory scowl and sat.

Allan waited while Donahoe took two deep breaths, then he pushed the play button.

"—ello, this is Willie. Sitting in the car in front of Miss Carrie's, making sure this thing works before I go to the door. Little light come on, guess it works."

A hollow bang. "Car door," Donahoe said.

The rattle of knuckles on a screen door. Repeated. Repeated again, louder.

"Miss Carrie, you come open this door." Willie's voice sounded shrill. "Miss Carrie. Miss Carrie, now, I own this house. You don't want to see no sheriff come evict you, do you now, Miss Carrie?"

A muffled crackling. Donahoe leaned forward, his face strained.

"Miss Carrie," Willie said, a greeting, uncertain.

"Say what you come to say," a fainter voice said, surprisingly like Willie's but gruff, almost guttural.

"I'm free of drink this evening, Miss Carrie. Just a poor old man come to make peace."

"You'll have no peace in hell, Willie Dixon."

"Yes'm, I know that, surely do."

"What you say about the sheriff come evicting me?"

"Well, now, Miss Carrie, a man get to thinking about when he won't be around no more, what things be like then. I been maybe thinking I should deed you the house now, Miss Carrie. You won't talk to me, how I gonna do that, you un'stand?"

After a few seconds an inaudible murmur. Allan quickly stopped the tape, touched rewind, increased the volume.

"Lord, lord, lord," Miss Carrie murmured.

"Old man gets to thinking, Miss Carrie. His heart wake him up in the night, a man get scared, you un'stand, laying in the dark thinking on all his sins. So if you be so kind, like to help me get right with the Lord, maybe teach me the way of praying, an old man sure be grateful, Miss Carrie."

Donahoe grunted at Allan and wagged his head.

"Lord have mercy on your soul if you're trying some con on me, Willie Dixon."

"Yes, ma'am."

The scrape and bang of the door.

Willie's voice, clear and loud: "That picture, Miss Carrie. Sure bring back a memory of New Orleans."

"That city is owned by Lucifer himself, Mr. Dixon. Now, if you come here to find forgiveness in the Lord, let us kneel on the floor and pray."

They must have knelt close together, Allan thought when the prayer began, "Oh Lord Holy Jesus . . . ," because the woman's voice boomed, fired by evangelical fervor.

Punctuated by Willie's occasional "Amen, sister" or "Hallelujah," the prayer—more of a diatribe against Willie's long life as a sinner—settled into a rhythm and rolled on and on.

"Hope he didn't run out of tape," Donahoe said.

Allan scowled and ran the tape back to catch what he missed.

"—girl who died in the shame of youth, a sinner of the flesh—"

Allan settled back.

"—sweet Jesus, take that child to your heavenly bosom, forgive those sins of the flesh—"

"Forgive the poor soul, Lord, who took that child's life," Willie's voice interrupted.

"Amen," the woman's voice, trembling.

"And forgive her, Jesus, for doing it in Your Name, like she think she should do being Your servant, Lord."

"Am—"

The silence must have lasted more than a few seconds, for the recorder had shut off and switched back on to Willie's voice: "—orgive Miss Carrie, Lord," spoken gently but with urgency.

"You leave," Miss Carrie said, cold as steel.

"You did it trying to save us all, didn't you, Miss Carrie. You figure the Lord have mercy on a girl killed like that, girl who she didn't really do the wrong herself, but have the sin passed on down to her, now ain't that right? You see that with her gone, there nothing left of our sin, either. 'Cause you killed her mamma, too, all that time ago. Now our sin all gone from the world, now ain't that right? Except for us. Except for you and me. And we be gone soon enough. You just cleaning up our mess, weren't you, Miss Carrie."

"It was your blood," Miss Carrie said calmly. "Tainted. The Lord knew. The Lord told me. He told me in my heart to kill you that night you lay sleeping. But I disobeyed the Lord—I took the laws of man above the Law of God. And I was the vessel passed on your evil blood. In my heart I knew.

"And Sabrina's mamma, yes, I prayed it ended there. My sister, she swore the Lord would cleanse the baby, not to harm that baby. Sabrina. Sabrina, that girl laughed in the Face of the Lord . . . like you, Willie Dixon. Just like you."

"So you cut her dead."

"I sent her purified to God."

"Why you not kill me?"

"Because I'm a fool."

"You're no fool, Miss Carrie. Never was a fool."

Sobbing. It took Allan a moment to recognize the sound. Sobs ripping a woman's heart.

"Just you and me, Miss Carrie. Who's to know?"

The sobs lifted into a wail, a furious squeal, piercing, then fading like feedback from a speaker.

"Mr. Allan," Willie's whisper, stirring the hair on Allan's neck. "She gone to the kitchen. Now I don't want you to worry yourself about this none—now hear me good. Doc says nothing he can do, my pump gone bad, you un'stand? She coming. Lord forgive us, you forgive us too."

The bellow gaining from the background nearly drowned the last words.

"My God," Donahoe whispered.

Allan shut off the tape. Donahoe stared at him and closed his mouth and swallowed.

"I can see why that screaming brought the neighbors," Donahoe said. "Whew."

Allan shifted his chair so that his head was turned.

"Aren't we gonna listen to the rest of it, professor?" Donahoe asked.

"Not right now," Allan said.